Pem

Books should be returned or renewed by the last
date above. Renew by phone **03000 41 31 31** or
online *www.kent.gov.uk/libs*

Libraries Registration & Archives   CUSTOMER SERVICE EXCELLENCE   CSE   Kent County Council kent.gov.uk

'Elizabeth Gill writes with a masterful grasp of
conflicts and passions hidden among men and women
of the wild North Country'
Leah Fleming

C334158979

Elizabeth Gill was born in Newcastle upon Tyne and as a child lived in Tow Law, a small mining town on the Durham fells. She has been a published author for more than thirty years and has written more than forty books. She lives in Durham City, likes the awful weather in the northeast and writes best when rain is lashing the windows.

Also by Elizabeth Gill

Available in paperback and ebook

Miss Appleby's Academy
The Fall and Rise of Lucy Charlton
Far From My Father's House
Doctor of the High Fells
Nobody's Child
The Guardian Angel

Available in ebook only

Shelter from the Storm
The Singing Winds
Under a Cloud-Soft Sky
Paradise Lane
The Foxglove Tree
Snow Hall
The Preacher's Son

. . . and many more!

Snow Angels

Elizabeth Gill

Quercus

First published in Great Britain in 1999 by Hodder & Stoughton
This edition published in 2017 by

Quercus Editions Ltd
Carmelite House
50 Victoria Embankment
London EC4Y 0DZ

An Hachette UK company

A CIP catalogue record for this book is available
from the British Library

PB ISBN 978 1 78648 220 4
EBOOK ISBN 978 1 78206 177 9

10 9 8 7 6 5 4 3 2 1

Typeset by Jouve (UK), Milton Keynes

Cover design by Debbie Clement

For Doug – brother-in-law, drinking
partner and friend

Prologue

It was a cold wet November afternoon when Abby Reed's mother died. The doctor had said she would probably go quietly in the night, but Bella Reed had never done anything quietly. She clutched the lapels of the doctor's jacket, her thin hands like chicken claws, and begged him not to let her leave this world and, though he had looked shocked, fifteen-year-old Abby could only agree with her mother. It was all very well for those who were convinced of paradise, but her mother knew that there was nothing beyond a box in the ground of the local cemetery and it was hardly a prospect to be faced with equanimity.

'My dear lady,' he said, 'you must prepare to meet your maker. There is nothing more that I can do.'

'Idiot!' she said, falling back onto her pillows. 'Get

him out of here, Abby. I don't want him at my damned deathbed!'

The doctor, shocked even further at the dying mother's foul mouth, almost ran. Abby could have told him it was nothing special. Her father proudly said of her mother that she swore better than any docker. Abby didn't see him out; she stood in the gloom at the top of the staircase which dominated their house and Kate, their maid, appeared from the kitchen to deal with the doctor and the door.

Wind and rain bespattered the entrance hall and the doctor stood for a moment before he faced the darkness. It was past four o'clock and the weather had ensured that what light there had been had gone as the afternoon started. Kate struggled to shut the door and Abby went back to her mother. The room was cosy. She had lit the lamps and the fire had been on in there not just all day but for many weeks while Bella's illness progressed. Bella was lying with her eyes closed.

'Abby?'

'I'm here.' She went over to the bed, sat down and clasped her mother's hand.

'I love you.'

Tears rose in Abby's eyes and in her nose and in her mouth and seemingly everywhere. Her mother did what they called in the area 'naming a spade a bloody shovel'; she always said what she meant. Other people might skirt around a subject, but Bella never did. Abby had been astonished as a small child that other mothers did not treat their children with open affection, that they did not spend time with them, that they did not appear to have any joy in them, but she had always known because her mother had always told her and always shown her. They both knew that Abby would never hear the words again on Bella's lips.

'You mean more to me than anything in this world. You've given me more pleasure than you could possibly imagine. I'm not afraid of death, I just don't want to leave you. Come closer.'

Abby kissed her thin cheek and Bella put a hand on her head.

Her mother didn't even ask for her father. Since her illness, he had taken refuge in his work. Abby didn't blame him for that. There was nothing he could do, and to stay around his wife's bedroom would have been an admission of her coming death on both their parts. He would be back soon, Abby thought, and there was life in her mother yet. They would have time to say goodbye. She lay for a little while with her head on the pillow beside her mother. She had not slept properly in several days and nights and she was so exhausted that she let herself drift for a while. Suddenly she heard the door. She had not expected to feel relief and, when she did, got up to meet her father. It was only then that she saw his gaze was fixed on her mother.

'She didn't stay for me,' he said.

The weather retreated for the funeral, but the cemetery was slippery with mud. Abby had insisted on going even though the old Northumbrian way was for the men to go; the women would stay behind and prepare the tea. Her father needed her there. She was his only child, and even though people might look disapprovingly, she didn't care. She held up her head and clasped her father's arm.

It was easier when they got back to the house. They lived in Jesmond, one of the more prosperous areas of Newcastle, in a big semi-detached villa not far from the cricket ground. People were packed in to show their respect. Henderson Reed was a shipbuilder, not the biggest on the Tyne, but well known. Abby helped to dispense tea. It stopped her thinking about her mother.

Charlotte Collingwood, wife of William Collingwood, who was the biggest shipbuilder on the Tyne, came to her. Abby had tried to avoid her. Charlotte was a pretty woman of forty who had given her husband two sons, but Abby despised her. She sat at the top of Newcastle society in a way that Abby's mother had once likened to 'a fairy with a Christmas tree stuck up her arse' and Abby had never forgotten it. Charlotte had come from a top family, a branch of the Surtees who owned land and many fine houses, but William Collingwood had made his way up the social ladder. He was nothing more than the son of a boat builder. Charlotte had been well bred but penniless, and now enjoyed fine clothes, a huge country house and more money than she could spend. She had never read a book in her life. Abby treasured her mother's books.

'You must come to us for Christmas,' Charlotte said. 'The boys will be home from school and we'll be having a party. I know you won't feel much like parties, but the change would do you good.'

Abby felt guilty then. Charlotte was being generous, and she could imagine lots of things worse than seeing Edward Collingwood again. He was eighteen, fair and handsome. He went to a top public school, he was well spoken, beautifully mannered and rumoured to be very clever. The younger boy, Gil, as far as Abby could judge, was the opposite: dark, stupid and sullen. He was just a bit older than Abby. They had long ignored one another, but, thinking of Edward and wanting to distance herself from her mother's death, Abby was inclined to agree at once. The idea of spending Christmas alone here with her father and the servants did not appeal, though perhaps he would think differently.

Charlotte asked Henderson. He seemed agreeable and Abby knew a lightness that she hadn't felt for months. Bella had struggled with her illness, only giving in when she could fight it no more. It had been a long and dreary autumn and Abby thought that her mother would not have wanted her to grieve further. She had known that her mother was dying; her grieving was almost done. It would do her father good to get away from the house and shipyard for a few days.

The days before Christmas were short and wet and empty. Abby missed her mother all the time and wanted to weep, but she couldn't; it was as though a door had closed between her tears and her eyes and even when she ached to cry, she couldn't. She did her best to look after her father and cheerfully presided over meals which neither of them ate. She was tired, but when she lay down to sleep at nights, thoughts of her mother flooded her mind and gave her no rest. Everyone else seemed so cheerful because it was Christmas, wishing each other all the best. Carol singers came to the door. It even snowed. Abby thought of her mother lying in the cemetery with a fine white layer of frozen water above her and no future.

It was therefore with relief, just after midday on Christmas Eve, that Abby and her father drove the several miles out of Newcastle to the mansion which William Collingwood had built a dozen years ago when he became rich. Abby did not think about the North-umberland countryside; she was used to the big farms and wide fields. Castles were commonplace here, the kind of fortifications which had helped to keep out the Picts and Scots and Border reivers at different times. Some of the farms had half-ruined towers or castles right beside the house, which might have looked strange to foreign eyes but were usual to those who knew the area. It was prosperous: the fences were mended; the walls were straight and safe; the roads were good.

Bamburgh House was a monstrosity, Abby thought as they pulled in at the gates of the long mile drive. It could have been beautiful; the honey-coloured stone had been quarried from right beside it, but the architect had been having some kind of love affair with Greece. Four enormous pillars obscured the front of the house. It managed to look stately in the slight covering of snow, but Abby was not deceived. She had been there before and thought it the most stiff, unfriendly house she had ever seen in her life. In the summer great arrangements of flowers stood to attention in huge vases in all the rooms. Everything was swept clean; no dusty cupboards in Charlotte's house. The maids were uniformed and unsmiling. The food was always lavish and overdone, so that it put you off before you started, and Charlotte was fond of table centres such as iced swans and animals made from chocolate and marzipan. Neither William nor his wife had any taste. The house, though huge, was filled with furniture. There was not a corner that had not its share of paintings and ornaments and dead animals in glass cases or their heads on the wall. There were tiger rugs and elephants' feet and stuffed birds. It was an animals' cemetery, Abby thought with a little shiver, and the furniture was uncomfortable, all gilt and velvet, short-backed sofas and shallow chairs. Sometimes Abby was ashamed to be there considering that she was aware of how badly paid and housed were William's shipyard workers – her father was always saying so.

It could have been no pleasure to work in that house, because none of the servants ever looked happy, not like Kate and Mrs Wilkins at home, sitting by the kitchen fire no doubt and enjoying the cake and sherry and beef which her father's money had bought for them. She had made sure they had generous presents that Christmas because they had been kind to her all that time when her mother was ill. Abby had been glad also that her father had provided a big dinner for all his workers, gifts for their wives and children in the form of foodstuffs and confectionery and a bigger paypacket than usual for all the men. Some of them drank their money, which was why her mother had in previous years insisted that their families should be given gifts directly as well as extra money. Abby had made sure that this year was even better for them. They should not feel the difference because her mother was dead.

In the huge entrance hall of Bamburgh House stood

the largest Christmas tree that Abby had ever seen, glowing with candles. Holly festooned every corner and mistletoe peeped out here and there among the red berries and green thorns. The weather did its best to help, freezing neatly so that the snow turned solid and wet trees glittered as though somebody had put them in just the right place to catch the winter sunlight. Huge fires burned in the rooms. Throughout the afternoon, people arrived and everyone was to stay, some of them for several days.

Abby began to enjoy herself, to be pleased at the dress she had brought. An excited hum came from having so many people in the house and there were wonderful smells and sounds between dining-room and kitchen. Maids went to and fro downstairs until the long tables were laden. Musicians arrived and began to make music in the ballroom. Abby glimpsed Edward, but of Gil there was no sign. A little maid came to help Abby dress. She was very young and chattered more than she should have done, but Abby didn't mind, and it was of her that she enquired for the other boy. The girl's face paled.

'His da leathered him,' she said.

'Beat him?'

The girl nodded.

'Two days since.'

'Why?'

The little maid's face darkened.

'Not for summat you'd think. He didn't do nothin'

like lads do. Locked him up an' all, like a dog.' And with that, Abby had to be content.

The evening went well. There were good things to eat: jellies and creams and cold chicken and ham. Abby even had champagne. Edward asked her to dance and, although she shouldn't have because of her mother dying, her father insisted. The music and the champagne made Abby pleased with everything. The light from the chandeliers glittered inside and the frost on the snow glittered outside. Gil did not appear.

'Where's your brother?' Abby enquired of Edward as they stood against a pillar in the ballroom, flushed from dancing.

'In his room.'

'It's Christmas Eve,' Abby pointed out.

'He isn't there by choice,' Edward said.

Abby couldn't rest. She tried to. She reasoned with herself. She didn't like Gil Collingwood and as far as she knew he had neither looked at her nor spoken politely. It was strange. She kept thinking about her mother alone in the cemetery and Gil by himself, and it all got mixed up. She had refused a second glass of champagne and contented herself with lemonade, but her mind did not unmix. She danced with several boys, she talked to girls she knew and it should have been the happiest evening she had spent for a long time, but there was an emptiness inside her which grew and grew until

Abby could bear it no longer. She left the noise and the music, took a candle from the hall, wrapped a huge piece of chocolate cake into a napkin and then made her way up the first of two wide staircases.

From the rooms below there were lights and the sound of laughter. It was a big house but conventionally laid out, with the upstairs rooms around a central hall. The rooms were well set back. The hall was lit and Abby couldn't hear her own footsteps because there was carpet all along the floorboards. She didn't know what she was looking for, but she saw it anyway. There was a key in the lock of a door as far away from the staircase as possible. She listened hard, but could hear nothing.

Abby brought her candle down to the key and very slowly turned it in the lock. It made no noise. The door opened soundlessly. Abby drew in her breath at the blast of cold air that came out of the room. It was freezing; she could feel it through her dress, straight onto her skin as though she wore nothing. At first she thought it was an unused room. There was nothing personal about it and, though she looked as best she could in the gloom, the grate was empty and clean, there was no light of any kind and the bed was stripped. There were no ornaments, no books, no clutter. There was no carpet on the floor; the linoleum was like ice. The curtains were drawn back and from there the moon threw its white light in through the window. It was, Abby thought, shivering, the nearest thing to a grave. Nobody was in here. There was no sound. She turned to go and the candle flickered in the draught. Then she saw him.

Gil was quite tall, that Abby remembered, but he was curled up as small as he could possibly be at the far side of the bed, right against the wall, like a hedgehog. He didn't move or acknowledge her in any way and, as Abby saw him better, she recognised the whiteness of his shirt and the blackness of his hair.

'God Almighty,' she said.

Her first instinct was to run for help, but she stopped herself. She couldn't do that. Adults lived in another world, a powerful world where she had no place and no influence. If she spoke a single word she would get into trouble and get him into even more trouble, if that could possibly be. She mustn't be found out. She left the room with as little movement as she could. From the room next door she pulled thick blankets and two pillows and carried them back and put the blankets over him and the pillows down onto the bed.

'Gil, are you dead?' It was not the time for formality somehow. 'Gil?'

He didn't move. Abby touched him on the shoulder.

'Go away.' With a strength that surprised her, he shoved the blankets back at her. They enveloped her. She had to push them off. Her heart pounded. She really had thought that he was not breathing. It was her nightmare come back: lying beside her mother, tired from trying to come to terms with the idea that she might lose her, that somebody else would go out of this life and she would not be awake or not be there and be unable to do anything. Nightly she haunted herself, thinking that if she had stayed awake, her mother would still be alive. She knew that it was stupid, but she only knew this in the daylight. When she had been a child the night had held no fear, it was a velvet blackness. She had fallen asleep listening to her parents' voices coming up from below the floorboards. Childhood had been when life was for ever, when nothing would hurt her. Now the darkness was full of devils and they tormented her with guilt and inadequacy.

Abby stared at the window, glad of the moon. There were thick frost patterns on the window. She remembered her mother showing her all the different ones. They were coldly beautiful.

'I brought you some cake.' It was rather squashed by its journey. 'Chocolate cake.'

He stirred after a few moments and then very slowly turned over. Abby made herself not react. There was a big mark across one side of his face where somebody had done what her mother would have called 'backhanding him'. His straight black hair hid the expression in his eyes. He didn't touch the cake as she offered it; he just looked at it and then at her and said, 'You'll get into bother.'

'Nobody will know.'

There was a jug of water and a glass on the dressing-table. Abby went across and poured some and gave it to him and he took the cake and ate it very slowly. Abby was more accustomed to the room now and she could hear the faint sounds of music from the ballroom. It seemed strange here in the almost-silence, like another world. She wondered if her mother could still sense some things from the life she had left, whether there was any way in which sounds filtered through.

She began to cry and almost choked in embarrassment attempting not to. After all these weeks, she chose this moment in which to realise that her mother could not hear the music nor feel the cold. She couldn't touch her or speak to her or have the love between them like a shining light any more. It was all gone; it was over.

'Did you want some cake?' he asked as the tears flowed. Abby shook her head wordlessly and wished for a handkerchief, for control, for oblivion. The candle, which was never going to be anything spectacular, guttered and gave up and she was left in the cold, white moonlight with a boy she barely knew, a hot face, cold tears, a blocked nose and a terrible desire to sniff before her nose ran. It got worse, until she was blinded and everything was salt and even sniffing didn't help. She found a tiny stupid scrap of lace and cotton in the only pocket of her dress and blew her nose. It sounded like a train to her ears. She mopped her face on the edge of the nearest blanket and the hairs from it went up her nose. When the crying took over her whole body, she gave herself up to it until it wracked her. When the sobs quietened she found the blankets over her, and his body, which was surprisingly warm, close. Exhausted, comforted, Abby fell asleep.

At some time in the night she kicked off her shoes and settled herself against him and slept again. Then somebody was shaking her gently. When she opened her eyes he was looking down at her and saying, 'You'll have to go or they'll find you here.'

Abby was horrified. She had spent the night with a boy, slept close against him in a bed. She remembered – did she remember it – his arms around her at one point and then his body folded in against the back of hers. 'Spoons' her mother would have called it, as in polite households where the cutlery was carefully put away on its side, not like in her house where her mother thought people had better things to do like painting, reading and going for walks on Tynemouth beach and making sticky toffee cake. The old familiar loneliness punched at Abby's insides again, but it was not quite so bad today because she had cried and somebody had been there to hold her. At least, she thought that he had. The embarrassment ousted the other feelings and her face burned. She fled and it was only when she reached her own room that she remembered it was Christmas morning.

She washed and dressed and went down to the dining-room, where her father and several other people were breakfasting. She kissed him, but felt somehow as though she had betrayed him, as though she had done something wrong. She couldn't eat. People were merry and there were sausages and hot coffee, but the smell of food made Abby feel sick. She had a terrible desire to confess what she had done. Only the thought that William Collingwood would no doubt beat his son all over again stopped her. They would blame him. She wished that she had not left the party. She watched Edward across the table, sitting with his best friend from school, Toby Emory, and she could not equate him with the boy she had left upstairs, his silent tongue and closed expression. Edward and Toby were laughing and talking about horses. Edward's father had bought him a new hunter for Christmas and they had already been down to the stables.

Nobody noticed that Abby didn't eat. She went off to church with her father and the others in the nearby village. In church, she felt dirty and she was cross with Gil. This visit could have been so pleasant. Another girl, Rhoda Carlisle, who came from Allendale Town at the top end of Tynedale where it met Weardale on the fell-tops, chatted freely to her as they came out of church. She was here with her parents and two small brothers. Rhoda was a tall, pretty, brown-haired girl who liked books, and when they got back to the house Abby was happier. She had done nothing wrong. And then the happiness dropped away from her. Gil was there. He stood out, or was it just because of what had happened? He was taller than the other boys and stood away from them. Abby blushed until she couldn't blush any more and ignored him. It wasn't difficult to do. He didn't even acknowledge her. He didn't smile and to her he seemed unapproachable and aloof.

There was a huge meal and so many people that it ceased to matter. She wasn't seated near him, but with Rhoda, Toby and Edward. Edward paid Abby so much attention that she was flattered and pleased.

It had snowed all the way through the meal, but afterwards it stopped and they went outside and threw snowballs at each other until it was too dark to see anything. They called by the stables to admire Edward's new horse and Abby found herself asking, 'What did your brother get for Christmas?' Out the words came. She was astonished at herself and not surprised that Edward frowned.

'I have no idea. Whatever he asked for, I suppose. Why?'

'I just wondered.'

'You just wondered? Tell me, Abigail, what is this sudden interest in my brother?' His eyes danced. Abby could have hit herself.

'He doesn't seem very happy.'

'You wouldn't be very happy if your father had taken a horsewhip to you.'

'Why did he do that?'

'My brother is stupid. He came bottom of the class. No, I lie, second to last, except in geometry. Can you imagine?'

'I don't think that's much of a reason to beat somebody and lock them up.'

'My God, you like him!' Edward stood back, watching her from astonished eyes. 'What is it you like best about him? His elegant manners, his erudite conversation, his fine wit?'

Abby would have given a lot to have said, 'I liked the way he put his arms around me', but she couldn't. And that was the moment she realised she felt proprietorial about Gil Collingwood, as though some kind person had wrapped him up in paper and presented him to her on Christmas morning. She shook her head and laughed, but the feeling didn't go away, even when Edward had stopped teasing her. She understood something – that touch was the most important thing in the world between people, that because of it she would have defended Gil against anyone who tried to hurt him. It was totally irrational, but her mother, Abby couldn't help thinking, would have approved of the idea. No wonder older people kept younger people apart. There was nothing like sleeping close against someone and seeing the old day out and the new one in for bonding you together.

As she came into the house Gil was in the hall. There were shadows, it was growing dusk and the lamps were lit, but he looked straight at her and Abby looked back at him. His eyes were so dark that you couldn't see the iris in them. He didn't say anything and Abby didn't linger. Late in the evening, when she had danced with half a dozen different boys and hated every moment of it because he didn't ask her and she couldn't see him, she went outside just to get away. It was bitterly cold out there; she had put on her coat and boots. She needed the quietness. It was completely still, just like the previous night, with a huge full moon and a complete quota of stars. Abby walked away from the house on the crisp snow; the trees were thick with it. Further over, the snow became too heavy on one branch and dropped with a dull thud to the ground.

She was feeling a little melancholy. Everyone sounded so happy. It made her think of last year and what things had been like then. Her mother had been well and in her impetuous way had decorated the whole house, made two Christmas cakes and bought Abby every single gift she had shown an inclination for. She wondered whether her mother could have known that it was the last Christmas they would ever spend together and consequently had made it the best ever. Why was it, Abby thought, that you could not return to those times? She thought of her mother's sweet laughter. It had snowed then, too, on Christmas Eve and her mother had taken her by the hand and run outside and they had danced in the garden. Abby could remember the small, square snowflakes on her dark hair. And every year they had made the snow angels. Abby couldn't bear to remember it. It seemed to her now that her childhood was completely lost because her mother had given her that childhood. Her father was a kind man, but it was not the same. It was all gone; it was finished; nothing would ever be like that again.

She heard a movement behind her, jumped and turned around quickly. There was Gil. Abby couldn't help feeling irritated. Did he have to be there every time she cried? Except that she was not crying, not quite. He was taller close to, much taller than she was. Slender and in expensive dark clothes and a white shirt, he matched the night, blended as if he wasn't really there, just of her imagination. Abby couldn't help but compare him with his brother and find Edward wanting. Gil really was very nice to look at.

'You could have asked me to dance,' she said.

'Don't know how.'

'I got six boxes of handkerchiefs for Christmas. I didn't realise they would be so useful.' And she scrubbed at her face and looked at him. 'Do you know how to make snow angels?'

'What?'

She didn't explain further. She stood with her feet together and her arms down by her sides and let herself fall straight back into the snow. Then she swept her arms and legs into a semicircle and got up carefully so as not to spoil the impression.

'There,' she said.

He smiled. It was not exactly an earth-shattering event, Abby thought. He contained it as though the effort of anything bigger would have been too much and it went almost as fast as it came, but she saw it.

'Go on then,' she said, and to her surprise he did.

Gil got up and stood back and Abby looked approvingly at the impressions in the snow before they turned and walked back to the house, towards the music and the lights. Her mother would have been pleased, Abby thought, and she felt peaceful as she had not felt since her mother died.

Chapter One

They say that time heals, but it isn't true. If anything, as you get further and further away from the death of the person you loved, so you see them more clearly, remember them more frequently, wish for them with an emptiness which gets bigger and bigger. Her father didn't mention her mother's name after a while, so that in a way Abby wished she could think of her mother as 'Bella' and that she could shout her name out when she went to the cemetery or when she stepped into a roomful of people. Nobody spoke of her. There was nothing left.

Rhoda Carlisle's father died only a month after the Christmas party. Abby wrote, knowing exactly how Rhoda would feel because she had been close to her father. Abby remembered him. He was a botanist, a kind, unworldly man who cared for nothing but flowers and insects and butterflies. Although he came from a family with a great deal of money, he settled in a tiny dales town without society or worldliness and he had loved it there.

Rhoda soon had other problems. Within six months of her father's death her mother had married again, the son of a local farmer, several years younger than she. People sniggered and said that Jos Allsop had married the silly woman for her money and that she had married him to warm her bed. Abby could only be thankful that her father had not been equally foolish, though she knew that he was lonely. He could easily have married again, he was a prosperous, respected man. In the early days Abby had been fearful every time an eligible woman drew near, but it was as though he didn't see them, as though Bella's death had blinded him. And yet, Abby thought ruefully, he saw too much. Once, when they had come home from what had been an enjoyable party, he put his hand on her shoulder and said, 'Don't fret, lass, there'll be no mistress here but thee.'

Abby stammered and disclaimed, said that she would be glad to welcome into the house anyone of his choice. He kissed her cheek.

'Aye, well, some day.'

The day didn't arrive, and in the end Abby stopped watching for it, but she could not help shivering in gratitude when she met Rhoda and her mother in Newcastle one day and Rhoda's mother was big with child. Rhoda looked ill, Abby thought, white and skinny. Her mother chattered nervously. Abby went home to a big fire and a pot of tea. When her father came back she kissed him and thought how lucky she was. They had tea together and sat over the fire and it was only then that Abby recognised the feeling in her. It was happiness.

Two or three times a year they went to stay with the Collingwoods. Edward and Toby Emory had gone to Oxford and there, according to Charlotte, Edward had taken everything before him. Toby didn't care for Oxford – Abby had heard him say so a dozen times – but he stayed there to please his father. Abby understood why. She had met Toby's parents, who were kind, intelligent people. They had six daughters; Toby, the youngest child, was their only son and they were proud of him. They had a foundry which made parts for ships and Toby would join his father in the business when he left university.

As for Gil, Abby couldn't help herself about him. She tried to because he got nothing right. There were rumours that he had been asked to leave school, expelled, though Abby was not told why and Charlotte always said it was just that Gil wasn't very bright. So he went to work instead of to Oxford. What he did there Abby had no idea, because nobody told her. When they did meet he barely spoke to her. Other people might call him shy, but she didn't believe that. The parties he was forced to go to did not make him dance or seek her out, and pride forbade that she should go to him. Many were the parties when she danced and talked with other boys and missed him. Yet every time she tried to dismiss Gil from her consciousness, he did something to bring himself back to her.

She fell on the ice that first winter. He was there before anyone else and picked her up and carried her inside. The following summer, when somebody tried to kiss her in the garden of a house where there was a birthday and Abby had objected, Gil pushed the other boy into a pond. Somehow, like a reluctant angel of mercy, he would appear during a crisis.

He grew tall and remote and other girls, thinking there was a mystery and conscious of how he looked and who he was, tried flirting and encouraging him. Abby could have told them it wouldn't work. Even Mary Ann Emerson, who was beautiful and clever and whose father owned a Sunderland shipyard and who boasted that she could get Gil to kiss her, was forced to retreat with a red face and downcast mouth. The only way to deal with Gil was to ignore him. Sometimes, therefore, as they grew older Abby would stop talking to find him sitting or standing near, not joining in the conversation, just there, listening. She didn't encourage him; she didn't dare. Her father, more observant than most, said heavily, 'I wouldn't like that lad to get any ideas about you. There's something about him that doesn't please me.'

Abby was half-inclined to say 'what lad?' but she didn't. In fact, she was rather pleased that it was so noticeable that Gil liked her.

'He doesn't have any ideas,' she said.

'Oh no? Still waters run deep, that's what I say.'

Abby stopped herself from defending Gil.

'He's like his father,' Henderson said. 'I knew him when he was young: quiet and devious and, by God, he let nothing stand in his way. He came from a nice family, his father built boats and they were respected, but he shook them off because they weren't grand enough for his schemes. His poor mother broke her heart over it.'

Abby was about to reply briskly that Charlotte was unlikely to do so, but she caught her father's eye and subsided. William Collingwood frightened Abby. Edward was like his mother, slight and fair and talkative. Gil was taller than his father by now, but he was dark like him. William was quiet and brooding and would brook no argument at home or at work. Her father called him ruthless, devious, and she well remembered the night in Gil's bedroom, the mark on his face and the way that he moved so carefully.

Edward and Toby left Oxford and came north again to go into their fathers' businesses. Abby thought that if she had been either one of their fathers, she would have detected a slight lack of enthusiasm. She thought how difficult it must be when you were a young man with ideas of your own and your father assumed that you would follow him into the business. She felt guilty on that count not being a boy, even though she knew that her parents had adored her. Her father had no one to go into the business after him and Abby could not help but be aware that in the way of men in business, he would have given much to have been able to write Reed & Son over the gates of his shipyard. She knew that her father and grandfather had been shrewd men, had bought up the land on either side of their shipyard for when they wanted to expand, but her father had not done so and she thought this could be because he was unsure of what would happen next. Abby had tried hard for some time when she was younger. She liked cricket. She liked to go and see her father in his office and play with the type-writers and give out the wages on a Friday when the men lined up at the open window of the office, but the actual design and building and business was something which held little interest for her. She had inherited her mother's love of books, kitchens, flowers and gardens and inevitably she spent a great deal of time with her mother.

Her father seemed interested in nothing but the busi-ness after her mother died. It even occurred to Abby that there was no reason why he should not marry and father a son so that the shipyard would go on and, although she would have hated it all, she could not in honesty deny that it would have been a good idea.

The world of shipbuilding went up and down like a seesaw, Abby knew, from years of listening to her father talk. There would be a depression, then things would begin to improve. Then, just when it seemed that things would be good for ever, everything would go down again. She was proud of her father: he was a just, even a generous, employer and he did everything he could to help those less fortunate. Gil's father and the other shipbuilders paid their men as little as they could get away with, kept them in horrible little cottages beside the docks and did nothing to discourage drinking and immoral behaviour. When work was short they paid them off, to save their wages bills. How people lived in the meantime was not their concern.

Her father's greatest pleasure was to discuss business. She thought it was all he had in common with William Collingwood, so they continued to be friends. Charlotte was inclined to favour Abby's company. Sometimes she took her to see her family over at Hexham, a lovely town with an abbey and many fine houses in Tynedale, twenty miles to the west of Newcastle. Her immediate family had a huge house to keep going and no money, but some of her relations were rich and were the cream of county society. The head of the Surtees family in the area was called Robert. He had an estate in Northumberland and a house in London. Charlotte said that she had her eye on him for Abby.

Abby liked Robert Surtees. He talked to her, made her laugh. He was handsome, educated and had inherited everything early in life when his father died. He hunted, shot, fished, looked after his estate and spent the season in London and Paris. Abby noted with some amusement that his family, even the poor ones, considered themselves above people like the Collingwoods and thought the way Charlotte spent money to be vulgar. Luckily Charlotte was oblivious to this. She visited Hexham in her shiny carriage, wearing long furs unless the weather was exceptionally warm, and expensive dresses, dripping with jewels and playing the fine lady. At one such event, Abby overheard a woman say to another, 'She married a workman. My dear, what do you expect?'

It made Abby laugh to hear William Collingwood described as a workman, but it was well known in the area that he had come from the coal port of Amble, where his father had built cobles – small fishing boats. Nothing he did, nothing he had achieved, no matter how much money he made or business ability he had, could make him acceptable to the upper circles of society beyond Newcastle. Abby thought that privately it must have cost Charlotte many tears.

Edward was the saving grace. He had graduated from

Oxford with full honours of every kind and gone into business with his father. He kept returning to Oxford, ostensibly to see his friends. Then Abby heard that there was a girl. She was, the rumour said in Newcastle, incredibly wealthy and outstandingly beautiful, with wit, intelligence and a generous father. William and Charlotte were delighted and a betrothal was arranged for the summer.

Abby was in correspondence with Rhoda Carlisle, who wrote that her new brother, the son of her mother's new husband, was ill and they would not be able to come to the betrothal party, so Abby invited Rhoda to stay. The weather was warm; they could sit in the garden and visit the shops and she would be glad of the company. Rhoda arrived, thin but brown-faced from being out in the fresh air. She clearly enjoyed being with Abby, but when Abby tried to talk of her family, Rhoda changed. Her dark brown eyes clouded and her conversation ceased.

After a week of running along the nearest beach, plodging in the sea, eating lunch in the garden, reading books in the quietness of the shady trees, Abby thought her friend looked a lot better. Then she began to talk of having a shop.

'What kind of a shop?' Abby said as they sat in the afternoon shade, drinking lemonade.

'Oh, I don't know. Clothes, perhaps, or hats.'

'It isn't respectable. You're young and unmarried.'

'Lots of women do.'

'Not women like us.'

'I'll have to do something and soon.'

'Why?'

Rhoda looked everywhere but at her friend.

'Why, Rhoda?' Abby insisted.

Rhoda looked fiercely at her.

'You don't know what it's like with two brothers, the baby screaming and – and him! My mother . . . she can't see anything wrong in him. I have no place there. I want to be away.'

'I'll introduce you to a nice young man at the party,' Abby said, trying for lightness.

'There are no nice men. They're all horrible.'

'You didn't used to think that of your father.'

'I was a child then,' Rhoda said sadly, and Abby thought of her own childhood when nothing seemed to change. The days went on for ever and her parents were always there, her mother teaching her at home, joking and laughing with her, buying her pretty things, making the house light and warm as it had not been since. The best time of all was in the late autumn, when darkness fell across the streets and lights appeared beyond the bay windows. The leaves were off the trees so that the branches looked like long fingers in the gathering dusk;

the wood fire gave off its bright flame; the kettle sang; the tea was made; one of her mother's rich fruit cakes and the pretty pink-and-white china were laid out with a cloth. They would sit there together, sure in the knowledge that her father would be coming home to them. There would be dinner and closed curtains against the draughts, and the round globes of the lamps would take the mystery from the corners of the rooms. They would read and talk and her father would relate his day. They would talk of people they knew and of Christmas to come and they would make plans. Later, Abby would curl up in her warm, soft feather bed. From there she would watch the fire die down and, as it did so, she would close her eyes in the knowledge that everything was right with her world and Christmas would mean all the special things that it had always brought. They had been so happy then. Why did it happen like that: to know that everything was all right and then to watch it taken from you? To know such happiness and to lose it was cruel. Her mother was dead and so was Rhoda's father and there was no hope for the future. Childhood was long gone and all the lovely, endless days would never come again.

Chapter Two

That summer changed everything. It was funny, Gil thought, how you kept on believing that things were going to get better. He had had the feeling all his life that there had been some kind of mix-up and he had been born into the wrong family. His father was little and dark and dumpy and blue-eyed; his mother was little and fair and not quite so dumpy, and so was Edward; whereas he grew tall and dark-eyed and it was always known in the family that he looked just like his grandfather Collingwood. This was not a good thing to be.

Gil could remember his grandparents, and with affection, from when he was very small. They lived in a dark narrow street in a terraced house in Amble, and his grandfather built boats for the local fishermen. His grandmother had no servants. She had a big oven with a fire and there would be bread set to rise on the hearth. She always wore a pinafore. Her house was clean; the brasses sparkled; she made soup and in her kitchen was a big table at which she seemed always busy.

His grandfather had a workshop and a yard some way from the house on the edge of the village towards the estuary, with Warkworth Castle in the distance. The workshop had a floor thick with wood shavings, and the smell was sweet. His grandfather built cobles, without plans or any help, two a year at least. And he had his own coble. Gil could remember pushing it off the beach into the waves when they went to see to the lobster pots and sometimes his grandfather took him fishing for cod. Edward didn't go. Was he seasick? Gil liked being there. He remembered the thrill of fishing, of feeling the tug on the line, the excitement and pride in his grandfather's voice when he caught his first fish and took it home for his grandmother to cook for tea.

They had both been dead for many years, but Gil knew that there had been a quarrel after which the visits to Amble stopped. His father had called his grandfather stupid and unambitious and the worst thing that he could be – a bad businessman. William couldn't forgive anybody for that. Gil had seen him reading the morning newspaper and shaking his head over somebody's bankruptcy and saying, 'I knew all along that he was a bad businessman.'

*

Being good at things began with school. You were sent away to be frozen, starved and beaten and then you had to be good at lessons. There was nobody to help. If you had a brother that made things worse, because he was obliged to ignore you. No one ever spoke to their brothers.

Gil envied Edward. For a start, he looked like he should and then he was a success at school. He had lots of friends and, though he wasn't a swot, he was good at things. His reports did not send his father into terrible rages that made Gil shake with fear and then cry with pain because there was always a beating to follow and days of being locked up with nothing but a jug of water and a mattress. He would, he thought, be good at being in prison if he should ever do anything very wrong.

At first he had determined to try harder, but the lessons were boring and the teachers were miserable at best. As he grew older nobody noticed that he was quite good at geometry and drawing, though he wasn't allowed to do drawing. Edward was so good at everything else there was no point in trying. Gil could not compete. Luckily his father didn't notice him much. With each report, the horror subsided after the first few days and his father was too busy at work to think about him. His mother was always out, shopping or visiting, and when she was in she was dressing to go out. She wore beautiful dresses and smelled lovely; she wore gloves almost all the time to save her hands.

Edward had many friends at school. Gil hated the idea. He had to sleep in a room with twenty other boys. The idea of putting up with them for more than he had to didn't appeal. They were stupid. They cared about whether they reached the cricket team. Gil had almost got himself into the cricket team and had to pretend not to be good just in time or he would have had to rely on other people for something very intricate and that was too awful to be considered. The games master, a creepy man who liked watching boys strip off for games but who was intelligent, said to Gil, 'Be careful, Colling-wood, or you might have to do something more energetic than getting out of bed in the mornings.'

Gil promptly became very bad at everything and kept out of the way.

Then, long after he had wanted to leave school, when he was sixteen, there had come a day when he had an argument with another boy. Gil rarely got into fights. He was big so people avoided him, but this time they said he had lost his temper and thrown the other boy out of a second-storey window. At first he denied it because he didn't remember. All he could remember was that amazing rush of feeling that nothing could stop or hinder. Beyond it somewhere he could hear voices, but far off and faint and nothing to do with him.

The other boy had been lucky. He had escaped with a broken leg. Gil was sent home for good to face his father and to be told that he could go to work in the shipyard labouring since he was obviously no good for anything else.

It might have been all right, but it wasn't, because the lads who worked at the yard knew he was William's son. The very first day half a dozen of them got him down onto the ground and gave him a good kicking. Nobody wanted to be seen with him. Day after day there was the kind of work that until then Gil had not thought existed: carrying and moving heavy things. His nails broke and his hands roughened. The dirt wouldn't come off them. The other men used indescribable language, most of it obscenities which Gil soon learned to recognise. Some of them drank heavily and spat frequently and eyed him as though they were going to give him a good kicking, too, though they didn't. The fighting that Gil had done at school he came to be glad of, and that he was big, so when he had fought a couple of them they let him alone.

At first he couldn't sleep for all the aching muscles. And it was strange to spend the day in the dust and dirt among uneducated men and then come home to the richness of his father's house, where his mother expected good manners, punctuality and clean hands and the talk was of social events and people.

After six months his father moved him. It became a

pattern. He spent time in each part of the works, with the platers, the riveters, the patternmakers, carpenters, plumbers, while, it seemed to Gil, Edward, Toby and their friends had a good time at Oxford. Gil couldn't think of anything to say when he met people. It seemed to him that he came from another world, and that theirs was somewhere entirely separate and rather silly. They did not know what it was like when you had one wage and half a dozen children, when you couldn't read or write, when you drank all your pay the first night so that you and your family starved all week. Some men would vow not to do it the next time, but they always did because it was the only escape. Some of them were moderate people; some had been saved by religion, but that didn't stop hunger and cold and heat and monotony from being their daily enemies, it just meant that they survived in some way. At home, where his mother insisted on there being half a dozen courses at dinner and enough food for three times as many people, Gil found himself staring. Often the men he worked with were the brothers and fathers of the maids at home, so everybody knew that he went back to luxury each night.

When Gil moved into the offices, among the engineers, the designers and the drawing office, everything changed. He found enthusiasm. He had grown to love the noise and clamour of the shipyard, to see the various processes which put the ship together, but he cared even more for the place where the ships were drawn, planned, designed, calculated. It seemed to him then as though this had all been in his mind to begin with and somebody had just drawn back the curtains. It was like having extra sight. He barely needed any of it explaining to him; he understood immediately. He could see the ship built and fitted; he knew how it went together; he knew that it would live and be something very important, that it could give men freedom, riches, adventure and love. It could give them communication. It could wipe for them fear and distrust and ignorance and it could enable them to kill one another. He could smell and taste and feel the ship even when it was only on paper. He knew how mighty and dangerous it would be and that he cared for this as he would never care for anything again in his life.

Mr Philips, who was the head of the drawing office, saw the enthusiasm, told Gil that if he worked hard he might achieve something, began to teach him and to get the other experienced and clever men to teach him all the things that they knew. Gil left home very early and got home very late and quite often he stayed with Mr and Mrs Philips because they lived in Newcastle. They had no children and Gil could see that as much as he was taking from Mr Philips he gave them back, because Mrs Philips made big meals and was always happy to see him. Seven days a week Gil worked. His father didn't seem to notice. He was so busy initiating Edward into the mysteries of managing a shipyard that he had almost forgotten Gil. Also, Edward had met a girl called Helen Harrison while at Oxford. William, Gil knew, expected his sons to marry for the betterment of the shipyard and the family, and Helen had beauty, money and social status. Her fortune would be put to good use.

'We'll have to look round for a likely young woman for you in a year or two,' William said.

That summer, Gil thought a great deal about Abby Reed. The truth was that he was afraid of her. His father said that she was exactly like her mother and that Bella Reed did far too much reading and thinking for a respectable woman. Abby was clever; Gil knew she was. She would talk to Edward for hours. After her mother died she ran her father's house so competently that Henderson Reed didn't bother to marry again. She had a disconcerting way of looking at you from frank blue eyes that unnerved Gil. He had even heard her swear. Her father looked sternly at Gil whenever they met, which made Gil think he was doing something wrong even when he wasn't.

The best days of Gil's life were those spent near Abby. That night with her had been the best night of his life and he could not forget about it as they grew older. She had crièd until she slept, exhausted, but she was warm and soft and smelled like blackberry pie. He had drawn near to the warmth of her and put his arm around her and she had moved closer in her sleep. He had also been there to pick her up when she fell and he pushed Thomas Smith into a pond when he would have kissed her. More than that, Gil couldn't manage. He couldn't think of anything to say to her and, as time went on, Abby seemed to become more formidable. Like Edward, she had lots of friends and was always talking and laughing and dancing. Everybody liked her and wanted to be with her. Gil thought there was no room for him near her. He didn't think she liked him. Why should she? Other people were clever and they were smaller and neat. He was always falling over things. Dancing would have been torture.

He saw even less of her when he began to work seriously, but he thought of what his father had said and bided his time, thinking that when he was twenty-one William might consider him old enough to marry. That summer, his mother boasted at the dinner table that she thought she had found a brilliant match for poor little Abby. Abby was always poor and little to his mother, even though Abby was the most confident young woman Gil had ever met. His heart plummeted. Robert Surtees. Who on earth could compete with somebody of twenty-five who was his own master, fabulously wealthy, from the top drawer of society, who owned houses and ran his own life, and had known exactly what to say probably since he had been in the cradle? She would undoubtedly make a good wife for a man like him. She was pretty enough to flatter expensive clothes and jewellery, wise enough to run a rich man's household. Her father would be delighted at such a match, Gil knew. He looked in the nearest mirror and saw a half-educated, overgrown boy with no graces. He stumbled away from his mother's table and left the house.

It was a perfect summer's evening, the one before Edward and Helen's betrothal party, and it was a relief to get out of the way. His mother had been fussing for days about the food, the flowers, the airing of beds and the making up of rooms. It was her only talent, he thought, organising parties. Perhaps he took after his mother, being no good at things. Then he remembered the look in Mr Philips' eyes over some of the work he had recently done. His drawings and calculations were 'beautiful' Mr Philips had said, 'just beautiful'. Gil had remembered this over and over again. It was the first time in his life that anybody had praised him. Gil wished he could live in the office. He listened hard to every piece of advice he was given from the educated, experienced men who ran his father's shipyard. If he could have gone in any earlier and stayed any later, he would have.

'You've got talent, laddie, real talent,' Mr McGregor in the engineering department had said. Mr McGregor wasn't supposed to call him 'laddie' or anything else that was familiar, Gil being the boss's son, but Mr McGregor didn't notice and Gil didn't care. It was almost a term of endearment. Mr McGregor and Mr Philips kept him close to them and gave him important, detailed work to do and Gil felt like a sponge, taking everything in. It was not like school, where he didn't understand. Everything he was told now became clear and he soaked up the teaching and the information even more as they began to praise him. Gil wanted to hear it. Every day he wanted to hear that he was good and for the two men to smile and shake their heads in admiration. The looks and words of approval would never cease to be a novelty. He had managed to please somebody and that had never happened before. Gil felt like a high-wire act at the circus: among the height and the fear but out there in the middle, doing wonderfully clever things. He had an audience who urged him on to do more and more daring, adventurous and creative things and the results were heady and wonderful. Gil would have done anything to bring to their faces that special glow of satisfaction.

Neither of them said anything to his father, but soon some of the best work was coming from Gil. He heard reported that his father was pleased at the new ideas and the accuracy and skill. Gil would spend hours adding deft touches, making sure that things would work and fit. Mr Philips opened the world of numbers to Gil as ten years of schooling had not, and he could see it, he could see the patterns. They were like frost on the windows and rings on the inside of trees. He had felt like jumping up and down. There was order in the universe; there was symmetry that you could alter and change. You had power there; everything had a place and a purpose. Levels and seasons and time and music were all to do with numbers. There came a clarity to Gil's mind that nothing could shift. It was like a flowering, an excitement, a sense of being where none had been before. Gil loved Mr Philips' office as he had loved nowhere in his short life. There he was not clumsy and stupid and self-conscious. Mr Philips would shut the door and when the door was shut nobody dared enter. Very often he went out and shut the door after him, leaving Gil alone, and it was bliss; the day went by much too quickly. He was always disappointed when it ended and he had to go home. The office was dusty because nobody was allowed to move anything. Gil knew it was a measure of Mr Philips' growing regard for him that he let him stay there away from other people and other eyes and anything that might break his concentration, but Gil felt as if he could have worked in the middle of Grainger Street in Newcastle and it wouldn't have made any difference. That office, filled with rolled-up papers that had been designs for ships God knew how many years back, was a sanctuary, an escape into another, better world. In some ways, Gil knew he would never come out of it. He was at home here; nothing could hurt him. It was clean and assured. Best of all, were his ideas. He soon came to realise that there was no limit to these. Once you had let that extra eye open which was creativity, it could not be closed. If you nurtured it and gave it space and acknowledged it, the work came to you and it was wonderful.

He had thought to go on from there, that he would prove to people he was good enough to marry Abby Reed. Suddenly she would see that he was clever too and she would love him. They would have a house in town and he would spend the rest of his life in Mr Philips' office and that house. He would not have a hideous Greek mansion and a wife like his mother, who wore gloves even in bed. He had thought, after being at boarding school, that he would want to sleep alone for the rest of his life, but a night spent alongside Abby had buried that notion. He would marry Abby and live in town. She would run the house and they would have children and he would be kind to them. He would not ignore them or beat them or send them away to school. He would read stories to them and at night he would sleep in a big bed with Abby, who was warm and soft and would belong to nobody else.

But his mother had been busy finding a husband for Abby. His parents liked her, there was even that about it.

He could have pleased them. She was Henderson's only child; there could be no objection. And when Henderson saw that Gil could do these great designs and such good work, he would be glad too. But his mother had taken Abby to Hexham to visit her family and she had met Robert Surtees and there was no help for it.

Robert was coming to the betrothal party. Charlotte had been clever. Gil allowed himself five minutes to think about being in bed with Abby. He gave himself five minutes a day. He lay back in the warm grass and closed his eyes. He would be able to surprise Abby. Maybe it was not too late. He had learned to waltz so that he could ask her to dance. It had been a long trail. Even making the decision to learn and then following it through had been difficult. He had stood on the pavement outside the dancing school in the narrow street of Pink Lane in Newcastle's centre and hesitated. The door was open, but it was the upstairs room; he had to climb the stairs before him. That was the hardest part. Once upstairs, the middle-aged lady was alone but for the gentleman who played the piano and she had been kind and patient.

'I want to learn to waltz,' Gil said.

'Of course you do,' she said, as though it were the easiest thing in the world. So he learned, thinking of himself and Abby.

*

The betrothal day came, hot and dry, the last day of June. Light streamed in, denying the darkness even a slender hold, and from early day everybody was busy. His mother went back and forwards with lists, and all the servants moved faster than usual. Gil had not thought that his brother's betrothal would have any effect on him. Why should it? But he was aware that Robert Surtees was coming here to see Abby. From somewhere he would find the courage to ask her to dance with him.

The afternoon was hot. The flowers which had been brought into the ballroom were watered so that they would not wilt. As many doors and windows were opened as could be to catch the tiny breeze that fluttered a little way among the garden paths. Early guests walked in the shade of the quarry gardens, where it seemed the rhododendrons had burst into special splendour, their flowers as big as his hands.

His mother sat outside on the terrace and dispensed tea and angel cake and smiles. His father accompanied various ladies with parasols into the rose garden. Abby came in the early evening with her father and Rhoda and Robert Surtees at the same time. Robert ignored Gil, but spoke at length to Edward and Toby, who had come some time earlier with his family. Gil decided that it wouldn't take much effort for him to hate Robert, standing there speaking in refined tones, talking about

Cambridge and how much better it was than Oxford, teasing the other two, glancing now and then at Abby and smiling at her. Rhoda didn't have much to say, it seemed to Gil, and she was much thinner than the last time he had seen her.

Gil didn't want to be with any of these people; he didn't understand why. Suddenly, anywhere else in the world would have done. It was as though there were an electric charge in the air. Red butterflies clung to nettles in the stableyard as Gil walked down to talk to the horses and rub their velvet noses. In the evening sunshine, fluttering as though they had been caught and pinned, the butterflies were so still that he could see the tiny black spots on their wings.

Throughout the early evening, people arrived. The musicians played. The dancing began, but Helen Harrison did not arrive. Gil saw the anxious look invade his brother's face. Eight o'clock came and went. Half past eight and still they were not there. Then, before nine o'clock, while it was daylight and only the coolness and the long shadows foretold of night, a carriage came up the drive and stopped in front of the house.

His parents were outside at the bottom of the steps and so was Edward. Gil didn't want to go forward, but, almost as though the house itself propelled him, he went and stood in the doorway. It was a defence. He felt as if marauders had made their way through the gates and up the drive and were about to storm the house. They could have been sixteenth-century Border reivers on an October raid, screaming and yelling, the horses' hooves dull in the night as they rode in to steal everything they could carry off.

Two ordinary people stood beside the carriage, but there was nothing ordinary about the young woman who turned towards him. Gil had never seen anybody like her. Her hair was the brightest shade of yellow. Her face was pink and cream and her eyes were a cool, dark-blue liquid. He could already imagine what her mouth would taste like: strawberries and pepper. Her lashes cast shadows on her cheeks. He thought of her hair loose, of how long it was, past her waist, and of her breasts bared for his mouth and hands. Gil tried to back away from the shocking images, but he couldn't. He had never felt like this about any woman in his life. He knew from that very moment that it was not the first time they had met. He recognised her. Helen Harrison was meant to be his; it had been written, ordained. He could smell the softness of her skin; he knew how she turned in her sleep. He could see her belly rounded with their child. He could hear her distant laughter as she ran away from him in play down a path that led to a rose garden. She didn't move or speak, though her eyes held his. Gil felt like somebody who had been struggling endlessly upstream until he was exhausted. His arms and legs were leaden with tiredness and the water was pulling him down. Her gaze didn't flicker, even when Edward came to introduce them and, as she moved towards him Gil gave up the fight. He went down for the last time and the waters closed over his head.

Chapter Three

Rhoda hadn't danced with anybody all evening and Abby felt disloyal as she polkaed and waltzed. Her mother had once told her that dancing was the only respectable way to get close to a man outside marriage, and it was certainly easier than staying near Robert Surtees. She regretted, in some ways, having agreed to go to Hexham with Charlotte. She liked him well enough, but no more than she liked several other young men, except that he was handsome and rich, and those were not, she kept telling herself, good reasons for liking anybody. Her father had already noticed Robert watching her and had talked about how smitten Robert was. He called her his sly puss. Abby had brushed him off. All she really wanted was to be with Gil, yet well into the middle of the evening they had not spoken, except in greeting. Most of the time she couldn't see him, the crush of people was so great.

The evening was warm and Rhoda was disinclined to

dance, so they went walking outside and here, finally, Rhoda talked to her about Jos Allsop.

'He comes into my bedroom in the mornings, he and my mother, and they laugh and joke and he tickles me as though I was seven. Sometimes when my mother over-sleeps, because often she's up most of the night with that brat, he comes alone, getting on to my bed and . . . I'm in my nightgown. He tells me how pretty I've become and during the day he spends a great deal of time with me. He touches me whenever he can. I'm afraid of him. I feel as though he's the spider and I'm the fly.'

They walked back through the quarry gardens to the house and were in time to see Helen Harrison arrive. They stood at a distance.

'Isn't she beautiful?' Rhoda said, but it was Gil's reaction that Abby saw. He had not looked at her like that, nor at any girl that she had ever seen. Abby was wearing what she had thought was a pretty dress, but when she saw Helen's she felt shabby and provincial. It was pale yellow spotted muslin with a tiny blue-and-yellow iris pattern. It was fashionable and shrieked to her of Paris, sophistication, society, adventure and involvement. Helen probably knew all the right people. Her life seemed dull to her. She caught a glimpse of herself in a nearby mirror and saw her defects, the too-long nose, the ordinary brown hair, her thin figure, her square, capable hands. Abby could have wept.

Helen and Edward danced, but afterwards Helen did what no girl Abby knew would have dared. She walked all the way across the room towards Gil Collingwood and quite obviously asked him to dance with her. Nobody did so except in a ladies' excuse me and Gil had always managed to absent himself upon such occasions. To Abby's dismay, Gil took the girl lightly into his arms as the music started and they began to waltz. He had lied. He did dance. Their steps matched perfectly and there were not now so many people, somehow, because Abby could watch them. Some woman beside her said to her friend, 'Don't they make a lovely couple?' And they did, much more so than Edward and Helen. Gil, tall and dark, and Helen, slight and fair, waltzed elegantly about the room.

Abby thought of all the times when Gil could have danced with her and hadn't, but he had known Helen Harrison barely an hour before dancing with her and he was talking to her quite comfortably by the look of things. Abby was angry, jealous, resentful, all things which she had not been before. She hated Gil in those moments when he had his arms around Helen Harrison and was moving her so confidently about the floor and she was looking up into his eyes.

'Did you go to Oxford?' Helen said. 'I met you there, surely.'

'No.'

'Then where did we meet?'

'I don't know.'

'Did you go to Cambridge? I have an aunt there—'

'I didn't go to university.'

'My father says that education is the waste of a good childhood.'

'Wasn't he educated?'

'Yes, I think that's why he says it.'

'My father had little education and thinks the opposite.'

They didn't talk any more. They didn't need to. Gil had danced with no one other than his dancing teacher, but it felt as though he had danced with Helen dozens of times. It seemed as if he could almost remember it. She entranced him. Her eyes sparkled and she was soft and light in his arms. And at the back of his mind, he knew the place that they had met before. The walls were white and so was the bed. It was afternoon and they were inside because of the heat. The houses were white and so was the sunlight and outside fruit grew on the trees, oranges and lemons hanging there such as they never could in England. It was quiet. The floor of the room was bare wooden boards and there was not even a breeze to disturb the thin white curtains at the windows.

*

Abby went outside. Her feelings were all mixed up and tumbled as though she were an egg timer and somebody had turned her upside down. She told herself it didn't matter that Gil had fallen in love with his brother's betrothed, that he had not shown any preference for anybody before. She wondered why apparently nobody but she had noticed. Was it because she knew him so well? Yet she didn't. They had exchanged barely a dozen words in the past six months. She meant nothing to him and now he must mean nothing to her. She gave a little shiver in the warm night. No good could come of his regard for Edward's bride to be. Perhaps it was just a momentary thing, passing.

'Miss Reed?'

She was standing on the lawn in front of the house. She turned around. Robert Surtees, handsome and smiling, was standing behind her.

'I hope nothing's wrong.'

'It was too hot inside.'

'Would you like to take a walk around the garden?' he said, and offered his arm. He spoke so kindly that Abby liked to hear him and tried to say the right thing back. He made her feel easier. It was late, but the night was not dark. A star peeped through here and there.

'Helen Harrison is very beautiful,' Abby said, unable to stop thinking about her.

'She's the most beautiful girl I've ever seen,' he agreed.

'We've met on several occasions. I can't think why she's throwing herself away on Edward Collingwood. She could have had a title. She could have married old money and an old name. She took London by storm and now look at her.'

'What's wrong with Edward?'

'Forgive me, the Collingwoods are common.'

'Charlotte married one.'

He smiled just a little.

'There are people who have not forgiven her. The woman is vulgar.'

'She's very kind.'

'She introduced us. I'm thankful for that,' he said.

Gil knew that, having danced with Helen, he should have danced with other young women. He looked for Abby, but couldn't see her and then spotted Rhoda Carlisle standing alone. She refused. Gil was relieved. He had done his duty and could now go off to think about what had happened. He went into an empty room away from the noise of the party. Beyond the window, in the gardens he could see Abby with Robert. The night was finally beginning to steal past the trees, but he could see clearly in the fading light that they were close together as they walked back across the lawns towards the house.

*

Gil's only hope was that Helen would go home. During the next few days he did everything he could to avoid her. He stayed at work, but for once work had lost its attraction. He could not put Helen from his mind. She remained at the house. Each evening after Edward came home they would read together and walk in the garden. Charlotte took her visiting to all their friends. In the morning at weekends she would go riding with Edward. In church on Sundays, Gil could hear her sweet voice. Gil wished that she would go away. He wanted to be with her so much he was sure it must have looked obvious, but he could tell that nobody noticed anything different.

He thought that she would probably go after a week, but she didn't. She stayed on because she said she could not bear to be parted from Edward. There was much talk about a wedding at Christmas. Charlotte and Helen spent hours making plans and long lists. Edward and Helen travelled to Durham to talk to the vicar of St Oswald's. Helen's parents had bought a house in Durham so that they could be near to their daughter after the marriage.

Gil couldn't eat or sleep and Mr Philips was beginning to complain about his work. Helen floated in and out of his dreams. When he was with her, he was conscious of his hands because he wanted to touch her so much. Worse still, she seemed to like him and often met his gaze over the dinner table or across the room. Desperate to get away, Gil went to see Abby. He suggested they might go for a walk. Abby looked surprised, as well she might, he thought. For a moment it seemed as if she might refuse, but she didn't. They left the house and walked through the dene near her home. It was pretty, with a stream and trees and shrubs, a bridge and little waterfalls. There were lots of people about since it was a hot July day and Sunday.

'How's Helen?' Abby asked stiffly.

'She's going home this week, I think.'

He hoped. She was sleeping in the room next to his. Why did they have to put her there? He could remember being with her, watching her turn in her sleep, her soft sighs, the sunlight breaking across the room, the shadows against the white walls . . . He dragged his mind back. Abby was talking to him.

'What?'

She looked accusingly at him.

'You haven't heard a word I've said. Why did you ask me to go for a walk? You don't want to talk to me. You never do talk to me or dance with me. You told me you couldn't dance.'

The words stuck in Gil's throat like dry biscuit.

'I can't.'

'But you can! You danced with Helen as though you'd done it hundreds of times. Nobody who hadn't waltzed before could have done it like that. You've obviously known for years.'

'I haven't.'

She didn't believe him, Gil could see. And he couldn't possibly tell her about the little dancing teacher in Pink Lane – it would make him look foolish. The angry look on Abby's face silenced Gil. They walked back to the house, Abby almost striding. Henderson greeted him without a smile and it was then that Gil realised her father didn't like him. What had he done?

'Now, young Collingwood, what can we do for you?' He looked grimly at Gil. 'I hear there's to be a wedding at Christmas. Awful things, weddings. Folk standing around looking stupid and trying to find something to say.' And Henderson stamped off.

Gil waited for Abby to offer him tea. When she didn't, he felt obliged to leave and go home.

Abby ordered tea for herself and her father the minute that Gil had gone. Henderson came in, sat down and drank his tea, but his face was dark and she had not long to wait before he said, 'I don't want that lad here, Abby. I've no objection to being friends with them up to a point, but if I thought you were taken with him—'

'I'm not,' Abby said quickly.

'What was he doing here then?'

'I don't know.'

*

Helen went back to Durham, but each weekend she came to stay or Edward went to her house. The next Saturday that she was at the house, Edward was out of sorts and she wanted to go riding, so Gil was obliged to go with her. They went early before the heat should take the day, while the dew was still on the grass, and it was just as good as Gil had known it would be. He was a better horseman than his brother, and riding through the wide Northumbrian fields with Helen was as near to perfection as life could manage. She enjoyed it too, shrieking as she jumped a fallen log, laughing when they raced. He felt as though he were giving her up to Edward again when they got back to the stables.

Her pretty brown riding habit suited her, making her eyes look even bluer, and they sparkled from the exercise. Gil thought that she was nothing like Abby. He was determined to make things right with Abby and went into Newcastle the following day. He found Henderson alone, and he was uneasy following him into the study. Henderson obviously worked on Sunday afternoons. To Gil, from somewhere, there was an echo. Was this what people did when they were lonely? The room had the untidiness of concentration. There were papers everywhere.

Henderson's house seemed small to Gil after the mansion that he lived in, yet it was a big town house with gardens and a tennis court, a conservatory and half a dozen big rooms downstairs.

'This is getting to be a regular thing, isn't it, lad?' Henderson said, watching him.

Being called 'lad' was like being at home and Gil resented the intimacy.

'Jack Philips tells me you have talent.'

Gill had had no idea that Abby's father was on such terms with the head of Collingwood's drawing office. The professional in Gil resented that, but he personally resented Mr Philips talking about him, especially to somebody like Henderson, who couldn't have kept his mouth shut during a sandstorm in the desert.

'Your father is lucky to have two sons,' Henderson said gruffly. 'Abby is out. I presume it's her you came to see. She's gone for a walk with Robert Surtees. Aye, you may well look. He haunts us.'

Henderson was watching him, rather, Gil thought, as though he might grab the silver candlesticks and run out of the door.

'I've got nothing against you, lad. I don't even mind that you're a younger son. But I wouldn't want to think that you were getting in the road here. Surtees is a man of property and distinction with a fine name and good breeding. I'll be the happiest man alive if he asks Abby to marry him. The only thing I lack in life is a son and he's a gentleman. He's educated and clever and knows his way about the world. You're just a lad and you haven't exactly distinguished yourself so far.'

The silence which followed was a Sunday afternoon silence. Gil knew it well. The atmosphere that you got when you went pigeon-shooting on those cool, foggy November days just before dusk came down slowly like a thief. The woods were full of pigeons, but you could not hear the flapping of their wings, nothing but the thick white silence before they moved, before you put the gun up to your shoulder and pulled the trigger. Never a day off for pigeons, never a peaceful Sunday, always the possibility of death before teatime, blood staining their grey-and-white breasts.

He left. Henderson showed him the door and Gil went, Henderson telling him flatly that Abby could be hours so there was no point in waiting and that he had work to do.

There was nowhere to hide. The lengthening nights became a torment of sleeplessness and want. His mother complained that he didn't eat and questioned the cooking. His father finally realised that he was making a mess of things at work and moved him so that he could watch him. After that, working beside his father and Edward, Gil was so miserable that he made elementary mistakes. Finally, one afternoon that autumn, his father lost patience and hit him. It was the kind of blow that sent you into the wall and, since the wall had no give in it, you took the pain twice. He had been thinking about leaving all that week, going he didn't know where, and that strengthened his resolution; but his brother, who had never before defended him, sprang up from the far side of the desk, shouting, 'Don't do that to him!'

They were the sweetest words that Gil had ever heard. Edward was in front of him like a shield. He could hear the quiet threat in his brother's voice when he said slowly, 'Don't hit him.'

William laughed.

'How brave you are,' he sneered, 'brave on the back of your lass's fortune? You aren't wed to her yet. I tell you, you aren't much better than he is. We'll do a sight more when you've wedded and bedded her. Then we might get some work out of you!' And his father left the office, slamming the door. Edward turned around, glaring.

'What the hell is the matter with you?'

Gil could taste blood and he had hurt his shoulder and his arm, but he got out of the office and down the corridor and into the cupboard-sized place his father had assigned his office before the stone in his throat eased.

Helen had arrived when they got home. It was Friday evening. She was particularly bright at dinner. She wore one of her prettiest dresses and afterwards she played the piano. William had barely spoken and went away to his study. Charlotte sat with a book. Edward came to where Gil was standing by the window and said, 'Toby asked me if I would go into town and play billiards. Do you want to come?'

Gil was astonished and rather pleased. He couldn't understand why Edward should seek his company or want to go out since Helen was there.

'Just going out for a while,' Edward said generally to the room and, since nobody raised an objection – his mother and Helen were forever discussing the wedding – they went. There was a full moon and Gil realised when they got out that it was exactly what he had wanted to do. It made him feel powerful, getting away.

The billiard hall was another world, companionable, warm, comforting. Young men drank beer and smoked and the sound of the billiard balls meeting with a snap across the table and clunking down into the pockets was mixed with talk and laughter. Toby greeted them with obvious delight and Edward seemed happier here than Gil had seen him for a long time. He played several games. Gil didn't do much. It wasn't that he couldn't play, he just didn't need to tonight. He cheered his brother on and gave him lots of advice and Edward laughed and made funny remarks at him. He was surprised at how well they got on and was content to watch the evening go by. He wished, in some way, that he could hold the time. Toby and Edward were like a double act at the music hall, they knew one another so well.

'Did I tell you I'm leaving home?' Toby said to Gil as Edward paused, chalking the billiard cue and considering possible play. 'I've taken a house in Jesmond, just a small house, all to myself.'

Gil envied him. At work that afternoon all he could think of was leaving. Now it didn't seem so important. He was happy in Edward's company. His brother had taken his part, but would it last?

'I'm going to plan my garden, immerse myself in it.' He looked tenderly at Gil's bruised face. 'Been fighting again, old boy?'

Edward cleared the table.

'How about a game?' Toby said to Gil.

'He doesn't want to play,' Edward said.

Toby laughed. His teeth were white and even and his eyes sparkled.

'Are you sure?'

'He's quite sure.'

'But you'll play, won't you, Ed?' Toby asked him.

'Play if you like,' Gil said to his brother's enquiring eyes. 'I'll watch.'

Chapter Four

As Christmas approached, what Abby had both most hoped and feared happened. She was dreading the anniversary of her mother's death, as she did every year. Her father's house had ceased to be a refuge and became an emptiness, the house where her mother had been and where the ghosts and memories only served to make the present less bearable. Her father spent all his time at work and the optimistic tone which he had held to at first seemed slowly to evaporate like a pale winter sun in mid-afternoon. He hid among his work even more than he had before her mother died, and Abby felt as though she could hear every clock in the house ticking.

Robert Surtees rescued her. Abby, being truthful with herself, acknowledged that she would have accepted invitations from someone less entertaining and handsome than he was to get away. She would have suggested to her father that they should move, but she knew he would see it for foolishness. In any case, they could not leave Newcastle because of his work, so it would be pointless. He hated the country, so they could not move there. Robert provided diversions. This year he had suggested going to the cemetery with her, but Abby had other ideas so they drove to his house near Hexham and spent the day there among his family. Abby suggested to Henderson that he should accompany them, but he only said gruffly that he would go to work as usual.

Robert's parents were both dead. Rumour said that his mother had committed suicide after a miscarriage and that his father had taken to drink and followed her, but Abby found his family sane and kind. There was his grandmother, whom Abby could tell liked her, and various uncles, aunts and cousins. Coming from an empty house to a family who made her welcome was so pleasant that Abby could not tell whether it was Robert she liked or his house and family. His life was so easy, filled with pleasure, the opposite of anything she had been brought up to believe in.

In her world, men worked all the time. Robert had people to take care of everything: an agent to manage the estate, a housekeeper, reliable people to see to his possessions and, as far as Abby could judge, it went smoothly enough so that he could spend much of his time with her.

He would have bought her presents, but Abby refused, knowing that expensive gifts meant commitment. Her father did not hide his pleasure at her conquest. The pride in his eyes made Abby pleased with herself in ways she despised, and in her honest moments she knew that her mother would have laughed in scorn. Sometimes she thought that she heard her mother's voice.

'Going up in the world are you, Abby? It gives you further to fall, don't forget.'

If her mother had been alive she would not have seen so much of Robert, but there was nobody at home and she began to spend her days with him. Her father encouraged the friendship and was eager to go to the big house for Christmas. Abby thought of Gil then, making snow angels. She had not made them again since that first year, had no inclination to do things like that with Robert, though she did other pleasurable things. They went skating when the ice was hard that winter and roasted chestnuts and gathered holly. Abby liked going out into the cold air and coming back to see the lamps lit in Robert's house.

It was the kind of house she would have wanted for her own, so far removed from the pretentious Greek mansion of the Collingwoods as a house could possibly be. Parts of it were five hundred years old, and Robert told her that his family had lived in some kind of dwelling on that same piece of land for eight hundred years. Various members of the family had added on to the house when times were prosperous, so that it had no coherent heart to it. People like William would have hated it. There was no symmetry, no organisation, just a mish-mash of half a dozen eras. Abby loved it because it spoke of the personalities of the Surtees family, the silliness in the folly beyond the house, their fear in the tower which had protected them, their artistic merits in the long gallery which housed paintings by several famous artists of the past. There was a lovely garden where Robert's great-grandmother had grown herbs to cure ills, and a rose garden which his mother had designed shortly before she died. This was what houses should be about, Abby thought, the sum total of a family, not an image of one time, erected to impress people. It didn't impress the upper classes, Abby thought: they only laughed at it. Then she was ashamed of herself.

Beyond Hexham it was not too far to visit Rhoda, and when Abby went there to stay overnight, she understood why her friend was not happy. Jos Allsop looked Abby over as if she were a prize sow, Abby thought. His gaze lingered on her breasts and hips and legs. He came into the bedroom in the early morning when they were still in bed and his hot gaze upset Abby, even though he didn't touch her. Rhoda's mother was pregnant again and the house seemed overfull of noise and people. The small boy who was Jos's son was spoiled, shouting and screaming when he could not have what he wanted immediately, so that Abby's fingers itched to smack him.

There was plenty of money. The house was big, the food was good and there were servants, but Rhoda's mother ignored her daughter and her guest and Jos gave them too much attention. Abby was glad to leave the little town and go for a walk on the moors, even though the day was cold and bitter and up there nothing stirred.

'I used to love it here when my father was alive,' Rhoda said, her brown hair blowing about, for she had refused a hat. There was nothing to stop the wind. The stone houses stood as a testament to good buildings and materials. Abby understood how Rhoda felt. When you knew you were loved, you could abide in such an inhospitable place, but when that security was threatened, the bleakness of it seeped into your life just as the wet wind blowing across the heather had soaked her gloves so that her fingers were starting to go numb. There was nothing here for people who were lonely. She thought it strange that she could be so lonely amidst the elegant buildings of the Newcastle streets, and Rhoda felt just the same out here, where the wind and hail blew horizontally across the unfriendly land. She even felt sorry for the sheep, who were huddled in for shelter against the backs of the drystone walls. It gave her a little glow to think that Robert waited for her when she wanted to go back to the more civilised atmosphere of Hexham. Rhoda had no one and it was difficult not to feel sorry for her, though Abby knew pity for an unworthy sentiment.

Rhoda seemed to have lost her mother as well as her father, and Abby thought that this was true. In a sense, when one parent died you lost both of them, for the other one, being no longer part of a pair, was altered in some way. Rhoda's mother now belonged to another man and Henderson belonged to his work, which he had gone to as surely as some men went to whores' beds; but Abby knew that the most important part of Henderson, that which fools would call his heart, was buried alongside Bella Reed in the cemetery and that in some ways Abby would never get him back. He belonged to his dead wife and that was why he had not married again. Abby did not know whether to be angry that he had given up or to be glad that he had not made a bad second marriage. Neither seemed of benefit to anyone.

She walked a long way with Rhoda, beyond where she would have been glad to turn back, grateful not to face the savage wind which screamed across the felltops. But Rhoda seemed oblivious to the weather; she had so little to go home to that was of any ease or comfort. Jos's family would be there for Christmas and, though Abby had met them only briefly, she could see what kind of people they were. They were like Charlotte in a sense: they cared nothing for books, music or religion; nothing spiritual came near them. The men were crude and the women were vain. They had never seen beyond the dale nor hoped to and were secretly, she thought, afraid of everything outside it. Jos was one of them. She worried that he would be cruel and self-indulgent and that Rhoda would suffer. There was no longer a book in the house nor a piano. He drank and smoked, slept long and, Abby suspected, bedded Rhoda's mother like a rutting goat. He did nothing useful because Rhoda's father had left more than enough money for them to get by. Robert must have despised him, she thought. Abby made certain that there was nothing between the two men beyond pleasantries, though when she left she could not bear to look back and see Rhoda standing alone with her sheepdog outside the door.

'You will come and stay with us for the wedding?' Abby had begged, and it was not just for Rhoda but for herself. She did not want to go and see Gil's hungry gaze on the girl who was to be his sister-in-law, yet she had no excuse to offer for her absence. Rhoda would provide support and had promised to come unless there was snow and the weather prevented her.

The wedding was fixed for two days before New Year, and Abby watched anxiously from the windows as the sky darkened and snow began to fall. Rhoda was to come to her the day before and to stay for more than a week afterwards. Abby's plan was that it would snow then so that Rhoda would be obliged to spend several weeks with her in Newcastle during January and February. That way neither of them would be lonely.

Robert took Abby to several parties during December. Everywhere she went, Abby was accepted by Northumberland society because of the man beside her. He asked her if she would visit his London house in the spring and here he would show her the city and take her to see the sights. Abby had not been to London and was excited at the idea. She had grown comfortable with him and had ceased to hanker after a boy who had proved stupid enough to fall in love with a woman he could not have. Abby felt the armour of Robert's love and was content.

It had not at first seemed to Gil as though his brother had changed. All their lives, Edward had taken little notice of him and the day in the office when William hit his younger son would not make the difference. Gil assumed that Edward's sympathy would pass, so he stored squirrel-like in his mind the way that his brother had defended him and the evening spent in the billiard hall. But as each day went by and Edward did not revert to the superior scathing person whom Gil could not like, Gil stopped thinking about that day.

Because he could not have Helen, it seemed somehow that at least he had gained his brother and, more and more, it felt traitorous to him that he should want her. He tried to put the feelings from him, and it also seemed – and this was strange – that in some ways they changed places.

Edward's work became less and less competent so that Gil began helping him, covering for him, making sure that William's wrath did not come down on Edward. Edward was restless. It did not please him to stay at home by the fire – and the weather was foul. He would go into town and play billiards and drink and, to Gil's surprise, his brother drank a great deal. He always asked Gil to go with him, which was an even bigger and much more pleasant surprise. Sometimes, Edward would not have reached home without him.

At first Gil was flattered by the invitations, that his brother would introduce him to his friends, but it also occurred to him that if Helen had been waiting for him he would not have wanted to leave her. Sometimes she came to stay and Edward took her to the theatre or to see friends, but he did not often go to her parents' house in Durham. Night after night, Edward played billiards. He would drink and laugh and call on Gil to admire the best shots. Often, he drank so much that he was not sober by morning.

Sometimes they went to Toby's house. He lived not far from Abby, though it was a much smaller house. Gil thought it strange inside, unlike any house he had seen before. The walls were painted white and there were no carpets, just polished wooden floorboards. There were no ornaments; everything was simple and uncluttered. There was a big garden at the back, but not much to see, all black and brown and bare-treed in the winter weather.

'What do you think?' Toby asked Gil on his first visit.

'It's like a monk's cell.'

Edward laughed so much that he choked. Toby grinned.

'It's so . . . sparse,' Gil said.

Toby went to the window and looked longingly down the garden.

'In the summer I'm going to sit out there under the trees and drink wine.'

Edward was leaning against the wooden shutter on one side of the window, and Gil could see that he was also imagining himself there.

Edward was silent on the way home. Everyone had gone to bed by then, but he would linger, not because he wanted to keep the day, Gil thought, but because he wanted to steal as much of the night as he could, as if the morning held some kind of terror. The wedding was a week away.

'Come in by the fire and have some brandy with me,' he said, and Gil went.

In the small sitting room, which was truly the only comfortable room in the house and everybody tended to go in there, the fire was kept burning brightly and the brandy decanter shone in the reflected fire, the housekeeper having discovered that they would often finish their evening here. Edward poured the brandy and they sat down by the fire. Gil considered the dark liquid in his glass.

'Do you mind if I ask you something?'

'What?' Edward stretched out his legs. He looked happier now than he had looked all day, as though brandy and the fire were his only pleasures.

'Are you frightened of marrying Helen?'

Edward looked at him.

'Of bedding a woman? I have bedded women before.'

'No, that's not what I meant.'

'What then?'

'Of being different, the responsibility, the – the commitment. Does it weigh you down, only you seem so . . .?'

Edward didn't answer straight away, and then slowly.

'Yes, it's frightening and strange. What made you think that?'

'You go out so much and you drink such a lot and . . . you take me with you as if you had no company. You have Toby and your friends.'

'I wanted to get something back. No, that's not true. I wanted something I never had: to be close to my brother.'

'Toby's more like a brother to you than I am.'

It was a secret smile and an unhappy one that Edward gave. His face almost hid it and he shook his head.

'I wanted . . . what was it . . . I wanted memories, but when I searched for them in my head they weren't there. All I could see was this space and my father shouting at us and the smell of my mother's clothes, the smell of her powder. And she was always coming and going like something that's never still. I feel as if I'm losing something, yet when I search my mind there's nothing to hold on to. And that day in the office . . . I wished I had been kinder to you.' It was only drink, Gil told himself when his brother, embarrassed by the words, had gone to bed; but when Edward left the room all the magic went with him. Gil had not known until then that his brother held the magic. He had thought that it was the night or the brandy or the firelight. He realised then for the first time that the magic is only within people. The room was cool without his brother, and silent, and had nothing to do with him. Something was over and something new was just beginning, and there was nothing left to do but go to bed.

Chapter Five

Helen and Edward's wedding day was as white as the icing on their three-tiered cake, but didn't prevent anyone from getting there since the snow was decorative only and quite soft. The service was held in St Oswald's in Church Street in the middle of the small city. From outside, you could see the cathedral in the background. Gil felt that his father would have been better pleased if the service had been held there, but Helen's parents seemed determined that William should not be allowed to ask everybody of importance in the entire northeast.

Edward had been drunk every night for a week and on two occasions, nights when he had not asked Gil to go with him, had not come home. His mother would have protested, but his father said, 'Let the lad alone. He'll be leg-shackled soon enough.'

Durham couldn't help looking pretty in the snow, with its narrow streets, grey river and magnificent cathedral and castle, but when Helen walked up the aisle of the church she looked to Gil like some kind of sacrifice, as though the vicar were about to slay her on the altar. Gil had to make himself not stand in front of her to protect her from what looked to him like ancient rituals up to no good. For the rest of her life she would be Edward's, belong to him in the most basic way possible, sleep in his bed, bear his children, obey him, be there for him to come home to. It was like a cattle market, Gil thought. Edward didn't smile and Toby, who was his best man, looked so pale throughout the ceremony that Gil was convinced he would faint. But Helen shone. She wore a long veil and a cream dress and nobody in the history of the whole world had ever been as beautiful. If he had doubted that she loved his brother, he doubted it no longer. She looked as though she had waited all her life for this moment. Her responses were clear and precise, whereas Edward's were low and mumbled. Edward was better after the ceremony, laughing and throwing pennies for the local children who gathered in the street. Since the day was now bright and fine and the snow had retreated to lawns and rooftops, he insisted on walking with his bride on his arm the short distance to her parents' home down New Elvet and across Elvet Bridge to the towpath where her parents had a gate to their house on the riverside.

It was a big townhouse. They went in by the gate and up the winding path through bare trees to where the house stood with its front to lawns and the river and its back to Claypath, up the bank from the marketplace. The older people went by carriage but the younger ones walked, laughing and chatting as the sun made the snow glisten.

Abby had said nothing but hello to Gil, and he didn't speak to Robert, for whom he had developed a hatred. Rhoda Carlisle looked pretty in yellow, and when Gil ventured to tell her so, since he was beside her and had to say something, she smiled and said, 'Actually, it belongs to Abby. I haven't a decent dress to my name. Who needs dresses when you live in the wilderness?'

'I thought you liked it there.'

'I did. Things like dresses only matter when you have little else, don't you think? I used to love Allendale Common. Now, I would give almost anything to get away.' She stopped and let the others troop past and it seemed only polite to stay with her.

She stood looking out across the River Wear, taking great breaths of fresh air as though she needed to store them. When the others had gone up the semicircle of stone and in by the French windows at the front of the house, the quietness was pleasant, only the birds in the trees. Later they danced together at the ball that was held that evening in a huge hall at a nearby college. Gil danced with Helen, but she was so happy she couldn't speak. He asked Abby, but she refused.

'I'd rather chop my feet off,' she said. 'Why don't you go and ask your sister-in-law? You seem to like her well enough.'

'I suppose you're going to marry Robert Surtees.'

Gil couldn't believe he had said this, but they were far enough away from the music and other people, so he didn't need to be discreet. She turned cold blue eyes on him.

'He hasn't asked, so it would be indelicate of me to say much other than that he's a gentleman and you're a stupid boy!' She turned with a swish of her skirts. Gil was angry. He went after her even when she ventured outside. Snow was starting to fall in big, dangerous flakes.

'That's not fair!' he said and, when she wouldn't stop, he got hold of her bare arm and pulled her around. 'I came to you.'

'To me? Oh yes, I remember. Sunday afternoon in the dene. You bothered to come into Newcastle to see me and then you ignored everything I said.'

'You say too much.'

'You love Helen.'

For months now, ever since the moment he had seen her, Gil had denied to himself that his regard for his sister-in-law was love. He had called it misguided, immature, inexperience, all number of things, but he had not called it love and he did not expect to hear it on anybody's lips, least of all from Abby. He tried to think. He tried to be truthful and the images of the warm country and the white room flooded into his head.

'It's – it's in the past,' he said.

'What past?' Abby laughed and her eyes glinted with fury. 'You haven't got a past, not that kind. I'm not blind. I saw you when you met her. I saw how you looked at her.'

'I recognised her.'

'From where?'

'I don't know.' Desperation got Gil further. 'Please, Abby, I do care about you. I have always—'

'No, you haven't. You've always ignored me.'

'I didn't know what to say, what to do. Give me a chance, please.'

'This is just because you can't have her. Do you think that's what I want? Some other woman's leavings? She could have had you if she had wanted, couldn't she? She didn't have to marry your brother.'

'She loves him.'

'Does she? Well, good luck to her. I'm glad it's not me, marrying a Collingwood.'

Abby remembered later the things that she had said to him and she thought that her mother would have been ashamed of her, but at the time it felt as though Gil deserved everything she threw at him. And she did throw it. Words were such horrible weapons and he was defenceless; he had always been defenceless in that way. She thought he was a product of a cruel upbringing. He had never learned to talk his way out of anything because he had always been physically hurt. He waited for the blows in that kind of situation, he expected them, and whereas if she had been a man he might have defended himself with his fists, he couldn't do it, so he had nowhere to go.

'You're common. You're not a gentleman.' Robert and his friends and their company were to blame for this, Abby thought. It was true that Gil's grandfather had been a poor man, that his father had built a monstrosity of a house, that they cared for material things such as people of quality did not, but it wasn't something he could help. She threw insults at him and Gil begged and pleaded with her not to marry Robert. How scornful she was, how unforgiving. The worst part of all was that she loved him. She liked Robert well enough, she saw it all clearly, and she knew that marriage to him would be comfortable and easy because of his money and independence; but the young man in front of her was the person she always looked for when she walked into a room. All those evenings when they hadn't talked and hadn't danced didn't matter as long as he was there. When he wasn't there every party was boring. He had nothing to recommend him: no breeding, no talents; he didn't even love her. She was to be his escape from a love which he could not have, and she thought that she could not bear that he should want Helen more than he wanted her. Yet without him there seemed little point to anything. Her pride brought despair to his face.

'If you ever cared for me at all, don't leave me like this, please.'

Abby thought she would go to her grave hearing him say that, and she told him airily, while the snow provided a white carpet, that she would marry Robert and he could go to hell. Which was, she thought later, exactly what he did.

People began to leave as the snow fell heavily, but all the Collingwoods had to do was walk up the hill towards the Harrison house, where they would spend the night. Helen and Edward were not having a honeymoon. He planned to take her to Paris in the spring.

'Besides, Toby and I are going to the Solway to shoot geese at the end of the month,' Edward had said.

Gil's room had a big fire and huge floor-to-ceiling bay windows which looked out over the darkness of the river where the castle and cathedral were outlined as gigantic shadows against the white sky. They frightened him, those buildings. Anything frightened him which could exist for hundreds of years when most men were dead at sixty. How many suffering souls had looked on those same walls and made no impression? For how many more generations would they stand while people died in a thousand different ways? Gil hated buildings that lasted. They should fall as men fell, it was only decent.

Helen and Edward had gone to bed. In a room across the hall, his brother was enjoying his first taste of a woman who did not belong to him. It was as though Helen committed adultery, except that no one else but him would know the wrong of it. He tortured himself thinking of her in his brother's arms while his memory, or his imagination, or some part of his mind, gave him her laughter and the happiness of them both and the child inside her, his child, the only one she had. He could feel her, taste her, yet his arms were empty and the longing hurt so much that he would have cried to ease it except that he couldn't.

The snow laid a heavy look on the night. The fire died slowly in the grate. He didn't go to bed. He stayed by the window, saw the night through and told himself that it would never be as bad as that again. His brother would have deflowered his bride by now and you couldn't do that twice.

Chapter Six

Abby had not been kissed before and didn't know what to expect, only that the timing was wrong. She was still upset about Gil. It was sweet enough, standing in a shop doorway with Robert, quite alone with him, and having him put his mouth on hers, but she kept thinking back to Gil and wishing she had said different things.

She and Robert had lingered on the walk to where they were staying with friends, dropped back from the others.

'I want to make you mine,' he said. 'Will you marry me, Abby?'

Her first instinct was panic and refusal, but she had known for some time that he had been leading up to a proposal; he would not have spent so much time with her or asked her to go with him to London.

'May I talk to your father about it?' he said.

Henderson, she knew, would be delighted. He had not thought about such things as an advantageous marriage, but since it had happened, apparently of its own making, he could enjoy it. He didn't like Gil, Abby thought, but Robert was the son-in-law every man dreamed of. She thought that even her mother would have been pleased. The only criticism Henderson might have made, and he had not voiced it, would be that Robert knew nothing of industry and would be unlikely to want to take on the shipyard as Henderson got older. In a way, Abby could make this up by Robert's prosperity and position in society and also she could ease some of the hardships of her father's life both past and present. With her married and settled, his responsibility would cease and maybe then, she thought, he would consider his own life, feel less guilty about going out except to work, find a social life, even perhaps a wife. More than anything, Abby wished to free her father so that he could have some future. All the important things in his life seemed to be in the past.

The following day, which was Sunday, the Collingwood family travelled back to Newcastle in the evening. Edward had nothing to say. Both he and Helen were pale and Helen fell asleep in the carriage against Gil's shoulder. She was still asleep when they got home. Edward yawned as he got out of the carriage and, glancing back, said to Gil, 'Carry her, will you? I'm so damned tired and she'll fall over the step and break her neck if she has to walk.'

Gil carried her up the steps and over the threshold into the house. Almost awake by then, she thanked him in a small voice and went away to her room. His parents went to bed, but Gil wasn't tired; he felt as if he would never want to sleep again. It was almost midnight when Edward, to Gil's surprise, came into the small sitting room just as he had on so many nights before his marriage and poured brandy for them both. He sat down in the chair across the fire.

'You can come to the Solway with us,' he said.

'What?'

'Goose-shooting. Toby's going and Ralph Charlton. Come with us. It'll be fun. You don't get much fun.'

'I can't if you're not at the shipyard.'

'Father won't miss me. I do so little when I am there.'

'You have no feeling for it.'

Edward finished his brandy and went across and poured another. Gil hadn't touched his drink.

'Oh, I have plenty of feeling for it. I hate it almost as much as I hate him. The two are bound together so closely, how could I feel otherwise?'

'Is there something else you want to do?'

'Yes, I want to go to the Solway and shoot geese.'

'No, I meant—'

'I know what you meant,' Edward said and he sighed.

'When I was a child and did something wrong, he used to thrash me and I could smell the shipyard on him, that particular dirty smell, sweat and work and mud and water and grease.'

'The smell of the Tyne.'

'Docks and those disgusting hovels he keeps people in. Do you imagine he ever thinks about them?'

'No.'

'Do you think about them?'

'Sometimes.'

Edward downed his brandy.

'I knew you did. You're a good man, Gil.' And he yawned and wished his brother goodnight.

Gil managed to avoid the row, though even from his office he could hear his father's voice and then Edward's and at one point they were both equally loud. Helen's fortune had been put to the company's use and it had been a huge sum of money. Money altered the balance of power, Gil thought. Edward had been given a big office next to his father's. He cared nothing for it and Gil had lingered there, admiring the view and wishing it were his. From it you could see, or imagine you could see, the extent of his father's domain.

There was a steelworks, an engineering works, a huge shipyard. There were blast furnaces, foundries, machine shops and chemical laboratories. The noise was tremendous from thousands of men performing skilled jobs. Enormous chimneys poured out smoke; ships were on the water; ships were being built; men scurried everywhere and Gil knew that beyond it all, his father had had the great gates repainted at the entrance to the shipyard. They proclaimed: 'Wm. Collingwood & Sons'.

They had begun with iron, now it was steel ships, warships, battleships for various navies from China to Spain, and oil tankers. On the wall of his father's office was a portrait of a man called John Rogerson, the owner of the *Mary Rogerson,* the first ship, they believed, to take crude petroleum in barrels from America to London. Anything could be done; anything could be achieved.

The noise suddenly increased as the door was flung open and his father strode down the corridor and came into Gil's tiny office.

'I suppose you're going as well, are you?'

'Don't start on him!' Edward said, following him in.

Gil didn't think he had ever seen his brother so angry.

'Well, are you?' His father, Gil reflected, didn't frighten him any more. He hadn't realised.

'No, I'm not.'

'He doesn't want to shoot the ickle-wickle geese,' Edward teased him.

William threw Edward a black look.

'You're idle, idle and good for nothing!' He slammed the door on his way out. Edward pulled a face.

'Freedom!' he said. 'Nothing but me and the geese.'

Gil had imagined that the weather would be so bad that they wouldn't go anywhere, but Helen wanted to shop and for some reason she asked him to go with her, so he went. It was a perfect day. She wanted to try on various dresses. Gil felt that his mother would have been more use, but he quite enjoyed it, sitting on a chair while she came out wearing each one, asking him what he thought. The truth was that she looked lovely in them all, though he managed to persuade her not to buy a bright pink creation with feathers. It was easy. All he had to say was, 'I don't think Edward would care for that,' and her face would fall.

They went out for tea. They spent an hour in an art gallery looking at various portraits of Grace Darling, who had, with her father, gone out in a coble to rescue people from a ship foundering on the rocks. Gil could remember his grandfather telling him about it. There were other paintings of Tynemouth and local people and places. It was a cold, dry day and lots of people were about. Musicians played on the street corners and families gathered in cafés to drink tea. Helen ate cake, drank her tea and went home laden with parcels. In the evening she wore one of her new dresses and they stayed up until late. Gil was happier with her than he could be with anyone else.

She was so excited on the day that Edward came home. She couldn't rest and kept going to the window to look for the carriage. He was late and it was dark and cold, but she ran down the steps in greeting, her eyes bright with tears. She didn't leave Edward's side that evening until he asked her to play the piano and then she kept looking across at him and smiling.

'How many new dresses did you let her buy?' he asked.

She went to bed, but Edward lingered for a while and Gil stayed downstairs after that, enjoying the night and the fire. Then a white figure appeared soundlessly from behind him.

'My God!' he said. 'I thought you were a ghost.'

'Is Edward not here?'

'No, he went up ages since.' Gil stood up and he saw that she did not even have a dressing-gown or slippers.

A tear fell and then another and several more followed quickly. Gil stared.

'Helen?'

She backed as he moved towards her.

'Very silly,' she said, 'excuse me.' And she ran away.

Robert saw Abby's father, but it was a brief interview. Her father came out of the study looking like a short fat sunbeam and Abby was pleased to see that he looked happier than she had seen him look in years.

'I only wish your mother was here,' he said.

Her mother could not have fully approved of Robert, Abby knew, but she smiled and enjoyed her father's pride and pleasure. Her mother liked people to work.

'I don't mind admitting to you,' her father said later, 'that I thought you had a hankering for young Collingwood and in all conscience I couldn't have given you to him.'

Abby had seen Gil that day in town with Helen and they had looked so happy. They looked right together, it was strange. They were laughing and she had hold of his arm. They had stopped to look in the jeweller's on the corner of Pilgrim Street and Abby dodged back into New Bridge Street to keep out of their way. Gil would never care for anybody but Helen and she had been right to agree to marry Robert. They would be happy.

Robert wanted to be married straight away and she could see no reason why they should not be. There were arrangements to be made, but he, having no parents, cared nothing for a big wedding and she, knowing Henderson's hatred of weddings, cared nothing for it either, so they set the date for around Easter and made plans. He would have bought her the whole of Newcastle had she let him, stripped his house and had her refurbish it, turned all the flowers in the gardens to roses since she loved them and toured around the world so that she could see every wonder on God's earth. Abby did not want to go away for too long. It would be hard enough for her father, she knew, to lose her from his house so that he came home to no one but the servants. To leave the country for any length of time would be too much. He disabused her of this idea.

'Abby, I had my youth, I had my marriage and I was lucky, for your mother loved such a fool of a man as I was. This is your turn. Go away for as long as you like. I'm happy for you. I couldn't be more pleased. Have this time and enjoy it. It may not last long if there are to be children.'

'Would you be pleased?'

'Everything about you pleases your old father.'

Robert would take her to Paris, Rome, Florence, Venice and anywhere else that she wanted to go.

'We could spend the whole spring and summer away. We'll start in London and go on from there and you'll see the house and I'll introduce you to all kinds of people and you'll like the shops and the theatres and everything.'

Abby had not thought much about being away from home, but now the idea appealed to her. She couldn't wait to get away.

Rhoda had stayed with her until after Christmas, and Abby wrote to ask if she would be a bridesmaid and to tell her about the wedding, to ask if she would help to choose the dresses and the flowers and when she could come and stay again because there was much to plan and do. Rhoda replied immediately that she would be glad to come and stay, for there was now a new baby in the house, a girl. The baby rarely slept; her mother and Jos quarrelled continually; there was no peace. Abby wrote back to say that she could come and stay for as long as she liked; she would be glad of the company. Robert, she told him, ought to find someone of their acquaintance so that they could make up a foursome when they went out.

He looked at her.

'Rhoda Carlisle? I didn't realise that you were so close.'

'She stayed with me at Christmas, Robert.'

'I thought that you were sorry for her.'

'She's a very nice girl.'

'Forgive me, she's a country bumpkin.'

'She is not!'

'She knows nothing and she's strange. She goes walking up on the fells alone. She has a thick dales accent and she's very odd. She even had to borrow a dress from you, as I recall you saying, for Helen and Edward's wedding. No, I don't think so, Abby.'

'Her father left her a great deal of money.'

'Don't be vulgar.'

'I'm not sure I'm the one who's vulgar here.'

It was their first quarrel, Abby realised, watching his

face go white while he restrained his temper. Here in her father's house in the sitting room, where Kate and Mrs Wilkins would hear them, they were fighting, but she was upset to think that not only did he not like Rhoda but he was ungentlemanly enough to say so.

'I have asked her to be my bridesmaid.'

'Then let us hope you have so many that no one will notice her.'

'I wasn't planning to have more than one.'

'Perhaps after we are married you will choose your friends more carefully. Between Rhoda Carlisle and Gillan Collingwood, you have nothing to offer.'

Abby was suddenly furious.

'There's nothing wrong with Gil.'

'Everything is wrong with him,' Robert said roundly. 'Not least that every time he's in a room with you, he doesn't take his eyes off you.'

Abby wanted to faint for the first time in her life. She put one hand on the chair arm.

'He does not!' she said.

'He watches you dance.' Robert laughed. 'It's pathetic,' he said. 'He doesn't have the wit or the manners to ask you to dance, he just stands there. Don't tell me you didn't notice the poor boy was lovesick for you. Haven't you ever noticed him hovering? Can he speak, or is he really as stupid as he appears? You really weren't aware of him?'

Abby's hands shook when she and Robert had tea a few minutes later. She couldn't trust herself to pick up a cup and saucer. The cake which Mrs Wilkins had made so carefully and so lightly stuck in her throat.

February was a long, cold month and March was worse somehow, perhaps, Gil thought, because you looked for it to be better and it was not. He was only happy at work and even then it was difficult. His father and Edward quarrelled frequently and though it was not in front of him, the atmosphere suffered both at home and at work. It was a curious thing to find his father at odds with Edward and in harmony with him, and although Gil didn't like it, somehow it favoured him. He took to his old habit of hiding in Mr Philips' office and his father at long last realised what was going on and called Gil in.

The room was full of light that day. It was late March and the evenings were beginning to lengthen noticeably. His father had big windows in his office, so what light there was always benefited the room. Plans and designs were spread the length and breadth of the huge desk. As Gil walked into the room, his father looked up and then he smiled. Gil could not remember that having happened before and knew that for once he had succeeded in pleasing William.

'I wondered whose hand this was that I could see

here. I knew it wasn't mine and I know my men too well to mistake them. They're bright lads, some of them, but not at this level.' He looked hard at Gil. 'Old men make good judges, but young men make good designers. I'm a good businessman, but I was never a good designer. I remember looking through some papers of my father's once and realising that if he had had ambition, he could have held the whole world. How ambitious are you, Gil?'

At last William had called him by his name. Gil hardly dared speak.

'I want to build the best ships the world has ever seen.'

William clenched his fist.

'The best?'

'The biggest, the fastest, the most beautiful.'

William's eyes danced with pleasure.

'All right then,' he said, 'you will and we will find the business, sell the ideas, get the contracts. We will build this company into something the world will never forget.' He came forward and clapped Gil on the back.

It was the happiest day of Gil's life. He worked late and then he went home with his father. The next day his father gave him an office which was so big it was scary. It had in it a huge Turkey rug and was all brass and mahogany. He installed Mr Philips and several other people whom Gil had requested in the offices next to it, so that it was as if Gil had his own section of the works, and he had Gil's name put on the door in bold black letters.

'Well, well,' Edward said. 'What's this?'

Gil wanted him to be pleased, but he could tell that Edward wasn't. Edward walked around Gil's new office and said nothing.

Gil was almost sorry that his father had recognised his ability. He had enjoyed the brief time of having Edward's affection. He had liked being part of the magic circle of Edward's friends, the billiard hall, the bars. He had liked the way that he was accepted as Edward's brother. Now Edward was going to put him back out into the cold and Gil felt as though his new-found status at work was a very high price to pay.

'Father admires you,' he said thinly.

'I don't think he does.'

'He told me so. He thinks you have — what is that word — flair. You. When did you ever show any true ability for anything? Now, however, you have blossomed. That's what we must call you from now on — Blossom. Toby will approve. He loves flowers. What kind of a flower do you think you are?'

'Shut up!' Gil said.

'I wish you well. You can have the whole bloody thing as far as I'm concerned. I hate every last stone of it!' Edward strode out of the office. He did not come back to dinner, nor did he return later. Helen had been out buying new clothes again and Gil was called upon to admire her dress. His father said that he thought Helen had enough dresses to wear a different one every day of the month by now.

Helen had started to drink wine with her dinner. Although William didn't approve of women drinking he said nothing to one glass, but of late she had had two. Tonight she had three and stumbled when she left the table. Gil was standing beside her and hoped that he had obscured his father's view, but, left alone with his father and the port, he knew that William, pouring from the decanter, had seen what had happened.

'I don't approve of men going out every night like this,' he said now. 'Damn it, the lass is still a bride. Where is he?'

'I don't know.'

'You go with him, don't you? Women, is it?'

'Billiards.'

His father laughed.

'Is that all? Have a drink.'

Gil drank some port, but slowly.

'Women shouldn't drink,' his father said. 'It's bad enough that men do it.'

Gil thought it was ironic that, having lost Edward's company and confidences, he should move on to his father. They dined in the small dining room unless they had company, and he liked it. It had two big fires and was warm and it was close to the kitchen so the food was always as hot as it should be. His mother loved candles and it was all silver and white, and since neither of his parents cared anything for economy, it was lit with a hundred dancing flames which softened the features of older people and enhanced those of younger folk. He could hear Helen playing the wistful tunes of Mozart on the piano in the room next door and outside was the peace of the Northumberland countryside. He had never before relaxed in his father's presence, but he did so now.

'The lass plays well, even after too much wine. I did see.'

'I know.'

'No, you didn't, you thought to hide her. It's a fine thing is chivalry, even if she doesn't deserve it.'

'I thought she did.'

'Aye, mebbe. Hasn't turned out to be much of a husband, has he? Still, neither do most men. Do you think you will? I thought you might have had Reed's little lass, but I see she's to wed young Surtees. I wish her joy of it. His father was useless and his mother was worse. What about Rhoda? I like the lass. She's got eyes like fell water – bonny. Her father was a strange one but good company and clever and he left her a deal of money. What do you think?'

'I don't know,' Gil said, taken aback.

'Well, don't leave it too long. She looks ripe to me.' And his father finished his port and went off to the study, doubtless to move on to the brandy, Gil thought.

Helen cried when she went to bed. Gil couldn't hear or see her, but somehow he knew. And why should she not, he thought honestly. After that first night, Edward had had no regard for her, treated her as though she were unimportant to him, and all the dresses and all the wine in the world would not make up for that. He no longer went out riding with her; he took her out as little as possible; he took no pleasure in her company that Gil could see and often, as tonight, he did not come home. Gil knew because he waited up for him.

When he went to bed at one o'clock he could not pass her door without opening it. He wanted to make sure that she was well, he told himself. She was asleep and it was not surprising. The room smelled strongly of brandy and there was a decanter a third empty and a glass, well-fingered. She slept heavily; he could hear her breathing. He was tormented with the idea that, being unused to spirits, she would lie on her back and vomit and choke. He told himself that he was stupid, but he couldn't leave her. So as the fire died and the room darkened, he kept alight a candle and stayed there, watching at the window from time to time in case his brother should think fit to come home. He tried to will him there. He tried to go back to where they had been during the short time when he had basked in the sun of his brother's love. He wanted that again so much. He conjured up the billiard hall, red and gold, and the laughter of the young men and their carelessness. Edward wanted the sunlight for himself alone. He wanted Gil in the shadows behind him and now, in the dark depths of the unforgiving night, Gil wanted that too. I would have stayed there, he thought, to have you like me.

Helen stirred in her sleep. Gil went over and tucked in the blankets around her. The night was cold, but if he fastened the shutters he could see neither the room nor the driveway outside. Her hair was braided, but her features were slack with drunkenness and her breathing was all brandy. Gil took the glass her lips had touched, poured a brandy for himself, sat down halfway between the window and the bed and saw the night through. He dozed a little and when he awoke, red was streaking the sky. When he got up, he could see the snowdrops in the front garden which had blossomed within the last few days. Spring was coming to the Tyne valley. It was always late, but he loved it the more for that. The waiting was worthwhile.

Edward did not come home. Gil left Helen's room when the streaks of light showed through the sky. She was not sleeping so heavily then, though he could imagine the headache and the sickness that she would have when she awoke.

He went off to work and was busy there all day, doing what he had always wanted to do, so that he forgot about her. When he got home she was pale and listless, ate little at dinner, drank nothing and afterwards didn't attempt to play the piano. Then Edward came home. He had tickets for the theatre that Saturday evening. She was at once a different person, smiling and lively. She clapped her hands and became excited. Edward offered to play a card game with her and she agreed. They went off to bed together early, but later, when his parents had long gone up and Gil was trying to talk himself into making his way up the stairs rather than falling asleep on the sofa by the fire, she came down. The servants had gone to bed and Gil found her clattering about in the kitchen by the poor light of one candle.

'The brandy's in the sitting room,' he said behind her. She jumped and turned and the candle hovered dangerously.

He lit the nearest lamp and saw by its glow Helen in a long white cotton wrap, wide sleeves lace-edged and pearl buttons from neck to toe. She looked so small in the huge space of the cook's domain.

'I didn't come for brandy.'

'I should think not, after last night. Don't you feel ill?'

'What do you know about it?' she said.

'Why don't you go to bed?'

'I don't want to. It's silent there and the night is so black and—'

'I'll take you up.'

'I'm not a child.'

'Come on.'

He put out the light, lit another candle in the hall and led her up the stairs by the hand. In her room, half a dozen candles burned and the fire was almost out. Gil put some wood onto the fire to make a pyramid and it began to burn. He secured the shutters over the windows and pulled the curtains tightly across.

'Your maid is supposed to do that.'

'I didn't want her to. It makes me feel closed in.'

'It's too cold for anything else,' Gil said. 'Aren't you going to get into bed?'

'With you here? Hardly.'

'Go on, I'll tuck you in.'

He did so, but he knew that tears were close.

'It'll be all right tomorrow,' he said.

Helen shook her head. She looked woodenly at him for a few seconds and then turned away. She began to cry, silently and without moving. The room was changing. Gil couldn't help but notice it and was glad that he had not been drinking heavily, or he would have blamed it on alcohol. It seemed to him that the few candles gave out the light and flame of fifty and that the fire became amazingly hot so that it warmed the whole room. The night was well shut out, but the curtains seemed thin like muslin. From somewhere behind them came the faint breeze of an early summer night with the air gentle such as at the onset of the new season. The walls were coloured golden from all the flickering flames and the shadows were large upon the walls from the fire.

'Don't cry,' Gil said, hoping his voice would bring normality back.

'I'm not crying,' she said, and to prove it she turned over towards him. It was as though someone else offered the tears because she gave no indication of them. Her face did not tremble; her nose did not run. The tears, unaided and unacknowledged, poured down her cheeks as though somebody were standing with a bucket behind her eyes and she was just some vessel through which they were going. She didn't sob and her throat didn't work; only her hands gave her away. Her fingers closed on the bedcovers and clenched there.

Gil was sitting on the bed. He took hold of her frozen fingers and rubbed them to put warmth back into them. She sat up and smiled at him and the room was all white, just as he had seen it in his mind a hundred times since they had met. Could you recognise the future like that? He had thought it was the past. Where was it? If things had already been arranged, if fate was there, then her marriage to Edward had been threatened from long before. Perhaps his brother had not stood a chance because time was mixed. The past and the future were more powerful together than the present, which was all Edward had had to offer.

It was just as he had known. His recognition of her had been right. They knew one another well. Gil had never been with a woman, but her body was not new to him and half the delight was in touching her again, in having her back from whatever distance they had come to be together. After the first kiss he could not have left her, even if his life and the lives of half the world had depended upon it. He had been lonely for her for years, waited for her for decades, mourned her loss, dreamed her presence, seen her in the distance a thousand times, wished that other women had her face, her body, her voice, her laughter. She had never been another man's wife. She was his and she came to him confidently, surely. In his mind it was summer in whatever warm country they belonged to. The very stones of the house were bleached by the sun.

She came to him naked, joyful, greedy, as though she, too, had waited from a long way off, as if distance was a prison and she had escaped. Her body was warm and soft and her hair became loose from the tight braids which usually held it. She was not crying, she was not speaking, yet her voice was full of love.

He had wanted her for so long and nothing could

stop them from being together. It was like a fight, a struggle to be near and, though all the demons of hell should try to stop it, nothing could. Each kiss was better and each caress brought her body nearer, until near was not sufficient. He thought the light flickered, even the shadows retreated and beyond, he knew for a split second, was the clarity that told him it was a Northumberland winter's night. He felt the hesitation on her, a second's resistance. Her body fought and then yielded. All the devils in hell screamed and Gil knew triumph. She was his. It was meant to be and nothing could alter his possession of her. You could not go back from there; it could not be undone; it was too late. She gave a cry and he knew it for pain. The winter wind howled beyond the window. The room was cool and the dying flames of the fire threw twisted shadows upon the walls. The bed was a tormented mess of sheets and blankets, and Helen lay sobbing, half clinging and half resisting. He didn't let go of her, not until it was over, not until her hands released him and her body drew back and then he stopped and left her.

In the candlelight with the bedclothes thrown back, on the white sheets there was blood, enough for him to recognise what it was, sufficient for him to stare. She was turned away from him as though ashamed and crying softly.

'Helen?' His voice sounded hoarse, as though it didn't

get much use. She turned further away and tried to get in among the blankets, to pull them up to cover her body. He hauled them out of her hands and dragged her back to him. She protested and fought and he put her down so that she should look at him. She closed her eyes and turned her head away, but he waited.

'Helen?'

Resigned, she opened her eyes, though she still didn't turn her head or look at him.

'What?' she said with a hint of impatience.

'Tell me that was not the first time.'

She closed her eyes again, but only for a second and then she said, 'What would be the use?' Her voice was tired, almost hoarse, as if she had spent hours shouting and fighting and had no more to offer.

'Why?'

She smiled. She changed in that instant. She was not the person that he had thought, the pretty empty-headed girl. She was not as he had seen her.

'Do you know how I spent my wedding night? Alone. I spend all my nights alone.'

'I don't understand.'

'He doesn't love me.'

'If he hadn't loved you he wouldn't have married you.'

'He's afraid of your father. He married me because your father wanted my money.'

'No.'

She looked at him clearly.

'But you love me, I know you do. You loved me the moment you saw me and I knew you wouldn't hurt me.'

'I just did.'

'Oh, that.' She stretched like a well-fed cat. 'That was divine. If you knew how I've ached for you.'

Gil covered her body in kisses and caresses. She tasted like rich fruit, like peaches and she felt so soft. He hadn't realised that a woman would be quite so soft, all rounded and warm. He found that he could make her body lift for him, that he could make her desire him just as much as he desired her. He could make the tips of her breasts harden under his tongue and have small noises of need make their way past her lips. It was wonderful. Best of all were her eyes. When she opened them it was as if someone had lit a candle there, for they were blue shine. He felt as though he had discovered the perfect secret, the greatest pleasure. Her tongue was so pink and her teeth were so white and he felt as if he could do anything now. He had the whole world there in bed. Nothing else mattered. He thought that he would never be lonely again.

Chapter Seven

Edward came to Gil in his office in the middle of the following morning and said, 'I'm playing billiards with Toby and the others tonight. Do you want to come?'

Gil didn't know what to say. He couldn't look at him. Edward came further into the office and closed the door.

'I didn't mean the things I said to you. I'm not jealous, really I'm not, but I wanted to please the old man too and I can't, no matter what I do, whereas you seem to be able to do it all the time.'

Gil was too ashamed of himself, too guilty and wretched to speak.

'I thought I might taken Helen to Venice in May, try to make up for things. What do you think?'

'I'm sure she'd like that.' Gil was amazed at how calm his voice was. Could he be a natural liar?

'I'll surprise her. So, are we playing billiards tonight?'

Gil couldn't think of an adequate reason to say no.

Every minute hurt that evening, watching Edward

walk around the billiard table. It had been a wretched day. Gil couldn't work. His mind replayed his seduction of his brother's chaste wife with himself cast as the villain. The billiard hall had been a haven, now it was just another place. Edward had not changed. He smiled across and asked for advice and Gil tried to be the same. Toby was full of talk about his garden, the containers in which he had planted bulbs which were flowering and the flowers which he was growing from seed on the window ledges of his white house.

'There'll be roses and I'm going to have a lavender hedge at either side of the path so that when people brush against it there will be an exquisite perfume. Do you know you have eyes that change colour?'

Gil looked at him, startled.

'In the evenings they're almost black; during the day they look like sherry. Curious.'

The room felt airless to Gil, even more so than usual. He made an excuse and went outside. After a few minutes Edward followed him. The Newcastle night was full of sounds and the pub opposite threw orange light across the pavement. He heard Edward and moved away. There was a bridge not far and they walked there and listened to the water as it made its way down to Tynemouth and out into the North Sea. Further on were the docks and the shipyard where their father had made his fortune.

'When I left Oxford I swore to myself I wouldn't

come back here,' Edward said, leaning over the bridge and scowling into the dark water.

'So why did you?'

'I can't help it. I've tried to leave, but every time the train pulls out of Newcastle station my bloody stupid heart breaks. I don't know how to go. I want to, but I can't. If I was born a thousand times, it would always be here, Tynedale, or Tyneside and Bamburgh beach. It belongs to me. When I was at Oxford I used to wake up in the night because I thought I could hear the pipes.'

Gil didn't want to go back inside, and either Edward didn't want to or he understood that Gil didn't, because they took the last train home. The stars were bright and Edward sang local songs as they walked from the station.

Gil had half-imagined that Helen would be waiting in his room and dreaded it, but she was not and everything was silent. He made excuses to himself, said that it had only been once, swore that it would never happen again. Edward would take Helen to Venice and things would get better. He fell asleep thinking of this, so tired that he could think no more.

All that week Helen was smiling and bright, even though Edward went out each night and stayed out on the Saturday. Gil's hopes began to lift. He had made a mistake. Everybody was allowed a mistake. He didn't think of her all the time; he didn't even want her.

*

On the Saturday night when it was late, therefore, it could not possibly have been that when he passed her room to go to bed he opened the door and went inside and closed and locked it. There were candles and there was a fire and he had not even the excuse that everything changed, because it didn't. And she had not gone to him and she was not crying. Anyone else would have thought she was reading. There was a book open beside her and a glass of wine untouched on the table by the bed. She watched him lock the door and come to her and he knew then that she had been expecting him. Her hair was loose and brushed and shining gold and she wore a nightdress that showed off her arms and shoulders and breasts, and it had buttons conveniently placed down the front. Gil sighed and sat down on the bed.

'How did you know?' he said.

'I've waited every night.'

She leaned forward and kissed him, friendly and sweet. That was when Gil realised that the moment you think you have conquered an enemy, all is lost. He had thought he could make his mistake and go back to where he was before and it was not so. He had thought he was strong, that he didn't want her. That was laughable now. He had not thought that he would betray his brother a second time, but then he had not thought that he would betray his brother the first time. He was not the person he had hoped to be. All he wanted, or would ever want, was her. She got out of bed and kissed and kissed him like somebody starving and held him and begged and started to pull his clothes off until Gil helped. He couldn't understand how he had managed to keep away from her all that week. The part of his mind that knew this was wrong was deliciously employed like a parent, telling him what an evil person he was. He was pleased to show it how bad he could be, putting her down and taking her as if she were a whore without kisses or caresses, then cradling her in his arms and giving her wine and laughing and telling her all the things that he had not been able to say the first time.

The wind got up outside and they threw back the curtains to watch the stars in the clear night, which seemed bigger and nearer and twinkled on and off as if in entertainment while the candles guttered and the fire died and Gil wished that the morning would never come. She was so wonderful, she was so beautiful and he knew that she loved him, that she had always loved him, was born to love him. She was nothing to do with Edward, or anyone else, so it didn't matter that she had married him. They talked about silly things and when the fire was out and the candles were gone and there was no light from the windows so the last vestiges of respectability were finished, in the complete blackness they made love and Gil knew that she had never belonged to anybody but him and that she never would. The responsibility was strange. Finally she slept and he listened to her breathing and knew then that neither of them would ever die. He acknowledged that it was all stars and folly, but it was all there ever would be and he would have given up the rest of his life for the sake of these few hours with her.

Chapter Eight

Abby's wedding to Robert Surtees was not as she had thought it would be. It was almost as though someone else were marrying him. His family, and especially Charlotte, took over. She had to have half a dozen bridesmaids; there had to be five hundred guests. Robert, as Charlotte pointed out frequently, was the most eligible batchelor in the county and therefore certain standards had to be met. Abby wanted to deny it all, wear an old dress, run away, but for his sake she went through with it. If they had loved one another differently she would have suggested they should elope, but he was important and she was not, so she meekly accepted his cousins and friends to attend her on the day and all the ideas that the women of his family could devise. Later, she swore to herself, it would be different.

It was May, the best time of year to be married, with all the flowers out. Her father was so pleased. The wedding breakfast was to be held at Robert's house since it could accommodate all the guests, and the fine bright day meant that people walked in the gardens and sat about talking. Rhoda was her chief bridesmaid. The Collingwoods were all at the wedding, though Helen looked pale.

Edward had started coming home at night, though nobody knew why, and Helen had become nervous. Gil was already worried and would have kept from her had he known how to. Each day he swore to himself that he would not go to her and each night he went; but on the first night that Edward came home to dinner, Helen drew Gil aside after dinner and without looking at him said, 'It must stop.'

'I can't stop. I don't know how.'

He drew her into a darkened room along the wide main hall of the house and began to kiss her.

'We could leave. We could go away—'

'He came to my bed.'

'What?'

In the darkness Gil could see nothing.

'He came to my bed. He's my husband.'

'When?'

She didn't reply.

'When, Helen?'

'I don't want to talk about this anymore.' She wrenched away, tore from the room and when he followed her she was sitting close beside Edward by the fire in the drawing room.

Gil couldn't eat or sleep or work. As far as he could judge, Edward bedded his wife nightly and she made no objection. William began shouting at Gil in the office. Gil thought of various wild schemes and dismissed them, but he admitted to himself after days and days of denying it that Helen did not, in spite of what she had said to him when they were together, love him. Her eyes lit up when she saw her husband in a way in which they had not done for him even at the height of passion. He counted for nothing. When his brother was present, she didn't notice him.

On the day of the wedding she didn't leave her husband's side. They moved around together, talking and laughing with everyone, her hand through his arm. Edward looked so happy. Toby stood and watched them too and he came to Gil.

'How are you, dear boy?' he said.

'How's your garden?' Gil asked him.

'I could fill it with black tulips,' Toby said.

Gil became more and more miserable. Helen didn't look at him; Abby didn't speak to him and later when there was dancing, Rhoda refused. Her mother and stepfather were there and her brothers, including the small one, her stepfather's child, who tugged at her skirts for attention. Gil felt like doing the same.

*

Abby had once as a child had a pot doll dressed like a bride. It could not be played with because it was in white and would get dirty. It sat in a glass case, untouched and useless. That was how she felt on her wedding day, something to be looked at and not touched.

She had missed Rhoda. There had been no one to whom she could confide her doubts and fears, the way she didn't like certain members of Robert's family. She liked to listen to Rhoda's problems, too, but this time Rhoda had come with her family and would go back with them. She seemed different, less approachable and had nothing to say. Even though Abby's thoughts were caught up in her wedding, she was shocked to see how thin Rhoda had become. Rhoda excused herself by saying that she had not been well, but she was silent. Abby wondered whether she was slightly envious because she wished that she could get away from her mother and stepfather and her life in Allendale Town. Rhoda seemed more unhappy than ever and there was little Abby could do. She resolved to have her stay for a long time when they came home again.

Abby endured the day well enough, speaking to everyone, smiling all the time, finally escaping into the garden when everyone was dancing. She could not bear another silly remark about her marriage. It was still light, though a star peeped through. She walked in the cool silence and it was such a relief, until she came to a big pond in the middle of the garden and found Gil by himself. He, too, had lost weight. He glanced at her and then down.

'You look—'

'Like something off a Christmas tree. I know. I had a doll who looked like this. She was called Ethel and her underwear was stitched to her dress.'

She waited for Gil to laugh or at least smile.

'We're going away,' she said to fill the gap. She felt a wave of homesickness and she had not set off yet. 'We're going to Paris and Rome and Venice. We might see Helen and Edward.'

In the quietness Abby's mind replayed accurately the way that she had refused Gil and how Robert had told her Gil watched her when she danced. Robert had been right. Gil had no graces, no conversation. He didn't even look at her. He ought to have wished her well, basic manners decreed it. From the ballroom, Abby could hear the musicians strike up a waltz.

'I must get back,' she said and picked up her skirts and ran across the lawn towards the door.

Gil walked around outside for a long while and then back towards the house. At the side of the house in the shadows, he could see Rhoda and a man. She was obvious because of her bridesmaid's dress: they were all alike, pale blue. She was standing against the wall. The man with her had one hand on the wall as though he were somehow holding her there, though he was not. As Gil drew nearer, he saw that it was Jos Allsop. Rhoda looked distressed as far as Gil could judge, her body drawn back against the wall as far as it could be. Jos was speaking to her in low, soft tones. Gil's feet crunched on the gravel and Jos turned around, quickly taking his hand away from the wall. Gil didn't know what made him say it, but when Allsop challenged him with a rude, 'What do you want?' he said, 'Rhoda promised to dance with me.'

'She's changed her mind.'

'I haven't.' Rhoda looked up bravely, though her voice trembled. Allsop cursed and walked away. Gil couldn't understand why he was concerned about her. She didn't matter to him. She was trembling and kept glancing past him fearfully as though her stepfather might come back. She looked like someone who wanted to run far away, a creature who longed for the cold, dark moorland and obscurity. The bleakness of her situation struck Gil as much the same as the way he felt. He put her hand through his arm and walked her slowly back inside. They stayed together. Gil needed the support. Rhoda was like a wall between himself and the other people who were there. He was not flattered. If she left him she would have to go back to her mother and stepfather and, he realised, anything was better than that. They danced twice and when he went to get Rhoda a drink, his father came to him and clapped him on the back.

'Her father left a tidy sum, lad, and if she's happy at home then I'm a Dutchman,' he said.

Abby had not worried about her wedding night. Her mother had talked openly to her about such things.

'Men are not gods. If they had been, they wouldn't have such ridiculous bodies which can provide such intense pleasure. Be kind when you marry and generous in bed and with luck you'll enjoy yourself.'

Abby did enjoy herself and was glad that her mother had given her permission to do so. Abby had no one to compare with Robert, but for sheer enthusiasm and joy he was impossible to fault. He quite clearly adored her. She did think he very possibly had been to bed with a number of other women as rich young men were inclined to. He made her laugh, which was a good start. They had champagne and Abby was more certain than ever before that she had made the right choice. He was kind and helpful and didn't embarrass or upset her. She was so pleased at her decision to marry him and could not help thinking of what Gil would have been like – clumsy, most probably, because he would know nothing of women – but her heart thudded that she had even thought of him. Abby wished she could be sure that he was all right because he hadn't looked it that day and she was partly to blame. She wondered what he was doing now and she thought of Venice. They would be there, the four of them, among the wonderful buildings and churches, and he would be at work in Newcastle without anybody.

Waking up in bed with another person was a pleasant surprise. They set off for London the next day and Abby tried not to look back, thinking of her father. He had assured and reassured her but, since he had not been without her before, Abby did worry.

The Mayfair house was huge and terrified her, but she had to do nothing so the terror passed. The housekeeper there was used to running everything and, though she was polite and discussed menus and guests with Abby, everything ran smoothly without any assistance from her and she was relieved. All she had to do was be the hostess at her first big party, be advised by her personal maid what to wear, and smile and chat to all Robert's friends. This, Abby conceded, was not difficult.

A life of pleasure was something she had not had before and it was strange. There were parties, at least one every night, and concerts and plays and different people to meet. Being up most of the night, it would be lunchtime when Abby rose. There would be visiting; either people would come to her or she would go to them and after a while she began to recognise everyone.

They went to Paris several weeks later, but in a way it was similar to London because most of the same people were there. She liked the new sights and the warm afternoons. They stayed for so long that Robert said Venice was not the place to go next, it would be too hot and smelly, so they went to Florence and there again were people she knew. Abby would have liked to go off and explore Florence alone, but she was not allowed to do so, other people declaring that it was not safe, so she had to endure their constant chatter all day. If she picked up a book she was almost bound to be interrupted and she discovered it was not the done thing to read.

'Are you bookish?' she was asked more than once.

Robert seemed happy to stay in Italy or in France and when they finally made their way back home he was reluctant to go any further north than London. Abby felt that it would have been churlish to have insisted. They were together constantly, but he didn't always come to her bed and Abby found that she was quite glad of the quietness, since she was now rarely alone. He put her first in everything. He loved to see her in new dresses; he bought her expensive jewellery; they went to parties together. Other men went out without their wives and Abby was pleased when he began to do so occasionally; people had teased her that he loved her so much he couldn't bear to be out of her sight.

Before the winter began, Abby had a dream. She

dreamed that Gil was a child again and that his father was turning him out of the house. She dreamed this two nights running. On the third night she thought that she was standing on the beach below the castle at Bamburgh. It was snowing and he was calling her and she couldn't see him through the snow.

Abby dreaded going to sleep and would lie awake during the quiet – at least comparatively quiet – hours of the London night and try not to wish herself in Newcastle. She had nothing to complain about other than that she missed her father and longed to see him. Robert complained that she had nothing to say. She caught a cold, developed a bad cough, became reluctant to see other people and was always tired. All during the first dark days of the winter she thought about her mother and about her father all alone and finally she went to Robert.

'I must go home for Christmas,' she said, and he sighed and kissed her and reluctantly agreed.

It was William's idea that Rhoda should stay. At first Gil resented his father's high-handedness, but while Edward and Helen were away in Venice, it was pleasant to come home and find somebody there. Rhoda was the least demanding person he knew. She would go walking alone, but he could go with her if he chose. She loved riding and didn't ask for company, though if he suggested they should go out together she seemed glad of the company. She was happy reading in the evenings, but loved the theatre. She was quiet in company, but she would talk to him when they were alone. Helen and Edward were gone three months and during that time Rhoda came to stay twice. Both times she looked so happy to come and so miserable when she had to leave that the second time Charlotte persuaded her to stay longer, so when Edward and Helen finally returned Rhoda was still there.

On that first evening, Helen drew Gil aside in the hall and said, 'What is Rhoda Carlisle doing?'

'What?'

'Do you love her?'

'I don't see what it is to do with you.'

'You belong to me!'

She said it so loudly that Gil looked around in alarm, but there was no one near. Recklessly, she put one hand into his hair and began to kiss him. Gil did not remember a kiss having tasted better. He wanted to stop her, but he couldn't. He drew her into the nearest empty room, a sitting room, and there he said to her, 'I don't belong to you nor you to me.'

'I missed you. Venice is a place for lovers.'

'You love Edward.'

'He doesn't love me.'

'He's your husband,' Gil said flatly, 'and he beds you, isn't that right?'

'He does his duty.' Her words sounded so bitter and she stumbled over the next ones. 'You may as well know now – I'm having a child.'

'A child?'

'Edward's child. For all his ... lack of interest, he managed that.'

'Well then.'

'I miss you so much. I kept thinking what it would have been like there with you. It would have been heaven. Do you still love me?'

'There's no good in my loving you.'

'But do you?'

'You know I do. I always will.'

'What a foolish thing life is and what tricks God plays on us.' She came closer to him so that her breath was sweet and warm on his face. 'You can't marry Rhoda Carlisle. She's off the moor tops.'

'I shall have to marry someone. I can't lead the rest of my life like this.'

'Not her. Please. I don't think I can bear it. I'll have to lie there alone at night and you'll be with her.'

'That's what I do.'

'But Edward's hardly with me. You could be with me.'

'You can't treat me like that. I can't spend the rest of my life living just for being in your bed sometimes, watching you with Edward the rest of the time. You do love him, I can see it in your eyes. You can't want that for me, even if you don't love me. It isn't right. If you care for me even just a little, let me go.'

'What am I to do?' Helen said. 'There should be a time for us, I know there should. I'm so lonely and I missed you so very much. I can't live in this house with you married to another woman, not after what you've been to me. You make love to me as though you'll never have the chance again, as though it's always the first and last time. Don't do it, please.'

'Helen, I have to try.'

'No!' She cried and clung and kissed him and pleaded and begged. It reminded Gil somewhat of that day when he had tried to persuade Abby to marry him. He blamed her still for his unhappiness. Living without Abby was like this room, empty and cool; he was moving around, falling over things all the time, clutching at anything that he found, from despair. He somehow had to put Helen from him physically and mentally, and it was no good. In the end, she ran out of the room and up the stairs and finished her battle alone. He went along the hall in search of Rhoda.

When it was time for her to leave, Gil panicked. He did not want to be left there with Edward and Helen together and the longest ever nights. Rhoda had kept the edge from the loneliness and he did not want her to go. They walked in the quarry garden along to the ruined castle. From there they could look back across the fields to the house. It was late evening, well after dinner and everything was silent and still.

'You'll come back soon,' Gil said.

'If I'm allowed.'

'Are you afraid of Mr Allsop?'

Rhoda didn't answer.

'Has he done something?'

'No,' she said hastily, 'at least no more than many men. He can't replace my father and my mother prefers him, I can see that she does. I don't think she loved my father half as much as she does this man and he is – he's unworthy. He's . . . uneducated and uncultured, so stupid that he doesn't realise it and he knows I despise him and yet—'

'And yet?'

Rhoda looked at him from narrowed eyes.

'He thinks that young women like him. He's old – at least old compared to men your age, but he . . . he actually thinks that I desire him, whereas he disgusts and revolts me. His stomach sticks out and his hair is thinning and he drinks too much and he smokes and his breath and clothes—' Rhoda wrinkled her nose. 'If he was a kind man, none of that would matter but . . . I miss my father. Every day of my life I miss him. But I have liked being here with your family.'

'Enough to come back?'

'Oh yes. I would give anything to come back.'

'You don't have to give anything. You can come back any time.'

'I love your house and I like your father and mother and Edward and Helen and – and everything.'

Gil moved forward, very slightly. He couldn't think afterwards why he did it. Rhoda drew back sharply, fell over a rabbit hole in the grass and landed awkwardly. Gil got down to help. She was trembling and trying not to cry.

'I didn't mean to scare you.'

'You didn't. It was just . . . I don't want to go and leave you. I'll miss you. You're the first man who's been kind to me since my father—'

'Rhoda, look.' Gil sat down beside her in the grass. 'I know it isn't how it should be, but . . . we get on very well. If we got married, you wouldn't ever have to go home again.'

She was shocked by the idea, Gil could see. He was shocked himself, but he had to find a way out of his life as it was. A struggle went on behind her eyes, but she agreed. He had not expected, either, that he would be so happy when Rhoda said she would marry him. It made everything so much better straight away. When they went back to the house and announced it, Edward clapped him on the back, his mother cuddled Rhoda, but it was his father's reaction which satisfied Gil most. He said, 'Well done, lad!' and he told Rhoda she was the bonniest lass in the county.

Helen did congratulate them, though somewhat stiffly.

The reaction from Rhoda's mother was positive and after that either Gil went to Allendale Town to stay for the weekend or Rhoda came to Bamburgh House. Gil had long since decided that he disliked Jos Allsop and spending time at the square, stone dales house was not a pleasant experience. He imagined that it could have been if Rhoda's father had been alive.

Allendale Town was very pretty, the countryside around it two dales, the valleys of the Rivers East Allen and West Allen. The rivers went for a short distance before meeting the River South Tyne at Allen Banks, but each made its own way, separated by the moors that surrounded the town, a monument to the lead mining industry which had been its mainstay for a hundred years.

Rhoda had lived there all her life and knew everybody, but life inside her home was bleak. Allsop drank. He made good use of all the pubs in Allendale and there were many of them. When he came home, those who were wise kept their distance. Gil was unlucky enough to meet up with him outside the Rose and Crown in High Street.

'You're a brave one,' Jos said as he staggered into the

road, 'marrying that. Her dowry's the warmest thing about Rhoda. You'll get nothing from her. Like the January snow she is, pretty but too cold to touch.'

Gil had to remind himself that he was staying in this man's house and went off without saying anything.

They walked up on the moors and Rhoda was always ahead of him, dashing here and there to show him a special place that she cared for, her favourite view or a stream almost as brown as her eyes. She knew the names of the birds and the flowers. She could pick her way easily as though she knew every inch of the land. He liked to stand and watch her, slender with her brown hair blowing about. She reminded him of a young deer, moving surely, quite at home, and she was happy there, looking back from time to time and smiling or pointing ahead at something she had seen. Sometimes she would let him catch her up, but mostly she preferred to go on ahead so Gil would slacken his pace and let her show him the moors. He came to understand that she felt safe with him and it made him feel good to get something right. He bought a ring for her finger. Its pretty green stone suited her and Rhoda could hide behind that. Nobody could touch her.

That autumn, as Helen grew fat, Edward began once again to go out almost every night and William complained with just the three of them in the dining room after dinner, when Edward tried to excuse himself.

'By God, you're not excused. Where are you going?'

'I'm going for a game of billiards. Do you mind?' Edward spoke softly, but Gil knew that he was most unhappy at being questioned.

'I do mind, yes. It's the third time in four nights. We have a billiard room here. You can play against Gil.'

'He doesn't play my game,' Edward said, looking at the door.

'And what game is that?'

'You wouldn't understand.' Suddenly he looked at his father and there was anger in his face. 'I've given you an heir for God's sake, what more do you want?' And he left the room.

William was as white as the tablecloth and almost immediately went off to his study. Gil couldn't help feeling rather left out because Edward no longer asked him to go. What William didn't know was that quite often Edward didn't come home.

At weekends when Rhoda was there, he did stay at home or they all went out together. It was a happy time. Gil's father generously gave him a fortnight's holiday towards the end of the summer, Rhoda stayed the full time and they had picnics by the river and sat out in the garden under the trees. Helen had accepted that he would marry Rhoda and chose to make a friend of the other girl. They went shopping and came back with all manner of exciting things. There were parties both at their house and at friends' homes, expeditions to the seaside and even a short break at Warkworth just beside Amble, staying with friends.

'Doesn't your father like Warkworth?' Rhoda ventured when William had told them he didn't understand the foolishness of wanting to go there.

'He was born at Amble. My grandparents were very modest people.'

Rhoda insisted on finding them in the graveyard, which Gil had wanted to do but hadn't liked to mention. Someone, his father probably, he thought, had erected a huge marble angel at the head of their plot.

'Dear me,' Rhoda said, 'it stands out, doesn't it?' And she betrayed herself with a giggle.

'It's typical of him,' Gil fumed. 'He ignored them when they were here and insulted them by this monstrosity when they were dead.'

'He probably didn't mean to.'

'How can you defend him?'

'He's your father. He's very nice to me. I wish my father was still here.'

For the first time in weeks and quite disloyally, he knew, Gil thought of Abby. Abby was probably the only person who understood the relationship that he had with his father. He missed her. He had tried to stop thinking about her after she had married Robert Surtees and gone away, but the memories of her were good and sometimes made him smile. He was glad that she was happy. She deserved to be.

Chapter Nine

The emerald ring on Rhoda's hand glittered. Abby had read or heard that the darker the stone, the more expensive it was, and the emerald was so dark that it was almost black with green glints, subtle and as rich as velvet.

'It's nice, isn't it?' Rhoda said shyly, and Abby hugged her.

'You could have told me!' she said. 'You could have written.'

'I wanted to surprise you.'

'You have. Oh Rhoda, I'm so pleased for you. It's a wonderful ring. Who is the lucky man?'

'Gil Collingwood.'

Abby's heart fell. It really did, she felt it. She was jealous and upset to realise that not only did she not want Gil, she didn't want anybody else to have him. No, that was not quite true. She didn't want anyone she knew anywhere near him so that she had to hear the details about the relationship, and Rhoda was her closest friend. Abby wished she could shout at Gil. In a way it was as though they had both betrayed her, somehow, stolen one another away from her. Her sense of justice rescued her, but it was difficult to sound enthusiastic.

'Gil?'

'Yes, why not?'

They were in the sitting room of Rhoda's home; Abby had called as soon as she got back. She was pleased to see Rhoda looking so much better, but now that she knew the cause of it, pleasure was hard to pretend.

'No reason, it's just . . . I didn't think it. He's . . . well, not your style, I thought.'

'I had to get away. I had to get out.' Rhoda glanced at the door as though someone might come bursting in at any moment, but it remained peaceful.

'You don't love him then?'

'I couldn't love any man.' And Rhoda shuddered. 'Mind you, I do find that I like him. He doesn't try to grab me, though I was convinced that he would, and he is rather fetching, don't you think? So tall and good-looking. He's a gentleman too. I didn't know that. Kind and generous,' Rhoda said, moving her finger so that the emerald glittered.

'Does he love you?'

'No. No, I don't think so. His parents like me and of course they like my money.'

'That's very cynical.'

'I don't mind. He's not boring, either. Men do tend to be boring. I think he's clever.'

'Clever, Gil?'

'I think he is. We're going to America.'

'America?'

'He has been . . . what's the word . . . "negotiating" . . . with a shipping line to build an enormous ship, and after we're married we're going to America with the head of the shipping line and his wife, and if Gil is clever enough Collingwood's will get to build the ship. So he will be doing lots of work and seeing important people in New York, but I'm inclined to think it will be glamorous.'

Abby was inclined to think so too, and the sting of envy hit her like a train. It was stupid and illogical and she tried to dismiss it, but what she most missed about having a husband who didn't work was the excitement of industry, the problems, the tensions, the possibilities. She had never thought that not working might be dull, but it was. The days were not enlivened by talk that mattered, because nothing mattered except births, deaths and marriages. The rest was gossip.

Why should not Gil and Rhoda be happy?

'Do you remember me saying that I would have a shop? You said it wasn't respectable. This is and I like his family. I like being there.'

'Bamburgh House is hideous.'

'I love it! His parents are kind and Helen and I go shopping. They're a family like we used to be. I want that again.'

Abby was also jealous of the friendship which had apparently sprung up between Rhoda and Helen. She and Helen could never have been friends, and Rhoda was inclined to talk about her a lot and about the coming baby. Abby felt left out. She had not found any close friends among Robert's circle. Most of them were from the south and made fun of her northern accent. Abby had tried to modify it, but she could almost hear her mother's scorn. The women talked about one another and the men drank and played field sports. Abby thought that she would not have minded so much if Robert had taken any interest in her father, her friends or her home. He tried to keep her from them and talked of going back to London soon.

'We've just got here,' Abby had objected, 'and there's Rhoda and Gil's wedding.'

'Precisely. You don't really want to go? It's not the event of the year. He's nobody and she's a bucolic fool. They've only asked us because of who we are. Collingwood and I can't stand one another. I'm not going.'

It was the same whenever she wanted to go to Jesmond and spend a little time with her father. Robert always had a good reason not to go. Abby was worried about her father. He had lost weight and seemed distracted about work. Robert complained if she stayed overnight because he had social events planned, people to stay or just that he missed her.

'You could come with me,' Abby pointed out.

'I've no wish to stay in that dark little house in the dingy Newcastle streets when I can remain at home in the country. Your father could come to us.'

'He's working.'

'It's time he gave up working at his age,' Robert said. 'There are other things in life.'

Abby suggested this to her father and he stared at her.

'Sell this business?'

'There's nobody to take it on after you.'

'I'm not dead yet and you'll have children.'

She didn't like to tell him that her children were hardly likely to work in a shipyard, and was only glad that Robert was not there or he would have laughed.

'The yard has been my whole life since your mother died. What else would I do?' he said.

'You could retire and come and live with us.'

'Robert would like that,' her father said sarcastically. 'I suppose you think I can take up hunting and prance around in a bloody daft outfit like he does.'

Her father, Abby had realised lately, had only just given up on the notion that his son-in-law would develop a special interest in the shipyard. They had nothing in common, nothing to talk about. Robert saw her father as a foolish old man and Henderson thought Robert useless and shallow. Trying to keep the peace between the two of them was not easy. She knew that her father was lonely, that though he said nothing he hated her to leave and she felt sick and weepy each time, looking back at him standing by himself on the doorstep. Each time she tried to get away from Robert, he had found something to stop her: friends were to visit, they were to visit friends, or there was a social event which she could not miss. It was some time before Abby admitted to herself that social events and many of their friends bored her. She spent too much time with them doing nothing and it all seemed so empty.

For a long time now, Gil knew, it had been his father's ambition to build a ship that would cross the Atlantic faster than any other and take the Blue Riband. He was closer to his father than he had ever been and could do little wrong in William's eyes. His forthcoming marriage to a girl his father liked who had money was another joy. Gil worked hard, his father praised him and his ideas and Gil clearly demonstrated his ability for shipbuilding, designing and engineering. He was sometimes quite surprised himself. He had no idea where this ability had come from. Edward had none and, though his father was a shrewd and accomplished businessman,

he didn't have it either. Some men would have been jealous, but Gil knew by then that William saw his sons as
an extension of himself. This was why he had been so
upset with them as children when he saw that they
might turn into people beyond his control. He relied on
Gil very much at work and it was a huge burden. Sometimes it would have been a relief to be allowed to fail,
occasionally to make a mistake, but when he did his
father went into terrible rages. Gil's mistakes were fewer
and fewer. He had trained himself to think no longer
about Helen, and his growing friendship with Rhoda
was a big help. His mind returned to his work and he
kept it there. To lose his father's new-found regard was
too much. Helen would have Edward's child soon, and
a mother, Gil had discovered, was not nearly as attractive a prospect. If she had been growing fat with his
child, he would have adored her and the child, but the
fact that each day he was faced with a woman who more
obviously than ever belonged to another man discour-
aged him from wanting her. And there was Rhoda. He
was making her happy. Gil had not been able to do that
with anyone before, but Rhoda was easily made happy
and he liked it. He determined to be faithful, kind and
to look after her and he was convinced that once they
were married everything would be right.

In the meantime, he was happy at work and knew
that, happy, he turned out his best. His father came to

expect that everything he did he did brilliantly and Gil wanted more and more to bring that proud look to his father's face. He never again wanted to be that dreadful person he had been as a child and a youth. He knew that his father had despised him. Now it was different. William's gaze was soft on him and Gil knew that out of his hearing William was inclined to call his son a genius. Gil knew that he was far from it. He had limited abilities in almost every way, as though God had seen fit to endow him with one gift and take everything else from him. Gil had begun to build a reputation as a designer of fine ships. They had plenty of work. People were beginning to respect him.

For some time his father had cultivated a man called John Marlowe. He was a rich man, the owner of a shipping line. He lived in London but had a house in Newcastle, which had been his family home. William invited John and his wife Edwina to dinner at Bamburgh House. Charlotte was worried that they would not be good enough for the Marlowes and was surprised to discover that Edwina cared nothing for fashion and John ate sparingly. Afterwards, John sat by the fire with Gil and talked about his ideas and ambitions. The Germans had lately built very fast liners and the government was not happy that British shipping might be overtaken in this way. If the Germans could build bigger and faster liners, they could build bigger and faster battleships.

The government wanted to build two big liners and there had been much discussion for almost two years while they looked for the right shipbuilder, Gil knew. Collingwood's had already submitted a great many designs. The first big problem was the shape of the ship and experiments had to be carried out.

'We could make a model. It's been done before. A big model so that we could do testing to see whether the shape would work.'

'It's performance I'm interested in,' John said. 'The government will provide two and a half million at two and three-quarter per cent interest and an annual subsidy of one hundred and fifty thousand pounds. The structure and the shape do interest me, but it's the speed I'm counting on. You would have to guarantee it. How long to launch?'

'Eighteen months.'

'It would cost you money. The river isn't wide enough and you would need new machinery and sheds.'

'It's been my father's life's ambition.'

'And yours?'

'It would be interesting.'

John laughed.

'We would interfere a great deal, a committee from the Admiralty and from us. Would you like that?'

'It would be worth it. You'd pay in instalments.'

'Do you have the latest prices?'

'Of course.'

'I'm taking Edwina to America at Christmas. I understand you're getting married. We could do some real talking and there are people in New York I want to introduce you to.'

William had not been taking part in the discussion. Gil understood that. Later he went to his father in the study.

'He wants me to go to New York with him, to talk to people and, I think, so that he and I can talk properly about it and in private.'

'I want to build these two ships as much as I've ever wanted anything in my whole life,' his father said tightly.

'Don't worry,' Gil said, 'we'll get them.'

He called himself rash afterwards. He went to bed and worried, but he would have promised his father the heavens and the earth if William had expressed such a desire for them.

From time to time the shipbuilders of the river met to discuss ships and men and wages. Henderson was always there and Gil went with his father and Edward. After Abby was married and went away to France and Italy, it seemed to Gil that Henderson was different, quieter and less interested in business. At one time at these meetings he argued because he was a better man than most. He paid what other men considered to be high wages and was badly liked for it. Worse still, he would not join the federation that the others belonged to, where wages were kept at what they considered to be an acceptable level so that the men who worked for them could not cause problems by leaving to go to another shipyard which would pay better. Henderson built good houses for his workmen and Gil knew that he had financed schools and places of recreation. Bella had been a wealthy woman when she married Henderson and Gil thought that if Henderson had had a son, he would have expanded his yard, his father having shrewdly bought up much land on either side of the present shipyard. Now, however, it was as if the spirit had gone from the man. Gil admired the things he had done and hoped that when he married Rhoda some of the money would be used to better things for the men, though if their bid was accepted for the first of the two liners a great deal of money would be needed. He had estimated it would cost ten thousand pounds to widen the river and they would need huge covered berths so that they could work in bad weather and new electric machinery for faster production.

Gil admired Henderson from afar because he knew that Henderson disliked him. Quite often after these meetings the men would go drinking together, but

Henderson was never asked. He was lonely, Gil knew, at work and at home. He had no friends in the business and no son, and Gil thought that Henderson might have started to realise what kind of a man Abby had married.

At one of these meetings in the late autumn, when Abby was still away, Gil refused several invitations to go out afterwards. His father frowned. Henderson had already left. Gil ran along the streets after him as Henderson rounded the corner into Eldon Square, a pretty place right in the middle of Newcastle where musicians often played and ladies gathered in teashops.

'Mr Reed!'

Henderson didn't hear, or didn't want to. Gil ran, shouting again, only slowing down when Henderson stopped and turned. Gil stood, panting for a few moments.

'I almost lost you,' he said. 'Will you come for a drink with me?'

'No,' Henderson said and walked on.

'I know you don't like me . . .'

Henderson stopped again and looked squarely at him.

'Your father's a bastard,' he said. 'What does that make you? I'll tell you. You come from a long line of third-rate people. They may call you a genius, but that doesn't make you a gentleman.'

'It doesn't make you one either,' Gil said, losing his temper. 'You're rude! All I asked you was if you would go for a drink. "No, thank you" would have done. I don't need to hear how base I am. I've got nothing to gain, after all. Abby didn't ever want me. You had nothing to be afraid of then and you certainly don't now.'

'What do you want?'

'I just want to talk to somebody who improves houses and conditions and things.'

'I'm amazed you're interested.'

'Why shouldn't I be interested?'

'Because you're a bloody Collingwood and all they ever cared for was money.'

'That's not true. My grandfather was a boat builder and a good one. He built cobles.'

'I know he did, lad.'

'Don't call me "lad". I do have a name.'

'One drink,' Henderson said.

They had gone into the nearest fuggy little pub and played dominoes and been there until it closed. After that, they met at least once a week. Henderson wasn't easy. He tore Gil's ideas to pieces in a way in which Gil would never have survived from his father. He scorned what he called 'misplaced philanthropy' as though it were something he hadn't heard of, but Gil could see enthusiasm in his newly fired eyes. Also, Gil could talk to Henderson about anything, and that was new. Henderson didn't accept that he was brilliant or that he was stupid, just that he was a shipbuilder who was doing his best. They had long, complicated discussions. He told

Henderson his ideas for the liner, knowing that Henderson would not say anything to anyone. It was such a relief to be able to throw ideas around without having to prove anything and, after the ideas had gone back and forward a dozen times, it was as though the discussing of them fined them down, improved them. Gil became more sure, more confident; he trusted Henderson's judgement and he knew that Henderson enjoyed the discussions. He invited Gil to the house, something Gil was flattered to do. Nobody else knew. They played dominoes by the fire in bad weather.

Gil tried to introduce some of Henderson's ideas at work, but his father objected strongly.

'We're not bloody women, to go interfering in the men's lives. Stick to designing ships, I'll do the managing,' he said.

Gil had also tried to talk to his father about wages for Edward and himself.

'You have an allowance. You can hardly call it mean,' William said, 'and you can run up bills all over town. You go to the best tailor. We have accounts everywhere, jewellers', shoemakers'. What the hell more do you want? I keep you extravagantly.'

'It's not quite the same thing,' Gil said.

'Is there something you want? Name it.'

'No, there's nothing,' Gil said.

*

Abby was surprised to walk into her father's house one cold day after Christmas and find Gil and Rhoda there. She had not seen Gil happy before and he was almost like somebody different.

'I thought you didn't like him,' she said to her father afterwards.

'I can talk to him,' Henderson said.

'You mean he talks about work.'

'If you like, and Rhoda's a good lass. I think they make a very nice couple.'

Abby thought they did too, and was astonished. Rhoda was well dressed now as she had not been and was wearing sable against the weather. She wore a jaunty little hat and a big smile and she looked at Gil from time to time as though to make sure he was still there. If they were not in love, which Rhoda had assured her they were not, they certainly looked as if they were. Their families both approved, Abby knew, and they knew one another well and were comfortable together.

'You are coming to the wedding?' Rhoda said.

'When is it?'

'In April. Gil's mother wanted it sooner, but the arrangements couldn't be made in time.'

'I'm not certain that we can. We're going away.'

'Do try and come. It won't be the same without you.'

'She's got too grand for us,' Gil teased, looking at his bride to be. That was when Abby thought that he was no longer in love with Helen, which was not surprising. Babies were hardly conducive to romance.

Helen's baby was born in a snowstorm, so she endured several uncomfortable hours before the doctor arrived. They called him Matthew. The christening was delayed until after the bad weather, and Helen took a long time to recover from the birth. Edward continued to go out every night. He did not seem interested in the baby or in her. Gil was glad of Rhoda then because she was a big help. She loved the baby, spent hours with him and, when Helen wasn't well, sat with her, cheered her, even encouraged her to go out from time to time to distract her.

Helen did attend the wedding but looked as though she should have been home in bed. It was a mild day, the first week in April, and Rhoda was married from the little stone parish church in Allendale. Her stepfather gave her away and was doing his best to look pleased about it, Gil thought. The wedding breakfast was at their house on the edge of the town and he could not but think of how unhappy she had been there and of how pleased he was to be taking her away for good.

They were to spend the first night at a hotel in Hexham and then to make the journey south to meet the Marlowes in Liverpool to join the ship which would take them to America. They were waved away from the house. It wouldn't take long to reach Hexham, but Rhoda said more than once on the journey that she was tired. She had been so bright until then. Now she was pale. She said little during the journey and even less when they reached the hotel. Shown to their bedroom, Rhoda looked at the big double bed and turned away.

She ate nothing that evening, pushing the food around on her plate, and when it was time to go to bed and Gil asked if she would like to go on ahead, she nodded and escaped.

He stayed downstairs worrying and had a glass of brandy. He could not help thinking of Helen, of being in bed with her, of her beautiful body. Rhoda had not let him touch her; she was afraid. He didn't know why, but he had an idea that Jos Allsop had tried to put his hands on her. Gil had not done so; he had been careful and was prepared to be patient now. He made his way slowly upstairs and opened the door of the room. The bed was empty. She was not there. Gil wandered about upstairs for a few minutes and then went downstairs, trying not to look obvious, but she was nowhere that he could see. Finally he ventured outside, doubting that even Rhoda would have gone outside in such cold windy weather. It was difficult to see anything in the dark, shadowed streets though the abbey stood out against the sky and the houses around the little green in front of the hotel had street lamps. He could see a small figure some way off. He paused for a moment or two. What was she doing out here? Was she so afraid? He hadn't understood. He wondered whether to go back into the hotel and wait, then decided against it and began to walk slowly towards her so that she might see or hear him and would not be shocked. She was not wearing a coat and the wind was whipping down from Hexhamshire Common. Was she imagining herself there, wishing herself beyond his reach? Her folded arms were thin and her hair blew about. He didn't go too close in case she ran.

'Rhoda?' he said softly.

It was several moments before she turned, as though she had been in some other place. He went to her and took off his jacket and tried to put it around her shoulders, but she backed away, shivering.

'I used to stand up on the fell and watch the lights on in our house when I was little, knowing I could go in out of the cold any time.'

Gil searched for the right thing to say. He had heard of animals caught in traps who chewed off their own limbs to be free. Was that what she had done, limping to him, damaged? She drew further away and turned in the direction of the open country as though she might run into it and away from him.

'You don't have to be afraid of me. Come back inside. You'll take cold.'

She didn't say anything. Gil had known that she had

not the feeling for him that Helen had had, but he had not thought things as bad as this.

'Have I done something?' he asked.

She shook her head.

'Do you think I'm going to hurt you, because—'

'No. No.' Her head was down. When she looked up Gil was horrified by the bleakness in her face. 'I've deceived you,' she said.

The only thing Gil could think of was that she had given her body to somebody else and, if she had, it was considered a very grave sin, that she should have done so without marriage, that she should have married him regardless. She had a good right to be afraid.

'Tell me,' he said.

'I don't know how to.'

'You must.'

'I'm unchaste.'

Unchaste. What a strange word and what huge significance it carried. He was uncomfortably aware of the double standard: that she was meant to be totally inexperienced but that he would not have been censured for such behaviour, except that he had done something much graver and was in no position to condemn anybody.

'I don't care,' he said recklessly. 'Do you love him? Was it that you couldn't marry him? Was he married? Tell me before we freeze.'

She looked clearly at him.

'It was my stepfather,' she said.

Something in Gil signalled recognition, as though some tiny part of him had known and that was why he had tried to protect her, but most of him was revolted. He couldn't take his eyes off her. Fascinated horror gripped him.

'You went to bed with Allsop?'

Her face filled with anger.

'I didn't!' she said.

Coldness took a hold on Gil inside as well as out.

'He took you against your will?'

'You didn't really think I would have gone with a disgusting, awful person like that.'

'Why didn't you tell somebody?'

'Who was I supposed to tell?'

'Me, for a start.'

'You wouldn't have married me! I had to get out.'

'There are other ways.'

'Nobody would have believed me. You can still send me back! You haven't had me yet!'

She ran. Gil cursed himself and ran after her. When he caught her, she thumped and kicked him. He shook her.

'Stop it! Nobody's going to send you back!'

'I'm second-hand goods, that's what they call it. I'll go. I'll just go.'

'You're not going anywhere. Come inside. I'm bloody well nithered.'

He dragged her back into the hotel and marched her upstairs and into the bedroom. Luckily the fire was blazing nicely and the room was warm. Gil's feelings were so mixed up. He was rather inclined to smack her round the ear for deceiving him, but the idea of Allsop raping a vulnerable person like Rhoda was beyond belief. In any case, he had sworn to himself that he would hit no one except in self-defence. Part of him also wondered whether perhaps she was lying because she didn't want to go to bed with him. Rhoda wouldn't even come to the fire. She sat in the shadows, curled up in a chair.

'Come over here, for goodness sake.'

'You're going to hit me.'

'I am not. I'd have done it before now. Did you really like me so little?'

'I like you very well considering you're a man.'

'Then come to the fire.'

There was brandy and glasses. It seemed a sight more appropriate than the champagne which sat like a reminder of what they might have been doing. He poured brandy, gave her a good measure and she sank down onto the rug by the fire. Gil sat down in an armchair nearby and drank his brandy gratefully.

'Did you tell your mother?'

'I tried to. She called me a whore and took a stick to me, as though it were my fault.'

'But she believed you?'

'Does that mean you don't?'

'I haven't made up my mind.'

'Why would I lie to you?'

'So that you don't have to go to bed with me.'

'All you have to do is force me and then you'd find out anyhow.'

'I'm not in the habit of forcing women.' He thought that sounded arrogant, somehow, but he needed a refuge. This was not how he had envisaged his wedding night. He had imagined it happy, difficult perhaps, but he had liked Rhoda, liked the wild person in her, been confident that they would deal well in bed together. He had desired her, not like he had wanted Helen or loved her as he had loved Abby even, but he had thought that he could have her as his wife. To his shame, there was also a distaste that another man had had her first, either willingly or unwillingly. He had wanted her to be completely his so that he could try to remake himself into entirely hers and it was not possible, he could see that. If she was lying then she cared nothing for him and if she was not, then she wouldn't go to bed with him. Either way, there was no chance that he would be saved or could save himself from the slavery that his love for Helen had turned into. He was too shocked to be tired and too miserable to sleep.

Rhoda sat on the floor beside his feet with her legs

tucked under her, making herself very small, both hands clutched around the glass as she stared into the fire.

'I'm sorry,' she said.

'Yes, I imagine you might be.'

She turned her head and looked at him.

'You don't know what it's like! It was vile!' Her voice shook.

'Why don't you go to bed?'

'No!'

'Well at least get up off the floor. You must be in a draught.'

She sat in the chair across the fire for a while and then, without saying a word, got up and undressed without showing her body and got into bed. She lay down with her face turned towards the wall. Gil got up, went and stood by the window and sipped at his brandy and watched the storm throw itself at the little town with its abbey and stone houses and shops, solid black shadows in the night.

Eventually she fell asleep and Gil's mind gave him Helen and the nights that they had spent together. He ached for her, longed for her. The loneliness was intensified because of the girl who slept in the bed. He drank some more brandy. It was strange how you could fill up the loneliness with alcohol. You shouldn't have been able to, but you could. If you hadn't been able to, you would have gone mad.

He thought of the men in the shipyards. They were like Helen, some of them, they had been trapped by sex or circumstances, by disappointment, pain or betrayal. He and Rhoda were like that now, for she had trapped them both. Beer filled the emptiness because there was nothing else, no love, no comfort, no education, no opportunities. They could not even get away. Religion was like beer for some of them. They found God and swallowed Him in great gulps.

The brandy took a good hold on his mind and body and soothed and comforted, but he did not stop thinking about Helen. Edward would be out and she would be lying in bed alone and he was married and could not go to her again. Would it be worse now that he was married, or had it been as bad a sin before? He thought it had. It had always been as bad as it was going to get, a betrayal of his brother and his family and Helen's marriage, whatever that was. It was done and couldn't be made right. Nothing would change it.

It was almost morning and he was sweetly drunk when he went to bed. It was just as well, he thought, it really was all that was left beside the work. He could feel sleep coming at him just beyond, stealing past the brandy, covering him up, cuddling him, holding him. If he tried very hard he could remember Helen's caresses, feel them, taste her mouth and her body. He could remember the warm land with its blue sea and the white villa and the mountains, the garden with its orange trees, the breeze gently disturbing the curtains in the bedroom. She was smiling at him, kissing him. They were together and nothing else mattered.

Chapter Ten

The ship was not nearly as big as the kind of liner that John Marlowe wanted, but it was comfortable; indeed, to most people it would have appeared sumptuous. Gil interpreted how important his presence was to John by the suite of rooms they were given. Just yesterday, Rhoda would have run about exclaiming excitedly at the pretty furniture, the view from the portholes; now, she merely looked at the big double bed and said nothing. Gil had awoken beside a reluctant woman for the first time and he didn't like it. Neither did he like the hangover which sat on his brow. It was not a good start. She lay, silently turned away, so he turned over towards her.

'Rhoda? Rhoda, look at me.'

She turned to him. Her eyes were swollen with crying, though he hadn't heard her.

'Let's make a bargain, shall we? I won't touch you, so give me back the Rhoda I knew yesterday morning.

We're going to New York.' When this produced no response he said, 'I'm not going to do anything to you.'

'It isn't that! It's just that . . . I shouldn't have married you.'

'What alternative was there?'

'Somebody else, not you.'

'You mean there's somebody you like even less?'

'I do like you. I like you very much.'

'Why don't we leave it at that then and do the best we can?'

'I'm sorry.'

'If I ever meet up with that bastard again, I'll kill him,' Gil promised and got out of bed.

There were plenty of distractions on board ship. He was glad of them and more pleased than he had thought he would be at John Marlowe's presence. He was grateful to Edwina, who kept Rhoda occupied and, after a day or two, Rhoda seemed to relax and begin to enjoy herself. John knew a great deal about shipping but nothing about ships, Gil thought, but he also knew what he wanted. As they went over the ship, Gil explained in great, though not very technical, detail; he kept the problems to himself and they were vast.

For a long time now people had preferred intermediate

liners like this one, with lower running costs, but things had changed. Germany and America were becoming powerful and it was time for might and skill to be shown. The British had their face to keep up and, though the cost was high, it might be even higher if they did not. They could not afford to lose their hold on the claim that they were the greatest shipbuilding nation in the world. Gil knew very well that Germany educated its engineers and designers, that it trained better its skilled men, that it took more quickly to the ideas of new machinery. The British were rightly famed for their lack of schooling, their inability to move around. They clung to one piece of land as though every other part of the earth was foreign territory, like small animals in burrows. As for new ideas . . .

Gil stood by the rail and watched the water and thought of himself, his hatred of school, his love for Newcastle. There was something which mattered here that he could not quite comprehend. It was nothing visible, nothing tangible, he only knew that somehow the ship would be built at Collingwood's, that in spite of wrong ideas and mistakes and sheer pigheadedness, if he were given the word to build this new ship in a year it would be rising like a soft monster, dwarfing the men who had gathered resources, materials and skills. In a year and a half it could be a being such as had never been seen on Tyneside before, the greatest ship the world had ever seen. Part of him was still looking at his reflection and seeing lack of education and experience, but his father had been right. Designers had to be people with uncluttered minds, men with goals, without distractions, fresh, new, exciting. He could feel this ship inside his head and inside his heart, and he knew that it would be built.

To win a place on the Admiralty list to build large liners was what most shipbuilders dreamed of, and he would have it. Other people might tender for the liner, but it was his and he would promise John Marlowe the whole earth to gain it, recklessly propose dates and times and finance, skills and feats of magic. He would do anything to gain this ship.

Gil discovered that he liked John Marlowe. He had been prepared to cultivate the man for what he wanted, but during the voyage they became friends and that was more than he had hoped for. John was much older and when they had met Gil had seen disbelief in his face that a young man could produce anything close to what he wanted, but as the ship made its way towards New York they sat up into the night over a drink and talked and Gil could see that John's confidence in him grew with each hour. He was a rich, influential man who knew other rich, influential men. He was shrewd, so that in a way Gil began to see himself as John saw him and he was happy about this.

Less successful was his relationship with Rhoda. She avoided him during the day, but that wasn't obvious because the whole purpose of the trip was business and she had no place there. He knew that she was ashamed of what she had done and he was ashamed of the way that he had reacted, so when they did meet they spoke softly to one another as people might think newly-weds did. At night, Gil put a pillow between them that she should feel easier. He let the business matters sweep over him like a tide. It was important that he should not falter because his marriage was a disaster. The one had nothing to do with the other. He put them into different sections of his mind and dismissed the marriage. He treated Rhoda as though they were good friends and, as they drew nearer to New York, he could see the look change in her eyes. The building of the new ship was all his concern. If he could secure this contract, no one, least of all his father, would ever doubt him again.

If Gil had had nothing more important to think about he would have been thrilled with New York, its huge buildings – the skyscrapers – the different communities of people from different lands, the Irish, the Blacks, the Jews, the Italians. It was noisy such as London could never be. The Marlowes had friends there and in some ways, Gil thought with surprise, it was as class-conscious as anywhere at home. Your name and your background were everything. The women were very beautiful and extremely well-dressed. Abby, Gil thought, would have hated it.

John introduced Gil to his business acquaintances and to Wall Street and business in the city. Rhoda went to see Central Park, the animals in the zoo, the shops. They stayed on Park Avenue, and it seemed to Gil that for somebody from the felltops, Rhoda dealt with this sophisticated, scurrying life as though she had been used to it. John seemed to take great pleasure in showing Gil around. He took him to a German beerhouse on the Upper East Side and, in contrast, to the newly built Waldorf Astoria, but nothing touched Gil, not the glamour, the money, the music, the intricacy, the poverty or the people. Rhoda would come home with wonderful tales to relate of who she had met and how she had spent her day. She went to the opera and he was obliged to go with her. He hated it and all the time his mind did a tortured dance between the way that she would not let him touch her and the ship he might not be allowed to build. His dreams had in them the frenzy of New York and a hunger which went round and round. He couldn't sleep; he was full before every meal and, on the penultimate night of their visit, the worry and frustration were too much. She was inclined to chatter now in the bedroom, but he silenced her with his mouth, put her reluctant body down onto the bed and slid his hands inside her evening dress.

If she had fought he didn't know what he would have

done, but she did what he imagined she had done with Allsop. She pretended she was not there. He knew very well where she was, up on her beloved moors, probably on some warm August evening, when the bell heather was as rich as rubies and there was nothing but land, sky and the occasional cry of the sheep. Her face was turned away, the blood drained, her eyes distant and her body like marble. Gil saw himself and was revolted. He dropped her and got up off the bed.

'Christ Almighty, I'm sorry.'

It all seemed so incongruous. The room was enormous, and it had gold-coloured curtains. The bed and the other furniture looked as if it had come out of some French brothel, he thought savagely, having never been into a French brothel. It was all gold and white and spindly as though it would break from even slight ill-use. It was not often that Gil wished himself back at Bamburgh House; he did not often feel safe there, but he wished it now. He tried to get out of the room, but Rhoda, nimble-footed from the fells, reached the door before he did. When he turned, she put herself into his arms and said, 'Don't be sorry. It wasn't your fault.'

'I want to go home,' Gil said.

'We will and you will have the ship. You will, you will. It will be all right.'

'We will. We're fit to build the first express liner. We are.'

'Now let's go down to dinner.'

There were always eminent people there, but tonight John had made sure that Gil was seated opposite a railroad millionaire. Soon the talk was of shipping and railways. The little fat man with the clever eyes impressed Gil.

'The idea is that you could buy a ticket in London to pay for your passage to New York and then go on anywhere in America by rail. Does that seem like a good idea to you, Mr Collingwood?'

'It might if I could have some part in the deal,' Gil said.

John laughed.

'Mr Collingwood is my man,' he said. 'He's going to be involved in all my best endeavours from now on.'

'I think we did it,' Rhoda said when they got back to the bedroom at an advanced hour.

'I think we did it too.' Gil said.

When they got home, relations between his father and Edward were worse than ever, but it was his mother who told him.

'Edward has stopped going into the office and he comes home once or twice a week to see Matthew and Helen. I don't understand what's going on,' she said.

Gil went to Toby's house, but when Toby opened the door he was alone.

'Yes, he's here,' Toby said, beckoning Gil inside. They

went through the house and out into the garden. It was late spring and the day was soft. Toby offered Gil a wooden seat. 'He's in bed asleep. He was drunk.'

Toby gave him wine that tasted of gooseberries. The garden was filled with herbs, lavender and thyme, rosemary, a dozen different kinds of mint and various tall flowers which Gil did not recognise, pink and violet and white. The garden was like some kind of tapestry woven in Toby's favourite colours.

'Did you get the contract?'

'Nothing's signed yet.'

'But it will be.' Toby stretched out his long legs in front of him. 'You have to admit, Gil, you've turned into Golden Boy.'

Gil squirmed in his chair.

'I wish we could be as we were. I don't seem to be able to have my father and Edward.'

'Having everything is an extremely costly business,' Toby said.

'He spends a great deal of his time here.'

'He has spent a great part of his life away from here,' Toby said, looking at him.

'It's you, isn't it?' Gil said slowly.

'Of course it's me. What did you think it was? You knew. Don't pretend to be so innocent. You went to school. Tell me nobody tried to bed you, you with your sweet face. Didn't you ever?'

'No.'

'How very boring.'

'It's not that, it's just—'

'That you like women. I had noticed.'

'If it was you, then why did he marry Helen?'

'Because. Happiness is a myth. It's something either in the past or in the future. You think you can catch it if you say your prayers and eat your cabbage and please your father, but all you really have is now and pleasure. He did try very hard.'

'Who did try very hard?' Edward said loudly behind him. Gil looked into his brother's bloodshot eyes and knew then that he had always known what could now be spoken of.

'You did,' Toby said, putting back his head. Edward looked straight back at Gil before he kissed Toby on the mouth.

Gil thought of his father. There was no way William would ever believe that his son could love another man. Gil thought that if William found out it might kill him. Yet Gil could understand why his brother had fallen in love with Toby. There was something very special about him. He oozed peace and Edward had not known peace in his life. The small white house with the wooden floors; the books and cosy fires; the smell of bread baking and chocolate cake cooking, and beef with onions bubbling gently on top of the stove; the garden with its tall trees at the end of the paths thick with greenery in summer; herbs for the pot and the small secret places where you could sit and dream – who would not have wanted to escape to such a place, to a person who demanded nothing, was always on your side, to be loved without criticism, to be accepted without question? Women could not do that. The war between the sexes could never be over. In some ways it was easier to give in. Toby could understand Edward's problems as a woman could not. They had been brought up together, gone to the same schools, knew the same people.

'And how is married life?' his brother asked softly.

Chapter Eleven

When she was in Northumberland, Abby very often went to visit her father on Saturday afternoons. He usually finished work at lunchtime when the men did, and she would arrive in time to have a meal with him and to stay the night. Sometimes Gil was there, calling in after work or coming on Sunday afternoons, when he would have Rhoda, Helen and Matthew with him. The baby made Abby feel uncomfortable. Henderson seemed taken with the child and, although Abby did not think herself particularly maternal, she knew that it was expected she would provide an heir and at least one other male child. She had not thought about this when she had married Robert, but he seemed to take for granted that they would have children. So far nothing had happened and by the time autumn came, Abby was starting to worry. She also thought that if they had a child, Robert might not care quite so much for the socialising, or at least differently, though Matthew's birth had not encouraged Edward Collingwood to be seen about any more frequently with his wife. Helen was so pale and listless that she was no advertisement for childbearing, Abby thought. Gil was very thin. In fact, Rhoda was the only one of the three who looked at all happy.

Abby wished that Robert had been with her. She loved him and she knew that he loved her, but he would not go with her to see her father, much less anybody else's father. She knew that Gil went to see Henderson because they had business interests in common and Henderson was, surprisingly for him, delighted to see another man's success. Gil had gained the contract to build the biggest ever liner and Henderson was as proud as if Gil had been his son. It made Abby wretched to see them together. All Robert seemed to have in common with his friends was enjoying themselves and, while there should have been nothing wrong in that, Abby was uncomfortable with it. Robert would laugh and call her middle-class, but it seemed to her that money and position brought responsibility with it. He had frowned at that.

'Are you telling me that I treat my people badly?' he had said.

It was a source of pride to him that 'his people', as he called them, were well paid, well housed. He looked after them; he did more, Abby thought in honesty, than William Collingwood had ever done for his workforce.

Abby tried to tell him firstly that they were not his, and secondly that he could have done much more with his money to help other, poorer, people. He didn't understand what she was talking about, nor would he let her use any of his money for what he called her good causes. People who did not work for him were nothing to do with him. He had no sense of general responsibility.

Abby knew that he did much more than many people in his position – some of them treated their servants and their workmen very badly – but it seemed wrong to her; she thought that not to use power for the general good was another way of misusing it and Robert spent so much on big parties and keeping up his houses and things which she considered unnecessary. She tried to talk to him, but he called her his little do-gooder and tolerated her. Abby knew that she ought to have been grateful for such a generous husband. Gil had no independence. He had nothing, Abby reasoned, yet there was something about him which she found difficult to dislike, the occasional reluctant smile, the way that he was quiet and did not put himself forward as Robert did. He did not attempt to dominate the conversation. Robert was often loud, shouting across the room to people or manoeuvring the talk for his own ends, towards his own interests, regardless of other people. But then, Gil did not know that conversation was a tool, she thought. He used it sparingly.

Henderson talked to Matthew, took the child up to his shoulder and then into his arms as he had no doubt done with her when she was that small. Abby could tell that he was charmed and wished she could have told him that she was having a child. It seemed to be the one thing she could have done. Robert had people to do everything else. This was all she could do for him. Several of their acquaintances and friends had children, some who had not been married much longer than them. This was her place. Instinct told her that the more concerned she became, the more difficult it would be, so she went on partying and talking to people, buying new clothes which she did not want and putting up with those friends he cared for whom she did not like, as part of her wifely duties.

To his credit, Robert did not mention children. She didn't think he cared particularly, but the women of his family were prone to asking after her health very often and Abby knew it was for one reason. It was not that she and Robert did not go to bed together often, though not every night. Three or four nights a week he did not come to her bed and she was quite happy alone, though a little hurt to think that he would not come just to sleep with her, that there must always be a reason. At first she did not mind, but it soon occurred to her that after she had gone to bed, the house was very still. One night, she ventured into his bedroom to find it empty. The next time he didn't come to her, it was empty again. He was nowhere that she could discover in the house and even in a house that size what could he do at night but sleep, read, smoke or drink by the fire? Abby went back to bed and, if she had been the kind of woman who wept much, she would have done so at the suspicions which thereafter crossed her mind.

Over dinner the following evening she said to him, 'Tell me, Robert, do you go to whores?'

Her husband choked over a mouthful of beef. He took a long drink of wine, coughed until his eyes ran and, when he had wiped his face on his napkin, he said, 'Dear God, woman, what a thing to say!'

'Do you?'

'Of course I damned well don't!'

'Then you have somebody else.'

Robert took another swig of wine.

'Whatever happened to tact?' he said.

'Do you?'

'Abby, my life is mine.'

'You have a mistress, then.'

He looked severely across the table at her.

'Well-bred women do not discuss such subjects,' he said.

'I'm not well-bred, so it doesn't count.'

'Do you want me in your bed every night?'

'I certainly don't want you in anybody else's.'

He looked down at his plate for a second.

'How can I say this without sounding nasty? Women like bed. Ladies don't. I respect you and I also expect, as your husband, to come to your bed when I choose. The subject is closed.'

'How can you go to bed with another woman? I'm your wife! Aren't I a good wife to you? Is it because I haven't conceived a child? Is it?'

'It has nothing to do with any of that.'

'What has it to do with then?'

Robert sighed.

'Men have needs. I don't wish to discuss this anymore,' he said, and got up and walked out.

Anybody would have thought, looking at Rhoda, that she and Gil had the perfect marriage. She seemed happy. This was what she had wanted: freedom. She shopped with Helen, spent time with the baby, chatted with Gil's father and mother, ate chocolate and read by the fire when the weather was bad and spent many hours walking on her beloved moors. Each night she turned the key in the lock of the door between their bedrooms. Gil asked for nothing. Most of the time he stayed at work.

The contract had been signed and work was going ahead. It was going to be a massive task. It would take ten thousand pounds to widen the river and covered berths were to be built; he had insisted on that. His father had argued that they would be draughty and would exclude light, but Gil had promised John Marlowe a launch date eighteen months ahead and he was not about to go back on this. He had also built a self-propelled model of forty-six feet and was doing all kinds of testing in a specially built dock. The results were exciting. If he changed the shape so that it was slightly finer, he would need less power for better speed. The broader beam meant the river must be dredged and widened, but many shipbuilders, including his father and Henderson, had been gradually doing this for years and were only pleased at the proposal. They were not quite so pleased at having to contribute financially.

Gil would have stayed overnight often in the office, but since Edward came home so rarely, and only then to see Matthew, he didn't. He went home to his polite wife and his cold bed. His temper had suffered too. At work sometimes now he could hear William in his voice. Things which seemed obvious to him had to be repeated. People did not work efficiently enough or fast enough to suit him or John or the Admiralty, and from time to time they sent their dreaded committee to interfere. It took all Gil's self-control not to shout at them too.

One night that autumn, when Gil had gone to bed late, he awoke with a start in the darkness, knowing even as he opened his eyes that someone was in the room. It was Rhoda. She had a candlestick in her hand and her face was full of distress. The room was chilly because the nights were becoming cold and the fire had gone out long since. She looked ridiculously young, her hair in plaits and her nightdress long and white.

'I had a bad dream,' she said.

It must have been very bad, Gil thought, to get her into his room.

'Sit down,' Gil said. He pulled off the top cover, gave it to her and she wrapped it around her. 'Do you want to tell me about it?'

'It was awful. I was up on the moors and I got lost. I don't get lost because I know them, but it was dark and cold, so very cold . . . and I was alone. The wind was doing that sort of low moaning sound it makes when there's heather or bracken. I couldn't see and there was nowhere to go and I stumbled and fell and hurt myself and then—'

'And then?'

'That was all. When I woke up—'

'It's all right. You can stay here.'

'No, I—'

'It's all right,' he said again slowly, trying to reassure her. Rhoda hesitated, but when he drew back the bedclothes for her she got in and after a short while she went to sleep. He awoke briefly some time later to find her cuddled in against his back, sound asleep. She was still there when the maid came in with the early morning tea. Rhoda would have run like a startled hare when she had gone, but he said, 'No, stay there and drink the tea. I never have time. I have to get to work.'

'But it's early yet.'

'I always go at this hour.'

He bathed and dressed. When he came back into the room, she had drunk the tea and gone back to sleep.

That evening when he returned home, she didn't say much. She ate nothing at dinner, and as the evening progressed became very pale. Usually she went to bed early, long before he did, but tonight she lingered. Gil knew the courage it took to face the following night after you had had a bad dream.

'Shall I see you upstairs?' he offered in the end.

Rhoda looked like a child caught out in mischief.

'There's no need.'

'I'm going to bed anyway.'

He lit a candle for her and took one for himself, but when they reached her room Rhoda hesitated.

'I can leave the middle door open if you want.'

Still she didn't move.

'Do you want to come and sleep with me?'

She did. After that she slept in his bed every night. By day she rode her horse out on to the moors, took the dogs with her, or took them for long walks. She went shopping in town with Gil's mother and bought pretty clothes and ornaments for her hair. She went visiting with his mother and Helen. She seemed happy. Each night when Gil came home, if it was before bedtime she would run to him and kiss him. After a while, that winter, she grew bolder and would hug him. If they were alone she sat on his knee and snuggled her face in against his neck. She talked to him about her day and she would tease and kiss him and stroke his hair. In fact, apart from the way that she slept in his bed, she treated him very much as she had undoubtedly treated her father when she was a little girl, he thought. She would play games in the woods with him, hiding behind trees and having him call her and popping out unexpectedly. She wrote him silly notes and sat by the fire for hours in the bad weather reading novels. Gil realised by the end of the winter that Rhoda adored him. For her, he was her father come back to life.

He tried to get her to kiss him, but she backed away in horror at anything more than what she had allowed. He tried to get her to talk about Jos Allsop but it seemed that she did not understand; she had wiped from her mind whatever her stepfather had done to her. To onlookers Gil could see that his marriage looked perfect. Men turned envious eyes on him. Rhoda was beautiful now, safe with him, loved by his family, cared for in that great house, looked after. She could not be touched. When they went out, she clung to his arm, elegant and beautiful. Other men were of no interest to her. She didn't leave his side and Gil could see their envious glances as they imagined her smooth young body. She put on weight and became rounded. Her skin glowed; her eyes shone; her teeth sparkled. She was completely happy with him, Gil knew.

When they had got back from America and Gil had seen Jos for the first time, the other man looked so much as usual, so ordinary, that Gil was not convinced he had done anything. He was not sure that his wife was stable, so he kept both himself and her away from the man and was civil when he had to be.

She loved presents. Gil quite often took her to the jeweller they frequented in Newcastle and there he would let her choose earrings for her pretty ears, bangles for her slim wrists, chains to put around her neck where he was not allowed to kiss her. He bought emeralds to match her engagement ring and watched the pleasure come into her face. She was like a child at Christmas and she would thank him profusely, cover his face with kisses, rush from the carriage to show everyone what he had bought her. She told him how much she loved him.

Gil bought furs for her exquisite body and she leaped on him in bed and kissed him. She hated the smell of whisky and, before Gil had been aware of this and had drunk some one night before bed, she recoiled in front of him, her eyes wild with fear. He never drank it again. There was more than one triumph in this. Sometimes her mother and stepfather came to the house and Rhoda unwittingly played the devoted wife. She liked to touch Gil, mostly, he knew, to reassure herself that he was still here; but to other people it looked as though she wanted him. Gil could see the puzzled look in Allsop's face and saw himself as other men did. Young and married to her and she hanging onto his arm, wearing beautiful clothes. And she was lovely. Allsop was always at least half drunk when he saw them, so it was difficult to be certain what had happened. He ignored his wife in company and she was pregnant again. Rhoda didn't seem to mind his presence as long as Gil was there, but sometimes he detected a glitter in her eyes and when they had gone she would often disappear up onto the fells alone.

Right from the beginning, Helen believed that Gil and Rhoda's marriage was a success, he could see. She kept out of the way unless there was some outing planned. It was, he thought, the best that she had loved him, leaving him to make his marriage work. He wished that he could have said something instead of having to play out this painful charade for Rhoda's sake. There was no way to better things. Night after night, Helen went to bed early and Gil was sure that she drank herself to sleep. She didn't talk much anymore, or pay much attention to her child. Nothing seemed to reach her. She always proclaimed herself willing to go out with them, but sometimes she could be silent all day. He became afraid that life would always be like that, Edward coming back only to see his child, Helen alone and he pretending for Rhoda's sake that life was good. Only the work was any comfort and, as the weeks went by, he saw the ship begin to take shape and there was a kind of happiness in that. He solved each problem as it happened. He had, with Mr McGregor's help, seen the engineering problems, most of them from the beginning, and with the experts from the drawing office and the design team he had done tests, but even so he was worried. If they had got this wrong it would be the biggest mistake in the history of shipping. On a bad day he was convinced the new ship would be a failure; on a good day he could visualise it on the water. He reported progress to Henderson every week when he saw him to play dominoes and he wished only that they could have been together on this project. He dreamed of joining forces, of amalgamating the two shipyards, of being able to work with Henderson every day. He was an easier man than William.

Henderson's health, however, was another matter. Sometimes he was too unwell to go to work and one evening that summer he collapsed when Gil was there, so that Gil had him put to bed and sent for the doctor.

He also sent a message to Abby. The doctor had been and gone before she got there, white-faced. Gil knew that she was remembering her mother's illness and death.

'Doctor Brown says he'll be all right.'

Gil said this half a dozen times in the ten minutes after Abby had been up to see her father. He was sleeping, she said. Abby had never been a fat girl, but she was much thinner than she had been a year since, Gil thought, as she sat down in the garden and he gave her tea.

'Are you sure the doctor said he's going to get better?' she asked again.

'Certain.'

'He's not going to die. I don't think I could bear it. When I leave him he looks so lonely, but perhaps it's a reflection or it's my own loneliness that I see. I hate leaving him. It feels like a betrayal every time. I'm so grateful to you that you spend time with him.'

'It's not a hardship,' Gil said. 'I like him. I wish my own father was like him.'

'He and Robert don't get on. I thought they would. They seemed to like each other so well at first. If anything happens to him . . . Don't worry, I'm not going to cry.' She smiled bravely. 'Every time I see you I do it.'

'Yes, it's not very flattering,' Gil said, and her smile became natural.

Abby wanted to stay at the house with her father, but she couldn't. She had her marriage to think about. She had discovered that things could not be mended in the bedroom; even alone with Robert, other women got in the way. It was difficult to be warm towards a man who had told you that you were inadequate. She had discovered that Robert kept a mistress. Not a long-time mistress; he would keep a young girl for a while and then pay her off. At least Abby thought that they were young girls. They seemed to her to be much younger than she was but old enough for him. In bed he was no longer gentle with her. He kissed her once or twice and then mounted her as though she were a horse, Abby thought. He rode her until he was done and then got off. She wondered if that was how he treated his mistress and had to stop herself from asking. Night and morning he bedded her and Abby did not have to wonder why. The subject of an heir had become important and her husband came to her bed regularly. She was, however, determined not to send him from her into another woman's arms and pretended she was eager to have him with her, though the endurance was hard to bear. Robert was a man experienced with women; he could surely tell the difference between enthusiasm and determination. If he did, he gave no sign of it. There was no child and things were more difficult than ever.

Chapter Twelve

When John Marlowe's ship was ready to be launched it was a great day at Collingwood's shipyard. It would be another year at least before the ship was fitted out, but the hull was finished. Edwina Marlowe, John's wife, was to launch the ship, which would be called the *Northumbria*. For once, William had called for a special party for all the workers and their families and inside the shipyard offices themselves a feast had been brought in for the Collingwoods and their family and friends.

It was a cold grey autumn day. The Tyne looked leaden, but the crowds who had gathered to watch the launch were cheerful and so were the men who had built the ship, and who now lined its decks.

Helen was there with Matthew and her parents. Edward had come; Toby was there in the background; Abby and Henderson were there, and even Robert. Rhoda was bright-eyed, cosy in furs, holding Gil's arm and beaming at everyone, her cheeks pink from the cold. She knew that this was his moment of triumph, his first ship, and the biggest ship ever to be built here. He could feel the excitement in her, her pride at his achievement. Edward came to him.

'Well, little brother, what a day.'

Gil looked at him. He was drunk; not the kind of drunk that falls over and sings and shouts, but the slow drunkenness that is never quite sober. Edward smiled at Matthew and took the child from Helen. Gil was glad that he had caught the look that Edward bestowed upon his son. He thought it was the biggest love in his brother's life; nothing flawed about it. Edward loved his child purely. Gil hoped that he would feel the same when Matthew became a little older and was not just his son but a separate person. William had never been able to make that distinction. Even now Gil was 'my son, the genius', whereas he had turned his back on Edward. The only thing Edward had done that his father was pleased with was to provide an heir. It was the sole reason his father let him into the house or, on the odd occasion when he chose, to come to the works. Neither of them would ever be free of William.

Henderson had insisted on coming even though he was not looking very well. Abby was pale with the cold and Robert didn't speak to Gil. He couldn't think how she had persuaded Robert to attend a ship launch.

'Are you thrilled?' Edward said. 'You must be. The

biggest ship ever. You did want the biggest, the best, the fastest. It was what you wanted and it's beautiful.'

He was right, Gil thought, it was beautiful. No wonder men called ships 'she'. This mighty being which he had created in his mind, seen so long ago in his head, this ship would make his reputation. He knew with a sureness he rarely felt that it would cross the Atlantic and take the Blue Riband and that his father would fairly burst with pride. Collingwood's would be made for ever and ever. Even now, he knew, the men spoke of him with respect, were glad to work on his ship. Gil wanted to do more and after this he would be able to. William would give them more money, build them better houses, ease their difficult lives. Gil would have more power in the shipyard and be able to do things.

More than anything, Gil wanted Henderson Reed's approval that day. He didn't know why; it was bad enough constantly needing his father to be pleased. He felt like a spaniel, wanting to be continually patted and told how clever he was; but Gil had such respect for Henderson and he knew today that Henderson was there just for him, even though the older man neither looked at him nor spoke to him. He leaned against Abby as Gil had not seen him do before. He was standing next to Robert, but they ignored one another. Henderson's dislike of his son-in-law had grown.

Edwina moved forward in the cold Newcastle day and said the wonderful words.

'I name this ship *Northumbria*. May God bless her and all who sail in her.'

Rhoda clutched Gil's arm even more tightly and, as the bottle of champagne broke over the ship's bows and the contents spilled over its perfection, Gil thought that if he lived for another hundred years he would never be as happy again. The ship began to move very slowly down the slipway towards the cold water of the 'queen of rivers'. The Tyne opened its arms and received the ship into its depths and the water came up on every side. The men on board and the people round about cheered and took off their caps and threw them in the air and were still cheering when the ship came to rest in the middle of the river.

It changed in those seconds, Gil thought. He felt like the parent watching the child become an independent adult. It was a separation, a letting go, a loss, a farewell, a parting. There was still more than a year's work to be done, but he felt that it was not his as it had been. It was plucked from his imagination and was gone. Gil wanted to run from this mighty being that his mind had conceived. He was afraid it would turn into a tyrant.

They went back to the offices through the many hundreds of people who had come to see the launch, and it was easier there, drinking champagne and receiving the good wishes of his friends, of all the other shipbuilders who had come to the launch and many other important people of the city. Abby and Robert seemed at home there and went around chatting to their friends. Edward and Toby left as soon as could be considered decent, though Toby came to Gil and congratulated him warmly.

'My dear boy, I'm so pleased for you,' he said.

Henderson said nothing, but Gil didn't mind. The old man's eyes were light on him, so Gil went over to him.

'Champagne, Henderson?'

'No bloody fear. I'll stick to ale.'

'How are you Abby?' Gil asked her, as she reached her father at the same time.

'Very well indeed,' she said, and Gil knew that she was lying. He knew her so well. 'We're going away.'

'Anywhere nice?'

'To France, I believe. It's warmer there. I'm trying to persuade my father to come with us.'

'Can't leave the yard,' Henderson said.

'Aren't you ever going to leave it, Father?'

'Not before I drop dead.'

Abby smiled, but it was a forced smile. Henderson watched her go to her husband and then he looked at Gil.

'I want to tell you something.'

'What?'

Henderson's watery eyes turned paler as Gil watched.

'I was wrong about you,' he said.

'Why, Henderson, you couldn't have been.'

'It isn't funny. If we could only look into the future. I can't stand him. He's never done a day's work in his life. He hasn't contributed anything. "By their fruit shall ye know them." That bugger hasn't got any fruits. He hasn't even given her a child. I wish I'd let you marry Abby.'

'It wouldn't have been any good. She didn't like me and she's so bossy,' Gil said lightly.

'Takes after her mother. She was sharp was Bella. I wouldn't care if he made her happy. Runs after other women.'

That night there was a big party at the house. Everyone danced and the musicians played well into the morning. Helen wouldn't dance with Gil or with anybody else.

'What's the matter?' he asked her.

'I caught my leg on the table edge at home the other day.' She called her parents' house home, Gil noticed.

'Is it all right?'

'It will be, but it hurts just at the moment. Go and dance with Rhoda.'

'Helen—'

'I know. Go and dance with her,' Helen said gently.

Rhoda was unusually happy that night. Gil wondered whether she had been drinking wine, but since she didn't care for that and laughed when he suggested it and said, 'I'm so proud of you,' he didn't worry until they went to bed.

It was late and dark and the house was silent by then; they had been among the last to go to bed. Gil didn't want the day to end because he wasn't sure whether he would ever be able to have another that was as good as this one. She got into bed and sat there with her knees up to her chin and watched him as he lingered by the fire with a last drink.

'Gil . . .'

'Mmm?'

'Have you ever thought about having children?'

'What?'

'You know, that we might not.'

'Children?'

'Yes.'

'I can't say it bothers me one way or the other.'

'You wouldn't mind then, if we didn't.'

'I don't know yet. I might, yes.'

'I think I might too, in the long run, eventually.'

'We don't have to think about it now. We've got years and years.'

'Aren't you coming to bed?'

'Shortly.'

'Now?'

'I don't want the day to end,' Gil admitted, 'it's been so perfect.'

'Could it be better?'

'No, I don't think so.'

'Maybe it could.' She got out of bed and came over to him and sat down on his knee. This was nothing new, but the way that she kissed him was.

'I thought you didn't want to do this,' Gil said, stopping her for fear he had misinterpreted.

'I didn't, but you're not him. You've proved over and over that you're not and I love you.'

'Rhoda . . . I think the act is . . . always aggressive.'

'I don't think you're very aggressive,' she said, smiling. 'Don't you want me because of him?'

'My God, yes.'

'I would like a child and you're the kindest man I've ever met. You make me feel safe, completely secure. I think I might be able to . . . I don't feel as if I'm your wife. I feel rather as though I'm your child and it's nice and for a while it was . . . You love me. Nobody who didn't love me could have been as good to me as you have been and I love you. I've been lucky with you. I didn't know at the beginning. It was just a gamble and I was desperate to get away from him and . . . not just from him, from all of it, the memories of my father and the way that my mother had become somebody I didn't know and their foul children . . . I feel so lucky. I want to spend all my life with you. Come to bed now.'

But he didn't because she didn't get off his lap and she

giggled and kissed him. Gil tried to talk to himself, be very slow and careful because he didn't really believe she was going to give herself to him, not after all this time. It would make the day good beyond all reason and that had not happened to him before. There was always a hitch, always a flaw, always some bastard to spoil it and nobody had yet spoiled this day. He could spoil it now if he was clumsy or if the memories of her stepfather intruded and he was sure that they would. The act was a taking and he was not sure whether she could bear to give any more, whether there was anything left other than the child she had so far offered as herself. He tried to think what Allsop had been like apart from the obvious brutality. It had most likely been her bed, so as she went on kissing him he very carefully eased her down onto the rug in front of the fire and held her to him. It was difficult after so long not to want her too much for caution, but he had spent months building her confidence. One mistake now and it could all be gone. He talked to her, kissed her, remembered what had happened last time he got hold of her like this in New York, but it was quite different. She was warm, willing. She wanted him and it was much easier than he had thought. When she tensed even slightly, he stopped touching her and asked her if she wanted to stop, but she said no. There was a slight reluctance on her, but he thought that she had watched Matthew for so long and decided that she wanted a child. Since she trusted him sufficiently she would put up with this, the cost with him would be worth the eventual result. He realised now that Helen had wanted him almost to the point of madness. This was not the same, pale by comparison, but it was better than nothing unless it should break down the trust again and she should retreat into that wild being of the moors she protected herself with. He felt awkward, as though he might drop her and smash everything, so it was almost a relief to have her. She turned her face away. It was the first time in such an act that Gil had felt dirty and troublesome and ashamed. This must be what it was like when you went to a whore, somebody who didn't want you, who was doing this for a reason and not for pleasure. How could men enjoy somebody who didn't want them? And yet you could, he realised; biology itself said so. Having her even like this was ecstasy after so long. He wished he could have run to Helen. He didn't know why he hadn't gone to her on all those many nights when she slept alone and he slept alone and there was nothing to stop them. Even when Rhoda slept in his bed he could have sneaked out. She would not have known. And Edward was in bed at nights with Toby. Yet in a way he had condemned them all.

When it was over, Gil wanted her more. It was like having one sip of champagne, one chocolate after years of doing without. Helen had always taken him into her

arms, but Rhoda didn't, as though he were a dress she
had tried on and decided didn't suit her. Failing to please
was something Gil knew he was good at. He had spent
years trying to please Abby, his father, Henderson,
Edward. The one person he had not tried to please was
Helen. They had started off from the same place and
when they went to bed there were no winners and los-
ers, no lovers or beloved. It all balanced and worked and
had been right in so many different ways from the beginning, always new but always right, always safe and so
dangerous, so deliciously, spectacularly pleasurable. He
wanted to crawl away and find her, so that he could not
be in this permanent competition with himself where,
no matter what he did, how hard he tried, he failed
always as though some part of him was standing on a
high rock above, saying, 'no, not quite, just a bit more'
and he was hanging on to the rock by his fingertips and
slipping down. One day he would slip altogether and
after that there would be no more trying to succeed.

'Did I hurt you?'

'No.'

'Was it like as if it was him?'

'I don't remember.' She got up.

'You don't remember?'

She looked at him.

'I had pushed it from my mind, a lot of it. I just
remembered the brutality and the fear, but there was

none of that here. I wish it had been the first time, that's all. I'm your wife. I don't want to be anything else.'

She reached out and Gil put his arms around her. They went to bed. He couldn't sleep for wanting her, but in the morning she kissed him and encouraged him and this time she didn't turn her face away. She laughed and made rash promises and it was Sunday, so he didn't have to go to work. They stayed in bed for as long as might be considered decent among people who had been married for so long. They got ready and had breakfast and went to church as usual, but all the way through the service Rhoda made eyes at him so that he could concentrate on nothing but her. There were visitors in the afternoon and many people had stayed, so they had no opportunity to be alone or to sneak away. The evening was endless and the talk was of the great new ship. Gil couldn't have been less interested. All he wanted was to take his wife to bed. After dinner, they slipped away to his bedroom, pulled each other's clothes off and made love and it was, he thought, the first time then. And a miracle had occurred. Saturday had been a perfect day. Sunday was even better.

Chapter Thirteen

Helen didn't go back to Durham with her parents when they left that Sunday, even though they tried to persuade her. There was nothing at Bamburgh House for her now except that William and Charlotte loved Matthew and encouraged her to stay. Gil had been thinking too much about Rhoda that day to consider Helen, but the following morning early, when he got up to go to work, his mother, to his surprise, was already up. As he came downstairs, she had a worried frown on her face.

'Helen isn't well. I think I ought to send for the doctor.'

'She was complaining about her leg on Saturday, but I didn't think anything of it.'

'Was she? I didn't know there was anything wrong and her mother didn't mention it. She wasn't limping. She has a fever.'

His mother was obviously in need of reassurance, so Gil went upstairs with her to Helen's room. It had been a long time since he had been in there and he was not comfortable. He thought of the nights he had spent there in her arms, but when he saw her, thoughts like that left him. His mother was right. She didn't seem well. The sweat stood out on her forehead and her cheeks were burning. He touched her forehead with his cool hand and she opened her eyes and smiled at him.

'That's nice,' she said.

'Is it your leg, Helen?'

'My what?'

'Your leg. You said on Saturday—'

'Oh no, it's fine,' she said. 'This is just a chill. I need to sleep, that's all.'

She closed her eyes, and turned her back on them. Gil followed his mother out of the room.

'I hate to bother the doctor,' she said.

William came downstairs as they stood in the hall at the bottom.

'Helen is unwell,' Charlotte said. 'She says it's just a chill.'

'She knows her own mind, surely. Stop fussing, woman. Come along, lad, we're late.' And his father went off along the hall to the dining room.

Gil was happy at work. He was thinking of how pleasant it would be to go home to Rhoda and, long before the day was done, when the autumn light had gone and the cold evening had begun, he stared from the office window, thinking about his pretty wife and the homecoming she would provide. A single star was twinkling above his office window. He got up and watched it for a while and thought how lucky he was. He had everything. If it hadn't been for the fact that William insisted on them working until six, he would have gone home at half past four. Since then, he had not been able to concentrate. He had not thought he could feel so much joy. He let his mind wander past the ship launch again and the men throwing their caps into the air as the ship went down the slipway, the noisy crowds shouting and cheering, the party afterwards and how beautiful Rhoda had looked and everybody had been so pleased, then home to the second party. And Rhoda. She had completed everything. His wife loved him and he loved her and nothing could spoil it.

He was standing there when his father came into the office.

'Your mother won't be pleased if we're late for dinner,' he said, and they left.

Gil watched that same star from the carriage window as they drove home in the darkness. It was a cold, clear night with barely a cloud and the moon was full, so there was plenty of light. When they reached the house there was a horse and trap by the door. That was when Gil thought of Helen for the first time. The doctor.

He hurried inside, along the hall and into the drawing room. His mother and Dr Brown were in there and they turned towards him faces that told him nothing good.

'Is Helen ill?'

'She's not well,' his mother said.

'What is it?' He directed his look towards the doctor as his father came into the room.

'She has a badly infected leg,' Dr Brown said.

'Her leg? She said it was better.'

'I would say it has been increasingly bad for at least a week.'

'A week? Why didn't she tell somebody? Shouldn't she be in hospital?'

'I don't want to move her. She's too ill. Nothing could be done there which cannot be done here. I will arrange for nursing and we will do our very best to look after her.'

Gil stared at the doctor's careworn face. He looked tired.

'What does that mean?' he said.

'It means that her condition could deteriorate and quickly. She should have been looked after several days ago.'

'Didn't her parents realise?'

'Presumably not.'

'But she must have known. She . . . she must have,'

Gil said and there was a small, sick feeling which began in his stomach and seemed to make its way through his body like a snake.

'Sometimes these things seem unimportant, especially to people like mothers who have the concerns of their children to think about. They don't understand that neglect can lead to serious consequences.'

'Edward must be sent for,' William said from behind Gil.

Gil couldn't believe what they were saying. He left the room, ran through the hall and took the stairs two at a time, along the hall to Helen's room. When he opened the door, Rhoda was sitting on the bed with a cool cloth in her fingers, dabbing Helen's face.

'Helen?' he said, and she opened her eyes.

'Why are they fussing? I'm not ill. I'm not ill, am I, Rhoda?'

'No, of course not,' Rhoda said soothingly.

Gil sat down on the bed and took Helen's hand.

'Do you remember the house, Gil?' she said.

'What house?'

She laughed. Her voice sounded hoarse and her laughter was full of disbelief.

'The house in Spain.'

'Was it in Spain?'

'Where did you think it was?'

'I don't know.'

'At the top of the mountain. It was best at the top of

the mountain because we got what breezes there were. You do remember it?'

'Yes.'

'And the bedroom? The way that breeze used to catch the white curtains in the bedroom. You said it was as if they were doing a dance. The bedroom in the afternoons.'

Gil glanced at Rhoda to see if she was taking any notice, but she pressed his hand and shook her head to imply that she knew it was nonsense. His heart was beating so hard that it hurt. He and Helen had not talked about this before. He was not aware that she knew any of this and it was nonsense. It was. Before she had arrived at the house as Edward's intended bride he had never seen her; he knew that he hadn't. He had always told himself that it was the way he had justified wanting Helen, taking her. He had pretended to himself that they had had some other life, that they had been lovers before, but they had not talked about it. Yet here she was describing the very scenes that his mind had given him a hundred times. He could almost smell the lemons and oranges in the garden, see the blue of the ocean, feel that soft breeze which had made its way across the mountain, cooled in the high air above the valley wherein lay the little white town. He could see it clearly now, the neat houses and the palm trees, the long evening shadows. People would be sitting outside drinking wine and talking and children played games in the quiet streets. Yet his sensible mind told him that he had not been to

Spain. He had been to America. He had memories of New York, but they didn't seem as clear to him as the place where he and Helen had been and not been together.

Helen was watching him and her eyes were so bright that he could hardly meet them.

'You thought I didn't remember,' she said.

'I knew you did,' he said cheerfully.

'We didn't talk about it. I thought you might think it was silly. We were there together. It was wonderful. When I saw you again, do you remember, you were standing at the top of the steps here and I was talking to your parents below. I knew it was you.'

All this while Rhoda was applying cool cloths and looked as though she were taking no notice of the conversation. To her, Gil could see, Helen was a girl in a fever, unaware of what she was saying and he was agreeing with her to keep her as calm as possible.

Later, the doctor sent a nurse, but Rhoda would not leave Helen's side. She stayed there all night. Helen slept fitfully and she talked a great deal. Some of it even Gil couldn't understand. All night and all the next day she burned and sweated. Gil's father insisted on them going to work.

'There's nothing we can do here,' he said harshly. 'The doctor has it in hand. We have money to make and orders to see to.'

'Surely for one day . . .'

William looked severely at him.

'Is it a service to stay here with her? You'll be better off at work and so will I.'

His father was being practical, Gil knew, and so he went and in some ways it was better. There was nothing they could do and Helen recognised nobody that morning so it was unlikely she would know whether or not he was there. Edward had arrived at the house early that morning so, from his father's way of thinking, there were sufficient people. He and Gil would be in the way. Gil did no work. He sat at his desk and his mind flooded with guilt and responsibility and the heavy notion that she might die and he would not be there. He told himself that she wouldn't know him even if he was there. When, after the longest day of his life, they finally went home, though there were grave faces in the house she was not dead. Gil ran up the stairs and into the room and there he stopped just inside the door. The young woman in the bed was not the girl he had loved. She was shrunken and grey and her hair was like seaweed on the pillow. Her eyes had no life. She looked tiny.

The nurse and the doctor were there. Rhoda was standing by the window. His mother was crying softly in a chair and Edward was sitting in front of the fire, not looking at anyone. Her parents were there, too, and they all looked so distressed that Gil knew she was not going to get better. He had not noticed until then that the room was different from how it had been when he and Helen had shared a bed. In those days there were always flowers and books, writing materials, pretty covers on the chairs and colourful bedclothes. Now it was all white and there was nothing to relieve it, as though, he thought, scarcely able to form it in his mind, she had attempted to recreate their bedroom in the house at the top of the mountain. There were white curtains at the windows which would not keep out the bitter autumn weather. Where had those come from? Had she so desperately needed somebody that she tried to recreate that time?

She opened her eyes and said his name. She had aged several years since the night before and her face was almost transparent. So was the hand she stretched out to him. He went to her, sat down on the bed beside her and took her hand.

'I was waiting for you to come,' she said.

'I'm here.'

'It's so hot. It's always so hot. Ask for some water.'

Gil put the glass to her lips and she swallowed a little.

Beyond the white curtains he could see the cold winter night, with lots of stars. He could remember lying in bed with her, watching those same stars, the windows flung back wide in spite of the cold because she had said that night was too pretty to be closed out. There was a white sheen upon the lawns; he had seen it coming back in the carriage. He had been so happy the night before. He ought to have known that such things could not last more than a few hours. He wanted to cry. He wanted to tell her that he loved her.

'Everything is so white,' she said. 'Isn't that good? I do love you.'

'I love you too.'

The room was silent. It had been silent before, but the atmosphere changed then. They might think it just a sick woman's rantings, but it was hardly appropriate that, with her husband in the room, she should tell his brother that she loved him. Not that anyone would expect her to say such a thing to the husband Edward had been to her.

'Do you think I did this on purpose?'

She was quite lucid, Gil thought.

'No.'

'Perhaps I want to die.'

'I don't think you do. What about Matthew?'

'Children have a future. What was my future to be?'

Gil didn't know what to say to that. The sick feeling that hadn't left him since the day before was almost enveloping him. He wished that all these people would leave the room. He wanted to say wild things to her.

'You're not crying, are you, Gil?'

'No.'

'You look as though you are. It's the first time you've ever cried over me.'

'You didn't really do this on purpose?'

'What, to punish you? Do you think I would? I will see you again you know. This isn't the finish. Though I have to say that when I saw you here the first time, a great deal of the feeling I had had for you had already gone, but you did love me, more than you loved anyone else?'

'Yes.'

Rhoda turned from the window. Gil could see her from the corner of his eye. Would she go on thinking that he was just responding to a dying woman?

'I want to tell you something, Gil, something very important. I want you to look after Matthew.'

The silence changed again. It was not hostile, but it was as if the other people in the room felt left out, ignored, that they had realised she wanted nobody but him near her when she was dying. Her mother and father moved in their discomfort and Edward was watching him. Her voice was down to a whisper and even that seemed an effort, but everyone in the room could hear her words.

'Of course we will.'

'No, you.' She tried to get up from the pillows and couldn't. 'Matthew is your son. I'm sorry that I deceived you. I had to lie. I thought I was the only one losing by

it. Edward isn't fit to look after him and he isn't capable
of fathering a child. If he says he is, then he lies. When
he's drunk he thinks he's a man and he never was. Matthew is yours.'

The silence seemed to hang in the room for ever.
Then Rhoda gave a hoarse cry and broke it. She ran. It
was the only way she could ever meet disaster, by running away, Gil thought. If she had managed to pretend
that Helen was not in her right mind, then the moment
might have passed . . . Edward was on his feet. Charlotte went after Rhoda. Without looking, Gil could see
his brother. There was nothing to lose between them; it
had been over long since. He had known that his brother
had used him as a pawn in some complicated game and
that those evenings at the billiard hall were not for him.
The few days when Edward had seemed to care for him
and even want his company were dispelled on the afternoon Edward had looked at him and then kissed Toby
Emory on the mouth. They had not been born to love
one another, as perhaps brothers often weren't, though
it seemed so wasteful to Gil. People born of the same
parents were meant to go together like pieces of the
same jigsaw, but he and his brother had been born to
destroy one another and there was not even any pity in
it. You could not point to a time and say here was where
it went wrong. It was broken and lost and there was
nothing but the ruins of it now. And Edward blamed

him about Helen. He could understand that. He had always blamed himself over it and the shock of the child was cold on him.

Did Edward believe her? If he did, then in those seconds he had lost the only thing which kept him a Collingwood. If the child was not his, then there was nothing to hold him here. In a way it was what he had wanted. His freedom lay just beyond the door, but the pain of losing his son could not be worth it. As for the girl dying in the bed, he had betrayed her before she had betrayed him and her revenge was complete. Edward came across the room towards them.

'Matthew's my son, he's mine. He's mine! You said he was mine.'

Helen smiled faintly.

'I tried to forgive you. You can try to forgive me.'

'Never! I hope you burn in hell, you bitch!'

The confusion was somehow nothing to do with Gil. He took her into his arms.

'Don't worry,' he said, 'I'll look after Matthew.'

Edward was shouting and people were crying, but Helen lay quietly in his arms and smiled at him.

He didn't know what time passed before his mother came back into the room.

'She's gone! I tried to stop her, but she wouldn't listen

to me and she's gone out into the night and I'm so afraid!' Charlotte went to William.

Gil put Helen's body carefully down and then he swiftly left the room. He sped down the stairs and, pausing only to collect a coat, opened the front door. It was a savage night. Wind blew the rain almost horizontally. He could see by the hall lights, then he was out into the bitter weather and the door was closed behind him. He called her name, moving away, trying to think where she might have gone – not far, surely, in this. Then he thought of how she would be feeling, of what Jos had done and of what he had done. She might go anywhere. It was almost impossible to see, but he knew the countryside around his home so he went to all the places that they had gone together and those that had been her favourites. He shouted her name and the wind took it away a thousand times. He didn't know which direction to go in, so he tried to go everywhere.

It was the longest night of his life and he was soaked through within minutes. He stepped in deep water every so often, banged himself off trees where there was no light. The wind whipped rain across his face, his feet and fingers were numb and his hair provided a way for rain to make its way into his eyes so that it stung and inside his collar and down past his shirt. The rain turned to sleet and, halfway through the night, to snow and though some sensible part of himself said that she would have gone home, he stayed out in case she had not done so. When morning came the snow was worse than ever; it was a blizzard. When darkness fell again, he returned to the lights of the house.

There was an uneasy silence in the hall. He threw off his heavy coat and made his way into the drawing room. His mother and Helen's mother were there by the fire with Matthew. His mother looked up briefly, her mother not at all.

'She came home?' he said, but he knew the answer before his mother gave it.

'No. Your father and Edward and her father and all the other men are out looking for her.'

He found dry clothes and went back out, but the blizzard was worse than ever and the light began to fail in early afternoon. From time to time he heard her name shouted, but he didn't meet any of the others. He went on and on and felt as though now he could go on until the end of time. It was dark again and he was lost. He was trudging through deep snow and fell over something and knew that God was watching. Even a second or two without the knowledge would have been some consolation, but there was no doubt that he had found her. It reminded him very much of being small and watching farmers take their dead lambs from snowdrifts. She was too cold for there to be any life left in her. He knew then that everything that mattered was over, that all the promise of the world was finished and that whatever happened now was the merest detail. But for Matthew, he would have stayed there. Helen's words went round and round in his head. Edward would not take the child. His father and mother would take it and bring it up as they had brought him up. It was not a thought for men who scared easily. William, having only one grandchild, would not let Helen's parents have him to live with them. He would train the child for the business; he would beat him and humiliate him and . . .

He held Rhoda in his arms, much as he had held Helen those few hours ago. How strange, how unkind, how very terrible, to be punished with such sweeping purity so that there was nothing left that could be redeemed. He picked her out of the snowdrift and carried her home, away from the fells that she had loved so much, where she had left her spirit, where she had spent her last hours heartbroken because of what he had done. They would not meet again. He would go straight to hell and his sweet, precious wife, whom men had treated so badly, would go to God and nobody would hurt her again. And God had other plans for him, he could sense it; it was not over yet.

He slipped several times. She became heavy and the wind and the snow took his balance from him with the dead weight in his arms. He slid down slopes which had been banksides and fields before the whiteness devoured them. The night went on and on as though the Day of Judgement had arrived, which it had. There would be no daylight again. At last, however, he came within sight of the house. He was inclined to leave her body on the doorstep as the little black-and-white cat he had had as a boy would leave mice as offerings, but he managed to open the front door and make his way into the hall and from there to the drawing room.

They were all gathered. Rhoda's mother, who looked like her for the first time, burst into a screaming torrent of accusations and tears. Jos Allsop came forward and tried to take Rhoda from him and Gil swung away.

'Give me my daughter.'

'She was never your daughter, you bastard!'

'Give her to me. I'm going to kill you!'

They took her from him.

'She's dead,' Allsop said unnecessarily as he and Edward and William leaned over her, after they had put her onto the sofa and put a blanket around her. 'She's frozen, trying to get back to her mother and me, trying to get away from him and that mucky bitch!'

Gil glanced around. He had not noticed, but Helen's parents were not there. He didn't know what Jos Allsop was talking about. Nobody was dead. In a minute, Rhoda would open her eyes and smile and say how funny that he had been fooled and everything would be all right again. Helen and her parents had gone home. He waited and waited for her to open her eyes.

William looked at him. The soft look was gone. Gil backed away just a little. He was a child again and his father was going to beat him beyond pain and lock him into a room so cold that his body would go numb.

This was not happening. There was an old saying, what was it? Yes, he had it. Something about God only giving people what they could bear. Things like this didn't happen. Nobody could bear this, not even the strongest, ablest person in the world could bear this. Rhoda was asleep; she was cold; it had been a bad night. She was not dead. She could not be dead.

Allsop went for him, but his father and Edward were in the way. Gil was glad. His father knew and everything would be all right. His father cared for him now, because of the things he had done and would tell Jos Allsop that there was no place for anger here and no need and everything would be all right.

'Leave him,' William said.

'I'm going to kill him! Now or later, it doesn't matter to me.'

'Give me the child,' William said to Charlotte and her face changed. She held Matthew close to her and began to cry and protest. Gil couldn't understand why. Her crying was almost a wail.

'It isn't true. Helen was out of her mind with fever.

You know she was. You can't do this. I won't let you. He's the only grandchild we've got or will have now. If you can't think of anything else, think of the family. He's your heir. He's the only person to inherit. He's the only one we've got.'

They prised the child from her. Matthew was crying at all the upset. Gil wasn't surprised. His father thrust the child forward, for some reason, at him.

'Take him and get out.'

Charlotte was almost screaming. Gil stared at the small, struggling boy.

'It's too cold for him to go anywhere,' he said sensibly. 'It's a blizzard.'

The men were actually holding Charlotte back and she was fighting with them, his demure and elegant mother.

'Take him.'

Gil took the child if only to shut him up, for he had begun fighting and screaming too, just like his grandmother.

'You will never come back here again, do you understand? You are not my son. You are not welcome here for the rest of your life and neither is your bastard.'

Gil looked at him. There was an explanation somewhere, but he couldn't think of it and Matthew was not happy with Gil. He kicked and fought and great tears ran down his face.

'You could keep him here just for tonight. I would go and I could send for him when the weather is better.'

'Take him and go.'

'Right,' Gil said, matter-of-factly, and he took the screaming, kicking child and let two of the servants usher him beyond the front door. He stood on the step as they bolted the door behind him. He waited as though the weather was going to improve, when it was obvious that it was not. As the child's screams and kickings subsided because it was so cold, Gil undid his coat and put Matthew inside it. Then he began to walk away from the house, up the drive. Matthew was no longer fighting, though he was still crying.

Gil began to walk and his mind soon turned to practicalities. He had no money on him; he had nothing and it was snowing hard.

It took him most of the night to walk to Newcastle because the snow was so very deep and the wind had blown great drifts into the hedges and the insides of the road and on the road itself where there was no protection. He kept losing his way so although it was not a long way, it seemed it. It was early morning when he reached Jesmond and banged on the door of Henderson Reed's house.

Kate had just got up, by the look of her. She ushered

him into the sitting room and hastily cleaned the grate and emptied the ashes before assembling a new fire. Matthew had long since fallen asleep. Gil put him down on the sofa, carefully not bringing to mind the images of Rhoda. Henderson came down the stairs, fastening his dressing-gown.

'What in hell's name is going on?' he said, looking from Gil to the child and back again.

'I need a favour, Henderson.' To Gil's surprise his voice worked and it sounded clear and steady.

'Name it.'

'Will you keep Matthew here for a few days? It won't be long. It's just for now. It's so cold outside and he's so very little.'

Henderson was giving him a special look, one Gil hadn't seen before, as though Gil were a rather likeable imbecile and had to be humoured.

'I won't ever ask anything of you again as long as I live,' Gil offered. 'I swear it to you before God. Please.'

'Yes, of course,' he said. 'Come and sit by the fire. I was just going to have some breakfast. What would you like?'

Gil felt certain that he would not eat again before death.

'I can't stay,' he said lightly, 'but I will be back for him.'

'Mrs Wilkins has some particularly fine ham to cook. That with an egg or two and some coffee. You prefer coffee, don't you?'

Kate came back into the room bearing the coffee pot and cups and saucers, and milk and sugar on a tray.

'Has it snowed much in the country?' Henderson asked, pouring coffee and handing him a cup. Gil had not heard Henderson talk so much or be so convivial. Usually he was the opposite: grumpy and quiet. Perhaps the entire world had gone mad.

Gil swallowed some of the hot liquid. It was tasteless.

'I wouldn't ask you, but I'm afraid for his well-being.'

'Small children need looking after,' Henderson agreed.

Gil put down his coffee cup and walked out.

'Wait just a minute—' Henderson began.

Gil got himself out of the house very fast. It was still snowing.

Chapter Fourteen

Robert had insisted on going back to Europe. Abby was tired of it and she was worried about her father. She wanted to stay in Northumberland. It was raining in France, so she could not see the advantage of being there. They had travelled down through the countryside and in some ways it reminded her of Northumberland and made her ache for home. The little villages and farms and the countryside around made her long for her father. She was tired of all the endless moving about that her life had become; she was tired of Robert's friends and of doing nothing useful. She had discovered that where there was nothing but leisure there was no leisure, and though she had tried telling herself over and over again that other people envied her life, her husband, her houses, her dresses, her jewellery and her not having to work, anything which there was too much of could become monotonous.

If she could even have helped poor people; if she

could have given money to decent causes, assisted people who needed help, that would have been something; but Robert did not believe in change so she was allowed to alter nothing, not even a set of curtains in any of the houses. She was sure that the feeling he had had for her when they were first married had evaporated almost entirely. He spent most of his time in pleasures which had nothing to do with her, men's pursuits: shooting, fishing, drinking, playing cards, going out to clubs and to various sporting matches. Abby was meant to carry on their social life alone and it was a lonely occupation.

She was still not pregnant, though he came to her bed three or four times a week. He did that out of duty and she let him out of duty. Her mind, having nothing to do, thought long on Newcastle and her father. She tried not to think about Gil. She could see that he was happily married and that his work was going very well. People talked about him with respect. Abby tried to be glad for him, but it was difficult. She knew that when you had regard for people you should wish them well, but it was difficult when he was so happy and she was not. She was homesick and kept thinking of her father waving her away from the door of his house in Jesmond. Every time she did so the tears rose in her eyes and sometimes fell down her cheeks and she would chide herself and say that it was for lack of anything better to do that she was self-pitying and it was the worst thing anybody could be. She wanted to be home so much that the countryside around her made it worse. Though the weather was wet and cool, the countryside shone, the stones of the houses seemed bright and the fields were so green. Each morning she would walk up to the bakery and buy fresh bread for breakfast and it was the most wonderful smell in the world.

She was so afraid not to be there. She was afraid that her father would die while she was in France. She told herself to be rational; she told herself that it was unfair to Robert. He had wanted to show her this part of France, the countryside to the west of Bordeaux where his friends had a house, Perigueux, and the little villages around it. Robert loved being abroad. He spoke several languages fluently. It was one thing about him which Abby admired. He had spent most of his life going from country to country and knew French, Italian and Spanish.

The people they stayed with there, Veronique and Marcel, spoke little English. Abby found it difficult, stumbling along, not understanding their fast speech and there was no one around her who spoke English. She liked their way of life. They lived for food and wine and Veronique did not have servants as Abby did. She ran her own kitchen and from it every day came wonderful smells of onion, meat and garlic.

The surrounding countryside was peaceful and Abby

went for long walks when the weather was not too bad and spent what time she could reading by the windows of her room, which overlooked a huge pond. But she was not left alone long. They could not understand why she wanted to go out alone and either they or one of their friends insisted on going. They had lots of friends and there were visitors every day or invitations to lunch or to dinner.

When she had been there for two weeks, Marcel caught Abby in the dimly lit hall one night and tried to kiss her. When she showed that she was shocked at his behaviour, he only laughed. He was middle-aged and fat and Abby found him unattractive, but it did not stop him from trying to make love to her several times after that. Finally she suggested to Robert that they should leave.

'We've only just got here,' he said.

It was a month, a long, long month.

'How much longer did you think we would stay?'

'I don't know. Over the winter, perhaps. They're glad to have us and I'm enjoying myself.'

'I would like to go home.'

Robert groaned.

'What a provincial little person you are, Abby,' he said.

Abby endured Marcel's advances as best she could during the days that followed. But for that, life was pleasant enough. At least Robert was happy. They had been there another three weeks before Abby caught her husband coming out of Veronique's bedroom during the afternoon. Abby hated the idea of lying down in the daylight, but at least it gave her a chance of being alone to read. How could you possibly be tired when you had done nothing for years and years and it was not summer, it was not hot in the afternoons. She thought that she would go mad if she had to endure much more of this boredom.

She had left her room sooner than usual and then she saw Robert. She stared him out and went back to her room. It was a pretty place with a wooden floor and rugs, pale walls and pretty walnut furniture. He came to her.

'I want to go home,' Abby said.

'Must you be silly about this?'

'Silly?' She glared at him. 'You're the one who's silly, carrying on like that.'

'She gives me what you do not,' he said.

'And what is that?'

'Passion. She has more feeling in her little finger than you have in your whole body. You're as cold as the place you come from. You never loved me.'

'I do love you. I wouldn't live a life like this for somebody I didn't love!'

'I have given you everything!'

'I don't want to be given everything. I am going out of my mind with the tedium of it. I've never been so bored in my life. I'm going home.'

'Go then!' he said and slammed from the room.

Going home was not easy. Abby had to find her own way, but she had plenty of money. She had not travelled alone before and had a great deal of time to worry about the future. She thought that if only there could be a child, it would alter everything. He would be pleased, proud; they would have something in common, something important to share.

Her spirits lifted a little when she reached England, even though it was bitterly cold. As she travelled north, it grew colder. There were the remains of what had been deep snow in the hedgebacks and against the walls, but she was glad to be there and, with each mile that took her north, her spirits lifted. She didn't go off to her home in the country; she went to Jesmond. A bitter wind was blowing in Newcastle. She left the station and hired a carriage to take her with all her luggage to her father's house. She couldn't wait the short journey to get there; she thought her heart would burst. She gazed from the window at the familiar landmarks, the houses, churches and pubs. When the carriage stopped outside the house she got out and ran up the steps to the door. Her only fear was that Henderson would not be at home, though it was Saturday afternoon and by rights he should have been. She opened the door and was about to call out when she entered its warm friendliness, then she noticed that a child was standing at the far end of the hall beside the kitchen door. He was very small, watching her with the concentration that only children have. Even in the dim light of the hall she recognised him immediately. He had Gil's dark Collingwood eyes. It was Matthew.

Even when he had stopped using his own name, they had recognised him. Gil hadn't thought how well-known he was in Newcastle and how he stood out, being tall and dark and well-dressed. Every shipbuilder in the area belonged to the same federation as his father and they would not employ him. Nobody dared offend William Collingwood. There was also disgust on their faces as the word seeped out about what had happened. He could have gone to Henderson and Henderson might have taken him on, but then again he might not. Gil couldn't bring himself to ask. Even somebody as skilled as he was had no future here. He thought of leaving, then he thought of Matthew. He knew that Henderson would lend him money and he could have gone to Glasgow, to Ireland, even to Germany or America, but there was some stubborn feeling in him that wouldn't go.

He couldn't get taken on even in some lowly position amongst people who knew him, so in the end he pawned his clothes, took some which looked as though they should have been thrown out, let the stubble grow on his face, changed his voice and his name and got taken on, after a number of rejections, at his father's shipyard. It was ironic that the only person who would employ him was his father. Down at that level, nobody cared what your name was as long as you kept your head down and worked. Gil's hands were sore for weeks and his body ached from the unaccustomed physical activity, but in a way it was a relief. The other life was gone and he did not want to think. He worked and then he went back to bed. He had found lodgings in one of the houses his father had built down by the docks and it was awful. It didn't matter much. The food was bad, but Gil didn't eat. The beds weren't very clean, but he didn't sleep much. It was noisy because the area was full of pubs and dockers and people coming off ships; different languages were common and so was drunkenness. There were prostitutes on the streets; there were people sleeping in the doorways and the alleys. Gil drank quite a lot, but so did everybody and the men he worked with took him as one of them. You couldn't fake the local accent; a man from another area stood out immediately. The language was unintelligible to anyone else, it was so thick and spoken so fast, it was its own language, but Gil had heard it from birth and had worked among labourers before. Nobody asked questions and the talk was all about work, so he was quite at home.

There was the question of Matthew. Gil didn't feel like a father, whatever that was, and he didn't know what to do. He didn't expect Henderson to pay out anything for the child so he went to the back door of the house from time to time and gave Kate money. The shocked look on her face and the way she didn't ask him in told him what they thought of him, so he said nothing. He didn't even ask after the boy, he just gave her the money and left. What he had after that paid for beer, whatever he bought to eat and his bed at the house. The only way he could sleep was to drink and it had become a habit. You went to work and then you drank and then you went to bed. He knew that a lot of his mates were married and that they drank their pay. Gil no longer cared about anything or anybody. He wanted never to care about anything again. He didn't even care that he was doing the lowliest work beside the most beautiful ship that anyone had ever built. It wasn't his anymore. He could look on the majesty of this being he had created and feel nothing. In several months' time it would leave to do its work and he didn't care if he never saw it again as long as he lived.

*

Abby moved further into the hall and the child ran away into the kitchen to be scolded by Kate, but Matthew said something and Kate came into the hall.

'Why, Mrs Surtees,' she said, 'I didn't know you were back. Come in and keep warm. It's bitter out.'

She ushered Abby into the sitting room.

'Mrs Surtees is here, Mr Reed.'

Abby had longed to see her father so much, but now she didn't understand what she had been fussing about. Henderson looked perfectly well and he got up and hugged her; but he was so glad to see her that she was pleased she had come back. He urged her nearer the fire, Kate took her outdoor things and her father asked after Robert. He showed some concern that she had travelled alone. Abby tried to convince him that there had been no quarrel, it was just that she had badly wanted to come home and he had wished to stay in France. She didn't think her father was fooled. A man and wife should be together and they were not, and he knew her too well to think that her jovial attitude was real. Abby was not altogether happy, either. He did not explain Matthew's presence and for some reason Kate kept the child in the kitchen while Abby and Henderson had tea in front of the fire. Abby wasn't hungry. In fact, she felt sick and the feeling increased as she stayed. Her father was not natural with her and although he was well, he looked upset, and his eyes were dulled.

After tea, when he had still offered no explanation, she asked him, 'What is Matthew doing here? Is Rhoda in town? Is Gil coming to collect him?' Abby didn't really want to see Rhoda and Gil; her own unhappiness would seem worse against their apparently perfect marriage.

Her father looked down into his empty teacup, positioned it carefully back on the small table beside him and then he looked at her.

'I was deceived in him,' he said.

'What?'

'When he was young and I thought then that he was . . . that he was capable of doing ill, I was right. I was fooled. I thought he had changed. People don't change. I'm old enough to know that. There was a time when I wished that I had let you marry him. You did want to marry him. I'm so relieved now that I didn't allow it. I can't sleep for relief. I thought I didn't like Robert but he's good-hearted and kind and—'

'I don't know what you're talking about,' Abby said.

'I'm talking about that bastard, Gil Collingwood. He left his child here.'

'His child?'

'Yes, his child. Matthew is Gil's. Newcastle is thick with scandal.'

Abby couldn't believe it. Then she did, and coldly. Gil had loved Helen, he had always loved her. Why should it be any surprise that he had fathered a child on her? That was just the kind of thing he would do. But his own brother's wife . . .

'Helen is dead, and Rhoda and he . . .'

Abby couldn't take this in. She held her father's hands while he explained haltingly the things he had heard. They ended her love for Gil. She knew that she had always had a caring for him but, that teatime over the fire, she stopped loving him. How could anybody love somebody who had done such things and how could he possibly expect her father to keep his child there? Henderson was worried and upset about the child and Abby knew that worry and upset were the very last things he needed.

'Where is he?' she asked.

'I don't know. He's been back to the house with money, but only when I'm at work.'

Abby's heart banged with anger against Gil that he should do such a thing, that he should take advantage of a man like her father, who had been his friend. It played on her mind. When she went to bed she didn't sleep, thinking of Rhoda and Helen and what Gil had done. The shock went round and round in her mind and got louder and louder. She questioned Kate and learned that Gil looked different, that he looked like a workman. She asked her father where he might have been taken on, but Henderson said that nobody would do so. Mrs Wilkins came to Abby and said shamefacedly, 'I know where he is.'

Abby stared.

'How do you know?' she said.

'I just do. Found out. He stands out, even like he is. He's working at Collingwood's.'

Abby was amazed.

'But the men would know.'

'Wouldn't know their own mothers some of them. Don't care neither, labourers.'

'Labourers?'

'He's living in Hope Street.'

Hope Street. The very name was laughable, Abby thought. It was a broken-down place right beside the docks. Nobody respectable would ever go there. All the next night she couldn't rest and on the Monday evening, when her father was lying down, she ordered the carriage and to the driver's consternation insisted on going to the very worst area of the docklands. Abby tried to take comfort that she was not alone, but he was a small, slight figure who had worked for them for several years and never spoken unless he had to. Luckily it was a vile night, bitterly cold and sleeting, so nobody was standing around outside.

She told him to stop and then she knocked on several doors, had no answer from three and did not know what to say to the others since Gil was unlikely to be calling himself by his own name. She persevered. Seven doors later, she enquired of a short, fat woman whether she had a lodger and the woman laughed.

'Half a dozen of them. Anybody in particular?'

'He's tall and dark and about my age.'

'Down the pub, pet.'

'Which pub?'

'Over yonder,' she said and shut the door.

Abby told herself that she could not possibly go into a pub. If he was not there, anything might happen. Even less than respectable women didn't go into pubs. It was predictably called the Ship. Abby walked up to it and went inside. It smelled. It smelled of sweat and dirt and beer and bad breath. The men, in a cloud of smoke from both tobacco and the fire, were indistinguishable from one another in their caps and suits. There was a tremendous noise, but as Abby made her way from the door towards the bar, it began to die down and she could see the man behind the bar, his eyes getting bigger and bigger. By the time she reached him, there was silence. He flipped up part of the bar top and came out from behind.

'Eh, pet, you can't come in here,' he said.

'I'm in,' Abby said.

There were calls and cries.

'I'm looking for somebody.'

'You can take me home with you, petal,' some wit yelled and there was laughter. Abby looked around her for sight of Gil and admiring eyes met hers everywhere.

'Has he got a name?' the barman asked.

'No.'

'Well, that's a fresh one. Howay, out of here.'

He put a hand on her arm. Abby pulled away, knocked into somebody and fingers grabbed her bottom. Fury sent the blood into her face. She turned and there was further laughter. The barman started to drag her towards the door and another man said, 'Don't fret, I'll see the lass home.' He put an arm around her waist. Abby panicked, tried to get away and couldn't. The laughter was louder now and unfriendly, jeering, and he had a good hold on her. The barman, who suddenly seemed a friend, let go and retreated.

From the darkness of the corner to one side of the door a man who had been leaning against the wall straightened in the shadows and Abby recognised something about him even before he levered himself away from the wall and began to come to her across the room. His height declared it to be Gil so she didn't know what she had seen first, just that she knew, because in their lives he had walked across a good many rooms towards her. Some angel of mercy he made, she thought cynically, but her heart knew it for deliverance. The panic which had claimed her almost ceased, but when he got close and she saw him better, she was afraid of him for the first time in her life. His cap was pulled low over his eyes, his face was pale beneath several days' growth of beard and his eyes were narrow slits of black light. He was very thin, wearing the same kind of clothes as the other men, dark. He moved slowly and carefully like a watchful cat and Abby was not surprised when the man let go of her without being asked. All the man said was, 'Yours?'

'Aye.'

Gil walked out of the pub, leaving her to come after him and the men parted and let them through. As the pub door closed behind her the conversation started up again like a full tide. Outside it was snowing. Abby glanced up the street. The carriage was quite a long way from her.

He didn't even turn around. He looked the other way up the street as though something interesting were happening there in the darkness. Even at his worst, Gil had usually had manners. He didn't seem able to manage that now. Abby took a deep breath.

'I want you to take Matthew,' she said.

Gil turned. He looked her up and down and said nothing.

'I want you not to involve my father in your . . . business. You had no right to ask him to take the child and less right to leave him there. Do you want his friends and business associates to think that he has anything to do with you?'

Again his eyes took in the street. Then he looked her straight in the eyes and she wished he hadn't. She stepped backwards.

'I'll come for him in the morning,' he said in a low

voice and then he walked away. Abby breathed deeply once or twice, then ran back to the carriage as fast as she could and went home.

To say that her father was not pleased at what she had done would have been an understatement. He had not often lost his temper with her, but he did so then.

'You had no right to go to him. Did you think about the danger in such a place? Did you think about what he could be like? Did you even consider me?'

'I don't know what you mean.'

'I like having the boy here. I don't have much in my life any more. I like him.'

'And when Gil comes to you and asks you for other favours?'

'He won't,' Henderson said quickly.

'How do you know?'

'Because I know him.'

'You like him still,' Abby declared in wonder.

'No! Yes. I don't know. I just . . . I shouldn't say this to you. Having Gil around me was like having a son. I'm horrified at what he has done, but I miss him. I miss him a great deal and having Matthew here was like balm to the wound. Gil has let me down, he's let us all down, but the child . . . the child was a link with him and he was something I had not known before.'

This hurt Abby. Firstly because she was a daughter and secondly because she had not produced a grandchild. Thirdly she felt as though she should have been around her father much more, not gone jauntering around the Continent for no reason but pleasure. Her father was a lonely man and she had not helped and he had gone to people like Gil to make up for her neglect.

'He can't take the child,' Henderson said.

'He must.'

'And what is he supposed to do with him when he's at work? Leave him with some slut in Hope Street?'

'He said he would come.'

'You had no right to ask him.' Her father regarded the fire for a while and then said, 'How does he look?'

'Thin, poor, his nails are all broken and his hands are ingrained with dirt and—' She stopped. Henderson's body twisted in denial of what she was saying to him. She only hoped that when Gil arrived the next morning her father would either not be up or be at work. She didn't want them to meet. She had deliberately described Gil as he was so that there would be no shock if they did meet. 'He doesn't deserve your sympathy,' she said briskly. 'He doesn't deserve anybody's help. He doesn't have to come into the house and you don't have to see him.'

Henderson was still angry when he went to bed, but he said nothing more and Abby knew how disappointed he was. Not only that his judgement had been wrong but that he felt he had lost Gil and Gil had been a valuable part of his life. Gil had made him happy. All that was finished now. Abby was sorry to deprive him of Matthew's company, but she knew it was for the best. It could do no good for any of them to have Gil connected with the house, coming there. A clean break was best, she thought, but when she lay down to sleep she kept remembering what he had looked like and she couldn't rest.

The following morning Henderson was thankfully still in bed when Gil came to the back door. Kate came through, saying briefly, 'He's here.'

Abby would have thought Matthew would be reluctant. He did not know Gil as his father. Gil didn't look as he had. It was surely all too different for a small child to take in. She thought he might even be afraid, but the child went readily to the door and looked up trustingly into Gil's face. Gil got down beside him just like a workman did, a neat balance for a tall man, and smiled and spoke softly and confidingly to the child.

'Hello, Matt. Are you coming with me?'

Matthew put his fingers onto Gil's face.

'Yes,' he said instantly. Gil stood up and swung the child up into his arms, a long way for him, and Matthew smiled in delight.

Neither Kate nor Abby said anything and Gil didn't acknowledge Abby. He took the child, walked away down the yard, out of the gate and down the back lane without a word. Abby followed him and stood by the gate, watching. There was something that troubled her. She didn't know what it was and it was only a tiny bit of her that was concerned. Most of her was glad to be rid of him once and for all, she thought, and it would have been feckless to have kept the child here. She went back into the house, glad of what she had done. Her father didn't mention it or Matthew's absence. He ate little and went to work and Abby debated what to do. She didn't want to go back to the house in the country where she would be alone and at least if she was here when her father came home to dinner, she would be there for him.

All that day she put Gil and Matthew from her mind. Every time she did so, she saw the image of them walking away down the back lane and something niggled at her. She was ashamed to have done such a thing to a tiny boy and from time to time her cheeks burned with guilt. Her father duly came home at half past five and he had nothing to say. He pushed the food around on his plate at dinner and afterwards went to his room. The house was silent. Abby went to bed and slept, but she awoke in the depths of the night and couldn't get back to sleep. She saw the cold autumn day in and when it was a respectable hour and her father had gone to work she ordered the carriage and once again made the journey into the docklands.

It was a different world from anything she knew and so busy during the day. The carriage jolted seriously on the uneven streets; the roads were filthy and the houses the same. She got out and made her way along the street. She thought of Matthew alone in that house with that woman. Gil would have to leave him there. She thought of the small child in among the dirt and God knew what kind of people. She knew that she couldn't leave him there. She hurried along the street, banged on the door and after a short while it was opened.

'You again? Owes you money, does he? Or are you married?'

'Is the child here?'

'The bairn? Upstairs. Him an' all.'

Abby stopped.

'He's not at work?'

'Nay, he didn't go. I told him, he doesn't pay for the bed during the day, it's needed for others.'

Abby trod straight up the grimy, uncarpeted stairs. The dirt crunched under her feet. At the top of the stairs were two doors. The first door that she opened showed half a dozen people in bed, sleeping. The other room was tiny and had in it a small child standing at the window. She thought Gil had left him there while he slept next door until she noticed the bed in the shadows across the room. She closed the door. It shut out the snoring from the other room, though she could hear other noises from the street below, people walking and shouting and machinery grinding somewhere. Matthew watched her carefully, silently.

Abby couldn't believe that Gil could sleep like that while two people were in the room. He must be exhausted. The covers on the bed made Abby's hands itch to take them off and wash them. They were beyond dirty. He didn't wake up, even when she sat down on the bed. It was bitterly cold in the room. He didn't move when she said his name. He opened his eyes. The light had gone from them; they were dull smudges. She stood up and moved back.

'Abby.' He made as if to sit up and then changed his mind.

'I had second thoughts. Matthew can't stay here.'

The look on Gil's face showed such relief that she was glad she had come.

'My father's got used to him. Would you let me take him back?'

'I wish you would.'

He still didn't move. Abby couldn't understand it. She went across to the little boy, but he backed away from her.

'Matt?' Gil called from the bed, and the child ran across. 'Go, just for a little while, just for now.'

Matthew began to cry. It made Abby think of how a small animal would have reacted. Children knew things that adults had long since forgotten. She hadn't thought he would go so readily with Gil and she hadn't imagined that he would not want to leave this vile place. Matthew tugged at the bedclothes and Abby caught a glimpse of what had been a good shirt at one time. The light from the rain-spattered window showed what looked to her like blood. She tried to meet Gil's eyes, but he was concentrating on the child, talking to him and adjusting the bedclothes. Neither his face nor his eyes told her that there was any kind of problem.

She went to him.

'Go with Abby now,' he was saying.

'Is there something the matter?'

'No, everything's fine.'

She touched Matthew, drew him away a little. Then she pulled at the bedclothes. Blood, all wet and shiny and frothy, a lot of it, so much of it, all over his clothes and all over the bed, sticky, oozing, bright red, more blood than she had ever seen in her life. Abby's experience was cut fingers and knees. Blood was something that stopped almost immediately, but this was not. Her first instinct was to try to stop it, but when she touched him her hands sank in it.

'Oh God. Oh my God, what have you done?' she accused him, starting to cry. 'What on earth have you done?'

Hearing her, Matthew began to cry too.

'It's nothing,' Gil said.

The blood ran down Abby's hands, down her wrists and onto the white cuffs of her blouse.

'I'll be fine. Please take him.'

'Oh yes, fine,' Abby said. 'What are you going to do, lie here and die?'

'I'm not going to die.'

'No? No, of course not.' Why had she had not noticed the grey of his face, the pain in his eyes? 'What happened? What on earth happened? No, never mind. A doctor.'

Gil clasped her wrist in his fingers.

'No!' he said.

'I see,' Abby said, suddenly cold and crafty. 'You think you can just die on me and I will do nothing.'

'You don't have to do anything. You're not owing me. As long as you take him, that was all I was bothered about. Just take him and go.'

'And have you on my conscience for the rest of my life? I will not!' She dragged free, wiped her hands on her skirt, picked up the child and went carefully down the stairs. The woman came out of the kitchen.

'Don't close the door, I'm coming back in a minute,' Abby told her.

She ran down the street with Matthew in her arms and ordered the driver to take the carriage down the narrow road. When they reached the house she told

Matthew to stay inside and then urged the driver into the house. He was not keen and when he saw Gil, he was even less so.

'He's a goner,' he declared, 'might as well leave him here.'

'I will not,' Abby said firmly. 'Gil, I want you to get up.'

'I can't.'

He had never seemed as big to Abby as when she tried to move him. The driver eyed the blood with distaste, but, seeing her determination, pulled Gil out of the bed. They hurt him, but Abby knew that if she didn't get him out of here he would die anyway and she didn't want him to. She didn't think about this at the time because she would have said that she didn't care any more, but she felt responsible, she wanted nothing to do directly with anybody's death. Somehow they got him out of the room, Gil walked part of the way and he certainly walked down the stairs because they were so narrow and steep that he couldn't have been carried down them, at least not by a small woman and an old man. He was unconscious before they reached the end of the street, but all Abby had to do then was get him home.

Dr Brown was not a happy man. He tut-tutted over his patient.

'Knifed,' the doctor surmised, 'I would say. Nasty wounds. It didn't help moving him.'

'I couldn't leave him there,' Abby said, and the doctor looked surprised at her vehemence. She had discovered that guilt came in various forms and, stupidly, all she could think of was Gil begging her to marry him. She kept telling herself that it was a long time ago and of little consequence any more, but it did not make her comfortable. She engaged two nurses so that neither Kate, Mrs Wilkins nor she would have to go into the room where Gil lay half-conscious. She would have nothing to do with this and there was no reason why their servants should have anything to do with it either. She had sent a note to her father and he came back, quietly delighted to see the child, but he came out of the bedroom grave-faced.

'Doctor Brown says he may not last the night,' Abby told her father as they drank coffee in the sitting room.

'It could be the smallest funeral ever,' her father said. 'Why didn't you leave him there?'

'Would you have wanted me to?'

'You could have taken the child and come home.'

'He asked me to marry him once,' Abby said. 'I told him to go to hell.'

'He seems to have managed it very successfully. I'm so disappointed.'

Gil didn't die during the night. Abby went to bed and told herself she didn't care and was wretched. She knew because she went in, told the nurse to go downstairs for a while and put the kettle on, the fire would be bright all night. She sat down by the bed and watched him. The room was silent. Abby sat down on the bed, afraid that he was quiet.

'Don't die on me. I don't want your death on my conscience, you bastard. How could you? How could you do such a thing? You, of all people. Why couldn't you die before I got there? That would have been easy, but oh no, not you.'

Gil opened his eyes, reached for her hand and, when he found it, closed his eyes again and after that was quiet. When the nurse came back, Abby went to bed. She even dozed for a little while but she dreamed about him each time and then woke up, so in the end, when the daylight finally came, she pushed back the curtains. It was snowing. She thought of that Christmas time after her mother had died when she went to Bamburgh House with her father and Gil's father had beaten him for stupidity and she had taught him how to make snow angels. It was such a long time ago.

In the darkness of the corner in the pub there had been deliverance. Amidst the smoke and the talk of the mighty ship they were building he was vaguely happy. Anonymity there. It didn't matter who you were or what your name was. If they couldn't remember, or hadn't heard, they called you 'Geordie'. Everybody was 'Geordie' here. The beer went down like velvet nectar and settled there so soothing inside you. It took the edge off everything, so that you could look back on anything at all and it was bearable. Amidst the sing-song sound of the Newcastle voices he felt safe. He didn't have to say anything; he was accepted here, at home, warm and comforted and he could go back to the night with beer for a blanket and disappear beneath it until the morning came. The morning wasn't to be thought of, but then again there was only that gap between waking and working. Once he was working, the time went by because the men were there. They hid him. He could hide amongst them for a hundred years.

And then the door opened and a woman walked in. He thought it must be the first time a respectable woman had ever walked into such a place and she was more than respectable; she was quality. Such an entrance, such a dress. It was blue and his swift mind told him through the beer who it was, because she nearly always wore blue. Part of him was admiring, but most of him was angry because he knew straight away what she wanted. He drew back slightly into the corner and watched her. She couldn't win here, but she didn't seem to know that or care; she was ready to take on the pub. The landlord wasn't a bad man and Gil didn't worry until Eccles got hold of her. If Eccles got her outside she was done for, so he went over and got in the way. Eccles wouldn't take a chance, not on somebody a lot bigger than him, even for a bonny piece like that and she was trouble, even Eccles would know that. She had always been trouble. He was so proud of her and wanted to smack her face.

He went outside and she followed him. He didn't look at her because he was so angry. All she was thinking about was her father and herself. The boy didn't matter. Her father and her mother and herself had been the only people who had ever come into the magic circle of Abby's mind. He doubted that her marriage was a success. What would she be like in bed? Very bossy, probably. Poor Robert, given instructions. And yes, he had been right. She started up straight away, going on about how ill Henderson was. It was all guilt, because she wasn't in Newcastle most of the time; she went swanning about on the Continent, doing God knew what with all Robert's posh friends, idle and wearing clothes like she had on now, which some poor bitch had ruined her eyesight stitching. She didn't know anything and she didn't care about anybody. He listened to her ranting on, gave the answer she wanted and walked away. She stood there in the street looking stupid in her silk dress and her bonnet, or whatever the hell it was, standing there like Lady Muck.

He didn't go far. He couldn't count on Eccles or some other clever bastard not coming out of the pub before she reached the carriage, so he waited and watched from the end of the street until she got there and inside, the door slammed and the carriage moved away before he went any further.

He went home. My God, it was home. Beer and oblivion. He wouldn't care, but the woman had offered him free board and lodgings when he first got there in return for bedding her. When he had refused the offer, she got two lads to try to throw him out. Gil had put them both down the stairs, had listened to the sound of the way that they bounced. After that she didn't say anything and within days he was accepted in the area. Workmen were loyal to one another, at least in certain ways, so he had a tiny room to himself most of the time, though somebody else often slept in his bed during the day. He could not think now how his life had been, how complicated. Now it was simple. He went to work, he got paid, he got drunk and he slept. He let nothing else into his conscious mind except that twice he had gone to the kitchen door of Henderson's house and given Kate money. He had seen the disgust on her face, on so many people's faces. He expected nothing more, it didn't matter. There was the present.

He tried not to think about Abby. She came from another time and it seemed so far away now, like something in another life. He would have to take the boy. He decided on that before he went to sleep. He could feel the way that his mind emptied. The beer did that. It kicked out all those creepy, itchy thoughts that turned your stomach in the darkness.

The following morning he had to go early to Jesmond. It would still make him late for work, but there was no help for it. One of his workmates lived nearby and his wife had a small child, so on the way back he would ask her, if he paid her, whether she would look after Matthew. Also he would have to think about finding somewhere better to live. Matthew could not be kept in a hovel. There was not going to be enough money to pay her, somewhere to live and eat reasonably well, but he pushed that to a space at the back of his mind. First of all, there was Matthew to collect.

The funny thing was that he missed him. Discovering that he had a child had not been a pleasant shock, but he felt sympathy for the little boy because his whole life had been altered. He had lost his mother and his home, his grandparents, prosperity, security and the biggest shipyard the Tyne had ever seen. Almost everything had gone. What Gil hadn't known at the time was that Matthew knew him better than he knew Edward; though Gil had not seen the fascination for someone else's child, Matthew was used to him, to seeing him around the house, to him being part of the everyday furniture of his small existence and, because Gil was the only familiar person when Gil went to the back door and got down and spoke to him, the child came straight to him with gladness in his face. Gil had thought that he was beyond feeling, but when he took the little boy into his arms he knew that he was not and that he would try everything to get back a decent life for him.

He carried him all the way back. He called in at the house where he was hoping to leave Matthew and Jem's wife was agreeable, tried to tell him that she would take no money. People in Newcastle, Gil thought, had to be some of the most generous in the world. She didn't ask questions about where Matthew's mother was. She accepted the child and Gil promised that he would pay her. He even spoke to Jem about it at work and the young man, who was about his own age, tried to say that they would not take money for such a thing, even though they had so little. Gil said again that he couldn't leave Matthew without paying.

Suddenly the world looked better; it looked as though something might work out. At the end of the day he collected Matthew from Jem's wife and she offered Gil to stay and eat. He tried to refuse, but he couldn't because the smell of the stew she had made was like nothing he had ever come across in his whole life, so he and

Matthew stayed and Gil was actually hungry. The taste of the vegetables and the small amount of meat was heaven. When he set out down the street he didn't even want beer for the first time. Things had changed that day. It was the best day in so long. He got halfway down the street when he glimpsed somebody in the shadows and put Matthew down, but he was not quick enough because he didn't like to let loose of Matthew completely. In those few seconds his attacker came upon him and it was too late. The first cut was almost enough, the second had him on the ground, the third wasn't really necessary, yet all he could think about was the boy.

He couldn't think when it had happened. Was it dark or was it the next day? Could it have been light? Could he have gone home and slept and then come out the next morning? He didn't remember much. He remembered pretending to Matthew that nothing important had happened. He remembered crawling up the stairs and it was like mountaineering. He remembered gaining the bed and after that his full concern had been that he was going to die and there was nobody to take Matthew. He cursed Abby a thousand times for what she had done. If only she had waited two more days, then it wouldn't have been important. He was going to die and leave the child in such circumstances. And then she had come back. What he wanted was for her to walk out with the child and leave him. The world was nothing to do with him, but she had shouted and sworn and called him names and pulled him off the bed. The pain was unbearable, excruciating. She shouted and shouted at him, and the noise had brought other people near, not too close, blood always made them back off. Abby's fishwife act was so annoying that he managed to get down the stairs and into the carriage. After that, everything went black. He was glad to be dead.

When he opened his eyes he was in a very clean bed, in a great deal of pain, his head didn't feel right and the people around him weren't clear and he felt sick. There was nothing beyond the bed and from time to time things came and went at such a rate that his head spun round and he blacked out. There was nothing going on beyond the bed of any consequence. The pain filled his whole life because it wouldn't stop and it made him sick. Only unconsciousness worked, and then not much. He wandered in and out of it and the dreams were all of finding Rhoda up on the moors, frozen. He found her there again and again, a hundred times and then a hundred times after that and each time it hurt more and each time she was dead anew and it was his fault. And he couldn't die. He tried hard, but he didn't seem to be able to. Then it occurred to him that perhaps for people who had done such unforgivably dreadful things, this was what death must be like, continual pain, nothing but pain and finding Rhoda dead for all eternity because he had done it with his stupidity. Helen and Rhoda had gone to heaven but he had killed them and he would stay here in hell, in pain, for ever and ever.

Chapter Fifteen

Robert came home. It was inconvenient. Abby's monthly bleeding had not arrived and she was so excited by the idea that she didn't want anything to interfere. She felt as though his coming home would bring it on. She would not be pregnant and she wanted that more than anything in the world. But Robert was repentant. The moment they were alone in the house in Jesmond, he pulled her to him urgently and apologised.

'I've missed you and I'm sorry. I behaved like a bear . . . and worse. It isn't that I love her or any of the others, it's just that . . . that's how I've always gone on, it's how men do go on. I worried that something might have happened to you and I was angry and—'

Abby kissed him and held him close. She didn't want to tell him that she thought she was pregnant until she was quite sure. The door opened and Matthew came in.

'Who's that?' Robert asked.

'This is Matthew,' Abby said brightly. 'Matthew, this is Robert. Do you remember him?'

'Edward's son? At least—' Abby nipped his arm and he stopped until she had told Matthew to go to the kitchen for a biscuit.

'You heard.'

'I heard all right, even in London. What is the child doing here?'

'We have Gil staying.'

'What?'

'Somebody knifed him.'

'Pity he didn't kill him,' Robert said. 'Why is he staying here?'

'There was nowhere else.'

'He shouldn't be near decent people.'

Abby forebore to point out to her husband that he was in the habit of taking other men's wives to bed, though not his brother's of course. She wondered whether he would have done so.

'You shouldn't stay here where he is. And what about the female servants?'

'We have two nurses. Nobody has to go near him.'

But she did. She didn't tell Robert that either. She didn't tell him about the way that Gil had cried out Rhoda's name over and over when he went out of his senses. He had almost died. The doctor had said he was going to and she was pitiless, but her father had gone into the sitting room and wept.

'How can you still care?' she demanded.

'I can't help it.'

It was difficult to resist, Abby acknowledged. Gil had lain in that bed looking about seventeen with his hair all over the pillow and his eyes wild, calling out again and again for the wife whose death he had caused. He didn't speak Helen's name. The nurse held his hand and soothed him. Abby slammed out of the room several times, only to come back. She made herself leave the house. The weather was bitterly cold and windy. The rain threw itself all over the bedroom window and often she would stand there by the light of one lamp and the fire looking out over the dark, freezing streets. She wanted to choke his young neck for the way he had murdered her regard for him. She let herself think about Rhoda for the first time. It made her so angry, the waste of it. She walked the streets for hours during those first days; once, she walked all the way to the river and cried. In the shipyard, she knew, Collingwood's were busy with the ship which he had fought for, designed and built. In a few months it would be finished. He had been so proud of it, so glad to please his father, she knew. Henderson reported that Edward was back at work, that his father was grateful, that William had been petty enough to amend the sign on the gate so that it read 'Son' and not 'Sons'. Abby knew that she ought to have gone to see Charlotte, but with Gil in bed at home it hardly seemed right, and people were beginning to realise that he was there. When everyone found out, it would damage her father.

Gil started to get better. Abby didn't go into the room any more after that. She didn't want to speak to him. When they finally did come face to face she said, 'The minute you can walk, I want you out of this house.'

'It isn't your house,' Gil said flatly.

'My father has his reputation to think about.'

'Why don't you go away, you make me tired?'

Abby's temper flared, even though she knew he was right. He was still in bed and so white-faced and dull-eyed that she knew he couldn't cope with this.

'You ungrateful bastard, I brought you here.'

'Nobody asked you to! And stop calling me names. You have a filthy mouth.'

'I could call you a lot worse than that. I could call you things you deserve.'

Gil's eyes wavered.

'You don't have to call me them, I know what I am,' he said.

Abby hadn't meant to go that far. She got herself out

of the room and didn't venture there again and, since Gil was too weak to come downstairs, they were both safe for a while. When he finally did get up there was nothing but pleasantries between them. Abby watched Henderson with Matthew and hugged to her the idea that soon she would be able to tell him he would have a grandchild of his own. He loved the little boy and was open with him. When Henderson came in from work, Matthew would go to him straight away, sit on his lap by the fire in the evening and talk all kinds of nonsense. Henderson read him a bedtime story each night and there was often laughter from the kitchen when Matthew was in there. When Gil got better the child rarely left his side, and in the afternoons, when Gil would lie on the sofa by the sitting-room fire, Matthew would lie with him and go to sleep.

Henderson rarely spoke to Gil, but Matthew sensed the tension and would go from one to the other if they were both in the room so that very often Henderson stayed in his study and worked during the evening. One evening he was gone only a few minutes before coming back into the sitting room, thrusting some papers under Gil's nose and saying, 'You've been in there, haven't you?'

'Well, I—'

'You've been into my study. You've altered these plans.' He shook the papers at Gil.

'Just here and there.'

'How dare you?'

'I . . . The – the figures weren't right.'

'They were perfect.'

'No.' Gil finally looked up. 'They weren't.'

'How can you tell? You didn't have the other papers or figures that go with it.'

Gil looked apologetic.

'I just know. I can tell by the design, the shape of it and the – the other things. I didn't mean anything, I just . . . could tell and . . . it doesn't look right, you see, here and here.' He pointed. 'And you could alter it here and—'

Henderson cursed and walked out. Abby said nothing. Gil went to bed. A little later, when she thought he might have calmed down, she opened the study door.

'May I come in?'

'Everybody else has been in. Why not?'

Henderson rubbed his face with his hands in tiredness.

'Has he spoiled it?'

'Spoiled it?' Henderson threw down his pen and laughed shortly. 'It takes other men weeks to work out things like that. He can do it in half a day.'

'But why?'

'I don't know. I don't think he knows himself. I knew something was wrong with it, but I couldn't see what. He only has to look at something. I wish I had a man with half that ability working for me. I could clean up. I could better Collingwood's. He doesn't do calculations like I do; he can see the answer. It's God-given, that kind of ability. It's a pity. I'll lock the study door in future.'

In the bedroom and the sitting room Abby found scraps of paper with figures and lines and drawings. She kept throwing them away and it was almost as if they came back in or reappeared. He scribbled and drew. Sometimes she thought he wasn't even aware of it. Henderson started picking them up and taking them away into the study with him. Finally Abby took the pencils, pens and any paper she found and locked them away in the bureau. After that, Gil did nothing. He was not well enough to walk far so he couldn't go out and he would sit with a book on his knee and stare out of the window for hours. Matthew had coloured pencils and soon there were little drawings on the daily newspapers and in the margins. Irritated, Abby grabbed a blue pencil out of Gil's hand.

'Will you stop doing that? Look at the mess you're making! My father hasn't read that yet. What are you, a child?'

'I've got nothing to do.'

'You're not well enough to do anything. You can hardly walk.'

'I can draw.'

'You can't. My father doesn't want you to. It upsets him when you interfere with his work.'

'Pictures?'

Abby bought him some drawing paper and some pencils when she went shopping. His drawings were all ships. They were not calculations or designs, they were just ships, intricate beautiful ships, some of which she suspected were not built yet. Henderson tried not to take an interest, but since the drawings were everywhere, he ended up asking about them. From there, it was a very short space to how they were built, what they had inside, what made them work, what the future of shipbuilding was. Her father could not keep off his favourite subject, especially when he could discuss it with somebody who knew exactly what he was talking about.

And then Robert came home. Abby was torn. She wanted to go back to the country with her husband and repair her marriage and gloat over her possible pregnancy, but she didn't want to leave her father with his apparently increasingly pleasing guest who was not well enough to leave but was well enough to carry on intricate conversations about shipbuilding. She had seen that light in her father's eyes before. It was enthusiasm. Robert did not want to go and leave Gil there either, but when he suggested to Henderson that Gil had been there long enough, Henderson wouldn't listen.

'What do you want me to do?' he demanded, standing

before the study fire while they tried to talk to him. 'I can hardly put him on to the street. He can't work.'

'You could give him some money and he could go and stay in a hotel or find a house.'

'Give him some money? He's not getting any of my money.'

'It costs you to keep him here, doesn't it? And that child must be eating you out of house and home.'

Mentioning Matthew was a mistake, Abby thought. Her father doted on him.

'Children are cheap when they're little,' Henderson said with a parent's authority.

'Your father likes him,' Robert told her afterwards.

'Yes, I know. They talked about ships all day on Sunday.'

'How boring.'

It wasn't, that was the funny part, Abby thought. It wasn't boring, not like when Robert and his friends recounted the day's hunting. Perhaps it was just that in her home shipping and shipbuilding and politics and economics had always been discussed. Her mother was a business and political person, somehow, and over meals and over the fire and in the garden in the summer they had talked as Henderson and Gil did now and she found herself joining in and being listened to, having her views seriously considered such as did not happen in her world. She remembered her mother and father's friends, who read and were well-informed and came to dinner and talked over the important happenings of their world. That had all stopped when her mother died and she missed it. She kept forgetting who Gil was and what he had done. She wanted to be there because it was exciting. She longed for the evenings when her father would come home and they would sit around the dinner table and eat good food and drink wine and talk. The weather was foul even when spring came, but she was glad of that because there was nothing more satisfying than sitting around talking while rain poured down the windows. She even fantasised a little, ruefully, thinking that if she had accepted Gil's proposal all that time ago, this would be their life now. She left Helen out of the equation of course, that would have spoiled the picture. She imagined Matthew as her child and that she and Gil could have lived here as man and wife with her father. It would have been perfect. She shook herself out of this. If she had married Gil, she would be dead by now. His love for Helen had been his weak point. She didn't know if he loved her still, if he had ever loved or been kind to Rhoda. She kept having to remind herself that he was not really this polite, sophisticated person across the dinner table. He was wicked, evil, he had cost two women their lives. There was no way round that. What kind of man bedded his brother's wife under the same roof as he lived with his own wife? Had he gone from one to another? She dismissed that. He was not capable of it, but then he was not really the person he seemed to be. He was much too clever to let anybody see what he was really like. His survival depended on his ability to fool other people and her father was fooled and she had been close.

Robert didn't stay at the house and she only stayed one more night while she gathered her luggage and her thoughts, but she went to Gil, in his room, when he went upstairs to bed. It was the only place she could be sure of privacy. She knocked on the door and he opened it and she followed him inside.

'I want you to make me a promise,' she said.

Gil didn't look surprised.

'I know,' he said.

'How can you know?'

'You want me to leave.'

'Yes. Will you do it?'

'No.'

'For my father's sake?' When he didn't answer she said, 'Then for me. I saved your life. You owe me that much.'

'I didn't ask you to save it and I didn't want you to. I asked you to take Matthew and I'm grateful for that, but I have scores to settle, I have things to do.'

'I don't know what you mean.'

'You must take some responsibility since you insisted on keeping me alive.'

Gone was the urbane conversationalist. Gil's eyes were like black ice and his voice was soft and deadly.

'Responsibility?'

'Why don't you go back to the country?' Gil said, and turned away and eased his jacket off. He was still doing that carefully, she noticed.

'I don't want to go back to the country and leave you here with my father.'

'What on earth do you think I'm going to do to him?'

'I daren't think.'

'Don't be silly, Abby. Have you told Robert that you're expecting a child?'

Abby's heart lurched.

'What?'

'Have you?'

'I haven't told anybody yet. How did you know?'

'I remember what Helen looked like when she was pregnant. So beautiful.'

'She was always beautiful,' Abby said impatiently.

'But that special glow. That's what you look like. Your hair is all shiny and so is your face and your eyes and—'

Abby was offended, not just that he should know without her telling him that she was pregnant, but that he should dare to mention Helen in the same breath.

'You still love her,' she accused him.

'I shall always love her.'

'You're disgusting,' she said and went to her own room.

There was nothing left for her but to go home and when she had done so she was glad. She made a visit to the doctor immediately, who confirmed that she was having a child and she was able to tell Robert on her very first day back. She had not seen him as glad about anything. It made her think that perhaps now her marriage would work. He wanted to tell everybody that she was having his son. Abby warned him.

'It could be a girl.'

'No, it isn't possible.'

He insisted on having a party and Abby could not refuse because she wanted him to be this glad. Her home was pretty with spring flowers around it and the coming summer. She could envisage herself sitting in the garden with her new baby, how proud he would be. Everything would be right now. It was like the beginning of her marriage again. Robert didn't leave her at night; he didn't drink too much; he didn't go out much without her. People came to visit and the party was a great success. Everything she suggested, he agreed with. Abby was happy except when she went back to Jesmond, which she did each Sunday to see her father. The one thing Robert refused to do was be in the same room as

Gil, so he wouldn't go. Abby didn't blame him. It looked to her now as though Gil would always be there, he was so comfortably settled. He had been to her father's tailor and wore expensive clothes. When she complained to her father, Henderson said simply, 'He earns his keep,' and this was another thing she worried about.

Gil had started working, designing for Henderson. At first just at home and then at the shipyard. By the time her pregnancy was almost over, Gil was at the shipyard drawing office every day. When she went to the house, he was always working. There was another downstairs room which had been her mother's private room, where she wrote letters, read and sewed. They had turned it into another study and there Gil worked. It meant that she could have more time alone with her father, but it didn't please Abby. Gil was polite to her. She barely spoke to him, but Henderson was happier than she had seen him since before her mother died. It made things worse somehow. He was so enthusiastic about work and she knew that with Gil in his drawing office he could build bigger ships, take on competitors like Collingwood's and she feared that.

William and Charlotte had come to the party. Abby hoped they did not know that she had taken Gil back to her father's house in Jesmond and it was obvious by the way they reacted that they thought Henderson responsible for the whole thing. He was in part, Abby thought now. Henderson would lose his friends because of Gil. People would not endure such things. William did not mention Gil, but Charlotte said to her, 'William is in a dreadful rage and has declared he won't speak to your father ever again, that he will do him out of business. He had no right to take Gil in.'

'Doesn't he matter to you, Charlotte?' Abby said, thinking of what it was like to bear and bring up a child and have everything go wrong.

'Matter to me? How could he?'

'He's your child.'

Charlotte hesitated and then she said, 'You can't imagine what it's like having a child you don't care for. I tried hard to love Gil and now he's broken my heart. I'm so glad to have Edward, so pleased to have one who acts as he should. We didn't know that Helen had betrayed Edward, that that was why he had gone away. How awful it must have been for him to find out that his wife cared only for his brother. What a dreadful woman she was; don't let us talk about her. And as for poor Rhoda . . . We have Edward back now and William is so glad. They go to work together each day and it's my only comfort. Tell me, how is my grandson? Has Gil poisoned him against us?'

Abby didn't know what to say to that since Gil didn't

mention his parents and Matthew was too little to realise what was happening. Charlotte was eager for every
detail: what Matthew looked like, how much he had
grown, what he could do and say now that he couldn't
when she had last seen him, whether he was being
properly looked after. She soaked up each detail; her
eyes were hungry. Abby told Gil this, but he said
nothing and, when she spoke of Edward marrying
again and having other children so that Charlotte would
not feel quite so bad, he laughed and said that it was
unlikely.

'Why, because he broke his heart over you and his
wife? How could you do it?' Abby had long wanted to
say this to Gil. 'How could you take your brother's wife?
And what about Rhoda? I didn't think you would marry
anyone you didn't love, even to change things. I thought
you were happy together. I didn't know that you were—'

'It's nothing to do with you,' Gil said.

He wouldn't say anything more and Abby wanted to
think well of him, but she couldn't.

On a warm summer's night she went into labour and it
seemed like a very long time. In fact, it was thirty hours
of extreme pain before the child was born, and it was a
girl. Abby was only glad that the child was healthy and
that she was well soon afterwards, but Robert did not

trouble to hide his disappointment. The day after the birth he got very drunk and stayed out all night and Abby knew that it was not in celebration. He did buy her a beautiful diamond bracelet to thank her for his daughter, but it was too late by then. Abby realised that she had committed a faux pas. The christening for the little girl was very small, only immediate family, and she had to arrange it herself when she recovered. Nobody mentioned it. Neither did Robert appear to care what the child was called. She was immediately banished, to the upper reaches of the house, surrounded by nannies and nursery maids, so that Abby's vision of sitting in the garden with her child did not become reality. Even Henderson wasn't interested. Only Gil seemed bothered and she couldn't understand that.

'I thought you'd bring her to see us,' he said, looking at Abby's empty arms when she came to Jesmond for the first time after the child was born.

'I didn't realise your passion was for babies, Gil.'

'I can't say it is, but . . . she's your daughter. You look tired. How do you feel?'

She was tired. Nobody else had mentioned it and she wished anybody except Gil would be nice to her. She was tired of fighting to spend time with her daughter, tired of Robert not wanting the child around him. It was unfashionable to see your children except for an hour in the evening and babies didn't seem to count. If she went upstairs to the nursery, the nanny made her feel out of place; nobody asked after the baby. It was almost as though she didn't exist and Robert had been astounded when she had suggested taking the child out with them when they went to visit friends. No baby, Abby concluded, could ever have been so unwelcome and all because she was the wrong sex.

That Sunday afternoon she lay in the hammock in the garden at her father's house and swung gently, looking up at the blue sky, while Henderson dozed in a deckchair and Gil played silly games with his son on the lawn. It was so peaceful and she missed Georgina. She had not even been able to choose the child's name. How ironic, she thought, that they didn't particularly want her but she had to be called after her great aunt for some reason. Abby could not help remembering her own happy childhood, all the time spent with her parents, especially her mother. She determined that Georgina should not grow up like this, but when she looked around at other daughters she realised that they were not often with their parents, they weren't allowed to speak until spoken to and there were no careless, happy childhood days as she had had. They were packed off to schools or to the upstairs of the house or rarely seen. Abby thought that many of the men cared more for their dogs and horses than they did for their children. Georgina would be brought up in the country, not invited to go away with her parents to London or abroad to visit friends.

'You're making a fool of yourself,' Robert said, 'and of me, wanting to take her with us. She has to be watched all the time. Nobody can have a sensible conversation when a child is there. Really, Abby.'

'I feel as though she hardly knows us.'

'I can't think what you mean. Children need routine. Nanny has it all in hand.'

A month after the child was born her husband walked into her bedroom and to her surprised face he said, 'We have one female child. It won't do.'

Abby wanted to burst into tears. She didn't want him near her. She didn't want anybody near her just then, but he got into bed and there was no way in which Abby could refuse him. It would have been difficult to say who was the colder there. Robert did not waste his time on kisses. He had her as he might have had a street walker, but with less enthusiasm. After that, he had her night and morning except when she was bleeding and she bled with a kind of determined regularity so that his efforts were all in vain. She felt so old, so used up and so useless. She knew that he had to have a son, but nothing happened. Robert began to drink and gamble and sometimes he even stayed away from home that autumn.

Abby couldn't help being glad of it. She felt physically sick at the idea of a man in her bed. She didn't want to be pregnant again, but she thought that if she was he might at least leave her alone. It was not to be, and when she went to Jesmond on Sunday she watched Matthew growing up and was envious.

Chapter Sixteen

Gil went to see Toby. It wasn't far. He didn't know what his reception might be. It was early Saturday evening and it was full summer. Gil remembered what Toby's garden was like at this time of the year and how cool and elegant his house was. The young man who opened the door was barely recognisable, bearded, unkempt and so thin that his cheekbones stood out. He smiled brilliantly.

'My dear boy,' he said, 'how are you?'

Gil hesitated.

'Do come in. Do. Do. It's been an age.'

The house was different, and it was not just the atmosphere. It smelled cold, as though no fire had been lit in there for a long time, and though the garden was sunny and the day was bright the warmth did not penetrate the house. It was not very clean. Dirty dishes were piled up in the sink. Toby offered to make tea and then called himself silly because there was no fire to heat the kettle.

When he would have offered wine, there was none of that either. There was whisky, so Gil accepted that. In the sitting room there was a bigger muddle, as though nothing had been tidied away for a very long time; books and papers in great piles on the floor and on the chairs. They went out into the garden and Gil tried not to stare. It was completely overgrown. The lawn was high; the flowers had gone wild and were choked with weeds, but Toby didn't seem to notice. They sat on wooden chairs and Gil remembered being here with Edward and how he had kissed Toby. He had also thought that Toby might blame him for Edward's leaving him. He hadn't been sure before that Edward and Toby no longer saw one another, but he knew it for certain now.

'How are you, Tobe?' he said.

'Extremely well. How are you?'

'About the same.'

'Yes.' Toby smiled.

They sat in the wreck of a garden and drank whisky and it seemed incongruous.

'My parents are wanting me to go back and live at home,' Toby said after a while.

'And will you?'

'I expect I shall. I'm getting married.'

'Married?'

'My father is quite old, you see. I'm the youngest.' Toby looked seriously at Gil. 'Try not to blame Edward.'

'I don't!'

'Your father spent years telling him how he would inherit everything and how important the shipyard was and that he must provide a son. And it is important. One's family is important. If they turn you out, where have you to go? You know that. I have to go home now and pretend, just like he did. I love them, you see.'

'But would you have done so if Edward had stayed with you?'

'I would have given up everything,' Toby said. 'He blames me for what Helen did. He thinks if it hadn't been for me, she would not have gone to you.'

'She loved him,' Gil said.

'He did love her, in a way. I think as much as anything it was this house and the way of life, the simplicity. It wasn't just me. If he had cared so very much, he would have left altogether. I would have gone anywhere with him.'

Gil left Toby sitting in the garden, looking out over what had been perfection.

That night, for no reason, Gil awoke and thought there was someone in the room. There wasn't. He got up and made sure, but when he went back to bed he remembered his attacker and for the first time knew that it was Jos Allsop. He couldn't understand then why he had not known, but from somewhere his mind gave him an extra sight and, as if from a distance, as though he was an independent observer, he saw the man and the action and the knife. He saw the hatred and he could hear in his mind the way that Jos had reacted when Rhoda was found and, to his astonishment, he realised that Jos thought Rhoda loved him. In his twisted mind what he had done to her was what she wanted him to do and he bore no blame for the fact that Rhoda had died, whereas in Gil's better moments, when he was not completely blaming himself, he knew that Jos had played a great part in Rhoda's mind and that he had pushed her towards her death long before anyone else had had any part in it. That was not to say that Gil excused himself in any way. He knew what he had done, that if he had not given Helen a child, if he had been a stronger person and not gone to bed with her, that he could have had Rhoda as his wife. It was always there in some part of his mind that Rhoda's death was his punishment for sleeping with his brother's wife, but that was not the whole of it, that was not all of it. Allsop was a strange, twisted man and he had not done Rhoda any good. Jos Allsop had tried to kill him. Perhaps he would do it again. Gil had no idea of his whereabouts, but he would make enquiries and find out.

Sleep deserted him. The cruel night showed him his dead wife and his father's accusing face and the family that he had lost. The emptiness was such an ache and it didn't go away. Gil watched the night turn into morning. Mornings were never as bad.

And this one wasn't. Matthew came in and threw himself on the bed and laughed and Gil could not be sorry for everything because his son had come out of the liaison with Helen. There was nothing as precious in the world, in the whole of life, as a child, and he had been lucky there. He and Matthew had a pillow fight and after that they went downstairs to have breakfast with Henderson. It was a ritual. Matthew would climb up onto Henderson's knee and eat ham and eggs from Henderson's plate. He liked it best when Henderson was having boiled eggs because he would have the top from the eggs, which he liked to scoop out of the shell. Then he would have soldiers, digging his bread and butter into the yolk so hard that it spurted out of the top. Henderson would cut small squares of ham and feed them to him.

After breakfast Gil and Henderson would go to work and here Gil felt safe and increasingly happy. He had thought the men in the drawing office would not accept him because of what he had done and it was true that nobody said much, but they had already known that he was skilled and capable and they respected his work. Each morning he and Henderson would sit in Henderson's office and talk. One morning that winter they sat there watching snow falling softly on the shipyard beyond the window and Henderson said, 'I want to build a big ship.'

Gil smiled.

'What's funny about it?'

'Just that I thought you might. The place isn't big enough.'

'It could be. We have plenty of room.'

'It would cost.'

'If you got me the contract for a big ship, I would make you a partner.'

This was beyond generosity. Henderson got up, coffee cup in his hand, and looked out of the window at his domain.

'You did it before.'

'John Marlowe is a very respected man. He won't have anything to do with me and a lot of other people would go the same way if you made me a partner. You've given me a job, I'm grateful for that.'

'If I died the shipyard would be sold, there's nobody to take it on. I have this vision of me in a wooden box and Robert Bloody Surtees spending my money on drink and women.'

Gil didn't return the straight look Henderson gave him.

'Yes, he does,' Henderson said, 'dear bloody women. He would spend my money on high-class whores and backing horses. Do you think I want that? He gambles too. I don't like a man who gambles. Men are meant to work, not go on like that. I wish Abby had never married him. She isn't happy. He didn't even give her a son. If they'd had a son, everything would have been different and maybe I could have hung on long enough if he was a decent sort and liked ships. No, that's not true. No son of Robert's could tell port from starboard on a Tuesday afternoon. What do they do, these men who care for nothing? How do they live? You have a son. I can't say I'm overly impressed with how you got him, it was a sorry business, but he's there and he's going to be a good lad.'

'He might want something else.'

'Aye, he might, but in my experience things like business are in the blood and you can't change that. Get me Marlowe's next ship and I'll give you a partnership.'

'It would have to be better and faster than the *Northumbria*.'

'So tell him. You could have total planning control,' he said as Gil hesitated.

'If you made me a partner nobody would bother with you socially ever again.'

'If we built a bigger ship than the *Northumbria* they would have to. Anyway, I don't care about things like that. Tea and gossip, that's all it is. I like my office and my own fireside. To hell with other people.'

*

Gil went to Allendale Town that winter to see if Jos All-sop was there, but the big stone house was locked up and the curtains were pulled. He went into the nearest pub to make enquiries and found that, after Rhoda's death, Jos had been crazy with grief and left and that Mrs Allsop had taken the children and gone back to her family in London where she had come from.

Gil walked the streets for a while until the next train came, but he hated every minute of it. The little town had not changed. He paused. Rhoda's body was lying in the churchyard not far from the church where she had been married to him. He had not attended the funeral, had not felt the right to do so. People would have been shocked. He walked among the gravestones and picked it out, it was so new. They had put her unmarried name on the stone: '*Rhoda Carlisle, beloved daughter of Jos and Mary Allsop*'. Beloved daughter of his. Rhoda would have hated that. And she would have wanted her father's name on her grave. Gil wondered if her father had been the only person that Rhoda ever really loved. If there was a heaven, then she would be with her father and possibly happier than she had been on earth, but he sus-pected that Rhoda was not far away, walking on her moors, her hair blowing in the cold wind. People were already saying that her ghost walked the moors. Gil could believe it. He went back to Newcastle in search of John Marlowe.

Marlowe was easier to find. He had offices in New-castle. Gil had been prepared to make an appointment or even to be told that Mr Marlowe would not see him, but after the secretary went through into the big office that belonged to him, the door opened immediately and John came out. He didn't offer his hand, he just looked hard and said, 'Gil. Come in.'

The office was luxurious: thick carpets, oak flooring, wide windows, heavy doors, a huge desk. It was the only office Gil had seen which was bigger than his father's. John leaned back against the desk. He was a big man, heavy. He folded his arms across his massive chest and didn't ask Gil to sit down. Gil stood with his hat in his hands and said nothing.

'You're a long time with your apologies, leaving my ship like that.'

'It didn't need me anymore. All the important work had been done, it was just detail and the men were there to see to it. It'll be fine. I have nothing to apologise for. Is she finished?'

'Aye.' John stood up straight. 'The mightiest ship the Tyne has ever seen. I'm so proud of her and very angry with you.'

'I know.'

'Do you? The Admiralty was not pleased to have to deal with other men over this, that you turned out to be the kind of person who created the biggest scandal we've seen for years. This ship did not need any of that and neither did its backers.'

'It'll take the Blue Riband on its first voyage—'

'You don't know that!'

'Yes, I do. You couldn't have built that ship without me and you know it and they know it. You didn't have the expertise. I guaranteed you that ship and all it could do, and it will.'

'You're very confident.'

'I'm the best.'

John smiled grimly.

'You're the worst bastard I ever met, but yes, you're the best.'

'So, have you given the second ship to somebody else?'

'Not yet. Do you want her?'

'What do I have to do?'

'You could try living a respectable life, that would be nice.'

'You don't care, not really.'

'The Admiralty cares.'

'Sod the Admiralty.'

'Henderson doesn't have the shipyard to build it; he doesn't have the people.'

'He will have. He has space and money and me and I'll get the people.'

'From your father?'

'If I have to.'

'Business shouldn't be this personal.'

'As far as I'm concerned it's always personal in some way. I'll build you a better ship than the *Northumbria*, faster, cleaner, sleeker and in two years.'

Gil and Henderson walked around the site, the huge space of land around the shipyard. It was a cold, blustery day, the wind coming off the Tyne. Gil paused.

'Why did you buy all this land? I mean, it was a clever move, but you might never have needed it.'

'My father bought it.'

'Very shrewd.'

'He was a rich man, didn't need to work, but unlike fools like Surtees, he liked to be involved in what mattered. And Bella had money. I would have kept it for Abby but she hardly needs it.'

'She might.'

'When's this? He's rolling.'

'He's gambling heavily, so I hear.'

'We'll build a fine ship,' Henderson said in satisfaction.

'You'll need housing. You'll need new berths and sheds and cranes and—'

'What's all this "you"?' Henderson said. 'It'll be us. I'm going to put your name on the gate.'

'I'd rather you didn't, it'll upset Abby.'

Gil had other plans. He went to see Mr McGregor at home that Saturday afternoon. McGregor was a Glaswegian who had come from Scotland especially to work for William Collingwood. He was a top engineer; Gil could not have built the *Northumbria* without McGregor's help. He was also a Methodist, a clean-living man who had been married for twenty years, didn't touch a drink and had probably, Gil reflected standing in the middle of the living room, never had such a person as himself in his house. Gil knew also that McGregor had admired his mind and it was the only reason he had let him in. Mrs McGregor luckily wasn't there.

There was no fire in the room and the smell of polish hung in the air. Gil could see his breath. Mr McGregor didn't even offer him a cup of tea.

'So,' he said, eyeing Gil coldly, 'what can I do for you?'

'I need you.'

'How?'

'I'm going to build Marlowe another liner.'

'Mr Marlowe cares more for money than for principles.'

'I'm not talking about either of those things, I'm talking about expertise.'

'I've worked for your father for fifteen years and you think you can walk in here and take me on as if I was a docker?'

Gil paused.

'May I sit down?'

'You'll not be here that long.'

Gil looked at him. He had spent months working alongside this man, their minds were in harmony.

'I'm young. I made a mistake.'

McGregor glared at him.

'A mistake?'

'Have you not made any mistakes?'

'Not of that calibre. My wife hasn't taken her life because I lay with another woman. Dear God, man, what worse could you have done? Your father is . . . he's . . . he was proud of you. Aye, he's a hard man,' McGregor said before Gil could. 'He brought you up hard and what did you do? You designed the most wonderful ship on God's earth and then you threw it all away over a woman.'

'I'm going to build a better ship.'

'I daresay. And will you throw that away too?'

'I'd do it again for her.'

Mr McGregor shook his head.

'It was the proudest day of my life when we launched the *Northumbria*. If I live to be a hundred I won't feel that again.'

'You would if you came and worked with me. I'll pay you better, build you a new house . . . '

'I canna be bribed nor bought.'

'The chance to work on another big project. Will you get that at Collingwood's, something to test your mind to its limits? You want that, it's what you live for. You need the challenge.'

That was what persuaded McGregor, the opportunity to use his excellent brain. Mr Philips was easier. He didn't like William Collingwood and when Gil mentioned more money, more freedom and a better house he said, 'You only had to ask.'

Gil was pleased with his work. After that, he and Henderson organised the kind of improvements and expansion they would need and the contract was signed. Henderson didn't put Gil's name on the gate, but he did make him a partner, it was all drawn up legally. Nobody was told. Gil took every good experienced man away from Collingwood's, including almost the entire drawing office. He took the best-skilled men. They had been badly treated over the years by Collingwood's so they were eager to leave, pleased with the good conditions and more money and housing he was offering them. Gil began systematically to dismiss every man who did not work to the limit of his abilities so that Reed's would soon become the most efficient shipbuilder on the river.

He also travelled to various parts of the country and abroad to make sure that he lost none of the contacts that he had made during his time at his father's shipyard. Since they knew of the *Northumbria* and he could tell them that he had secured the contract with Marlowe and the Admiralty to build another huge express liner, they had sufficient confidence to promise him work, a great deal of which would have gone to Collingwood's.

The following spring the *Northumbria* left the Tyne and on her maiden voyage she took the Blue Riband for the fastest crossing ever between Liverpool and New York. It was difficult for Gil not to think of her leaving the Tyne and worse when she broke the record as he had predicted. He wished he could have been at his father's shipyard when the news was brought, but he knew that it was as bitter and sweet to his father as it was to him and that because of it his fame spread even further and it did him nothing but good. The orders came in, the shipyard was expanded, he and Henderson even bought another piece of land on the river and began setting up another yard to deal with the rush of work. Gil and Henderson were invited nowhere socially, but he didn't care and he didn't think Henderson cared. The work was so exciting and the light in Henderson's eyes made up for a lot, and when he came home in the evening there was his child and a decent meal and a good bed and a bottle of wine. They sat by the fire in wet weather or in the garden in fine and they talked about the ship-yard and about politics. Things could have been a lot worse, Gil decided. They had been and no doubt they would be again, so he took pleasure in the present and his friend and his child and his work.

Chapter Seventeen

Abby became pregnant again that summer and was so thankful that she didn't know what to do.

'This time it will be a boy,' Robert said, satisfied. After that he left her alone in bed and she could only be grateful.

She went to her father's every Sunday and there, to her anger, she was happy. The little boy grew more interesting and attractive every week and there was always beef for dinner and Yorkshire pudding. Her father and Gil sat by the fire and she talked with them and drank her wine. In the afternoons if the weather was good they would take Matthew to the park and sail boats on the pond and she was able to behave like a child, screeching and yelling as the sails on the boats filled with wind and they raced to the other side. She was even happy looking over the bridge at the dene, watching twigs or leaves in at one side and out at the other. She and Matthew would dash to the far side of the bridge to see if they emerged, or whether they had caught on the side or on a rock or a piece of something bigger which was floating past. She always told herself on the way home that she had been very foolish, that Robert would have despised her, but the simple pleasures were stored in her mind. She was as desperate as Robert for a son, not only because he and his family wanted an heir but because she had seen Matthew. Georgina was a difficult child who cried frequently and Abby found herself hoping that she didn't have to see much of her.

One Sunday in September, when her father had declined a walk to the dene because the wind was cool, she was standing with Matthew watching their twigs disappear under the bridge when suddenly a pain wrenched at her insides. Abby gave a cry and clutched her stomach, waiting for it to disappear. It came again, even more sharply. She slid down onto her knees and shouted and Gil came running over the bridge to her. She was fighting for breath amidst the pain.

'My baby.'

'No, it can't be,' Gil said, getting down beside her.

The tears began to run down her face from the pain. When it eased a little, Gil picked her up.

'You can't carry me all that way.'

'Save your breath,' he said, and urged the little boy to stay close.

'It's gone. I can walk. Put me down.'

'Keep quiet.'

The idea of losing this child was more than Abby could stand. She closed her eyes against his shoulder. She was not heavy, he could carry her, but she didn't want him to. She had lost weight during the last few years. Unhappiness did not make you fat, Abby discovered. Gil was big, but he wasn't very fat either. Sheer hard work did that. She was reminded of when she had hurt her ankle and he had carried her into the house. They had been so young then and Gil had been a different person. He didn't seem like a different person. If she could have forgotten about Helen and Rhoda, he seemed to her very much the same, only speaking when he had something to say. He was easier with the child, laughing and playing, throwing Matthew into the air and catching him when he came down, mock-fighting with him on the lawn or on the rug in front of the fire, sitting quietly with him reading stories or playing draughts with an old board and bottle tops. Thinking of Matthew made her feel even worse.

By the time they got back to the house the pain was excruciating and she could feel the warmth seeping between her legs. Gil put her down on the bed and ran to get the doctor. Kate helped her out of her clothes and into her nightdress, but the blood was not reassuring. Some hours later, with Robert and Gil in the same house downstairs, Abby lost her baby, a bloody lump that they wrapped in a cloth and quickly took away. With the physical pain gone and the doctor trying to quieten her, Abby cried and cried.

Robert came to her.

'It doesn't matter,' he said, 'we've got plenty of time for other babies. Don't cry.'

'I don't want another baby, I want that one.'

'What were you doing?'

'Nothing.'

'I didn't realise that you were spending so much time in that man's company.'

'I'm not. We took Matthew for a walk. There's nothing sinister or intimate about that. I don't even like him.'

'Then why go?'

'Because of Matthew. Why else?'

'You go out with a man other women would die rather than be seen with because he has a child? What must people think?'

Abby didn't want to talk about Gil or think about him, she wanted to think about the child that she had lost. She hid in the pillows.

'I think you had better stop coming here on Sundays. It obviously isn't doing you any good.'

Abby wanted to say that she came to see her father, that Matthew was a bonus, but she was so tired that she couldn't. Her father refused to go to the big country house, which was Robert's domain. Abby couldn't understand why men had to be so difficult. All she wanted to do was sleep, wake up, be pregnant like before and not feel that dreadful pain which had brought her to her knees and the horrible sensation of her child's life-blood running down her legs. She wished also that Robert was the kind of man who would put his arms around her, stroke her hair and tell her that he loved her. There was a time when he would have. She sensed his impatience, his disappointment with her and the failure that belonged to both of them because they had not produced a male child. The idea of him in her bed again pounding at her body was the least appealing of all. Abby didn't look at him. She feigned sleep until she did sleep, and by that time, somewhere in her vague uncon-sciousness, he left the room.

Gil had kept out of the way after Robert had arrived. He was working in his little office when Robert came downstairs and was surprised when the door opened and Robert glared at him.

'Stay away from my wife,' he said.

Gil knew that he was to blame for a great many things, but Abby's miscarriage was not one of them. Robert came into the room and closed the door. Gil wasn't very happy about this. This was his room. He stood back against the edge of the desk.

'Everybody knows what you're like with women and I haven't forgotten the boy that you were, standing for hours at the edge of the ballroom watching her dance. If you go anywhere near her, I'll see to you personally.'

He slammed the door after him. Gil winced. Matthew was in bed. He hoped the noise didn't wake him. Gil went through into the sitting room shortly afterwards, saying hopefully, 'Has he gone?'

'Aye, thank God. Couldn't stay under the same roof with you and me, not even for her sake, poor lass. I don't think she'll have any more.'

'Why not?'

'The same thing happened to Bella,' Henderson said sadly. 'We wanted a big family. She used to talk about how lovely it would be to have them all gathered around us. A dynasty, a whole family of Reeds, that was what she wanted. She lost two before Abby and another after her and there were no more. If that was what he married Abby for, he's going to be disappointed. He seemed to care for her so much.'

When Gil went upstairs to bed he found Abby on the landing, a thin white figure, vague-eyed. Gil was about to ask her what she was doing up when he realised that she wasn't awake. He led her gently back into her room and put her into bed. She woke up, looked accusingly at him and said, 'What are you doing here?'

'I'm tucking you in.'

'Why?'

'Because I adore women in white nighties. Lie down and go to sleep. It doesn't hurt, does it?'

'Not anymore.'

'Good.'

'And I will have lots of other children you see. Lots. That one didn't matter. It's gone. It's gone.'

Gil sat down on the edge of the bed and Abby said, 'I never want to go back to the dene again ever,' and started to cry. 'I want my baby.' She put her arms around his neck. Briefly there was the feel of her face and hair and then she drew back and said, 'What am I doing?'

'Lie down and go to sleep.'

Abby lay down and he tucked in the bedclothes, left the lamp burning for her and went to bed.

When she went home nobody mentioned the baby; it was as though the child had not existed. Christmas came and Abby wasn't well. Robert did not come into her bedroom. She thought the doctor had talked to him so at least she had peace there, but she was tired and her spirits were low. Quite often on Sundays she didn't go to Jesmond. Occasionally she would visit friends in Newcastle and call in to see her father on Saturday evenings. Robert was resentful of her absence, but with Robert saying he wouldn't go to Newcastle and her father refusing to go into the country, Abby grew tired of them both.

At Christmas she saw William and Charlotte and even Edward. She tried to talk to Edward about work; she thought that at least might interest him. He looked at her.

'Is it true that you saved my brother's life?'

Abby had no idea that anyone knew, though she also knew how difficult it was to keep a secret in a city like Newcastle where people were so closely involved in business and one another's interests. She managed what was meant to be a smile.

'Me? He stayed at my father's house. He's still there, though I wish things otherwise.'

'I have heard lurid stories, though God knows how they could be worse than the things he had already done.'

'My father has done himself a great deal of harm keeping your brother there.'

'He hasn't done us any good either,' Edward said grimly.

'What do you mean?'

'Don't you know? Gil's trying to destroy us. He's taken all the best men, left us with the rubbish. He's taken all the best work, and he's taken the contract which my father fully expected to get. We built the *Northumbria*, but when it came to the same thing again, the Admiralty gave the bloody contract away. To him. The devious bastard. Here we are, the greatest shipyard on the Tyne, scrabbling around for bloody work and him . . .'

Abby rarely saw Gil. On Saturdays when she went to the house he was usually still at work, or if she went in the evenings he didn't come out of the office. She saw Matthew unless it was late and he was in bed. The visits were unsatisfactory. Henderson, tired after a week at the shipyard, had nothing much to say. Abby could remember a time when she and her father had delighted in one another's company, when she had hated leaving him, had looked back from the carriage until she couldn't see him any more and he stood waving her out of sight. Now he didn't even get up, but wished her goodbye from his armchair, and the house did not feel like her home any longer. Gil seemed to have taken it over. Perhaps that was what he had done with the shipyard, though she couldn't have said. Nothing was altered in the house; it was exactly the same as it had always been, but somehow his presence had made everything different.

She had dismissed from her mind the rumours that Collingwood's were having a bad time. Business was like that; no one knew better, but Edward talked so bitterly about his brother. There was hatred in his voice. Abby was not surprised at that, but she had thought the cause was Helen's betrayal and therefore Gil's. She had not considered practicalities and she had not thought Gil devious. When she did see him he was usually with

Matthew, laughing and playing silly games, and she could not see him now in any other role.

Edward did not look like Gil's brother. He had grown fat and looked older, worn and weighed down by loss and disappointment. William was silent. Charlotte was the only person to discuss Abby's miscarriage and Abby wished she wouldn't.

'You must take better care, stay in bed, rest. A child is vital.' Charlotte gave her advice on what to eat and what to do until Abby itched to be gone from her. Charlotte was not the person to advise anybody on children, Abby thought. Her sons were no credit either to her or to William.

Abby did not see her father before Christmas, but on Christmas Day she grew restless. They had guests who had been there for several days and she was tired of them. She went for a long walk in the early afternoon. The sky was heavy, but it hadn't snowed and she decided that she would go into Newcastle and call in on her father. She could stay overnight with friends if she wished. Robert was playing billiards, several of his cronies around him, all rather drunk and laughing, and he paid little attention when she said she was going to Jesmond.

'Tell your father I wish him all the best,' he said, waving a billiard cue at her.

'I just want to make sure he's well,' she said.

She took the carriage, called in on friends not far away, was assured that if she wanted to go and see her father for an hour or two she could come back to them if she liked. It was the middle of the evening when she knocked on the door of Henderson's villa. Nobody answered at first, but after a while the door opened and there stood Gil in his shirtsleeves. Abby was determined to be merry and wished him all the best, and Gil ushered her into the house.

It was silent, that was the first thing that caught Abby's attention. There was no Christmas tree, no lights or decorations. There were no revellers; there was no smell of meat or pudding or brandy or any of the trappings which went with this day and the house was cool. At her house there was a huge Christmas tree. Holly and mistletoe hung everywhere and people were laughing and drinking and playing games. Tomorrow there would be hunting; she would go along to drink a stirrup cup with them and everybody would be warmly wrapped to see them away. It was a wonderful sight and traditional. Then they would all troop home to big fires and delicious food and champagne.

Gil led the way into the little office.

'The fire's lit in here,' he said. Abby stared. He was quite obviously working. 'Your father's in bed, I'm afraid. He was tired and so was Matthew. Kate and Mrs Wilkins have gone home.'

'You let your servants go home for Christmas? How very modern and how uncomfortable for you.'

She looked with distaste at the papers on the desk, the small fire in the grate and the way that the curtains were still open, letting in the draught. Snow was falling. Gil looked like a clerk, not an important man. His sleeves were rolled back and his fingers had ink on them.

'My father isn't ill?'

'He's fine. He was tired.'

'He works far too much.'

'Yes, I have tried to talk to him, but he loves it.'

'I was talking to your brother. I saw your parents and Edward; they came to a party at our house.'

Gil tried, she thought, to disguise the hunger in his face, but he didn't quite manage it.

'How is he?'

'He's got very fat. I expect he eats too much.'

'He takes after my mother. She used to have full weeks when she didn't eat for fear of not being able to fit into her dresses.'

'Are you trying to take everything from them?'

'Am I doing what?' Gil said, obviously taken aback at the question.

'He said you have taken their best men and their work and that you have a huge contract to build a liner. I didn't know that. I didn't know that you were involved in such projects.'

'It's just business,' Gil said.

'Is it?'

'Your father wants to build up the shipyard, to make it bigger, to handle bigger ships. I think he's always wanted to do that, but it was too much for him on his own.'

'And now he has you and can.'

'Something like that.'

'You got the big contract yourself.'

'I did build the *Northumbria*.'

'I thought it was Collingwood's who did that.'

Gil looked at her, and there was something about the look which silenced Abby, and he said softly, 'I am Collingwood's. Edward knows nothing and my father . . .' He didn't complete the sentence.

'And you have stolen their best men.'

'I haven't stolen anything. I pay them better.'

'It's about money, then.'

'When is business about anything else?'

Abby determined to change the subject.

'Working on Christmas night. I don't know. You could offer me a glass of wine.'

He went off to the kitchen and came back with glasses and a bottle. It was not, Abby thought, tasting it, the kind of thing she was used to. It was very inferior, thin and white.

'So,' she said, waving her glass, 'no parties? Is this what you do every night?'

'Yes.'

'My father often goes to bed early?'

'Quite often.'

Here at the back of the house it was strangely silent. She had forgotten. There was nothing but the darkness of the garden and the softly falling snow. How strange that this was the town and so quiet, whereas in the country where they lived it was so noisy.

Gil's conversation, Abby thought, was almost non-existent. He had no social graces nor needed any because he was asked nowhere, not even on Christmas night. She thought of all the socially adept men she knew who would entertain her, talk to her, make her laugh. They would have done more if she had just said the word. It was no secret that her marriage was difficult and that her husband had frequently bedded other women. It would have been little fault if she had gone to any one of the rich, handsome men she knew and they would have been glad.

Gil was not her social equal. He was nobody. He was, it was allowed, good in his field, but work was not the criterion by which men were judged in her world. Even their tailoring was more important. Their hunting prowess, their shooting ability and their bedroom manners mattered and not one of them would ever have sat here without a jacket, with ink-stained fingers and expected her to sit there with them, silent, drinking a not particularly good wine. He didn't even look up much, but Abby knew him too well to think that this meant he was particularly concerned about any of these matters. The seeming vulnerability and his jacketless, tieless state, the confusion of the room, the quality of the wine, entertaining a lady in a scruffy little room with papers strewn on every surface and books on every chair – he had had to move some so that she could sit down – none of it registered with him. He didn't care about the silence between them or that she was not entertained.

Gil seemed so young, sitting there looking down into his wine, waiting for her to go away so that he could get on with his work. Nothing had touched him; none of the tragedy had brought lines to his face. He seemed years and years younger than Robert and his friends, though he had worked all of his life and they had not.

'Are you worried about him?'

'What?'

'Your father,' Gil said.

'I'm afraid that he will die.'

'I am looking after him. We come home early in the evening and have tea with Matthew and he doesn't work after that.'

'I'm sure you are doing your best.'

'You think it's all too much for him.'

'Well, it is.'

Gil came to her and Abby was confused as she wasn't

with other men. He was so tall and his hair was black in the lamplight and so were his eyes.

'You always blame me for everything.'

'That's not true!' She looked up at him and wished she hadn't. His eyes were guarded. He moved back slightly, as though he hadn't meant to get that close.

'It's just that' – Abby couldn't get the words out – 'having lost my mother I was hoping he would live to be old, and . . . I'm afraid that if he goes on working too hard . . . I don't want to talk about it, not even the possibility. This wine isn't very good.'

'I don't know much about wine.'

Abby thought she should go home. He clearly didn't want her there, interrupting his work. 'I should go, you have a lot to do.' She indicated the papers that were overflowing the desk. She was going to put down her half-full glass and managed to tip the contents down the front of her blouse. Luckily the blouse was the same colour as the wine, more or less. She scrubbed at the mess with a handkerchief.

'A wet cloth would help,' Gil said.

'I don't want a wet cloth. It wasn't much. I'd drunk nearly all the wretched stuff.'

And then she looked at him and he was very close. She could see the base of his throat where the top button of his shirt was undone. She reached out and touched his arm.

'Gil—'

It was like the night they had spent together, Abby thought, and all those other times. He was the only person in the world who could reduce her to tears without doing anything. All those men that she knew and flirted with, men she called her friends, couldn't have made her cry if they had broken her arms. And then he did what she had wanted him to do when it would have been all right for him to do it all those years ago. Now, when it was not permissible, when she was married and he was disgraced, when they didn't even like one another, he took hold of her and put her against him and kissed her.

Abby had never before kissed a man she was not supposed to kiss, so she was not sure whether it was the illicit bit of it that she liked best or whether it was that she had waited such a long time. She knew at that moment why she hadn't bothered with other men and presumably the illicit bit would have worked just the same. And all the hundreds of times that Robert had touched her, he had not kissed her like this. His kisses had been ungenerous somehow, impatient perhaps, or was she doing him a disservice with hindsight? Robert was a very experienced man with women; he knew all about kissing. Robert knew a great deal about everything when it came to this, but she saw with a frightening clarity that all the times when he had, did not make her his as even this single kiss made her Gil's. She had always belonged to him, perhaps even before that freezing cold night in the bedroom. That had been Christmas too, almost to the day.

It wasn't that he tried to seduce her; he didn't. Any other man having got that far would have had his hands on her in seconds, but Gil put his arms around her as though she were distressed and it was only then that Abby realised she was. All she had was her father and of late they had not got on. He didn't care for Robert and Robert disliked him and that made it difficult. Gil didn't even kiss her a second time; he held her in against him so that nothing could hurt her, with his arms between her and the rest of the world and she didn't cry. It was as though he was used to her there; she was meant to be there. This was really what women wanted from men, Abby thought, comfort, a little protection, a place to go to be safe from time to time.

The last person Gil had kissed like this had been Rhoda, and the memories came back: the triumph of the launching when the ship's hull was finished, that weekend which had been the best of his life only to turn into the worst, the way she had run, the looking for her and the greatest misery, finding her cold and still in the snow on the moors. This made him want to deny that she was dead, to pretend to himself that he had her back, that nothing had happened, that she was in his arms. He couldn't do that. Perhaps he could have with another woman, but not with Abby. He cared for her too much to do that, fought with himself and won, remembering what had happened when he gave in to what he wanted. He drew away but she followed him, kissed him. She didn't hold back at all. She got her hands up to his neck and touched his throat. Gil could smell the wine down the front of her blouse, the sweet and lemon scent of it. He could feel the way that her fingers slipped to the first button on his shirt. He was astonished that she should do such a thing. Abby hadn't altered at all. She was still the bold girl who had gone upstairs to find him, turned the key in the lock, covered him in blankets and given him chocolate cake. She looked at him, smiled at him, put her hand into his hair in caress.

'You could at least take off your hat,' Gil said.

'Shall I?' She took out the hat pins as if she were doing tricks. She took the pins out of her hair, too, so that it swung down past her shoulders and she took off the jacket that she wore and started to undo the buttons on her blouse. He grabbed hold of her and she laughed. The smell of wine seemed to fill the whole room. The images of Rhoda faded. All he could remember was that he had wanted her when she was sixteen and all the nights when he had been alone and all the days and the evenings when he had done nothing but work. Months and months of not being able to touch anybody. Now he could. She didn't stop him from unfastening the garments that hid the rest of her body from him and then he could touch her, put his mouth on her, draw her close to feel her skin against his skin.

Abby wondered if her father had ever drawn her mother down on to the rug in front of the fire in this room. It seemed doubly wrong to be doing this here. A man she was not married to, a man who had the kind of reputation which excluded him from society, was making love to her in her mother's sewing room. The papers got in the way from time to time and fluttered about her. Some of them slid off the desk when Gil moved away from it and into her arms and his ink-stained fingers were slow and cool and a little uncertain. Not like Robert. Robert was always certain, but then Robert did not prize her except as the mother of a child as yet unborn. It would be funny, she thought, it would be so funny if she could have a child from this night. After all, Helen had done it. Helen had had his child, but that was not just from one night, that was something that went on for months and months, didn't it? Abby did not believe that he was the kind of man who would bed his wife and another woman in the same house. Gil wasn't made like that. He couldn't have done it, she knew that he couldn't. Yet he had, apparently. Robert would have. He had done it in France and any of his more decadent drunken friends might have done it merely as a pastime, but Gil was not a drunk and he was not an idler. His eyes were clear and his mouth was sweet and he had not spent years swigging whisky and laying women and smoking foul-smelling cigars. He was also, Abby thought a little gleefully, the kind of man who had concentration. You could tell that from his work. He thought about one thing at once and gave it his entire attention and just now he was concentrating on her. She would have bet a thousand pounds that there was nothing going on in Gil's mind which reached beyond the edge of the rug.

The firelight turned his skin to gold and put a halo around his shiny hair. All the times that Robert had made sexual advances to his wife meant nothing more to Abby than the papers that had fluttered to the floor. She felt sorry in several ways, because it all seemed so base and meaningless and so utterly pointless. She was angry with herself, too. It seemed to her that she could have and should have married Gil. She would have wrested him away from Helen and he would not have gone through all the hell that his life had been and she would never have lain under a man like a victim and endured the invasion of her body. Her life with Robert was nothing to do with anything that she had ever wanted, she could see that now.

He was being more and more careful, as though at any minute she was going to deny him. Slower and slower the kisses and caresses became, even though Abby had yielded her body long since. It was ironic, she thought savagely, that Robert did nothing but take her and that she was actually going to have to ask this man to.

'For God's sake!' she said into his hair.

'Are you sure?'

'I'm dying here,' she said with a little choke of laughter. 'Please.'

'I didn't think you would.'

'What the hell else do you think I'm doing here, bare on a bloody rug?'

'You have a foul mouth for a woman.'

Abby got hold of his hair.

'I love you. I love you and I want you. Now.'

He took her at her word. Abby closed her eyes and after that she couldn't think at all or even want to. Her mind fought briefly. It was wrong. She was not married to him, but that only served to make it better. It was exquisite, nothing like the way that Robert came to her, but that was duty and obligation, it was all about contracts and commitments and the carrying on of names. It was not the act which was important it was the result, whereas this was purely pleasure. This was like chocolate and ice cream, chilled wine on a hot day, fire-light on a winter's evening. She could feel the fire, not near enough to burn, and the rug which was thick and the draught which came under the door because the fire had begun to die down and the logs gave off a sweet scent in the grate.

Outside she could hear the wind lifting the snow, but the house was silent. Robert was prone to whispering obscenities into her ears, but Gil didn't even tell her that he loved her, as though speech had nothing to do with him. He said not a single word and there was no grunting or labouring. In the silence Abby bit her lip so hard that she could taste blood, as though there had been some kind of agreement that nothing should escape her lips beyond a sigh. There had been times when she had wondered at herself whether she felt any real passion at all. In the early days of her marriage, the intimacy had been sweet but it had not been like this. Robert had called her cold and she had thought the fault lay with her. Other women seemed to like him well enough. She had come to the conclusion that she was the kind of woman who preferred affection, but it was not so. She craved Gil like food after a long fasting and the more she had of him, the more she wanted. She only hoped that her body might turn out to belong to some other woman so that afterwards she would not have to go under a table and hide somewhere for embarrassment. Robert had not had this response from her; he had not been hers like this; she had not felt like his. She liked Gil better and better. She felt so triumphant, so powerful, so wonderfully, screamingly alive. She felt as though she would never be alone again; he would belong to her for all time. There was nothing to go back to and no need. Everything was in the present.

Gil was only dimly aware of the room, the silence, but he could feel the forces around him trying to stop him. All the intelligence and all the guilt and responsibility had hounded him to here. He had kept away from women. He had thought he would never hold anybody again and the Puritan in his upbringing told him sternly that he was not entitled to, that he had committed too many grave wrongs. He could not free himself of Helen dying and of Rhoda up on the fells. He found himself entitled to nothing but his work and his child and, since it had been offered him, the friendship of the man he admired above all others. If Henderson knew what he was doing now ... He was going to lose Henderson. The man was his only friend, he was not well and was gradually getting worse. He didn't tell Abby that. He didn't think he needed to, but he was all Gil had. At work, the men did as he told them. His business reputation meant that not only did they not question him, but neither did they feel themselves to be his equal and it was difficult to be friends with people who weren't. All he had was his work and his child and Henderson and a third of the triangle was about to be lost for ever.

This was just momentary, he knew. She was going to hate him afterwards when the magic had died with the firelight. He was not entitled to her, was taking something he was not meant to have. But she had wanted him and there had been so many nights spent alone. When he hesitated because he knew how wrong this was, he had given her a way out, she had told him that she loved him. Gil knew that it was nearly always men who did that. Was she doing it for what she wanted? So he gave her what she wanted and part of him felt so calm, so cool, so detached, whereas the other part of him wanted her so much that he couldn't see beyond it. That part took over until only a vague sorrow and awareness remained and he could not have identified it. He took her past reason, past thought, past the kind of control where she had put her teeth into her lip until she cried out. Helen had taught him a lot about pleasure, about the things that women wanted men to do to them. Somewhere beyond him he had an impression of white curtains fluttering in the breeze. Then they stilled and the Newcastle night threw snow at the window. He didn't care that somebody might hear her cries, or that the tears spilled or what might happen afterwards, just that she would remember, that it would matter, that nothing would ever be the same again.

*

The fire had darkened in the grate and the lamp was low. The draught under the door made Abby shiver. It was worse than she had feared. There was no easy escape. They were not in bed, so she could not turn away and bury herself in the bedclothes. She was naked on a rug with a man who was not her husband in the room where, as a little girl, she would sit on her mother's knee and learn the clock. Somewhere above them her father slept. The room was full of shadows. Abby was glad of that. At least she could not see herself or him very well. He began to dress. She watched his beautiful, lean body disappearing behind his clothes, ordinary working clothes. She did not understand why he had such an effect on her except that he was so good-looking. He was nobody.

He glanced at her from dark secret eyes and said lightly, 'Regretting it already?'

'I have to go,' she said. 'I'm staying with friends.'

He didn't argue. Robert would have put up a fight, tried to get her to go to bed with him so that he could have her again, so that they could sleep together. There was no question, either, of her walking there by herself. She put on her coat and he found his in the hall and they stepped out into the street together. It wasn't the kind of weather for talking, but even if it had been a summer's night she thought the only sound would have been their footsteps. She directed him briefly as they went and when she reached the front door, he wished her a brief goodnight and left her there.

It was as though nothing had happened. Abby went inside by the fire and sat for a while with her friends, talking about small matters. Then she went to bed. She couldn't believe what she had done. Men did that to high-class whores, walked in, spoke of love, had them and then left, without any kind of affection or relationship. They paid, too. Short of offering Gil money, she had done all that. She couldn't sleep. She watched the long night finally fade into morning and then she went back to the country.

It felt so normal there so that she was easily able to convince herself that nothing had happened. She tried to put Gil from her mind, to excuse what she had done, but she couldn't. She stayed at home, glad of the safety, able to play hostess to their friends and go to various social events. Everything was bearable until the evening almost a fortnight later when Robert wandered into her bedroom rather drunk. It was late and she was almost asleep. Without any ceremony at all he got into her bed and tried to take hold of her and Abby refused for the first time.

'Whatever is wrong with you?' Robert demanded.

'You've had too much to drink.'

'If I'd had too much to drink, I wouldn't be able to do this,' he pointed out.

'You're not going to do it.'

'Goddamn it, you're my wife.'

'No!'

Abby punched him in the eye and he laughed, but it wasn't funny. She did not want Robert to touch her; she felt as though it would wipe out the existence of the lovemaking between Gil and herself. Abby knew that Robert was entitled to her body, that there was no reason he would see that she should refuse him and that he would not expect it, since she had not refused before. He didn't mean to hurt her, but he insisted on having her so she gave in and let him, after which he said he couldn't think what all the fuss was about. For several days afterwards, as his eye went dark red and yellow with bruising, he bragged that Abby had acted like a prize fighter.

He staggered off to his own room to sleep and didn't appear until noon the next day, when Abby was having lunch with friends. By the time she came back, people had arrived for dinner. To her surprise he drank nothing and when she went to bed he followed her there, putting up both hands in surrender.

'I'm sorry,' he said. 'I've wanted to say it all day. I do most sincerely apologise. I was drunk and you were quite right and if I've hurt you . . .'

Abby began to remember why she had married him.

'I'm not hurt,' she said, but somehow she was now much more so than before. She was hurt for him because she should not have gone to Gil, wished she had not, was glad that she had left him. It did seem, though, as the days went by that Robert was drinking more than ever and there were other nights when he came to her room. She didn't refuse him again, no matter how drunk he was.

Sometimes he stayed out all night and one morning that spring he came home as Abby was breakfasting. He looked tired, unshaven, defeated. He sat down near her in the dining room and refused everything but coffee. When the maid went, he got up and walked to the window. It was a cold rainy March day and the daffodils in the garden had been knocked over by the weather, as they were every year, Abby thought.

'I have a confession to make,' Robert said.

'What's that?' Abby thought it must be a woman or some social thing he had agreed to while drunk, so when he said calmly, 'I've lost the London house,' she was astonished.

She looked up from her toast and marmalade and coffee.

'Lost it? How can you have lost it?'

'At play.'

'You gambled away our house?'

'I had to, Abby. I had to do something. My losses were huge. It was either that or blow my brains out. Perhaps you'd have preferred that?'

'It would still have been a debt of honour, so that wouldn't have helped,' Abby said dryly.

'You know these things so well.'

'How could you have lost so much?'

He turned away from the window, came back to the table and sat down with a sigh.

'I wasn't going to get involved but I keep promising myself that I won't drink and when I don't drink I have to do something, you must see that. When I'm drunk I'm disgusting to you. It's not a road I want to go down. After all, I have no son to leave it to. I'm sorry, I didn't mean that. I don't mean to reproach you. It's my own fault.'

He talked and talked; he paced up and down; he became more and more upset all morning. He began drinking when they had lunch, 'just a glass of wine', a bottle and then another. After two glasses of brandy he fell asleep on the sofa in front of the fire. By teatime he was awake and they had tea and cake and then a carriage arrived. It was late in the day for anyone to come to the house uninvited, so Abby's heart beat hard and she was right. It was Kate with a note from Gil. Henderson had collapsed at work.

Robert offered to go with her, but he had no

enthusiasm and was still recovering from his lunchtime drinking. Abby had imagined it would be difficult to go back to the house in Jesmond, but she didn't give that a thought now. Her concern was all for her father. She ran into the house, stopped short as Gil came into the hall.

'Where is he?'

'Upstairs.' He caught her arm as she would have gone. 'Easy, easy. Come into the sitting room a minute.'

'He's dead, isn't he?'

'No. He's asleep. Have some tea.'

'I don't want some bloody tea!' She twisted away from him, though it wasn't necessary, he wasn't holding her.

'The doctor says he should make a complete recovery, but he won't be able to go back to work for some time.'

'Who cares anything about that? I've begged him to stop.'

'It's his heart,' Gil said. 'He loves his work, you know that.'

'If it hadn't been for you he would have been content with the way things were. He's too old for all these ambitious schemes. He would probably have given it up long since.'

'That's not true. His work is all he has.'

'He has me and you and Matthew.'

'People aren't enough. All he's really had since your mother died is his work. He isn't the kind of man who does other things. He's even bored on Sundays.'

'He hasn't been well for a long time, it's just that you haven't told me,' Abby guessed.

Gil had not been surprised when Henderson was taken ill. He had seen it coming and for a number of days had suggested to Henderson that he should stay at home, but Henderson wouldn't. He was too involved in what was happening and Gil understood because he had felt the same way when the first express liner was being built. It was wonderful to watch it take shape and to be involved in all the different processes as they went along. He knew that Henderson had had the same ambition as his father, he had just not put it into practice for lack of help and support. He had that now and was enjoying himself, but he was also ill and the illness made him frustrated. He would not stay at home no matter how he felt. Gil didn't feel quite the same about the second ship. It was not lack of novelty, it was what had happened since. He didn't trust anything any more and he was proved right when one of the men ran into his office to tell him that Henderson had collapsed. Finding the older man on the floor made Gil's own heart misgive. He knew then that it would only be a short time before he did not have Henderson either to work with or to go home with. He couldn't imagine what that would be like. He didn't want to. He sent for the doctor and sent a note to Abby. When the doctor said Henderson could go home, he took him.

He and Abby hadn't met since the night they had made love on the rug in the little office, but he could tell when he saw her that that had gone completely from her mind. All she wanted was for her father to be better and they both knew that wasn't going to happen. She stayed the night, sitting up in her father's room while Henderson slept. Gil wished he could reassure her, but the words would mean nothing so he didn't say them. He looked after Matthew, read him a story, went up to make sure that Abby was all right, put Matthew to bed and then did some work. It was only when Abby came downstairs late that he could tell she remembered what had happened between them, because she came into the office to see him.

'He's sleeping peacefully now,' she said to fill the silence.

'You're not going to stay up all night with him, are you?'

'I think I might. If he takes another bad turn I want to be there. You go to bed.' Gil began to protest, but she said, 'I'd rather you did.' So he went.

He didn't sleep. Having lost so many people whom he loved in so many different ways, Gil didn't think he could stand Henderson's death. He went through it again and again to try to arm himself for if it should happen, when it would happen, although he knew that you couldn't prepare yourself for something like that. The idea of being completely alone with nobody but a child for company was impossible to face, so it was not just for Henderson's sake that he was upset, it was for himself. Henderson had done so much for him, much more, he knew, than he deserved. He was aware that Henderson would not live to see the big liner built and it seemed cruel that he would not achieve his ambition. William had done that, though it must have been a sour victory when the *Northumbria* left Tyneside and he was not there to see it. He wondered how his father had felt, why there was no pure pleasure, no undamaged triumph.

In the darkest hour of the night he left his bed and went through into Henderson's room. Abby had fallen asleep in the chair, but her father was breathing freely and easily and the rest would do him good, Gil thought. He went back to bed for fear of disturbing her. He was glad when daylight came and he could go to work and leave Abby in charge. She stayed almost a week and during that time they did not have a private conversation. Gil stayed at work as much as he could. She sat upstairs with her father in the evenings. At the end of the week she went home and Henderson was strong enough to tell Gil that he was glad she had gone.

'She fusses over me.'

'She worries about you.'

'She can worry about me from the country.'

He stayed at home for the first two days of the following week, but insisted on going in for an hour or two on the days after that, even though Gil tried to dissuade him. He had dragged from Gil every detail of every happening and even when Gil came home in the evenings he questioned him closely, as though he couldn't know enough about what was going on in his shipyards. Gil was happy to tell him as long as Henderson didn't want to go back full-time. It was difficult for Gil to manage both shipyards, but when he suggested putting a manager in at the smaller yard Henderson lost his temper and called him names. Gil knew it wasn't good for him to be upset, so he went away to the little office and worked. An hour later Henderson put an apologetic face around the door.

'All right, all right, I'm sorry. I shouldn't have shouted and cursed like that. Yes, we'll have a manager and yes, I'm a silly old fool. Being old means having to give things up and I'm not ready to do that yet.'

'I wasn't asking you to give anything up.'

'Yes, you were. You and Abby both think I shouldn't be there. I want to see that ship finished.'

'The big yard needs all the help it can get. It needs both of us.'

'It's a good thing you didn't go into the diplomatic service, you're totally transparent,' Henderson said. He came into the room and closed the door. 'I've got something to say to you, something I should have said before. It's serious and you aren't going to like it.' Henderson looked down at his feet and then straight into Gil's eyes. 'You're very like your father. I know you don't want to hear that, but it's true and until you got here he was the most successful man on the river. Now he isn't because you've taken it away from him. People can't help their nature. You have one advantage over him: you're cleverer than he is and it's good for us because we are using that for our gain.

'I've talked to my solicitor recently. I've changed my will. I've left you everything.'

Gil went cold with shock.

'You can't do that.'

'I have done it.'

'Henderson—'

'I know the argument, but let me just say this first. I was mistaken in Robert Surtees. I regret it. He hasn't made Abby happy and I don't trust him. I'm not saying you would have made her happy. I think your personal life has been deplorable, but I trust you in other ways. I don't want him to get his hands on anything that belongs to me. I've heard lately that he has gamed away his London house. God knows what more he will do. I wouldn't care if he was a sensible, honourable businessman, but he isn't and I'd rather he didn't get his hands on a business which has been my life's work and belonged to my father. You know what you're doing and you have a son.'

Gil didn't say anything immediately. It was such a long, complicated speech. Then he got up from where he had been sitting at the desk working when Henderson walked in.

'Abby would never forgive me,' he said.

'I would never forgive you if that bastard ruined my business. They don't need anything from me and Abby has no legal comeback. She's not my dependant; I can leave my assets as I choose. They're rich. The only thing I ask is that if he were to gamble everything – I'm not saying he will, mind you, but disappointed men do strange things – if she needs help I want you to look after her. Promise me.'

'What do you mean "a disappointed man"?'

Henderson's eyes were red and watery, but his look was direct.

'You know what I mean.'

'No.'

'She loved you. I kept her away from you. He loved her in the beginning but I don't think she ever loved him. She married him to ease my mind. I think he realises now that Abby didn't care for him as she cared for you.'

'It might have been the worse then if we had married.'

'Possibly, I'm not saying otherwise.'

'There are other ways. You could give me a share and give her financial control—'

'No.'

'Then half.'

'That would make it worse. I want it all in safe hands.'

'Robert isn't a bad man.'

'No, worse than that, he's a fool. Abby's like Bella was. She would rather do without if she couldn't have everything. Abby would have broken her heart when you were unfaithful to her, but she didn't love Robert sufficiently to break her heart over him. That's about all I have to be thankful for. Now, I've said my piece, I'm going to my bed.'

When he had gone, Gil let himself remember how he and Abby had been that night in this little room because it was clear to him now that it would not happen again. She had lied to him that night, told him that she loved him. It was not true. It had been once, but it was not anymore. His behaviour had altered that, but this would finish everything. When he lost Henderson he would lose her too and this time for good. She would think he had put his own interests before her father's or hers. She would not forgive him.

Chapter Eighteen

Gil and Henderson were invited to Toby's wedding and they went, not least because the girl he was marrying was a cousin of John Marlowe's wife Edwina, and they could not afford to upset John and Edwina. Toby privately told Gil that 'there's no need to worry, old boy, it's a rush job, she's expecting.'

'You got her pregnant?'

'I sincerely hope so. If somebody else did it I'm not going to be very pleased. Don't give me that naive look, it doesn't suit you.'

Toby's parents looked so pleased and would hardly be any less so when they found out that their new daughter-in-law was having a child. It was what they had wanted.

John and Edwina very sportingly, Henderson said later, stuck with Gil and Henderson. Abby came over to say hello. Robert didn't. It was difficult for Gil because all his family were there. To have to sit across the room from Edward and his parents at the reception was one of

the hardest things he could think of. It was miserable.
John made him laugh and Edwina squeezed his hand
and promised to invite him to dinner. After a while,
when the food had been eaten, the toasts had been made
and the speeches finished, several people drifted across
to talk to John and he introduced them. They could not
afford to offend him and so stayed talking. Gil would
have given almost anything to have his brother speak to
him. Edward didn't look at him. Charlotte chatted, seemingly oblivious, to all her friends and William glowered
in the corner and said little.

It was a lovely day and the wedding meal was held at
Toby's parents' home. The guests walked through the
gardens and sat about outside on stone walls with champagne glasses in their hands and chatted. Matthew ran
round the garden with the other children. Gil did not
miss the way that his mother looked hungrily across at
his child and he thought of how she must have missed
him. He was her only grandchild and she had been so
distressed when everything went wrong. She didn't go
to Matthew, so Gil thought she must have been given
clear instructions by William, but he could see the longing in her face.

Edward avoided Toby except for what was polite. As
the day drew towards evening, when everything had
been said and done, Toby came to Gil and said, 'Spare
me some time or I shall go mad.'

They walked some way to the river with glasses of wine and sat there out of the way of other people. There was a tiny stone bridge. Toby sat down, let go of his breath and said, 'Tell me it's the right thing to do.'

'How can I after what happened to us?'

'It isn't like that.'

'Don't you love Edward now?'

'I wish it was as simple as that. She is a very nice girl.'

'She seems so.'

'We have a great deal in common. She loves gardens and good food and wine. We've bought a house and I really did enjoy that since she has taste. I think we shall deal very well together. Your brother and I are in the past. He has nothing to offer and I have too much to lose.'

'But you love him?'

'I shall always love him. Other things matter, other kinds of love, I didn't think that I would want a child, but I find that I do, isn't that strange?'

'I don't see why it's strange.'

'You love yours, don't you?'

'More than anything on earth.'

'Anything?' Toby said, looking up as Abby approached.

'The dancing has started,' she announced. Toby excused himself and walked back to the house. 'You're meant to ask me.'

'I don't think that's a very good idea.'

'Why not?'

'You know why not. You shouldn't be seen with me.'

'If my father is, then I can't very well ignore you and I'm determined that one day you will. There is nothing wrong with now.'

So they went back to the house and waltzed twice. People watched closely. Gil was inclined to think that he would fall over his feet or hers, but he didn't, though he couldn't talk to her and dance at the same time and there was little pleasure in it. Gil had thought in years past of what it would be like when they danced together and it was so disappointing, he so potentially clumsy and Abby aware of the watching eyes. Later Gil danced with Edwina and she invited him and Henderson to dinner the following weekend. Gil was astonished at the social success of his day, though when he looked up after that dance his father and mother had left. Edward left soon afterwards and Henderson was looking tired so they went too. Gil put Matthew to bed and, when he came downstairs, they sat in the garden and drank brandy and talked about the wedding and the various people.

'You should try to make it up with your father,' Henderson said.

'No.'

'He'll die one day and your guilt will be all you have left.'

'No, it won't.'

'No? There is too much at stake. A parent gives to a

child so much that the debt can never be repaid, even a harsh parent. People only find that out when they are parents. Hating him is not the way.'

Gil took his brandy and went to bed.

Edwina did her best to admit them to her social circle, but Henderson didn't want to go out much, he was too tired, and though Gil had thought that he longed for company he found that it was not so. If he took Henderson they had to come back early; if he went alone he missed him and he had always found conversation difficult, especially with women. He realised that the only person he wanted to see was Abby and since, if she was in the area she came every weekend to see her father, he had her company, after a fashion, which was to say that she avoided him as much as possible. Gil was not insensitive. He kept out of her way as much as he could, and if that was impossible, he was as courteous as he could be.

Henderson began visibly to fail. He no longer went into work for any length of time and Gil was so concerned about him that in some ways it was easier if he didn't; but when he was at work and Henderson was at home, he worried because he was not there for him. The ship was taking shape and Gil was inclined to hurry it because he was determined that Henderson should live to see the launch. All through that long, hot summer and into the cool of autumn Gil worked until he was dizzy. He didn't sleep much; the problems of the two shipyards made him over-alert because they were too much for him without Henderson. He had lots of very good help, but it was not the same. Each day when he came home, no matter how late, Henderson always wanted an account of how the day had been and since there were almost insuperable problems all the time, Gil was obliged to invent a good deal of pap for Henderson's ears so that he would feel there was nothing to worry about. His story-telling abilities seemed to have improved a good deal, until one day when Matthew said to him, 'I want to hear a story like you tell Grandpa Henderson.'

Henderson either didn't notice that Gil had become a fairly accomplished liar or he didn't want to know and he would sit with shining eyes and listen to the tales from the shipyards, but Gil became so exhausted that he couldn't eat or sleep and kept nodding over his desk in the afternoons.

The idea of a social life became a dream. He could not mix freely with people and they did not want him in spite of Edwina's efforts. So Gil worked and watched Henderson lose weight, watched Mrs Wilkins try to tempt his appetite with delicious food and Kate hover over him on Sunday afternoons while he slept; he watched at the way Matthew would approach him cautiously and move quietly about the house.

By November the hull of the ship was nearly finished and Gil was pleased enough to congratulate himself on having managed that. He took half a day off on the Sunday, went home in time for the big meal in the middle of the day. When Henderson slept that afternoon by a big fire in the sitting room, he took Matthew to the park to sail boats and for once enjoyed being with his noisy child as they raced their boats across the pond and the cold backendish wind filled the sails of the vessels. Gil thought about the launch; he thought of Henderson's face as the big ship slid down the slipway, how proud he would be, how pleased. It would be a punch in the face for all those people who did not acknowledge them; perhaps it would even make up for the hardness of their life. It was a bigger ship than the *Northumbria* had been, yet a sleeker more modern ship because this time he had used the full extent of his creative powers. His father was not there to keep a bridle on him in any way. Henderson would stand admiring and only criticise what he knew, and that was not design. This ship looked what it was, entirely his creation. Sometimes Gil would stand back and be surprised that he could have done such a thing; it was not possible that men built such huge and terrible things. Mr Philips was a happy man these days, with the kind of pay which enabled him to buy good suits and take his wife to Blackpool for her holidays, and Mr McGregor, though he said little, was ready to build powerful engines for all the work which should have been his at Collingwood's and was his behind the gates of Reed's.

Mr McGregor had a guilty conscience about William, Gil was aware. They had as much work as they could handle and he knew that he was seriously damaging Collingwood's shipyard because times were hard, orders were lower than they had been and yet his order book was full because his fame had spread abroad. When he went occasionally to the Marlowes' for dinner it was not for gossip and pretty women, it was to meet clever, influential men, often from other countries, men who cared nothing about his former life and knew much about his work. Gil felt as though nothing in the world could stop his success now.

He went home for tea in the gathering dusk that afternoon, Matthew dancing ahead of him carrying the boats. It was cold. There was the promise of rain, he thought, sniffing the air. Matthew ran into the sitting room to be there first to see Henderson, while from the kitchen came the sound of teacups rattling and the smell of an orange cake which he knew Mrs Wilkins had made earlier, Henderson's favourite. Matthew, chattering, left the boats in the hall and ran through into the sitting room and Gil followed him. Henderson was still asleep in his favourite armchair. Matthew ran off to the kitchen to help bring in the sandwiches and cakes. Gil warmed his hands by the fire and waited for Henderson to wake up. He didn't. When Gil got down beside him, he knew that Henderson was dead. He tried to convince himself that it was not so, but he had seen death too many times not to be sure that it had claimed his friend.

He went to the kitchen and told Mrs Wilkins, and she and Kate kept Matthew in the kitchen while Gil went for the doctor. When he confirmed that Henderson was dead, they moved him upstairs into his bedroom. Gil had sent for Abby and when she came he went into the hall to meet her. She was thin and white and looked terrified. He had said little in the note, not wanting her to travel into town knowing for certain that her father had died, but he knew that it was in his face.

'Where is he?' she said in a voice just above a whisper.

'Upstairs.'

Abby looked at the stairs as though they were a mountain.

'Shall I come with you?'

'No.'

'He's dead, Abby.'

She nodded and went on up. Gil went back into the sitting room, where his small son was making quite a good job of crying and eating orange cake. He sat down and took the child onto his knee. Abby was upstairs such a long time that Gil wanted to go to her, but he didn't. He put Matthew to bed; shock had made him exhausted. He went straight to sleep. Kate had cleared the crumbs and dirty plates and when Abby finally came down she made tea. Abby sat and did not drink the tea and stared into the fire.

They had lost a good many of their friends as well as their London house that year. It was strange, Abby had thought at the time, how the two went together. The house had belonged to Robert's family for so long that nobody spoke of it, but his losing it alienated people, they were so shocked. Charlotte had been vocal in her disappointment, but Abby thought that if she had been the kind of person who criticised, she certainly could have done so with the Collingwoods. Their business was starting to go downhill, the competition from German and American and Irish yards, on top of Scottish and the damage Gil was doing, was too much. They had tried to replace their top men, but clever, skilled men were difficult to dislodge from other yards and William would not offer better wages and housing and other schemes such as schools and churches, which many shipyard owners did in other places. He preferred the old ways, relying on his business ability and reputation. It was not enough. Gil had made Reed's the premier shipyard on the Tyne and when people spoke of him now it was not about scandal but with respect because of the mighty ship which would make his name and the kind way in which he treated his men. Unlike other yards, he didn't lay them off when times were hard, but then he seemed to have insured himself against hard times. There was always work and if there wasn't Abby knew that Gil went abroad in search of it, unlike many of his competitors. Men fought to work for him because they knew that they were almost guaranteed security. Her father had loved the business which Gil had built up; he had loved being part of it.

Robert was away when her father died. She did not know whether to be pleased or not. He had gone shooting with some cronies. Strangely, now that they had no London house Abby longed to be there as she had not before and to be reassured that they still had lots of friends, though she did not know what she might miss about those who had deserted her. She told herself that it had just been a house, that it didn't matter, they still had the house in Northumberland and it was so much more spacious. But the loss of prestige was huge and she knew that when Robert was sober, he was disgusted with himself, which was the world's best reason for not staying sober. The comfort was that he did not gamble when he was drunk. Shooting, he was neither drunk nor gambling so Abby tried to be happy that he was not about when her father died. They had not liked one another at all towards the end she thought: Henderson because he considered Robert an idler and Robert because Henderson had been ill on and off for a long time now and he thought that Abby was in Newcastle more often than he wanted her to be.

Abby felt lost, as though she had no one. Robert was not to be relied on and she could not ask Gil for any help. She did not need help with the funeral arrangements, having taken care of everything when her mother died. It was strange how Gil acted the part that her father had then. He went to work and she stayed at the house. The one thing that was different was Matthew, and he was a comfort to Abby, diverting her mind when she would have been sad to everyday things such as playing games and reading stories. He had started school and could read and write very well and was inclined to read to her when he thought she was more upset. They went shopping together and he entertained her. She took him out to tea in Eldon Square.

Robert came to the funeral, sober, beautifully dressed in an expensive suit, smiling and attentive, saying all the right things. Matthew stayed at home with Kate, and Abby got through the entire service and burial without weeping. It was Gil who was no help that day. Wearing a dark suit, speaking to no one, she could not hear his voice when the hymns she had chosen were sung and during the burial she did not see him at all.

Back at the house, people who had barely spoken to Henderson for years gathered to drink tea or sherry or whisky and talk about old times. She heard her mother's name mentioned. Kate had taken Matthew out to tea. Abby was grateful to both her and Mrs Wilkins, who had helped to organise the food and drink and kept going around making certain that nobody was without a glass or a cup and saucer. John and Edwina were there; even Toby had come. Abby was grateful to them. Toby's wife was not there. She had only a few days ago given birth to twin boys and, even though Toby's dark suit and sober expression were correct for a funeral, he could not suppress the triumph in his eyes and the happiness which shone in his face.

'What have you called them?' Abby managed to ask.

'Frederick after my father and Richard after Henrietta's father. Don't you admire the tact?'

'A very good move,' Abby said.

Gil did not come back. Even after everybody had gone and she had read Matthew a story, put him to bed and gone up a little later to make sure that he was asleep, he did not come home and Abby was angry. She was used to this, to men leaving women to do everything. Then they would come back, drunk and useless. It was only when she heard the front door at around ten o'clock when everybody had gone to bed, that Abby got up ready to make stinging remarks. Then she remembered she had no right. He was not her husband. One night could not call him her lover and he was certainly not her friend, but she had needed him that day and he had not been there. He should have been and he was not. She went out into the hall.

'Where have you been?' she said.

Gil was taking off his coat.

'Work.'

'To work?' Abby was shocked. 'Today?'

'Things don't stop, you know.'

He was certainly sober, she thought.

'I would have thought that out of respect you should have given the men the day off, closed the shipyards.'

'Your father wouldn't have wanted that.'

'How do you know?'

'I just do,' he said, and went into the little office and shut the door.

Abby was too angry to do what she knew she should have done and let it rest. She followed him there.

'I've had a houseful of people all afternoon. I didn't see you at the burial.'

'I didn't go.' He was shuffling papers on the desk.

'You weren't there?'

'I have a ship launch next week.'

She stared.

'You can't launch that ship now.'

'It's ready and it will go.'

'It would be a sign of disrespect. Besides—'

'Besides what?'

'Well . . . there will be things to sort out, the will

and . . . I have asked Mr Brampton to read the will tomorrow. Perhaps you could find time for that. You – you ought to have closed the shipyards. I presumed you had.'

'Time's money.'

Abby looked down. She didn't want to continue this conversation. She and Gil had been living in the same house for several days and she had not thought about him, but in this room it was impossible not to. She wished fervently that she had not given herself to him, most especially she wished that it had not been here. She left the room and went back to the sitting-room fire, but the room was more empty than it had ever been without her father, so she went to bed.

There was always a fire lit in the little office, but no doubt Kate, like Abby, presumed that he would not work that day, though what else they thought he was supposed to do Gil couldn't think. He had had to go to work. Everything was going wrong and had been for several days, as though the yard knew that Henderson had died. He had to be there to sort things out and it was just as well: he couldn't bear the house; he certainly couldn't bear the church and the idea of the cemetery was not to be considered. He thought of all those people in Henderson's house. He knew they would come, people who hadn't even visited when he was ill, some who had turned their backs when he took Gil into his house. Where had they been when Henderson was recovering from his last illness? Where had they been when he was lonely? Where had they been after his wife died? They had been at home among their families and now they had the audacity to pretend respect.

Robert had not even spoken to Gil, as though Gil were allowed to feel no loss, yet he knew well that people would count Henderson Robert's loss and would no doubt have offered their condolences, shaken his hand, sympathised.

Gil had said his own farewell to Henderson that afternoon beside the big ship that Henderson had not lived to see launched. He had seen to it that the ship would be ready next week, that she would move cleanly and swiftly down to her baptism in the water of the river that Henderson had loved so well. Henderson was not in that wooden box in the cemetery and he was not in the church; he was in his office at work and walking among the men and standing admiring beside the ship, looking at it with proud eyes and winking at Gil in joy. He would always be there and it was the only place that Gil could bear to be.

They gathered in the sitting room alongside Kate and Mrs Wilkins for the reading of the will the following afternoon. Abby already hated that room since finding out that her father had died in it, as though the room were somehow responsible for his death. She wasn't much concerned about the will. She had been her father's only child and it would be good to have her independence. She knew that with what her mother had left, the two shipyards and the house, she would walk out of here a rich woman. She had of late been concerned about the loss of their London house through Robert's gambling, though to her knowledge he had lost nothing since. The others were there for small bequests. She only wished that Gil would sit down, but he didn't. He walked about the room until the solicitor was ready to begin and then stood at the window with his back to everyone.

Mr Brampton was all that you imagined a solicitor to be. He coughed a great deal as though he had a permanent cold and he didn't shift around in his chair like other people because he was used to sitting all day. He wore a suit, not as expensive as Robert's but very nice, and he was small and slender and precise.

First of all, Abby discovered that her father had left some money in trust for her daughter. Mr Brampton said, hesitating and coughing, that this could not be touched until Georgina came of age and was for her alone. Abby was rather pleased about this. How far-sighted of her father to have provided so well for his only grandchild. He had not mentioned it nor given any indication that he cared particularly for a child he had rarely seen. Then Mr Brampton went on to the house. She was looking forward to this because this was her home. She had always loved it; it had been a sanctuary, the place she had been happy with her parents. She had never had a house completely her own. She loved every piece of furniture, every room, the paintings, the conservatory, the garden. Her ears deceived her then as she listened to Mr Brampton's politely monotonous voice. Her father had left the house to Gil. She ran the words over in her mind for mistakes. He could not have done such a thing. In stupefaction she listened. Robert was to have her father's watch and she was to have the ring he always wore on his little finger – a wedding gift from her mother – and Mrs Wilkins and Kate were to have five hundred pounds each. They both gasped with pleasure at this. And that was all. It was over. She listened for further words but there were none. Abby couldn't move for shock and disappointment. Mrs Wilkins and Kate went out and Robert went to Mr Brampton and said what she had wanted to say.

'That can't be right.'

Mr Brampton looked severely at him above his spectacles.

'I assure you, sir. I dealt with Mr Reed all his life and it is exactly right.'

'But what about the works? What about the shipyard?'

Mr Brampton glanced across the room towards Gil.

'That has nothing to do with this, sir. The shipyard did not belong to Mr Reed and was therefore not his to leave.'

'It didn't belong to him?' Robert's face was getting redder and redder, like coals with bellows at them. 'The shipyard has been in the Reed family for two generations. How could it not belong to him?'

'It belongs to me,' Gil said.

Mr Brampton coughed again and tried to excuse himself, but Robert objected, glaring all the while in Gil's direction.

'How could that be?' He had gone from scarlet to white, whiter than Abby could remember him being.

'I was made a partner almost from the beginning and then gradually, after he knew that he was ill, Henderson made it over to me. It's perfectly legal. Mr Brampton here is a stickler for the law.'

Mr Brampton nodded sagely.

'It can't be right. You came here with nothing.'

'I went into the business with a contract for the biggest express liner ever to be built. Such a project is worth a great deal of money.'

'So you bought your way in.'

'That's what people usually do.'

'I knew nothing of this.'

'Why should you? You haven't shown any interest in

the yards. You haven't put any money into them. You've yet to set foot past the gates that I know of, and you know nothing about shipbuilding or industry. It would take a foolish man to leave things so badly.'

'But it's worth a great deal of money.'

'Only as a business.'

'It could be sold.'

'It isn't going to be sold. It's going to go on exactly in the way that Henderson intended.'

'I shall get my solicitors onto this. I don't think he would have done such a thing to his only child.'

'You'd be wasting your money,' Gil said.

Robert was almost sneering.

'I see I've been duped,' he said. 'Everything they say about you is true. You've done a gullible old man out of a fortune. You complete and utter bastard. I'm not going to sit down under this. I'm going to put you on the street. I'm going to make sure that you have to do what you should have done – what any man with any honour would have done after you caused your wife's death and that of your sister-in-law – I'll make sure that you leave the north and can never come back!'

He slammed out of the room. Mr Brampton followed him, coughing and taking his papers. Abby and Gil were left alone. She didn't know what to say. She thought that she had never been as angry with anyone as she was with Gil now. She could barely speak.

'How could you take everything? I trusted you.'

'I haven't taken everything.'

'What more is there? The business, the house with everything in it . . .'

'You can have anything that you want from it, that was just an oversight.'

'You didn't even tell me. You could have, surely you could have. Why didn't you refuse when my father suggested that—'

'He didn't suggest it,' Gil said, finally looking at her, though with caution. 'He went to Mr Brampton and did it.'

'But you must have been there, when the partnership was set up.'

Gil didn't answer that.

'So legally everything is yours. Morally it belongs to me and if you have an ounce of decency in you you will give me what is mine.' She looked at him and Gil met her eyes.

'No,' he said.

'You have known about this for a long time, haven't you?'

The trouble was, Abby reflected, that Gil never had been any good with words. He couldn't talk his way out of anything. Words were no use to him. Drawings now, he could do that. His genius was for shipbuilding, but he was a seriously flawed person and inadequate.

'Everything comes down to numbers with you,' she said. 'It didn't matter that while you were – while you were screwing me on the floor' – he flinched over that, Abby noted – 'you were in fact the person who was about to steal my inheritance. You weren't even man enough to tell me!'

Gil wasn't looking at her any more. Abby was reminded unbearably of the boy he had been, silent, unapproachable, not asking her to dance, not talking to her, eyes downcast. She could see his eyelashes. And the anger and the feeling that she would weep if she didn't do something made her go over and hit him. She smacked him hard across the mouth with an open palm. Afterwards she wished a thousand times that she hadn't. The sound echoed around the room like a shot, it was such a clear clean noise. Gil didn't react at all and Abby knew that intimacy with physical violence did that to you. It reminded her of the night that they had spent together so long ago and she had thought he was dead. He had been knocked across rooms and beaten beyond endurance many times. This was nothing. He just stood and waited to see if she was going to do it again.

'You let me give myself to you knowing that you were going to inherit almost everything,' she said through her teeth.

'What did you want your father to do, let your husband waste everything?' Gil's eyes fired.

'He could have left it to me. The law does give women rights.'

'Like shite it does! Nothing is tipped in your favour. A decent lawyer could get it all from under you in days. Then what would happen?'

'I'm not a child!'

'Abby, I would rather it hadn't been left like this . . .'

'Of course you would. What would you want with a house and two shipyards?'

'Your father was concerned about you. He wanted to secure it.'

'He's certainly done that. Did you talk him into it?'

'That's not worthy of you.'

'So, you screwed me on the floor and all the time you were stealing what was mine. And even after you had me, you didn't tell me.'

'I didn't know. And as for the rest, you wanted me to.'

'Well, it couldn't have been very good because I don't remember wanting you to do it again. In fact I distinctly remember leaving. Do you remember that?'

All he said was, 'Don't.'

'You haven't changed at all. You're devious and cowardly and I wish I hadn't gone to you. Do you know what I discovered? That you think every woman is Helen. I imagine you called Rhoda "Helen" in bed or at least thought of her that way.'

'Do you have to throw that at me? You couldn't run

the shipyards without me and that's all that's important. Your father wanted it to be the best and it is. How long do you think it would go on like that without me? Or did you think that I would work with Robert telling me what to do?'

'I thought it would go on as it is.'

'You think I'd do this for a wage? You mistake me for somebody else.'

'I think I have,' Abby said, and with as much dignity as she could, she walked out of the room, out of the house. All she wanted to do was get away, whereas in another sense it was the last thing she wanted. She wanted to be there with her father and even possibly with her mother. She wanted the past, the time when everything had seemed to be in front of her, when nothing had gone wrong. It was hard to think of Gil as an interloper and a thief as well as everything else.

Robert talked. She would have said nothing, but he told everybody that Gil had taken his wife's inheritance so that people were shocked afresh at Gil's behaviour and no doubt, Abby thought with some satisfaction, it would destroy what social life he had carefully managed to build up. After that day she couldn't bear to go past the house, so she kept away from that part of the city when she came into Newcastle, but she missed her father more and more.

*

The following week the ship was launched. Gil provided extra money for the men and a big feast for their families, which was what Henderson had wanted, but it was a subdued affair because of Henderson's death. Local dignitaries stayed away. Edwina was there with John, but she was very quiet, and Gil surmised that he had seen the last of her dinner parties. People who did come complained about the bitter cold of the day, but Gil felt nothing. He watched the big ship slide down into the water and all he could think was that Henderson had been robbed of his triumph and that people thought he had cheated the old man. He went home, had tea with Matthew and put the child to bed. A little later, when he was sitting by the fire, Kate came in and hovered.

'Can I have a word?'

'Certainly.'

'I'm getting married. Jack McArthur.' Jack was a plater at the yard, Gil knew him well.

'We'll have to find a good house for you.'

'We're leaving. Jack has been offered a job on the Clyde.'

Gil gave her his congratulations. Later still, Mrs Wilkins came in. Gil knew, though this lady had said nothing, that once Henderson was dead she would not stay. She thoroughly disapproved of him, though she had not even by a look given him to think she disliked him, but he understood. They would both think Abby should have everything. She was the daughter, he was an outsider and much, much worse.

'I don't want to stay here without Kate and I've worked long enough. I have a sister in Alnwick. I'm going there.'

Gil wished her well. He was about to lock the doors when somebody banged on the front door. When he opened it, John Marlowe stood there.

'Thought you might like to go out,' he said.

The pubs were shut, so Gil had no idea what he meant. John didn't drink or gamble to excess and he couldn't take Gil anywhere respectable because nobody would want him there. He went without asking because John had done a great deal for him, but when the carriage stopped and they got out and went inside the building, he realised where he was. The hall of the house was brilliantly lit and gaudy. A beautiful woman dressed in a blue satin dress came along the hall towards them, smiling. Her shoulders rose creamily and bare.

'Mr Marlowe, how are you?' she said.

Gil wanted to go home. He would have said so had the man been anybody but John. John introduced them. He was obviously a valued client. Very soon Gil found himself in a bedroom with a blonde-haired girl who was prepared to do anything for him, so she said. Gil couldn't afford to offend John Marlowe, so very reluctantly he went to bed with her. To his surprise nothing devastating happened. The roof didn't fall in, somebody didn't haul him out of there complaining that he was doing wrong, but something went cold in Gil's head, it was the only way he could think to work out what he felt. He didn't care who she was or how she had got to here or what might occur afterwards. She was an object to be enjoyed. He had her and then he drank some wine and then he had her again and then he went home. He didn't even offer to pay; he presumed that John paid. He went home and slept well.

Chapter Nineteen

Abby dreamed about her parents. She dreamed of being a child and of the happy times. When she awoke she was miserable. She could no longer take refuge in her father's house. People were right: Gil had not cared for Henderson; he had played the old man like a fish and taken everything from him. It was proof enough, they said, that he did not come to the churchyard or attend the funeral tea, and that he had gone to work that day and that he had launched the ship just as he intended a few days later. Charlotte wept bitter tears as she stood in front of Abby's drawing-room fire. Gil was never to redeem himself. She had seen Matthew at Toby and Henrietta's wedding that summer and William would not let her acknowledge the child.

'Edward is obviously not going to marry again. Indeed, I don't know what he does. William complains that he is not at work, that he is often absent. Sometimes he doesn't come home at night, so whatever women he does see are not respectable. Was ever a woman so cursed in her children?' Charlotte turned a wet, red face on Abby. 'William says we must sell the house.'

'Sell it?'

'We cannot keep it up. He had that house built for me.'

If Abby had been frank she would have said that Bamburgh House was a small loss, having never liked it, but it was Charlotte and William's monument to their success and she knew how much it meant to them. But how would they sell it? Nobody of any taste or discernment would buy it.

'William says there is a house in Westoe which would do very well.'

'Westoe Village is pretty,' Abby said, thinking of all the elegant Victorian houses in the little village just outside Newcastle. Some of them had big stone walls and behind them big gardens. 'It would be very convenient,' she said.

Charlotte was upset at the loss of prestige as much as the loss of the house, Abby thought. It was a very big house for just the two of them. Perhaps at one time they had expected to found a dynasty; now they had no one. But they would not think of it like that. This was a matter of pride and Charlotte's pride was almost all gone. Abby privately thought that if Charlotte could learn to hate Gil, it might help. William obviously did and so did she. The loss of her father was all caught up with the feelings that she had for Gil. She had not realised, either, that she needed to have the house to go to. It had been somewhere to get away from her life in the country, from the husband who was rarely at home and the child she hardly saw.

Charlotte had grown very fat and when Abby did see William he looked like an old man, tired, disappointed and angry, but she had not thought things in such a way that the big house would have to be sold. She knew how she had felt when Robert had lost the London house. It had changed things, their place in society, their friendships and relations between them. When she looked back, Abby could see that her husband had been proud and confident. Now he stayed away a lot and came home drunk or penniless. Abby felt that she had no one and began to take her child away from the upstairs of the house, where she seemed like a prisoner. There were lessons in the mornings, so Abby insisted that in the afternoons she should see Georgina. This meant leaving the house because if she did not, Nanny would interfere and people would arrive and take up her time. They didn't do much. They went shopping or out to tea, but it was Abby's only pleasure. Going into Newcastle was a mixed pleasure because it had been the city of her childhood, but in a way she saw herself and her mother doing just such things and for the first time she enjoyed her daughter's company. She refused Robert's wanting to go abroad as they had done so often in the past. He went by himself and she was glad of the respite, because he did not allow mourning. When people died, Robert's reaction was to ignore them. Since Henderson's death he had not mentioned her father, nor would he permit the wearing of black. It seemed to Abby that Robert was pretending that nobody ever died, most especially nobody who mattered. Somewhere inside him his parents lived, she thought, because he could not bear that he should lose anyone.

If there had been anything decent about Gil at all, Abby thought, she would have gone back to the house, if only to talk to somebody about her father. She found herself outside in the street across the road several times and she was afraid. She didn't know how she had got there, only that she couldn't leave. She remembered Gil saying that she could have anything she wanted from the house and the truth was that many of her personal possessions were still there. She wanted them; she wanted something to remember her father by, but she could not make herself go there either when he was not there or when he was. She had heard that Kate and Mrs Wilkins had left, so the new servants would not know her sufficiently to let her past the doors. They certainly wouldn't allow her to take anything from the house and Abby wanted not to see Gil again.

*

Gil had chosen new servants from out of the area, chosen them for their backgrounds and ability. He paid them well and expected high standards. The house was always perfect. Meals were on the table at exactly the right moment; cupboards and drawers were orderly; his clothes were put out daily, washed and starched and ironed. Everything was in its place just, in a way, as it had been before, only more so. He had altered nothing. The house was just as it would have been and daily he expected to find Henderson there. His not being there was, in Gil's mind, a long, long corridor where Henderson was just out of sight, just far enough away so that Gil could not wave at him.

He went to work except on Sunday afternoons. He came back at teatime every day so that he could spend some time with Matthew, but when the boy went to bed Gil worked. One day the spring after Henderson had died – it was late March and it should not have been warm but it was – the sun was pouring in through his office windows. Usually he would have ignored it and gone on working, the outside world did not intrude here, but for some reason he couldn't stand it any longer and he left the office and went home.

It was a Saturday afternoon, that would be his excuse. The men weren't there. Some of the office staff were, especially, he thought smiling grimly, those who expected to be noticed. The air beyond the shipyard was soft, spring-like, so he went home early. When he opened the front door he could hear laughter and when he opened the sitting-room door, Hannah, the general maid and Matthew were playing some kind of game, hands crossed, spinning round and round in the middle of the room. She didn't see Gil at first, or hear the door.

Gil hadn't seen anything much of this girl except her obedient demeanour and the way that she cleaned and polished the house to a high shine. Gil had kept the new servants in their place; he didn't want intimacy of any kind. He didn't want to regret their leaving when they went as he had regretted and resented Kate and Mrs Wilkins. For several months the house had been like the office, well-run, almost military. He blamed the old servants for going, even though he knew there was no reason why they should not have done and they had been right to go; but they had taken from him the last vestiges of his life with Henderson. Day by day he carried with him the stone of Henderson's death and the way that Abby had left him. He had known what she would do and say; he had known that they would quarrel and she would hate him, but the knowing of it before it had happened had made things worse in a way because there was nothing he could do to stop it. Her love had counted for nothing in the end. He didn't care that Robert was going pretty much to the devil; in some ways he was glad. Henderson had foreseen all that and planned carefully. Gil missed him every minute, he missed the old servants and he felt betrayed because they had been part of the family and had left his son just as though he didn't matter. Matthew had cried a lot because things had changed so much and Gil had thought he was the only adult in his child's life, but it was strange how things moved on. His child had obviously developed a close relationship with this girl from Yorkshire.

They spun round faster and faster, giggling and shouting, until they were obliged to let go. Then they collapsed into a heap on the thickly rugged floor, helpless, out of breath, triumphant. In those moments Gil remembered what youth was meant to be like.

Her cap had come off, the pins loosened. It reminded Gil uncomfortably of the girls he paid for on Saturday nights. Hannah was no different, it was just that she had been luckier and he held her fate in his hands just the same. He paid her well to clean his house. His sense of justice would not let him take anyone's labour for less than he thought they deserved. His servants were higher paid than anybody he knew. John Marlowe laughed and called it indulgence, but Gil knew well by now that money meant independence and it was more important than anything. This girl had no independence from him yet. If he chose, he could put her on the street and then she would end up, if she was lucky, pretending to some man that she enjoyed being put down and laid for money.

And then she saw him. She blushed crimson. She had pretty brown hair and deep blue eyes and she was breathing very quickly, partly from the exertion but partly now from shock and fear, he knew. Gil hadn't realised until then that she was afraid of him. He was never rude to his servants, he never made difficult demands, so he thought. It was his power over her that she feared. She retrieved her cap as she got up and stood there in front of him like a condemned prisoner, lowering her eyes and handling her cap nervously.

'So,' Gil said lightly, 'what about some tea?' and he smiled at her.

She looked up, bit her lip and was for a second Abby, biting her lip to bleeding on the rug in the study. Her colour came back to normal. She said, 'Yes, sir,' and scuttled out.

'You frightened her,' Matthew observed.

'What am I, an ogre?'

Out of breath, Matthew flung himself onto the sofa.

'Yes,' he said.

It was the following day that Abby went to the house. She made herself. She wanted so much to see the place and to have something belonging to her father and, although she dreaded going, she could stay away no longer. She tried to shield herself against Gil before she got there, to think that probably she would see Matthew, which would make it easier, and that she had only to speak a few words to Gil. She could envisage what it would be like. He would be working because he always worked. She would not remember what they had done in that little room and he would most likely be frigidly polite. He might let her collect her things and take something of her father's and it would be formal, not as bad as she thought it was going to be. She would get through it. She had to.

She knocked hard on the door and was surprised to find it opening immediately as a small boy ran at her.

'Aunty Abby!' he said in obvious delight and hugged her. 'You never come to see us and now I'm going out.' He indicated several small boys on the pavement whom she hadn't noticed, and an adult, presumably somebody's father, armed with a cricket bat and a ball and cricket stumps. 'We're going to the park. Will you still be here later on?'

'I will try.'

'You'll be staying for tea. I'll be back.' And with that he waved and ran off, shouting behind him, 'Daddy's in the sitting room. Go in. Hannah's half-day.'

Abby went into the gloom of the hall, except that it wasn't gloomy because the spring sunshine poured in through the stained glass of the inner door. She stood there expecting any second to hear her father's voice.

There was the faint smell of Sunday dinner, roast beef and Yorkshire pudding. She paused by the little office, but since Matthew had said Gil was in the sitting room, she made her way there. He hadn't lied. Gil was in the sitting room. He was asleep. He was lying on the sofa. The fire burned softly in the grate and through the windows the garden was full of daffodils and other spring flowers in small cream, blue and red clumps beyond the lawn.

He didn't wake up even when she moved around the room. It was exactly as it had been, her father's chair in its usual place. She thought of the reading of the will, the last time she had been in here, her anger, Gil's stubbornness and the way that she had hit him. She could not reconcile any of it to the young man who was asleep on the sofa. He looked so harmless, lying on his side, obviously very tired. His waistcoat and trousers were dark, his shirt was white and his eyelashes were so . . . He opened his eyes and the impression disappeared. His gaze was cool like tap water. He sat up slowly. Abby glanced at the door.

'Matthew let me in,' she said. 'I know I have no right to come here,' Abby had rehearsed this, but she hadn't counted on her throat being so dry that she couldn't get the words out, 'but . . .'

He got up. Abby wished he hadn't. He was much bigger than she. She knew very well that he could dominate a room just by his presence. He didn't, but he could if he chose. She had known businessmen all her life and she could imagine him in the boardroom, saying nothing and reducing other people to blancmange.

'You can come here as often as you like, though it hadn't occurred to me that you might want to.'

'You said . . . that I could take something. My things are here and . . . some things which I think my father would have wanted me to have.'

'Help yourself,' Gil said.

Even getting out of the room was difficult. It seemed to Abby to take a long time because he was watching her, or at least she thought he was watching her. She closed the door with a slight bang, not out of temper but because her hands were sweating. How could he manage to be so predatory without doing anything, she thought in irritation. It was because you didn't know what he was thinking or what he would do to further his ambition and she was well aware that he would do anything to get what he wanted while all the time looking so civilised. It was a veneer, nothing more.

She went upstairs to what had been her own room and, to her surprise, it was exactly as she had left it. It was clean; everything was dusted and polished, but the things she had left here were undisturbed. It looked as though she had gone away for a while and would be back. There were books on the bedside table. Some of them had been her mother's. One of them was open and she picked it up. It was open at the very page where she had left it. Her combs and hairbrushes were on the dressing-table. She had not taken those because Robert had insisted on buying her more expensive ones. Her old wooden jewellery box was there and a brooch that her mother had given her as a child, two silver owls with emerald eyes. At least, she had thought at the time that they were emeralds and her mother did not tell her otherwise and spoil the dream. There were various wooden bangles, a silver chain with a cross her parents had given her on her first communion and a silver ring with a pink stone which her parents had brought back from Cornwall. It was like being a child again. There was a jar of cream and in the top drawer, pins and some papers. She closed the drawer. And then a thought occurred to her and she could not resist it. She left the room and stole across the landing towards her father's bedroom. When she opened the door she was so shocked that she couldn't move. Nothing had been touched.

She opened the wardrobe and there were all Henderson's suits, his shirts, his ties, his shoes. She even thought she could smell the cigars he sometimes smoked. The bed was made up and she thought at any moment he would walk in and her heart would piece back together again. The view from the window was of the tennis court. She remembered him picking her up when she was little and standing her on the window ledge to watch her mother playing tennis down below with a friend.

Feeling rather like Goldilocks now, she went into the room next door which was where Gil slept. For some reason, she was not a bit surprised to see that it was empty. She thought at first that he must have moved into another room, it was so bare, and then she thought of his room at home. It was completely cleared of any mess or any sign of possession. There was no book; there was no evidence of anyone's stay; it was like an unoccupied hotel bedroom. Only when she opened the wardrobe were Gil's clothes to be seen and it was so neat that it frightened her. Nothing was an inch out of place. It was symmetrical; everything lined up; it was mathematical in its precision.

'Find anything interesting?' he said from the doorway. Abby spun round and looked at him. He looked so enquiring but friendly. She held his eyes steadily.

'Why do you keep my father's things?'

'You can have them if you want them,' Gil said.

'You've kept the house exactly as it was when he was alive and this is . . . this is—'

'My bedroom,' Gil said. 'I don't remember you having any particular inclination to be in here before.'

'I was just curious.'

'About what? There's nothing to see.'

'So I observed,' Abby said and went past him to stave off any more questions.

In the end Abby took very little, some books which had been her mother's before they were hers, some cuff-links which were not valuable and had been left on her father's dressing-table, the little silver owl brooch. She sat upstairs in her father's room and stayed, dry-eyed, thinking of him there. She hadn't realised how long she was there until Matthew burst in.

'You are still here! I hoped you would be. Come downstairs. Daddy says the tea is ready and there is chocolate cake.'

Abby tried to say that she wasn't staying, but the boy's face fell.

'You must stay! I haven't seen you in ever so long.'

Abby went. Her idea of fun was not eating chocolate cake with Gil, but Matthew chattered all the way through tea, eating rapidly and talking at the same time, so that Abby thought nobody had ever told him to do one thing at once. Even though being there was difficult, it was worth it for Matthew's shining face and boyish talk. She thought that he was very advanced for four. The children she knew of that age clung around their mothers and didn't talk. Matthew didn't stop talking and knew a great deal about cricket. He seemed so happy she could not help but think that if Gil had got nothing right in his life but this, he certainly seemed to have got the hang of parenting. Obviously his son had never been beaten or shouted at or made to feel at all unwanted. When he had finished his tea, Matthew went back outside to play with his friends. Abby waited until the door was closed and then she said, 'He's a very nice little boy.'

'You can never tell. Presumably I was a very nice little boy.'

'You hated cricket.'

'Team games,' Gil said scornfully.

'Isn't Reed's Yard a team?'

'No, it's a dictatorship.'

She almost smiled.

'I thought you'd have had the gates repainted.'

'Why?'

'It isn't Reed's any more.'

'Abby—'

'No, don't,' she said quickly.

'You don't know what I was going to say.'

'You were going to plead your case and it's not something you're any good at so you might as well save your breath.' She got up. 'I only stayed because of Matthew.'

'If you want to come back—'

'I don't. You may keep my father's belongings, but there's nothing left of him here, I can see that. I shan't come again. Goodbye.'

Abby chose to go back past the gates of the yards, but the first just said 'Reed's' on it as it always had and the newer yard said 'Reed's Yard No. 2' as though it were some poor relation and not the biggest shipyard on the Tyne. She could not help being glad that Gil left that at least as it was. Her father would have been pleased about it, his name still there.

John Marlowe had in some ways taken Henderson's place in that he had become a friend. It was a strange kind of friendship. Gil was not invited to his home and John didn't come to his house. Often John was away. He had other houses and he went away on business frequently. Sometimes Gil was away, so there were long periods when they didn't see one another. On Saturday nights, however, if they were both in Newcastle they went out to dinner and for a few drinks. Then they went to the high-class brothel to which John had introduced Gil.

Sometimes John called in at Gil's office unannounced. He knew that Gil would go home early, have tea and spend some time with his son, but that invariably he went back to the office. John usually turned up late in the evening and Gil would talk over their work with him as he had done with Henderson. He would call unannounced, timing his visits well when everyone had gone home. Gil imagined that this was deliberate. Although they were business acquaintances, it would have done John no good to have cultivated Gil as a friend. In the office they could talk undisturbed. When they went out, they went to obscure places. It was almost, Gil thought with humour, like having an affair with a married woman. Nobody must know; it was furtive and secretive and had about it an air of intimacy which he liked. John Marlowe's mind was always full of new ideas.

Gil had copied his father's way and had windows which overlooked the river. As the evening drew in, he would sit with his feet up on the desk and drink whisky. John would call in, and in the summer months when the sun stayed late they would watch the shadows fall across the river and they would talk.

On one such September evening, when the shadows were beginning to darken in the corners, they had spent an hour talking about politics when John said suddenly, 'I hear your father's house is up for sale.'

'I gather, yes.'

'And there is a buyer.'

'Is there?' Gil looked across the empty desk at him.

'You know bloody damned fine there is, Gillan, it's you.'

'That's just a guess.'

'Playing cat and mouse with the old man, are you? Does he know it's you?'

'I don't know.'

'You've done it through a third party? Do you want

him to find out? You want him to see how badly he needs to sell, is that it? You can't really want it.'

'How do you know?'

'What are you going to do there? Remember your wonderful childhood?'

'I don't intend to live in it.'

'What if there's another buyer?'

Gil laughed.

'Who the hell would want it?'

John considered his whisky glass.

'Are you going to pull it down? It's a nice site.' John swilled the whisky around in his glass as though it were brandy. 'What are you going to do with it?'

'I don't know yet.'

'It was his goal, his main ambition, it was part of his dream. Your father clawed his way up the ladder. He did everything he had to do to get there. He even cast off his parents. Now you're ruining him.' Gil didn't answer that. 'What are you really going to do with it?'

'Nothing. I'm going to do nothing.'

He had bought Bamburgh House not knowing and not caring whether his father knew who the buyer was. That winter, when he had a free day, he went out to the house.

Winter was never the best time for such outings, but he was pleased with it. There were no animals in the fields, the grass was long on the lawns and it had about it a neglected air. The front door had come open; someone had thrown stones at most of the windows so there was glass on the floors; the snow had blown inside. It was a bitterly cold day and Gil stood in the middle of the room which had been his father's study and remembered the harsh words, the blows. He went upstairs to what had been Helen's bedroom and thought of the nights they had spent there together, the only truly happy nights of his life.

He had debated with himself whether to pull the place down, but in the end he decided that it would be a fitting monument to the Collingwood family to let it go to ruin slowly so that people would point from a distance, the grass would grow knee high around it and the birds would find a nesting place.

A bird – he couldn't decide what kind, small and brown – flew into him on the stairs and Gil knocked out some more glass so that it would have plenty of room to get out. It found the exit when he had gone downstairs. He watched it fly away in the direction of the quarry garden and a bitter wind moaned through the hall. Glass crunched under his feet. The window ledges were thick with dirt. The windows that had been left intact were streaked with rain, and because there were no curtains the grey winter light filtered into the hall where the Christmas tree used to stand.

There was one room he didn't go into and that was his bedroom. As a child he could remember the morning sunlight twinkling in there because it faced east. Edward's room had been comfortable; he had rugs and a fire and books, but William decided that Gil behaved so badly at home and at school that there would be no comfort. What might have been a refuge had been nothing better than a dungeon until the night Abby had spent with him. Gil went back to Jesmond, back to the servants who were polite and competent and to his shipyards where everything was done as it should be and he didn't want any of it. All he wanted was his child; it was such a relief to be able to go home to Matthew.

Chapter Twenty

Abby couldn't believe at first that Gil had bought his parents' house. She knew how much he had always hated the place. Charlotte and William did not know about the sale until afterwards, but since they did not have another buyer they would have been obliged to accept Gil's offer, she thought, even if they had known that he was the purchaser. But she wondered whether William would have been prepared to endure the humiliation of knowing that his son had bought Bamburgh House. They would have waited a long time for another buyer, she thought.

They moved to Westoe and bought a house there. Although much smaller, it was a great deal prettier than Bamburgh House had been, but Charlotte and William hated it from the beginning since it reflected their reduced circumstances. They needed fewer servants and only one gardener and Robert reported that there was no saying how long they would be there. The depression deepened.

William put the men on short time and finished many of them so that he would not have to pay them while times were hard. Abby tried to talk to Robert about helping them financially, but he said that he could not afford it. She didn't argue. She privately thought that he considered it none of his concern, but she had heard talk that Gil bought houses and took people off the streets, that he set up facilities so that people at least had hot food, drink and shelter, especially when the weather was cold, wet and windy, which it so often was. It did him no good in the eyes of other shipbuilders. They despised philanthropy of any kind, thinking that if the men were given that kind of help they would not work.

'He's soft,' William said of his son. 'He was always soft. Does he think he's going to save the whole world?'

Robert laughed.

'There's nothing like a good hard winter to rid the streets of rubbish.'

Gil gave work to as many people as he could afford and helped a great many others. Henderson, Abby thought, would have approved. She could almost see her mother smiling. Abby went into Newcastle to help. She told no one and she didn't see Gil because he was not doing the work personally, he had delegated it, but it was done and she was proud of it. She used what little money she had and what influence she had to get other people to give. She could not understand that they would not give up even one of their many comforts for the plight of those who were without food and shelter.

Abby sometimes passed Bamburgh House on her way to and from Newcastle and she only hoped that Charlotte had not seen the destruction that the winter weather and Gil's neglect had wrought here. It was a deliberate act of destruction. How angry William must be, though he didn't show it, how frustrated that his son could afford and would allow this monument to William's ambition to fall slowly into ruin. Gil could not have thought of anything better to upset his father.

Charlotte rarely came out to the country to visit. She was so envious of the beautiful house which Robert and Abby owned. It had been, Abby admitted to herself, one of the reasons she had married Robert. She loved it in all its seasons, in all the different times of the day. Its mish-mash of styles betrayed the affection in which the family had held their home and there was one big comfort about it: Robert could not gamble it away; it was entailed through the male line. Abby knew therefore how important it was that she should produce another child, but Robert was drunk or absented himself from home so often that this seemed unlikely. When he was there he did not come to her bed and Abby did not want him there.

She knew that they ought to have had other children, that it was not considered wise to bring up an only child and though she had been an only child herself, there had been many times when she had wished for family. When things had gone wrong, a sister or a brother might have been of some help. Especially since her father had died, she had nobody. Gil had always seemed like almost family; she had known him such a long time and he had been closer than anybody else in that respect, but that had gone too since her father had died. Gil had become the enemy. Abby thought she liked that least of all. Since Henderson had died, she had lost them both. There was no one to talk to who understood anything important. Sometimes it was all she could manage not to go to Jesmond and tell Gil she wanted to be friends, she needed him and she would have to remind herself of what he had done. Even now, she could not believe it.

Gradually the paintings, the furnishings, the horses, everything which could be sold, was, as Robert gambled more and more. Abby even tried to get him to stay at home. The day came when she went to her jewellery box to find nothing of value left in it. The presents which he had given her to commemorate their betrothal, their wedding, anniversaries, birthdays – sapphire and diamond earrings, diamond bracelet and necklace, half a dozen beautiful rings and even the emerald set which had belonged to his mother and been in the family for many years – it all went. Abby tried to talk to him, but she could hear her words and she had no new argument to give him. He had not listened to her before and there was no reason why he should do so now except that, she said, 'Soon there'll be nothing left. Then what will we do?'

He gave her a clearer look than he had given her in years.

'I loved you,' he said.

'I loved you too.'

'No.' Robert shook his head. He was rather drunk. It was the middle of the afternoon and the shadows were stealing across the lawn beyond the drawing-room windows. It was Abby's favourite kind of day in winter, cold and wet but if you were inside with a fire and plenty of food, you could rejoice in the cold weather.

'You never loved me,' he said sadly. 'You always loved that bastard Gillan Collingwood.' And he got up and wandered from the room and closed the door with a tiny click.

He didn't come back. Abby didn't worry at first. She didn't worry until the following day, because although he sometimes stayed out overnight it was rare that he stayed out for longer than that. She worried, too, for how lucid he had appeared, for how bitter he was. Therefore in the middle of the afternoon when a carriage pulled up outside the house, she got up in agitation. Two policemen were shown into the bareness of the drawing room and for once Abby did not think about the lack of good furniture, the marks on the walls where the paintings had been taken down, the silver that was gone, the ornaments. She was watching their faces and she knew before they said anything that the news was not good. They were very sorry – they weren't sorry, it was just that they didn't know what else to say – they were very sorry, there had been an accident. Mr Surtees had been shot. The truth was, Abby thought brutally, that her husband had taken a double-barrelled shotgun to himself, so there couldn't have been much left of him. Still, he must have been recognisable. One of the many Surtees cousins had found him in their barn. Why, Abby thought idiotically, didn't he do it in his own barn? They had concluded that he had fallen over and the gun had gone off. It was a ridiculous notion, but of course a Surtees could not have killed himself. His father had not drunk himself senseless and killed himself. The trouble was that it was the name of intelligent, honourable people and if he had killed himself then he had dirtied the name and there was no room for that. Abby, like everybody else, would have to pretend that there had been an accident.

Abby blamed herself. She tried not to, but it was difficult. She thought of all the things she might have done, of the help she could have given him, of the love she had withheld and he was right, at least he had been at the beginning. She did not love him and, although she no longer loved Gil, it had always been too late for her to love Robert, so many things had been in the way. They had been too unalike and yet people said that opposites attracted and they had been that.

She tried to shield Georgina from the knowledge of what had happened, but she had to tell her child that her father was dead. It would have been harder still to say that they were penniless and homeless, because that was what happened.

The family gathered in the house, even Charlotte, full of concern. It was Charlotte who said to her – no doubt there had been a family meeting at one of their houses and she had been nominated because she knew Abby so well – 'You can't stay here.'

Abby stared.

'Not stay?'

'The house is entailed and you have no place here. You have no son. It all belongs to Robert's cousin Gerard, and he and his wife and family will want to move in immediately. You'll be able to stay for a few days until you find somewhere else, but no longer, you must realise that.'

'I have nowhere to go.'

She thought that Charlotte might have cared sufficiently to say, 'but you must come and stay with us,' only she didn't. Abby thought that in a way Charlotte was rather pleased at what had happened. Abby was worse off than she was, whereas of late she had had to watch Abby in the loveliest house in the county while she made do with a polite Victorian stone house in a village. It did not suit Charlotte's ideas of who went where. This was her triumphant moment. Abby had not borne a son and was to be turned out of doors like a stray cat.

Nobody offered her refuge and she had no money. There was nothing left. The stables were empty; the furniture was worthless. Robert, Abby thought grimly, had made sure that he cleaned them out before he shot himself. Had he not, just for a moment or two, considered if not his wife then at least his child? It seemed he had not. She did not recall a single instance when he had spoken to Georgina or asked for her company. The child shed no tears except for her mother's distress and Abby was so angry with her dead husband that she could find no sorrow or grief.

Abby could not believe that his family or his friends would not offer her some help, but they didn't. They all came to the funeral and she was obliged to find food and drink in the house. The only good part of Abby's day was when she noticed Gil had come to the funeral. That, she thought, was kind of him. People didn't speak to him, but he seemed oblivious to that and although they had no conversation, she was aware of him in the church and afterwards at the house where he stood alone, not clutching a glass as some men might have done if they were left to their own company but standing quietly by the window as though he were waiting to see what would happen. Abby didn't have to wait long. The cousin who was inheriting showed her no mercy.

'You must leave and within the next week or so,' Gerard said. 'Anthea has plans for the house. We have a great deal to do here, so much to alter,' and he looked around the drawing room as though counting the cost. 'The builders are to begin soon.'

Abby stood there in her drawing room, in what had been hers, she reminded herself, and panicked. What was she to do? Suddenly she hated them all. They were eating her food and drinking her whisky and there was practically nothing left. Her own comfort was that when there was no more whisky they would go, but it seemed that Gerard intended to move in that very day. Could he not have given her a little time, a few days to consider? She thought he would have liked her to leave right there and then. As she stood by herself in the middle of the house which she no longer owned, Gil walked across the room to her.

'Considering your options?' he said.

'I don't have any, it seems.' Abby wished that her voice was more steady. 'The stables are empty, the cellar's empty, the bloody coffers are empty, there's nothing left, there's nothing—'

'And the scavengers are here,' Gil said, nodding in Gerard's direction. 'Is there somewhere we could talk?'

'What about?'

Gil didn't answer that, so she led him into the nearest empty room and it was very empty. Even the furniture had gone from here. It had been Jacobean, hideous but worth money, and there had been a number of good though also dark and hideous paintings on the walls. The afternoon sun threw its relentless gleam onto the empty walls and the bare floor.

'Did it himself, did he?' Gil asked softly.

'Of course he did. They blame me. I blame me too. Why did he have to do it? I'm not going. They aren't going to turn me out of here.'

'Abby, look . . . you do have somewhere to go. Your father only left me the house on condition that if you ever needed it you should have it.'

Abby looked straight at him.

'How could he have known?'

'He told me that he wished he hadn't talked you into marrying Robert.'

Abby sighed and went to the window. She couldn't believe that she would have to leave this place. It had been one of the main reasons for her marrying Robert and she didn't believe Gil.

'My father didn't talk me into it. I wanted him. He was the catch of the county. I thought—'

'What?'

'I don't know now, I don't remember.' She sighed. 'You can't give me the house.'

'Why not?'

'Because everybody will think I'm your mistress if you do.'

'Straight to the point as always.'

'It's true.' Abby turned from the window and smiled at him. 'They'll say, "what other reason could he possibly have? Nobody is that generous."'

'I loved your father.'

'I know you did.'

'No, you don't. You think I was nice to him for what he could give me.'

'That too, perhaps. I suppose you're going to tell me that he gave you the business for the same reason.'

'He gave me the business because he had nobody else to give it to and he wanted it to go on. There's a great deal of money, Abby. If you won't have the house then you could buy a house—'

'And you think people would be deceived? You know a lot about ships, but you don't know much about people. My reputation wouldn't stand it; things are bad enough.'

'And what use will that be when you end up in Hope Street, selling yourself because you don't have any money?'

Abby laughed. She hadn't laughed for a long time and it eased the great boulder inside her.

'I don't think things are quite that bad,' she said. 'I could go and be a barmaid at the Ship. Do you remember the Ship? You came across the room and rescued me. You can't do that this time.'

'I could if you let me. Wouldn't you rather do the dignified thing and leave?'

'What, with you? It would ruin me.'

'Your husband has killed himself. You don't really think you're going to be asked to polite parties? Come with me. We don't have to see each other. I'll move and you can have the house all to yourself. It's waiting for you.'

Abby allowed herself a few seconds of longing for the home that she had loved so much.

'Where would you go, Bamburgh House? It would almost be worth it to see you there, hating it so much. I don't think you ever loved my father or me enough to let yourself go back there.'

'The choices are gone. Where's Georgina? Go and get her and pack a bag.'

'I'm not going with you. Nobody would ever speak to me again.'

Abby left the room, wandered through the hall, striving for breath because there were fifty people in the drawing room and none of them should see her cry. They would be talking about her, what a bad wife she had been, how she had not provided a son, how they had known all along that she was a silly choice, that she was middle-class, beneath him, with different ideas, that she was not beautiful and read too much and was too opinionated. They wanted to get rid of her. Abby was wretched. She knew that she had not been a good wife to him, she wished that she could begin again.

She ran away upstairs. She did not want to face Gil, afraid that she should change her mind. She watched from the window until his carriage left and then she went back downstairs to face the mourners. She had been right. Gerard had no intention of leaving. He moved in that very day and, although she questioned the solicitors, apparently he was entitled to do so. After all, her husband was dead. His family followed swiftly and they began immediately moving in their possessions. It improved the look of the house straight away since there was very little left. New servants were employed and they ignored Abby. At the dinner table she was fed and so was Georgina, but they insisted on her moving out of her bedroom, which was the second most important, and no one spoke to her.

She made a trip into Newcastle to find work, but the work which she could have found in a shop or a factory she was turned down for because, even at her shabbiest, she would not fit into such a place. As for office work, she could not learn to type in a week. There was also the question of Georgina. Where would they live and who would look after her? The winter streets were wet and gloomy, or was it just how she felt? The problem seemed insoluble. After a full day trudging the streets, she found herself getting on a tram that went to Jesmond. She hadn't intended doing that, but it was dark and cold and had rained for most of the afternoon and she could not go back to the comfortless house which had been hers without looking at the house where she had spent a happy childhood, the best time of her life. She got off the tram and walked. She stood in a puddle and her feet were soaked. She stopped across the street. Lamplight was soft in the windows. It was evening now. Gil would be at home. She could not resist crossing the street and banging on the front door. She heard footsteps in the hall and a maid opened the door. Beyond her, Abby could see the hall just as it had always been. The tears which she had not shed for so many days threatened her now, half convinced that her parents sat beyond the sitting-room door. She was ushered in and the door opened. Gil and Matthew were sitting by a big fire, eating cake and drinking tea. The teacups winked in the firelight. Abby thought her heart would burst. Matthew shouted his hello and bounced across to her and Gil pulled a chair close to the fire and gave her tea and cut her cake.

The night closed in around the house. Abby tried halfheartedly to leave, but Gil dissuaded her and it was so easy to stay. Georgina was safe at home. It was just one night to remember how things had been, but she could not even do that. When Matthew was safely in bed and they were having a meal, she said to him, 'I need some work. You employ women.'

'Not women like you,' Gil said.

'What do you mean? I can learn.'

'You wouldn't like it.'

'I don't have to like it. I have nowhere to go and nothing to do. Please.'

'You were married to Robert Surtees, you can't just—'

'Then what can I do?'

'I told you, you can come here.'

'I don't want to do that. If you let me work . . . I could work . . . Please, Gil.'

'Stop begging. It doesn't suit you.'

'What are my alternatives? I have to work.'

Gil got up and came across to her and he got hold of her hand.

'Look at that,' he said. 'You've never worked a day in your life.' And he turned her hand over and touched the soft palm. 'Women who work are either considered as little better than prostitutes or they live in reduced circumstances, and what would you do with Georgina?'

'I would manage. Please.' Abby wrenched her hand away and got up. 'You are so—'

'What?' When she didn't answer, he said flatly, 'I'm all you've got left, you can't afford to turn me down. You can have this house and part of the business. You could marry again eventually.'

'Whatever makes you think I want to do that?'

'Abby, if you go out to work you would lose your reputation just as badly as if you came and lived here with me, no matter what the circumstances. Socially you're finished.'

'Well, thank you. Out of the frying pan and into the fire, that's very nice.'

'There are worse things.'

'I shan't ask you to name them.' Abby stood for a few moments and then thought of something. 'Why haven't you changed anything in the house?'

'We could go back and collect Georgina in the morning and you could pack your things and bring with you whatever you want.'

'I don't have much. What are you doing this for, you can't want me here?'

'It was part of the deal. I got everything and when you needed it you got it back.'

'I don't want it all back. I don't want you to leave and I certainly don't want the business.'

'Why not?'

'Because you would leave that too, I know you would. Besides, it isn't the business which was my father's. You built it.'

'There's enough to go round,' Gil said roughly.

The next morning they drove into the country and collected her child. She packed her clothes and her few possessions and left the house which she had gone to so optimistically such a long time ago. She felt nothing but relief. Gerard and his wife and children waved her away from the front door. Abby didn't look back.

Chapter Twenty-one

Living with Gil was not as difficult as she had thought, but then nothing could be. To anyone who was not suffering from her husband's suicide it might have been considered dull. There was no social life, no invitations came and there were few visitors, only the tradesmen. She had nothing to do. The house was run rather, Abby thought, as he probably ran the works; she was just glad she didn't have to work for him. He didn't say anything, but the servants minded him, as her mother would have said. It should have got on her nerves that the whole thing moved like an army camp, but it didn't. She was so glad to be back there, it was coming home both literally and in her head. She had not eaten or slept properly for a long time, but she did now and the two children liked one another immediately. Georgina was happy, therefore it was difficult for Abby not to be.

No one came in drunk; nobody gambled anything away. Gil came home promptly at half past five for tea.

At seven o'clock he either went back to work and was there long after she went to bed, or went into the study and was seen no more. He left for work at six in the morning. Sometimes she heard him. Occasionally he went out and came back late, but Abby considered it none of her business, which was quite refreshing and, although he did drink sometimes in the evening, it was never to excess so after the first two or three times of seeing him do so Abby relaxed. Gil did not get drunk; he did not shout and lose his temper and empty the house of everything which was comfortable. He would take a glass of brandy into the office or, if she stayed up late, there was the faint smell of whisky, but it did not affect his speech or his actions, so she didn't care.

Nobody talked about marriage. If the local gossips thought she was sleeping in Gil's bed, let them think it. She hadn't lived with a man like this since her father, and it was rather comforting. He didn't make demands; he didn't complain; he didn't make her feel as though she ought to be responsible for anything. He insisted that she should open a bank account and he paid money into it each month. That had been a hiccup.

'Why?' she had said to the suggestion.

'Presumably you need to buy things. Think of it as the start of what I owe you.'

That put it on a different footing. It was a handsome sum but, considering he had taken her inheritance, Abby didn't care and spent it freely. She thought that she was a kept woman, but was doing nothing for it. That was not quite true. She had undertaken the caring of the children. Matthew seemed delighted that she and Georgina had come to live with them and treated her straight away as he would a mother. For somebody who couldn't remember his mother, she counted this as a bonus. He had started school. She took him there each morning. Since Georgina was quite desperate to go, watching all the other children, Abby talked to the kind woman who ran the small school and Georgina was soon going in the mornings. Luckily it wasn't far to walk, because she had to collect Georgina at lunchtime and Matthew at teatime. There were only a few pupils and it was really just one room with a yard behind, but the children seemed happy there and quickly learned their letters. She or Gil read to them both in the evening before bed. It was all so civilised, Abby thought, rather like marriage was meant to be and probably never was.

Georgina had fast caught onto the idea of having two parents and would listen for Gil at the door, run to him and throw herself into his arms. Having had one father who ignored her, she was not about to start calling him 'Daddy' as Abby had feared, but called him by his first name. In vain did Abby point out that this was not considered respectful, but since Gil called her 'Georgie', something else Abby didn't like, she left the whole problem to resolve itself. Georgina adored Gil and Abby thought it was not surprising. Robert had not shown his child attention or affection, but Gil managed both. He would throw her up in his arms and she would scream in delight when he caught her again. He would listen to endless tales that the children told about school, read long stories, sometimes the same one over and over again so that he would lean back against the bedroom wall, eyes shut, and relate word-perfect whichever story it was that had been requested. He told her her paintings were brilliant and her numbers and letters were superb. Abby feared that Matthew might feel left out, so she took him to the park to play cricket when it was fine and to sail boats when it was windy and encouraged his interests. She took both the children shopping and out to tea and for various day trips in the fine weather.

That summer when the children were at school Abby would steal time and lie in the hammock in the garden and imagine to herself that she was young again. The garden had not changed, it was just as her mother had planned it, and although they had a gardener, she spent time there, helping and suggesting and generally getting in the way, enjoying the various plants in their seasons. She wasn't unhappy; she didn't mourn Robert and her vague feeling of guilt soon went away.

It took a long time before she felt restless, before the day she went upstairs to her father's room and decided that it was time to clear it out. She was half inclined to do so without saying anything to Gil, but when the children had gone to bed one autumn evening and he had retreated to the office – still the little room which had been her mother's, he rarely ventured into the study which had been Henderson's – she knocked on the door and went in.

'You don't have to knock.'

'I don't want to disturb you.'

Abby no longer thought of this room as the place where they had made love. She had come to terms with that. She went in and stood for a moment and then said, 'I thought I might clear out some of my father's things from his bedroom.'

Gil frowned.

'I did mean to do it,' he said.

'People could use all those clothes. Some of them are good, and it's past time – and other things.'

'What other things?'

'The dining-room curtains are dropping apart.'

'I thought your mother had chosen them.'

'It was a long time ago. They're in a terrible state.'

'I don't mind what you do.'

'Right.'

Abby emptied her father's bedroom. When she had finished there was nothing left but the furniture and, much as she had dreaded doing it, she felt better. Then she bought new curtains for the dining room, but once she had done so, the rest of the room looked shabby and out of place. After that, it became a compulsion. The house had been her mother's and then her father's, though it had not been Gil's. Now it seemed that it could be hers and there was something unstoppable in her that wanted to make it so. She had not refurnished a house before. She had been allowed to touch nothing in Robert's houses, things were so old and valuable, whereas here her mother had been sensible, practical. Gil objected to nothing. For one thing he was too busy and for another he either liked what she did or was too cautious to tell her that he disliked it. He paid for it all without complaint, though Abby questioned him more than once as to whether it was costing too much. She was fearful of ending up like Robert, caring more for property than for people. That winter when the cold weather came, she spent a lot of time at the houses that Gil had set up for homeless people and at soup kitchens, providing hot food and clothes and bedding, and she was glad to be useful.

The depression that had been creeping up for years took a hold on the area and many businesses closed down. One of the first to go was Collingwood's shipyard. Abby thought that she could not feel sympathy for Charlotte, but when Gil's parents had to leave what they had thought of as a modest house in Westoe and live in a terraced two-bedroomed property in a street in

Jesmond, she did feel sorry. Charlotte had had nothing to do with her since Abby had left Robert's house and gone to live with Gil. One day when the weather was for once less bitter, she took the children to the park. There she spied a little fat figure of a woman watching them from across the way. She left the children playing happily and walked slowly across. The cold wind blew the woman's hair about where it escaped from her hat.

'Hello, Charlotte,' she said.

Charlotte wasn't looking at her. Her eyes were fixed on the small boy who was giggling.

'That is Matthew?'

'It is, yes.'

'How big he is for his age.'

'Doesn't he look just like Gil did at that age?'

'Oh no, Gil was sullen and difficult. He would hide a lot and not come out and he wouldn't learn to read or write.'

'I believe excessive ability often takes people that way,' Abby said stoutly.

'Is Matthew clever?'

'Average.'

'He must take after Helen.'

Abby was amused, but careful not to let it show. Just then, Matthew bounded across.

'Come on, Aunty Abby, we have to get back. Hello.' He beamed at Charlotte.

'I'm your grandmother, Matthew. Do you remember me?'

'Are you?'

'You have two. Your other grandma lives in Durham.'

Abby tried to move him away, but he was intrigued, as well he might be, she thought.

'You have two grandfathers. Don't you know anything about them? And an uncle. Do you remember your Uncle Edward?'

'Is this true?' Matthew said, turning Gil's dark eyes on Abby.

'We have to go. We must get back. It's teatime.'

Abby had almost to drag him away and she was not pleased with herself. When Gil came in shortly after they got home, for once Georgina was not first down the hall and Abby could hear him from the sitting room. 'I met my grandmother. You didn't tell me about her. Why didn't you tell me?'

'Did you now? Where was this?'

'In the park near the entrance. She was standing there by the railings. Why don't we see them? She told me I had another grandmother and two grandfathers, but we never see them.'

'They don't want to see us.'

'But she did.'

'They didn't before now.'

'Why?'

'Because I did something wrong, something they

didn't think I should have done and your grandfather, that's my father, he turned us out of the house.'

There was a short silence. Abby wished she could have stopped her ears.

'It must have been something very bad.'

'Yes, it was.'

With a wisdom well beyond his years Matthew said, 'You don't want to talk about it, do you?'

'No.'

'I would like to see them.'

'We'll have to think about that.'

Abby couldn't eat. Gil didn't reproach her; he didn't lose his temper; he didn't say anything. She had not faced anybody with that much restraint and it was just as bad as if he had called her everything he could lay his tongue to. She didn't meet his eyes all the way through tea and was so glad to get up from the table that she hurried. He went to the little office and stayed there. Abby dealt with the children, but by the time she had put them to bed, she couldn't bear it any longer. She walked into the office without knocking, slammed the door and said, 'All right, say it, say it! I shouldn't have gone across. I didn't think. She was in the park and it is a public place. They live here. What did you expect? They live ten minutes' walk away. You knew this, you knew what it was like, that Collingwood's had closed, that they have lost almost everything. What did you expect me to do?'

She waited for the onslaught. Robert would have made the house ring.

'Matthew followed me,' she said, starting up again quickly. 'I thought he was playing.'

Gil was staring at the wall.

'I saw her on the street the other day,' he said slowly. 'She looked so little and fat and old.'

'Does this mean you're going to let him see them?'

'No.'

'And when he asks?'

'I'll think of something.'

'Don't you think he's entitled to see them?'

'I think we've discussed this sufficiently.'

'You wrecked the house, you put him out of business, you ruined their lives. Isn't that enough?'

'He did it himself.'

'He'll die some day and then you'll be sorry.'

To her astonishment, Gil laughed.

'Do you know that's exactly what your father said. What on earth makes you think so? I'll dance on his grave. I've bought the property.'

'What property?'

'Collingwood's.'

'Don't you own enough of the riverside?'

'I couldn't resist.'

'He's an old man and he's finished. What pleasure is there in that?'

'I got it cheaply,' Gil said, 'so very cheaply. I'm going to put "Reed's Yard No. 3" on the gates. Then I think I'll be satisfied.'

Abby was angry.

'And what are you going to tell your son, that you didn't bed your brother's wife and your own wife at the same time?'

'Hardly, even though it's the truth.'

'Is it?'

He had not spoken about this before, at least not to her, but he was sufficiently upset, she knew, to do so.

'You really thought it of me?'

'Men do.'

'You mean Robert did, bed other women?'

'He did it all the time.'

'I cared about Rhoda and Helen very much and I didn't betray either of them; it was my brother I betrayed. I thought I loved him. I thought he meant more to me than anybody in the world, but I took his wife and his child. Matthew was the only thing that mattered, the only person he really loved ever I think. I destroyed it and Rhoda and Helen both died because of it, but I never played any woman false. I never did.' He got up and was out of the room before she could have stopped him or said anything, though what she would have said or done Abby wasn't sure. It was undoubtedly the longest speech of Gil's life, and she believed him.

She went after him, at the time she wasn't quite sure why. He would have been better let alone, but she went, along the hall and he was standing there in the gloom as if not sure where to go or what to do. She decided it for him because he turned around as she approached and drew her to him and tried to hold her and kiss her. For some reason all Abby could remember was the last embraces that her husband had given her and her regard for him surfaced. She did not feel guilt about his death; she felt resentment and anger.

'Take your hands off me!' she said and before Gil could turn back into himself from being Robert she had spoken in rage and he backed off and walked out. He left the front door open. It was a vile night. Wind and rain threw themselves in as he opened the door. Abby hesitated only just before going after him, but it was too late. The street lamps told her that the street was empty, so where he was she had no idea.

'Gil!' she shouted in case he was close enough to hear her, but even if he had been it was doubtful whether it would have turned him back. Abby cursed herself, but then she realised that it was true. She didn't want any man near her, not after what Robert had done.

There was nowhere to go, Gil discovered, nowhere except work and that wouldn't do. In the end, after walking the streets for a short while, the weather drove him to make a decision, so he went to the brothel where John had taken him. Mrs Fitzpatrick who owned it welcomed him with a smile. He hadn't been there in the short months since Abby had come back to Jesmond and it was only now he could see how much he had hoped that he could gain her affection again. He and John had done some late-night drinking, but he had refused to go to Mrs Fitzpatrick's. John had laughed.

'Why bother when you have it at home?' he said.

'It isn't like that.'

'It isn't like that for me either. Edwina withdrew her bedroom favours a long time ago,' John said with a sigh. 'Women. If the pretty little Mrs Surtees isn't giving you what you want, why do you keep her? The whole world thinks you're bedding her and the odds at the clubs are that you'll marry her.'

Gil could see now that Abby wouldn't marry him, that she wouldn't let him near her, even after he had just told her that he had done nothing dishonourable towards women. She wouldn't believe him. Why should she? Men were like that, Robert had proved it and after Robert why should she want anyone else? She had what she needed: a roof, money, comfort and security for her child. He could not turn her onto the street. Gil could see them going on like that for years and years. He had known that she did not love him, but he had not known that she was disgusted with him.

Mrs Fitzpatrick knew that he favoured blondes. When he came here all he thought of was Helen. He didn't have the same girl twice; he didn't want anything to do with them other than bed. They were all blonde, they were all pretty, they were all the same to him. He was directed upstairs and went and knocked on the door. The rooms were all the same, too, as though Mrs Fitzpatrick wanted to encourage anonymity. Men could be anything they wanted here and the girls could be anyone they wanted, which was why he came here. After the first time he had tried to make himself not go, but the memory of being able to have a woman like that stayed with him. It was the only way he could think of Helen.

He opened the door. The rooms were all sumptuous, huge beds and lavish bedhangings. It was a very expensive place. The girl was blonde, of course, and dressed in red underwear which would have looked ridiculous except that it didn't at Mrs Fitzpatrick's.

'Good evening.'

'Hello, stranger,' she said smiling.

'Have we met before?'

'Everybody knows you. The girls have all dyed their hair yellow, hoping you'd come back.'

'Whatever for?'

She stood up. She was very pretty and went in and out in all the right places.

'Because you tip better than everybody else. Lucky old me. You're the most generous man in Newcastle, my petal. When you've been here, somebody always has new dresses and new scent and oh, all sorts of things. Now it's my turn. Some men are mean, they're mean all over, but you . . . you're a star.'

Gil took off his jacket and took her into his arms and held her close and it was such a relief.

'My dad works for you,' she said.

'What does he do?'

'He's a joiner.'

'So what are you doing here?'

'I like it.'

'Nobody likes it.'

'It's my work. It's what I'm good at. Some days are awful and some days are . . . not so bad.'

Gil laughed.

'That sounds like work,' he said.

She was good. He insisted on knowing her name, which was Sylvia, but to him she was Helen. They were all Helen. He didn't drink much when he was there, but he needed a couple of whiskies to complete the illusion and then she was Helen, so beautiful in his arms. He was back there in that house with the narrow cobbled street outside and the smell of breadmaking in the alley in the early morning and the sweet scent of lemon flowers. She was all he would ever need or want there in the soft white sheets. He was making love to her and she was giving herself to him freely such as nobody had done since. It was only there that he acknowledged his life to be a nightmare. There was nothing in it beyond her, there never had been. He had never had his brother's love or his parents' affection; Rhoda had been all need and Abby had married a richer more eligible man than he was, but here Helen would give herself to him completely and it was all he needed.

He stayed the night with her and the illusion was complete. He could even come back into reality as far as to imagine the house that he had let go to ruin way back during those wonderful stolen nights when he had been happy. That brief time had altered everything, finished his life, but now he remembered why he had done it, that it had seemed worth it, that he had wanted nothing but her.

In the morning the magic died. She was just a pretty girl in bed with him and beyond them the Newcastle streets were busy from the early hours and the room seemed tawdry in the harsh morning light. He drew back the curtains and it was still raining.

'Do you have to go?' They always said that. Mrs Fitzpatrick had trained her girls well; they always pretended they were reluctant to see you go, even if they had wished you in hell several times during the night while you made good use of your money and their time.

'I should have been at work an hour ago.' He washed and dressed and she watched him from the bed, her bare shoulders so kissable and inviting. He would pay on the way out, but he always gave the girl some money. This time she recoiled from the wad of notes.

'I can't take all that!'

'It's only money.'

'Missus will think I've robbed you. I'll be on the street.'

'Go back to your old man then.'

'No fear.' She took the money and laughed and kissed him. Her breasts were so soft and her mouth was so warm that Gil wanted to stay. He walked out into the cold of the Newcastle streets and thought how unremittingly cruel life was, how spiteful. People were always going on about what a wonderful world it was, but it wasn't true. It was shite. The deserts burned you, the sea drowned you, the ice froze you, you dragged some kind of existence out of it all, taking the bread from another man's mouth if necessary, and then you died.

He walked to the office in the pouring rain. It was a long way and took most of the morning and he had had several meetings planned. His secretary would be having fifty fits. He reached it and shook the rain off his jacket and she came pale-faced to him.

'You have a board meeting and—'

'Yes, yes.'

'Mrs Surtees is here.'

Gil slicked back his shiny wet hair and went into his office. It looked so comfortable against the grey of the morning and the greyer river and the thick dark steel of the sky. The fire was burning, the lamps were lit and Abby sat there with her hands in her lap.

'You didn't come back,' she said, just above a whisper. 'I was so afraid when you didn't come back. I didn't mean it, I was just—'

Gil went back to the door and ordered some coffee and then he went to her.

'You thought I was going to shoot myself, yes?'

'No . . .'

She made him ashamed, sitting there with that anxious look on her white face. He got down beside her as he did with the children and said, 'I'm sorry, I should have understood better than that. It won't happen again.'

'But—'

'Go home. You look as though you haven't slept. We'll have some coffee and everything will be all right.'

She had been hurt too many times. Gil resolved not to do it again, but things changed. After that he quite often stayed out all night, there was nothing to go home for beyond the children. Sometimes he went back and had tea with them and read them a story, but more often he stayed at the office until late and then went either to Mrs Fitzpatrick's or drinking with John Marlowe. John seemed to have time on his hands unless he was working and Gil surmised that his home life was no better. Edwina was, John said, absorbed in the world of culture. He said it in such a funny way, as though Edwina had been caught in a mouse trap. She sat on committees and chaired meetings to do with the local arts and had other ladies to tea in the afternoons. She did not drink and abhorred smoking. She went to bed early and got up early.

'She's pure, blameless,' John said with a laugh.

One evening he persuaded Gil to go to the billiard hall with him. Gil didn't want to go. It was the same place that his brother and Toby had frequented in the old days but, since there was no alternative except the office, the whorehouse or the pub, he went. It hadn't altered. It was just the same with the big baize tables, the low lights focused on them and men standing around drinking beer. He had always liked the atmosphere, the talk. It didn't matter what you did or who you were here, you were accepted. You didn't even have to play, you could just be there.

To Gil's surprise, Toby was there with another young man. He seemed pleased to see Gil.

'If we weren't in public I would hug you.'

'I can get by without it,' Gil said.

'This is Everett. He's quite charming, not as handsome as some people but very talented.'

'What about Henrietta?'

'My dear boy, we have the perfect marriage, two lovely little boys and she is expecting another.'

'You amaze me.'

'Why should I? It's the simplest thing in the world, rather like threading a needle. You should try it some time.'

Gil laughed. He couldn't help asking, 'Do you see my brother?'

'Yes, often.'

'You do?'

'We're the best of friends, we always were. He's working for someone else. I think he likes it.'

'Nothing could be harder than working for my father,' Gil said grimly.

'He's not well. You should see him.'

'I don't need any advice.'

'Families,' Toby said with a sigh. 'Would you care to play with Everett?'

'Thank you, I've got John somewhere.'

'It's your loss.' Toby said and went off, smiling happily.

Abby relived that evening again and again. It was funny, she thought, how the smallest things mattered. Nothing had happened and yet Gil was different after that. She had not thought that he came home to her or for her. She had thought that his life carried on as it had before she arrived, but she could see now that that was not true. He had liked coming home to her. Now he didn't. The only reason he came back was for the children. All the charity work and all the time spent with Matthew and Georgina seemed dull because, even though she hadn't known, she had looked forward to him coming back. It was too late. He didn't give her the chance to redeem herself. He stayed at the distance where she had put him. She could smell perfume and whisky and cigars around him and she knew what that meant. Robert had always smelled like that, decadent, indulgent.

Gil went to work every day but Sunday and then he and John would go to the pub and come back at around three, very much the worse for beer, eat a huge dinner and then fall asleep. Many was the Sunday afternoon when the weather was fine and warm and the children were about, but Gil was no longer available to take them out. At first they complained, but it was in vain. He didn't hear them. Then they complained to Abby and she tried to talk to him and, though he listened and agreed, it didn't make any difference. Gil's life had taken on some pattern he imposed upon it and he didn't choose to alter it for anyone else. He would stay out all night on Saturday, go to the pub, have his dinner, sleep and go out with John in the evening. On Mondays and Tuesdays he stayed at the office until late, on Wednesdays he stayed out all night and on Thursdays and Fridays he played billiards. It was as rigid an existence as he had had before, but different. His room was always a complete mess now, though the maids didn't complain, they just cleared up all the clothes from the floor. The office at home was clean and empty because he didn't work there. It was like living with someone else and all for . . . Abby didn't know, for a few moments when he had tried to touch her and she had stopped him?

She had another problem. Matthew had started disappearing on Sunday afternoons. Gil didn't notice. When questioned he said blithely that he had been to the park playing cricket with the other boys. Since it wasn't far it seemed a perfectly plausible explanation, but Abby had the feeling that it wasn't true. It happened the next Sunday, too, so the one after that she left Georgina playing by the fire – it was not a fine day – and followed him. She had suspected what he was doing and so it proved. She had difficulty keeping up, though she thought she knew where he was going. She had to see him go in the front door. She kept back a little way but was close enough to see the short fat woman who embraced him. Abby walked slowly home through the poorer streets, uncertain what to do.

Matthew came back with glib tales of cricket. Gil

went out. Abby put Georgina to bed earlier than usual and she stood Matthew by the fire in the sitting room and said, 'I know where you went.'

She could see his small face deliberating. Was it worth a lie? Might it work?

'You went to see your grandparents.'

Matthew frowned. He looked a lot like Gil when he frowned.

'They are my family,' he said.

'And what about your father?'

'He doesn't care,' Matthew said bitterly. 'He doesn't care about anything except the shipyard. He never comes home and when he does he brings that man with him.'

The children, Abby thought, didn't like John Marlowe. They didn't say anything, but they called him 'that man' and blamed him for keeping Gil away from them. Georgina no longer ran along the hall at teatime; she no longer listened for Gil's footsteps. Like most other men Gil had compartmentalised his family, but then, she reasoned, they weren't his family. She was a leech and Georgina was her daughter. He kept them separate and mostly ignored them. He provided money and not his time or attention or regard and she had done it.

'What if he finds out?'

'Will you tell him?'

'What if I don't tell him and he finds out?'

'He won't. He doesn't notice anything.'

'If I promise not to tell him will you stop going?'

'I don't see why I should.'

Abby didn't see why he should either.

'Because he will be very angry.'

'He's never angry.'

The opposite was true, Abby thought now. Gil was permanently angry, it was just that he didn't shout or lose his temper or give any signs other than obscure ones.

'Matthew, your father doesn't like being crossed. A great many men have regretted it. I know he looks . . . even-tempered, but you are a very small boy and you must accept that your father would not like you to see your grandparents.'

Matthew became the small boy that she was speaking of and started to cry.

'My grandfather is ill. He stays in bed and they are poor and my father did it. He did it! He did! I hate him!'

He ran upstairs. Abby went after him.

'I hate him! I hate him!' In the room that was his own, Matthew shouted again. 'I know what happened. I know what he did. My grandfather told me. He's a horrible man. He's horrible and when I am older I shall go and live with Grandfather and Grandmother and never speak to him again!'

Abby didn't know what to say.

'What did your grandfather say your father did?'

'He made them poor. He took the house and the

business and everything and they have nothing and he – he—'

'What?'

Matthew looked straight at her, his dark eyes spilling tears.

'He killed my mother,' Matthew said.

Chapter Twenty-two

Gil couldn't remember her name. Was it Sylvia? It could have been Desirée – where had she got that name from? – no, no, it was Chloe. He was convinced that Mrs Fitzpatrick named her girls as one would name a new puppy. They were probably all called Ethel and you couldn't possibly call a girl Ethel in bed. Ethel and Agnes and Agatha. He was sweetly drunk. Not so drunk that he couldn't take her, just drunk enough so that her name didn't matter. He listened to her catching at her breath in the silence. It was three o'clock in the morning and the Newcastle streets were deserted. It was his favourite time. You could conquer the night by not asking it for sleep, he had found that. He no longer had to pretend that she was Helen and the vision had gone. He could not, even the worse for half a bottle of whisky, conjure the images of Spain in his mind so that they flooded the room. Helen was dead. Each night he knew it and it was so unforgiving. You couldn't distance yourself from such things, yet he was a long way from her now, so far that he could not remember what she tasted or felt like. The life that they had had was no closer than the way someone would see it in a book, with words and paper between you and it, nothing of substance, nothing there. She was gone from him as though someone had closed every door between them. All he had now was the work and the whisky and this girl whose slender thighs were parted for him. It was all there was and he had been a fool not to know it.

Gil felt nothing when he saw his brother from across the billiard hall. He had not expected that. A thousand times he had pictured them meeting again, what he would say, what he would do. All the years when they had not seen one another and not spoken he had missed Edward more than he missed Rhoda and differently from how he missed Helen. He missed him in a way that said 'it's your own fault'. He wanted to see his brother, but he did not feel as though he deserved to do so. It was hard, too, because Edward was always near, at first either at the works or at Bamburgh House and then a hundred times Gil thought he saw him in the Newcastle streets. He was always mistaken, but each day he looked just in case. Even to catch sight of him would somehow help, but until the night in the billiard hall he had not. They could have met face to face on any of the big streets. People who knew one another met every day;

the chance of it happening must be great, but they didn't meet. He couldn't understand that. At Toby's wedding he had not looked at Edward because of his parents, but in the billiard hall they were not there and it was different. Night after night in the loneliness he had dreamed that they met. The best dreams were where it had all been a mistake and it was the old days and he was at home. In fact, it was not the old days because there had not been a time when they were as happy as he saw them in his mind, when they were both married and their parents had smiled on them. No such time existed except in Gil's subconscious, but he would awaken and feel cheated and then guilty. He could not free himself from what he had done. He knew that he never would, that he must learn to live with the person he was because he had made too many mistakes and could not go back and undo them. Neither could he make reparation. There was nothing to do but go forward and hope to try to do better in the future. He was beyond that, too. He didn't want to do better, he wanted to drown in whisky and women and never sleep again while it was dark. No more of those nightmares which had Rhoda and Edward and Helen in them. Gil had discovered that if you could sleep during the hours of light you didn't have nightmares. It was as if they were not allowed. You could sleep a damned sight more peacefully when there were not deep shadows in the corners pulling faces at you.

His daytime dream was that Edward would come to him, forgive him, that everything would be made right, but when it happened it was not the lovely summer day that his mind built into it, it was late at night in a billiard hall and even though Edward must have been fully aware of Gil, he ignored him just as though he did not exist. Toby was with him, even came across, greeted him.

'My brother?' was all Gil could say.

'I don't think he wants to talk to you.'

'What is he doing here?'

'He comes here a lot, we always did.'

'With you?'

'Who else?'

'But . . . your family.'

'Don't be silly, old boy, they aren't old enough to play billiards,' and Toby departed, smiling.

'Do you want to go?' John asked, seeing his expression.

'Yes.'

'Mrs Fitzpatrick's?' John said when they got outside into the street.

'My God, yes.'

With Chloe in his arms, Gil felt happy.

'He didn't kill your mother, Matthew,' Abby had said. 'How could you think such a thing?'

'Grandfather said so.'

'Your father has looked after you all those years. Who are you going to believe first?'

'Grandfather and Grandmother have wanted to see me but my father wouldn't let me. You know that's true. Grandfather says that my father is a bad man.'

'He has done many good things,' Abby said. 'He helps people who have nothing. He gives them shelter and food and he gives thousands of jobs to men in Newcastle.'

'He doesn't like me.'

'That's not true.'

'Then why do I not see him?'

'He's very busy.'

'He's very busy going out to the pub with that man,' Matthew said.

'This must stop,' Abby said, 'and you must not go and see your grandfather and grandmother again. Do you hear me? If you disobey me I shall smack your bottom until you can't sit down. Do you understand me?'

'You can't do that!'

'Try,' Abby threatened.

She went to see Charlotte and she could see by the look on Charlotte's face that she knew Abby had found out. The house was tiny and gloomy and William upstairs in bed.

'What's the matter with him?' she asked.

'I don't know, he just isn't well.'

Charlotte's furniture, what she had left of it, was far

too big for such a house and dwarfed each room. It looked incongruous, towering there. The walls were painted brown; the fire smoked; the windows were tiny and from next door came the sound through the thin walls of somebody having an argument. How had Charlotte come so low and did Gil really want his parents like this? She couldn't believe that he did, that he had brought them to this and would let them survive there as best they could. She took Abby upstairs and Abby had to go even though she didn't want to see William. The man in the bed looked old and grey and smaller, but he said, 'What are you doing letting his whore in here?' and closed his eyes.

Abby said nothing until they had gone back down the steep, narrow stairs again.

'Do you think that of me?'

'Everybody does,' Charlotte said.

'It's not true. Just because we're living in the same house . . . You know why I'm here. Matthew is not to come here again. If Gil finds out, I don't know what will happen.'

'What more can he do to us?' Charlotte said simply. 'We love the boy. We have nothing.'

'I have told him that he is not to come back and if he does it will be the worse for him. If he does turn up here, you are to send him home. Are you listening to me, Charlotte?'

'No, why should I?'

'William has poisoned his mind against Gil and Gil doesn't deserve that.'

'It was only the truth. He won't let us see Matthew, has told him stories about us.'

'That's not true. You must send him home.'

The following Sunday Abby tried not to let Matthew out. Unfortunately he went anyway, but she followed him and banged on Charlotte's door. When nobody answered she walked in, searched the lower storey and, finding nothing there, went upstairs and dragged Matthew out of William's bedroom. They couldn't stop her. William couldn't get out of bed and Charlotte wept. Matthew resisted. He twisted and turned, he kicked her and thumped her and when she got him into the street it was worse. It took her a long time to get him home and her patience and temper were worn out by then. She smacked him until he howled.

Unfortunately Gil chose that precise time to come home. Sober as water and neat as a new penny he looked gravely at her as she walloped his child, the first time that anybody had done so, Abby knew. He didn't interfere; he left her to it on the sofa in the sitting room. She sent Matthew to bed, put him there herself and then she went downstairs, listening to Matthew's sobs beginning to quieten. She went back into the sitting room, hoping that Georgina's presence would protect her, but Gil came in.

'Georgina would you mind going to your room for a little while?' he said.

'Have I done something too?'

'No, I just want to talk to your mother. You can go to the kitchen if you would rather and see Hannah.'

'She isn't there,' Georgina pointed out as she left the room.

Abby wished she could go to her room too.

'I wasn't expecting you,' she said.

'Obviously.'

'It wouldn't have made any difference. He knew what would happen, I had already told him.'

'He's seven,' Gil said.

'He understood perfectly.'

'Are you going to tell me what he did?'

'Why, are you going to unsmack him if you don't agree?'

Gil looked hard at her.

'Tell me.'

Abby gave in.

'He went to see your parents, not once but several times and I told him not to do it again. He lied to me and then he disobeyed me and your father has told him that you killed Helen and he hates you. Is that enough?'

'It's ample,' Gil said.

'I thought it might be. However, if you spent less time

screwing women and drinking whisky and playing billiards, I daresay things might not have come to this.'

Abby had to leave the room because she had never smacked a child before in her life and she felt sick and wanted to cry. She was bruised and battered from trying to get Matthew home while he kicked and punched her. Luckily there was nobody in the kitchen, it being Sunday afternoon, so she busied about there, instead of crying. She made some tea and sat quietly at the table, pretending to eat chocolate cake which had been made early that day and was still fresh, and drinking three cups of tea before she could even think of moving anywhere.

After a while Gil came in. She made more tea and cut him a piece of chocolate cake and they sat in the kitchen as they had never done before. He ate his cake. Men were so insensitive; they could eat even if somebody was dying.

'Did you see my father?'

'He called me your whore.'

'How did he look?'

'He looked defeated. He's old and tired and you've beaten him and now I've beaten your child. No wonder we are all so happy.'

'You think I ought to take Matthew to see them?'

'I think you ought to allow him to go. I think you should arrange for Helen's parents to see him if they want to. You could write to them. After all, they can hardly blame Matthew for what happened. He is the only grandchild any of them has. How could they not want to see him?'

'Because he's mine?'

'That's not his fault.'

Gil took a deep breath.

'All right, I'll let him go. Will you take him?'

'There's nobody else,' Abby said.

Gil didn't write. He went to Durham the following day to see whether he could locate Helen's parents, but it was as he had feared. They had moved. The people who were living in their house didn't know where they had gone and neither did anybody else that Gil could find. Determined, he travelled to Oxford, but they had not gone back there and he knew that if they were in London he was wasting his time because they could be anywhere. He came home and went back to work. He tried to talk to Matthew, but every time he walked into the room, his child got up and walked out. He caught hold of Matthew once and tried to get the child to talk to him, but Matthew just looked past him.

'I have said that you can go. What more do you want me to do?'

Matthew continued looking past him, so Gil let him loose.

*

On the Sunday Georgina stayed at home. Gil made sure he was there to stay with her and Abby took a silent Matthew across the streets of Jesmond to where his grandparents were living. Abby had sent a note to say that he could come and had received nothing in reply, but she assumed that Charlotte would be agreeable. Where else did they have to go on Sundays? She would have left him at the door when Charlotte opened it, but Charlotte's distressed face told her this would not do. She ushered them inside to the fire and then she looked tearfully at Abby.

'William died last night,' she said.

Life could not be so unkind, Abby thought. It could not do this to them. Matthew ran to his grandmother and huddled in against her skirts and she held him there with one pudgy hand.

'Oh Charlotte, I am sorry.' Abby's mind did swirling things. How on earth could she ever tell Gil that his father had died without seeing him and that he had given his permission too late.

'Did Edward see his father before he died?'

'Of course. He lives just around the corner. He's so good. He comes every day. He has a good position, you know, he works for Blade's. They aren't as big a firm as we were, but they turn out solid ships, William always said so.'

'You didn't think that perhaps—'

'Abby, you know William. I did suggest that he ought to see Gil, but he wouldn't. They're so alike, so unforgiving. What am I to do?'

'I'll talk to Gil.'

'No. I couldn't. I shall manage.'

'You have a family.'

Charlotte managed a wry smile.

'They're as badly off as I am in that great tomb of a house they have. I never thought to go back there. The house takes everything and it's so uncomfortable and so cold and . . . I don't want to go there.'

Abby gave her some money. Charlotte tried to refuse it, but it was only politeness.

'Leave the boy with me a little while. I'll bring him back. Gil isn't there, is he?'

'He is at the moment, but—'

'I'll bring him to the back door and then I don't have to see him.'

Abby walked slowly home, wishing that it was four times as far. She even went round by the dene, but she knew that Gil was expecting her just to drop Matthew off and come back, so she could not be too long. Even so, she lingered. Gil was not a happy man, she knew that. Happy men did not behave like he was behaving. Happy men, Abby thought savagely, did not go to bed with whores. She had a sure idea that if a man was bedding a woman at home, a woman he liked and desired,

he would not go out to pay for it, not unless there was
something seriously wrong with him. And that was her
fault. He was a man. If she had gone to bed with him he
would have stayed with her. Men were not so complicated. All they needed was warmth and time, like bread.
Robert had taken everything from her, at least that was
how it felt. She had nothing left for Gil and he had desperately needed somebody. She didn't want to be
touched, not in that way. Comfort would have been
nice, but men were not much good at comfort alone, not
until they were very old presumably. He had gone to his
work, like her father had done, but he was much younger
than her father and had found time to fit in whisky, billiards and women. What would he do when he found
out that his father was dead?

She went reluctantly home and he was hovering in the
hall.

'You were a hell of a long time. What were you doing?
What did my father say? Were they pleased? How long is
Matthew staying?'

'Come into the sitting room.'

What difference that would make she couldn't think,
but somehow it seemed better than the hall. She knew
Gil very well, but she didn't know how he was going to
react.

'Gil—' She looked up at him and she didn't have to
tell him. 'Your father—'

'No. No, not now, not now. No.'

'He died last night.'

'Of what?' Gil said, as though this was important, as though it could not have happened.

'I don't know, he just did.'

'No, he can't have done, not like that. He would fight, he would—'

'He's been ill for some time.'

'Nobody told me. I didn't know. No, I did know. I didn't think . . . Couldn't I have seen him? Would my mother have let me see him?'

Abby lied valiantly.

'I think the end was very quick.'

'No. You said he had been ill for some time. It couldn't have been. Was my brother there?'

Abby cursed Gil's quick mind.

'Was Edward there?' he persisted.

'I really don't know.'

'Yes, you do.' He was watching her closely. 'My brother was there. My father said goodbye to him. My brother was there. He didn't want me there, did he? He didn't want me there. And my mother . . . my mother didn't.'

Abby tried to take him into her arms, but he wouldn't let her.

'What about Matthew?'

'Your mother wanted him to stay and it seemed sensible,' Abby said, trying to be normal.

'Are you going for him?'

'In a little while, yes. You were going out with John, weren't you? Why don't you go?'

Gil went. There seemed nothing else to do, she was right. But when they went to the pub he wasn't thirsty and, although John talked to him and especially about his father, Gil couldn't hear. They went to Mrs Fitzpatrick's, but he walked out. All he wanted to do was go home, but when he got there he didn't want to be there either. Abby was still up, she was sitting by the fire.

'Matthew came home?'

'Yes.'

'What about my mother? I was thinking about her. What will she do?'

'Edward will take care of her.'

'Edward?'

'Yes. He has a house you know, not far away.'

'I'm sure he does. I see him sometimes, in the billiard hall. He's got very fat. He takes after my mother.'

Gil went to bed. He stole into Matthew's room and watched his son sleeping. He knew now all the things that were unholy to know, all the things that if God had cared about anybody, he would have told them before they were born instead of letting them go crashing about destroying everything. The trouble was that you had to live a life and lose everything, to suffer and then to die, yet you didn't know that when you set out. You didn't know how to lose everything, so God demonstrated it to you. This was the last thing he had to lose, the very last person, so he made a bargain with God: if Matthew should leave him he would die, he would deliberately die. He would take away the gift that God had given him; he would take it away to punish God for expecting so very much of anybody. He would cut off that life so that he would never again see the tide full on Bamburgh beach.

He went to bed and his mind gave him the good times. It was laughable. There hadn't been any good times. His mind would not be stopped, it dredged itself. Sick sentiment gave him the light in his father's eyes the day that the *Northumbria* was launched. He remembered how proud his father had been of him the day that John Marlowe had signed the contract for the *Northumbria*. He thought of drinking brandy with his father and how William had given up port because Gil didn't like it, the hand on his shoulder and the way William had bragged to his friends about 'my son, the genius'. He wished again and again it could be that night when his father had said casually to the butler that from now on there would be only brandy after dinner because that was what Gil preferred. And he wished that it could have been different. He wished more than anything that his father had even just once told him that he cared. He never had and he never would. William had gone to his grave without saying it and he wished that he had never been born. William had not loved him. He could have plucked the moon and the stars down from the sky; he could have prevented the sun from rising and the night from falling and William would not have loved him for it. The magic that he had made in ships was admirable and William had admired it and called upon other people to admire it, but it was not love. And yet he had given Gil so much, all the things which his own father had not given him: prosperity, security, education, high position and the chance to succeed in a business which his father had built so very high. Gil had destroyed that business and his father's house and his father.

Chapter Twenty-three

Gil did not go to the funeral. Abby could not help being relieved. She had had the feeling that if he went, there would be trouble of some kind and more trouble was beyond what he could bear. Besides, after all this time it would be an empty gesture and he could afford none of those. He had been unpredictable. She had thought he would go to some whore and stay there maybe for weeks, or that he would get drunk and go on being drunk, which was what Robert would have done, but he didn't. He kept on going to work each day, he came back at teatime and he was silent. It was the silence which irked Abby. Gil had been silent for most of his life and quiet for the rest of it.

The funeral was very small. It seemed sad that a man who had helped to shape Tyneside's future should be ignored now because he had failed. Failure was not allowed in this world of business and being poor was not to be thought of; indeed, people thought it was catching. They stayed away, all the people who had money and influence, they did not come to see Charlotte through her ordeal and, although for years Abby had thought Charlotte silly and trivial, she felt sorry for her that day. Money had meant everything to Charlotte because until she had met William she had so little of it. Now she had little of it again. Abby resolved to ask Charlotte how badly off she really was, or whether Edward would look after her. He was much in evidence that day, putting his arm around her, supporting her in the almost empty church. No more than a dozen people had come to see William laid to rest. Abby was ashamed of the people of Newcastle that they could treat anybody in such a way.

Charlotte cried throughout the service. Abby sang as loudly as she could because Gil was not there and because her father was not there and because William was not there and she felt angry because Charlotte had been let down by other people.

Afterwards they went back to Charlotte's horrid little house, where somebody had provided tea and cake. Abby couldn't swallow a crumb. She thought of Gil at work. She had kept waiting for him to drop to pieces. Nothing had happened, or maybe it was just that people dropped to pieces each in his own way and Gil had done so without anybody noticing. You couldn't watch somebody's heart break. Abby scorned that as silly and she knew that it was not what she meant, it was just that people were silently desperate. That was what Gil was like and she didn't think there was anything to be done about it. He had destroyed William, had wanted to destroy him, had wanted to take some measure of revenge, but William had died and there was no revenge as complete as someone's death. He had seen his father as young, as able to fight him, as able to come back from his corner like the prizefighter he had always been. He had not known, or had not chosen to acknowledge, when his father was beaten. To Gil he was the same man he had been when Gil was a little boy and defenceless. He was mighty and powerful; he was not in a wooden coffin in the earth, finished and done for.

She came back to a silent house. Hannah had taken the children out for the day. The last thing Abby had wanted was for Matthew to demand to be taken to the funeral. Funerals were not the place for children, at least this one was not for him; but after he was told that his grandfather had died, Matthew reacted as Gil would have done and said nothing. He did not cry or ask questions and when she had suggested that Hannah should take them out for the day, he seemed eager to go. Abby didn't blame him. It was what she wanted to do, to pretend that none of it had happened, that they did not have the future to face.

Hannah and the children duly came home and they

had something to eat and Abby put them to bed early and read them a story. Georgina fell asleep in the middle of the story, worn out from her day by the sea – Hannah had taken them to Tynemouth and Georgina had spent a considerable amount of time excitedly relating her day to Abby. William's death did not touch her at all; Abby was glad of that. Matthew must not have mentioned William that day and Georgina did not know him. It had been a good day out to her. She had seen the gulls and been on the beach and been bought sweets. It was all she needed to make her happy. Abby wished that adults could be like that, needing so little to produce happiness. Matthew needed more. She sat down on the bed and cuddled him. He drew back slightly. Abby thought he would probably not forgive her for smacking him and she didn't blame him.

'Are you all right?'

'What will happen to Grandmother?'

Abby would have been interested to know.

'I expect she will go and live with your Uncle Edward.'

'Couldn't she come and live with us? I suppose Daddy wouldn't let her.'

Matthew's dislike for Gil over the past weeks was making things worse.

'He would if she wanted to. She is his mother.'

'I don't know much about mothers and you certainly aren't like one. You hit people who are smaller than you.'

'I didn't know what else to do. You were so bad.'

'Was I? I'm like my father then, aren't I?' And Matthew drew away, turned over and pulled up the bedcovers.

Abby went wearily downstairs, the truth ringing in her ears. She asked Hannah for some wine. At least that was one thing that had improved since she came here. There was none of that thin vinegary stuff that Gil thought was wine. It was thick and red and went down wonderfully. She had two glasses before Gil came back for dinner, and felt a lot better.

They ate. At least, he ate. Abby couldn't manage a single mouthful. He didn't ask her about the funeral; he didn't drink any wine. He retreated to the office. Abby sat there, drinking wine until her hands shook. She didn't hear the knocker. The first inclination she had of anybody was when Hannah came through into the sitting room, saying, 'Mr Edward Collingwood's here.'

Abby stared, sobered immediately, said, 'Bring him in here,' and went across the hall into the office.

Gil didn't look up, he was working.

'Edward's here,' Abby said. He looked up then, stared at her, through her. 'I've had Hannah put him into the sitting room. Do you want me there?'

'No, it's all right,' he said.

He went out. Abby stood leaning against the desk in the office, shaking.

*

Gil was used to what his brother looked like, had spent so many hours watching him covertly from across the billiard hall. That place had been a sanctuary at one time and, more than that, it was the place where his brother had shown him friendship. Gil knew very well that the best thing brothers could be to one another was friends. Those first days at the billiard hall he had loved Edward like never before, had been a new person in that he had thought his brother cared for him. In his best hours he could imagine them as old men, sitting around the fire talking about their lives, comparing the good times and the bad and speaking of people they had known, and having their grandchildren around them. He thought that they would grow more like one another as they became older. He had heard of brothers doing that, of them starting the same sentence in the same way, pausing at the same time, laughing together. It would seem a nauseating similarity to the young, but he had for so long wanted something from his family that would show their regard, that he had loved Edward too much. Expectations of that kind were never fulfilled, yet he had believed it so. He knew now that he had been Edward's alibi for the kind of love which was not acceptable. Edward could not go home and tell his parents that he loved another man. What kind of society, what frightened people would deny a love like that? And the struggle against it had been costly.

His stupid heart was hopeful, was ready to begin again, to draw near. He reminded himself that there was no place to go here, nowhere near his brother was there a space for him.

'I thought you might have come to the funeral,' Edward said.

'Don't you think that would have been a little hypocritical?'

'Hypocrisy has its place at these affairs.' He paused for a moment and then said, 'I wanted to see you this once before I go. I'm leaving. Strange how it took my father's death to liberate me. Before, somehow, I couldn't go. Of course there was money. I've been keeping them for a long time.'

Gil's insides suddenly had a pair of iron grips around them, the pain was so bad that he could hardly speak.

'Where are you going?'

'France.' Edward smiled faintly. 'We always did intend to. Toby has found us a house not far from Bordeaux. A few acres, a big garden.'

Gil could not believe this.

'Toby?'

'Are you like everyone else and deceived? How could you be with what you know?'

'But he has children, sons and a wife.'

'It's no good,' Edward said. 'No matter how hard you try, it doesn't work.'

'He'll lose his family, his parents and . . . everybody.'

'That's what passion does, isn't it? We have tried so hard and now we can't try any longer.'

Gil couldn't think of anything to say.

'Wine, decent bread, a few flowers and Tobe's happy. The rest was just from wanting to please other people and there's never any good in that. I won't be back. I just wanted to see Matthew one last time.'

You could be jealous of a child, Gil discovered, even if that child was your son and you loved him. Somewhere inside he was shouting, 'Me, me!' but no words came out. Words were weapons that he didn't know how to use. He was afraid of them, they could undo you in seconds.

'I haven't forgiven you.' Edward said this with a smile and Gil was only glad that he had no heart left to break, there were so many pieces by now that the damage was limited. Sometimes he thought comfortably that middle age would find him smug because there would be nothing left.

'I didn't expect you to,' he said.

'I know that you'll look after Matthew. Can I see him?'

Gil took him upstairs to where the child was sleeping, but a strange feeling began to gnaw at his insides. It was a familiar, sick feeling as when something was about to go wrong. When it happened you felt as though you should have known, as though you should have looked around you, located it before it got that far. Edward spent a little time upstairs, seeing Matthew at his best. Then they came back down again and stood in the sitting room. Edward looked at him and the gladness that Gil had felt when Edward had arrived evaporated.

'I did love Helen,' Edward said. 'I know you think I didn't, that I used her like some kind of shield because of Toby, but I didn't. We were just friends then, at least I liked to think so, wanted to. I think he cared for me differently than I cared for him. There are many different kinds of love. I did love her. I didn't really marry her because our parents wanted it, I craved her. And she was pleased enough with me until I brought her to Bamburgh House and she saw you.'

Gil looked into the darkness beyond the windows and remembered how Helen had looked when he had first seen her.

'After she saw you, my love affair was over,' Edward said.

'No.'

'It was an instant thing, wasn't it? I couldn't have been deceived about what you felt for one another. You loved her from the moment you set eyes on her.'

'Yes, but it wasn't—' Gil said and stopped.

'Wasn't what?'

'I can't explain. It wasn't the first time we'd met, or it seemed not to be.'

'Where had you seen her before?'

'I don't know.' He couldn't tell Edward about the house in Spain, or how he thought of their past that way.

'That's ridiculous, Gil.'

He sounded so normal, so natural, as though they had not been estranged for years and Gil's mind stored up the remark in case his brother should not be civil to him again this side of the grave.

'Are we talking about other lives here?' Edward said sceptically.

'No, of course not.'

'Then what?'

'I don't know. It ruined my life too!'

Edward pondered for a moment or two until Gil regretted the outburst.

'On our wedding night she wouldn't have me and all the nights that followed I wasn't you. I longed to be you.'

'She said you didn't want her, that you wanted to be away from her.'

'I had no choice. I shouldn't have gone through with the marriage, but I thought it was one of those passing fancies that women have and the settlements were all sorted out by then.'

'She loved you!'

'But she went to bed with you. Yes? My wife was a virgin when you had her, was she not?'

'God help me. I was second best.'

'You were never second in anything,' Edward said flatly. 'You don't believe in being second, you've proved that again and again. Don't you see yourself as you are? You're totally without principles. You will do whatever is required to reach what you choose. Your mind is with your – your reckless ambition and your taste for revenge. Even Abby. Look at her. You could have married her.'

'She wouldn't have me.'

'Was this before you seduced my wife or afterwards? Look at yourself, Gil, what success, what achievements and what cost. And as for Father, you took away everything, even his dignity.'

'You hated him too.'

'Not sufficiently to make him watch the house he loved fall into ruin and the gates of his shipyard locked against him. I didn't reduce him to taking handouts from his elder son, or dying in a mean, shabby hovel. How could you hate anybody that much?'

'He turned me out.'

'Oh yes, now we come to it. You bedded your brother's wife, deceived your own wife and each of them in her way killed herself over it.'

'No!'

'Yes, they did. But Helen won. Her child lives. And you think that he's yours.'

The sickness was a headache now and a dizziness, but Gil said calmly, 'Are you going to tell me that he isn't?'

'No.' Edward looked clearly at him. 'The plain fact is that my wife had you and me together, if you'll forgive the bluntness. Contrary to what you believe, I do like women, I have enjoyed their bodies and even though my wife chose to give herself to you, she was so beautiful and I wanted her so badly that I took what she offered me. How naive you were. We were both bedding her. I don't think she knew whose child it was. I certainly don't.'

'But you let me think . . . and you let me take him. You let me take the blame. You watched Father put me out because of it. You let me leave with him. If you thought he was yours, why didn't you fight for him?'

Edward's gaze was patient.

'You're the most capable person I've ever met. You had more to offer.'

'I had nothing!'

'I knew that if you believed he was yours, you would move heaven and earth for him. And you have. He's happy and that's all I care about. How happy would he have been if there had been more fighting, if the truth had come out? How could he have been shielded from it all? It was bad enough that he should lose his mother. He needed a solid background. You've provided that very well. I have no intention of upsetting things and I'm about to make the life for myself that I want. I have Toby. In a way it's so much easier to love another man, and he loves me as no one else in my life ever has, completely and to the exclusion of everyone else. All I want is a little peace. I owe you nothing, you took what you could. I have to go. Toby is at my house making a daube, practising his French cooking. The smell of it will be halfway down the street by now. I don't suppose we shall ever meet again. I hope not. Goodbye, Gil.'

When he had gone, Gil went to bed. He pulled a pillow to him and closed his eyes and willed sleep to come to him. At least it was night, at least it was cold, at least it was October. He couldn't have borne that it should be summer and the stones of the house should be baked hard and the white curtains should catch the breeze beyond the bed and billow like sails upon the water.

Chapter Twenty-four

That autumn Gil went out to the country to see Bamburgh House and was ashamed of his handiwork. The house itself looked affronted. Birds flew in and out of the empty windows. Inside, everything was wet and in bad repair. It looked worse in the winter weather. The lawns were knee high; the bare trees were as black as mourning and there was about it an unnatural silence such as he had heard only in graveyards before now. He had to suppress the desire to close the outside doors in some futile form of protection or reparation. He wished that he had not gone there and when he went back to his neat house in Jesmond images of the house haunted him. Even at work he could not put from his mind the sadness which he felt. He no longer remembered with bitterness being thrown out of there or the bad way that his father had treated him. All he could remember was standing in the drawing room and hearing Helen play the piano. He had had to stop himself running toward the sounds.

He wanted to pull it down so that all evidence of her would be gone, but he couldn't. His inclination was to repair it and go and live there. It was, he knew, the only way in which he would get his mother out of that awful little hovel where his father had died. She insisted on living there as though it were some kind of shrine, rather than a gloomy little street house. Gil gave her money, but she mourned William and insisted that she could not move since Edward would be coming back. There was no point in telling her that he would not do so. She believed that he would and she would not listen to the gossips who said that Edward had run off with Toby. Her son could not have done such a thing and therefore he had not. She told everybody that Edward had endured a dreadful life because of what Gil and Helen had done, that it had been too much for him and he had gone, but he would come back. Many other people did not believe that men could do such things; his mother was not alone in her ideas. They could not have run away together, they had both gone but they had gone differently, separately. The Emorys, anxious to stem the talk, agreed with this and put about a tale that their son had worked too hard and that his mind was affected. Insanity was the easier option.

Charlotte would not see Gil. He did go once, but she would not answer the door and took to shouting at people through the letter-box. After that, when Abby went to see her, the doors would be locked and the house in darkness. Abby knew that Charlotte rarely went out. She thought that people were speaking about her and laughing on the streets. Abby tried to persuade her to come to them, but she would not move.

'There is one thing which would work,' Abby said, confronting him in the little office one November evening when the rain had poured down the windows for two days.

'What's that?'

'You could take her to live at Bamburgh House again.'

He was surprised at her perception.

'She wouldn't.'

'I think she would.'

'It's in very bad repair.'

'You could put it right. You have nothing else to do with your money. I think you owe her that.'

'I owe her nothing!' He got up. He didn't intend to, but he couldn't talk about this calmly.

'What will you do then? Let her stay there and go out of her mind, because that's what she will do.'

'Always straight to the point,' he said savagely.

'Don't you care about her at all, not even a little?'

'No!'

'Then why did you let her see Matthew?'

'That was for his sake.'

'He's not going to think very highly of you if you don't help her.'

'I don't want to go back there.'

'I think you should.'

Gil looked at her. She hadn't changed from being a young girl. Her eyes were so blue and intense and there was that strength, that steeliness, which insisted on doing the right thing.

'I'll do it on one condition,' he said.

'Which is?'

'That you come with me.'

'Me?' Abby's blue eyes rounded. 'I'm not going to live there. I always hated it. Besides, I love this house. Are you trying to tell me that you can't afford to keep two houses?'

'No.'

'Well then, I shall stay here.'

'Then so will I.'

'Gil, this is my home. I was born here. I spent the happiest childhood anyone could have. My mother and father both died in this house. I love it.'

'Then we won't go anywhere,' he said.

Abby couldn't move him. She knew it was wrong. She tried telling herself that it was his fault alone that his mother was behaving as though she should be locked up, but as the days went by and all she could get from Charlotte was crying from the far side of the front door, she lay awake at night worrying about the responsibility. All she knew was that she had been unhappy away from here, that all those supposedly exciting times in London and Venice and France and all the other places Robert had taken her were times when she had longed to be here in Newcastle. She could not give up this house for anybody, much less for a woman she had always despised as weak and stupid.

Even Matthew could not get his grandmother to open the door. All the contact they had was that if they left groceries outside, Charlotte would take them in. She allowed no visitors and she did not leave the house. Abby looked around at the four walls she had chosen instead of Charlotte and despised herself. She despised Gil even more for making such terms and didn't talk to him, but when he did come home, which wasn't often, he had missed tea and had to eat separately. Abby, from politeness' sake, had to endure his company and make conversation and not throw her wine glass at him across the table as she longed to do.

'Couldn't we keep the house on?' she asked eventually.

'What would be the point?'

'It's always better to own property. We could rent it out.'

He looked at her across the table.

'Have you ever considered what you might do if your parents really died?' he said.

Abby went white; she could feel herself.

'I don't know what you mean,' she said.

'Yes, you do. You're keeping them alive by staying here. You still have your mother's books and your father's cufflinks and—'

'Those are keepsakes. I've changed a lot of things in the house and you shouldn't say such a thing!'

'Have you ever loved anybody as much as you loved them?'

'No, I haven't and if you had an ounce of decency you wouldn't hold your mother to ransom over something as stupid as a house! You waited until your father died before you did anything. Are you going to wait until she does?'

'I don't know, am I?'

'You're low!' Abby was on her feet with temper. 'Low and devious! I don't think you care about anything, you unscrupulous bastard!'

Gil sat there as though somebody was being rude at a dinner party and it was nothing to do with him.

'When I think of what you used to be like,' Abby said breathlessly, 'when I think—'

'Don't think too long,' Gil said, and he got up and walked out.

Abby lasted three more days and then she went to Charlotte's house, shouted her name through the letter-box and, when she could hear her breathing from the other side of the door, she said, 'What if I told you that you could go back to Bamburgh House?'

There was no answer.

'Charlotte? Can you hear me?'

There was another short pause and then Charlotte said, 'I can't though, can I?'

'If Gil had it repaired you could. Would you like that?'

'We were happy there when the children were little and we were young. We were happy. We had everything. I had jewellery and furs and beautiful gowns from London. And we had lots of servants and grey horses and . . . William was a good husband to me. I miss him.'

This had not occurred to Abby. Nobody thought of William like that, but his wife obviously did.

'I couldn't live there alone.'

'We would come with you.'

The sentence was out. Abby heard it and knew there was no way in which she could retract it. There was silence from beyond the door. She wished that Charlotte would refuse, prayed that she would. Abby thought all that was keeping her upright was the fact that she was living in the house that she loved so much. She could not give that house up for Charlotte, there was no reason why she should, yet things were not good at home. Gil had given up any pretence at family life and was coming home less and less. Abby was haunted with the way that Gil had behaved as they had grown further apart. She tried to reason with herself. They were not married; she was not responsible for him, but since Edward had left and his father had died, Gil seemed barely to notice anyone or anything beyond work and whatever he did when he was not at work and not at home. And Abby knew very well what he was doing. She had to tell herself not to panic, that Gil was not weak like Robert. He would not ruin them financially no matter what vices he took up and he would not take a gun to himself; he wasn't made like that. William had been strong in some ways and Gil was like him. She was quite certain that, no matter what happened, Gil would be at his desk at work by seven in the morning. She wished sometimes that she could just go over to make sure that he was, because more and more he didn't come back at night.

The day after she had made this announcement to Charlotte she actually tested this theory. Gil hadn't come back that night and she had wanted to talk to him and not wanted to. Wanted to win and so, early the next morning, she got up and made her way across the town to the number two yard. It was the big place and he spent most of his time there. Work was fully started when she reached the office. The clerk in the outside office looked surprised to see her, but ushered her inside without a word. There was Gil looking as though he had gone home early the evening before, had dinner and gone early to bed. He was bright-eyed, immaculately neat and scrupulously polite. Abby did not know how to get past this kind of defence. She wondered where he kept his clean clothes, whether whores were offering a laundry service as well as the other kind these days. Nobody who had drunk brandy half the night and screwed some little bitch into the mattress could look like that, Abby reasoned.

'Coffee?' he said, having greeted her.

She shook her head.

'Tea?'

'No! I didn't come here for . . .'

He looked at her attentively.

'I want to talk to you,' Abby said. 'When are you coming back?'

'Six o'clock?'

'No, I mean when are you really coming back?'

He didn't look at her. He leaned back against the front of the desk and regarded the rug in front of it with rapt concentration.

Abby sighed.

'I have suggested to your mother that we should go and live at Bamburgh House and she has agreed. If I come with you and give up my father's house, will you come home?'

He stood for a few moments before he said, 'All right.'

Abby only remembered to breathe when she had left the office.

It cost her a good deal to say goodbye to the house she had loved so much. She felt wretched, but there was nothing practical to be done. Gil sold the house quickly, presumably in case she should change her mind and as though he had had buyers waiting in the wings. Once it did not belong to them, Abby was downhearted and wished to be gone before she could bear no more. Charlotte came to live with them and Matthew spent a lot of time with his grandmother. He and Georgina stayed up for dinner, although Georgina was inclined to nod before it was over. One such night, just before they moved, Matthew surprised Abby by saying, 'All my friends are going away to school soon. Do you think I might be able to do that?'

Abby knew that Gil wanted to be friends with his son again, but the colour drained from his face.

'Boarding school?' Abby said, to fill the gap.

'I could be in a proper cricket team and Harry English says they have great larks in the dorm after lights out. If I don't go I shall be left here for weeks and weeks and they'll be coming back telling me all about it, and Harry's brother, Timothy, is going.'

Gil said nothing.

'When is Timothy going?' Abby said.

'Next autumn. Could we go and look at his school?'

Abby glanced across the table at Gil. She knew that Matthew would not appeal directly to Gil.

'Grandma thinks it's a good idea,' Matthew urged.

'Education is very important,' Charlotte said. 'William always thought so. Boarding school is good for boys. It makes them independent and strong.'

Gil let the silence empty and widen. Luckily the meal was over. Everyone left the table. Gil went into the little office and closed the door. Abby deliberately made herself not go after him. She had no place in there and if he had wanted conversation, she reasoned, he would not have gone in. She put the children to bed. She occupied Charlotte until it was late and then she went to bed. It was a thankless thing to do. Sleep did not arrive. She put on a dressing-gown and went back downstairs. Softly she opened the door of the office. He looked up.

'Maybe we could go out and look at the house sometime?' she said.

Gil sat back in his chair.

'Is it nearly finished?' Abby said.

He stood up.

'I've got the plans somewhere.'

'You didn't tell me.'

'I didn't think you were interested.'

'Show me.'

He located rolled-up papers, which she had assumed were work, and spread them across the desk. Abby went and peered hard at the different drawings, the front of the house, the sides, the back.

'It doesn't look the same.'

'It isn't meant to.'

'You took the columns away!'

'They weren't actually doing anything important, holding anything up, they were just . . . decorative.'

'That's a matter of opinion.'

He smiled.

'It makes it look entirely different,' Abby said.

'This is the inside. We've moved the kitchen and chopped up the hall here—'

'I rather liked the hall. Has your mother seen these?'

'No.'

'Bathrooms!' Abby said.

'And proper heating. It was never warm.'

'I'd like to see it.'

He rolled up the plans.

'You don't have to humour me,' he said. 'Matthew can go away to school if he wants to.'

'That wasn't why—' Abby began and then stopped.

'Maybe you should go to bed.'

Abby's face went hot with temper, but she controlled it.

'I'd like to see the house.'

'You'll see it when it's finished.'

'Did you do all the designing alterations yourself?'

'Of course.'

'Did you pull down the bedroom where we slept the night, or the bedroom where you spent the nights with Helen, or with Rhoda? Do you seriously believe you can go back there and live after that?'

'It's all different,' he said. 'If you'd looked closely at the plans, the upstairs is altered beyond recognition.'

'And you won't remember?'

'I've done all my remembering. I'm going to go back there and have it for mine now.'

'Isn't that what your father did?'

Gil didn't answer that.

'It was your idea,' he said.

They moved in the middle of the summer which helped, she thought. It was one of the hardest things that Abby had done because the house in Jesmond had been sold. She felt like a deserter. The garden was full of all the flowers that her mother had loved and she was aware that once she left, she would not be able to come back again. It felt so cruel to leave this place that she loved and move to one that she despised. The last few days, while they were packing, she barely looked at Gil or spoke to him, but every moment she was aware of what she was losing.

The children were so excited. They knew that they were moving to a big country house, that they could have ponies, that there would be lots of space, that they could choose their bedrooms and they could have big parties, Grandmother had said so. Abby was inclined to think that they would miss their friends, but she didn't say that to them. She didn't want to dampen their enthusiasm. She kept busy, packing, making sure that everything went well. On the moving day she was too miserable to say goodbye to the place. When she reached the first sight of Bamburgh House, it was such a shock that she forgot she had hated it. It did look different; it looked welcoming. The huge pillars were gone and the front of the house was open to the light and the day. The long windows were filled with sunshine and it seemed to Abby that she could see Gil's hand everywhere after that. Inside, where there had not been huge windows there were now, so that the house caught every bit of sunlight. The walls were no longer dark and dingy; the stairs which had been stone had been replaced with wood; the hall which had had huge stone pillars and stone walls had been altered, too. There were fireplaces and wooden floors and it was warm. Upstairs, there were bathrooms between the bedrooms with doors leading in on both sides and there again were more windows, but it was warm from the central heating and there were thick carpets.

It was barely furnished apart from that. Gil had done nothing other than basic alterations and the furniture they had brought with them disappeared into the huge spaces. Charlotte and William had furnished every inch and nothing much was left, but with the evening light coming in through the drawing-room windows, Abby could imagine what it might look like. Abby thought Charlotte would want to begin at once making it as it had been, but when Abby tactfully suggested that she might like to help she looked horrified.

'I did that once, I don't want to have to do it again.'

Charlotte, Abby thought, had recovered quite remarkably. She looked well, happy, even thinner. She liked being with the children.

Abby began to furnish the house. She did it slowly and could not help being pleased with the results. There wasn't much you could do with a library where the walls were oak-panelled, indeed, she rather liked that room; but the dining room she did in varying shades of yellow and when the morning sun came in and they had breakfast in there she was comfortable with what she had done.

The summer was here and she discovered the gardens and the various flowers that she knew her mother would have liked. She talked to the new gardeners, made plans for next year, read books; she thought that the one disadvantage about her father's house was that you couldn't make progress in the garden, as much had been done as could be, whereas here everything could be altered apart from the way that the quarry garden had its rocks and the various trees. Much of it was a wilderness and she was keen to begin again. She hadn't realised she was talking so much about it until she noticed over dinner one night that Gil was not listening. He was the only one there, the others had all gone from the table when the meal was finished. She shut up and listened to the silence.

'I didn't mean to go on about it,' she apologised.

'No, no, it's nice. Do you still miss the other house?'

'Not much. Not as much as I did, not since I learned to bore you over the dinner table about the garden.'

'It looks fine,' he said, 'so does this room.'

'Do you think it does? I'm worried you won't like things.'

'Why?'

'Because you don't say anything. I can't ask you, either, because you aren't here or you're in the study working. I have to just go ahead and hope you don't hate it.'

'Why worry?'

'Well, because you have taste.'

'God preserve us, do I? Don't tell anybody.'

Early that summer they went to look around various schools for Matthew. He was so enthusiastic. He ran around talking to people and asking about the sports teams and enthusing over the dormitories. It all looked wonderful, Abby thought, the huge and imposing buildings, the great stretches of green playing fields, the hundreds of boys all wearing the same clothes. Gil tried to talk him out of it, saying that there were perfectly good schools in Newcastle. Charlotte took the opposite view and Matthew was more inclined to listen to her these days.

'Why doesn't Dad want me to go?' Matthew said wistfully to Abby one evening when they had come back from looking at a well-known school in Yorkshire.

'Because he hated school,' Abby said, on her knees weeding a border. She liked doing this, it made her feel better and she needed to feel better. Gil was working fourteen hours a day and was silent when he came home. She tried to make herself talk to him or, even better, go to him, but she was convinced that if she went to bed with him, Helen would somehow be there. There was an atmosphere in the house. She was convinced it was of her own making and sometimes she thought she heard the faint sounds of a piano when no one was playing.

'But I'm not him,' Matthew pointed out reasonably.

Abby sat back on her heels and looked at him through the sunlight.

'He knows that and you may go if you wish. He hasn't said that you can't.'

'I know that.' Matthew dug his toe into the soil. 'But he doesn't want me to, does he?'

Abby couldn't say that Gil felt he had lost his child, firstly to his mother and then to his parents' hatred for him and now he was going to lose him physically to the kind of establishment which he despised.

'If you're happy there he won't mind, and if you aren't happy you don't have to stay.'

'Did he have to stay?'

'Yes, he did.'

'Why?'

'Because your grandfather insisted and . . . he wasn't very clever at school.'

'But he is very clever,' Matthew pointed out. Abby rather wished Gil had been there to hear the pride in his son's voice.

'It's a different kind of cleverness.'

'I'm good at cricket,' Matthew said. Abby watched him go racing back up the garden path towards the house and thought that Matthew would probably do very well at boarding school. He would be the sort of boy who wouldn't mind getting up for early morning cricket practice and he had a good memory for all those dreadful lessons. A great many men got through life with little more.

There was a part of Abby that became happy that summer. Georgina loved the country and Gil bought her a pony and taught her to ride. He spent more time with her daughter than he did with her, but Abby let him. She knew that he needed to be with the child. On Sundays when he was at home, he and Georgina went riding in the fine weather and she always declined the invitation. Abby couldn't abide horses. She thought they were the stupidest animals on God's earth, but Georgina adored her pony as only little girls can, and Abby had to stop herself from objecting to the time she spent at the stables. She was convinced that the grooms used bad language and said things to Georgina that they shouldn't, but the effect was that she turned into a lovely girl that summer and she had something she had never had before, a secure home with a man who came back, even if he was late. Abby could have forgiven Gil a lot for that. He was also a safe man, she thought, remembering Jos Allsop and Rhoda. Georgina could climb all over him, hug and kiss him, know that he would throw her into the air and catch her, tease her and that she would remember him later as the father to her child, when she was grown up. Abby remembered Henderson with such affection and it was important.

She knew also that Gil was taking comfort in the fact that Georgina was not going away. That autumn Matthew went to school. For days and days there had been arrangements to make, clothes to buy, the big trunk open in his bedroom. The maids named socks and packed pyjamas and then they all went by train to Matthew's school in Yorkshire where his best friend was going too. He didn't even mind leaving Gil and Abby; he ran off, not looking back. Abby thought she had never seen a boy so right for boarding school.

That night when they got home Gil prowled the house as though he were going out. He didn't go, but Abby watched carefully. He eventually shut himself into the study and then, when it was very late, he went upstairs. Abby had gone to bed hours since, but she hadn't slept so she got up, tied a dressing-gown tightly around her waist and knocked on the door. She couldn't hear anything and hesitated, but when she opened the door he was standing by the fire as you might at an inn when you had just come in from the cold, fully dressed except for his jacket and holding a whisky glass in his hand. That made her hesitate again. Men and alcohol were such a dangerous combination. She had not forgotten what Robert was like after several drinks, insisting on going to bed with her, the whisky sour on his breath and his actions so uncaring, mechanical, cold.

'At least close the door,' he advised.

She came into the room and shut the door.

'Are you thinking about Matthew?'

'Leaving him there was like being ripped in half.' It was not, Abby concluded, his first drink. She waited for maudlin reminiscences, for long drawn-out sentences, for a tirade on the horrors of public school, but nothing happened. Robert was too much in her mind. Drunk, he had said everything he thought. Drunk or sober, Gil did not, she surmised, say even a tenth of what he was thinking and he sifted it all first. This sentence had slipped past the whisky, but it was the only one.

'He'll like it,' Abby said helpfully. 'He'll be on the cricket team in no time.'

'It's the wrong term,' Gil said.

'Oh. Yes. Rugby?'

Abby made herself cross the room to him, but he didn't encourage her, he didn't even look or make conversation. It was rather like opening the door of an ice house and hoping for even a small blaze.

'I thought you might have gone out,' she said. 'I thought to Newcastle to that dreadful Irishwoman's establishment.'

'She's Scottish,' he said.

'I thought you might have.'

He said nothing. Gil might not have the hang of conversation, Abby thought, but he had definitely mastered the pause.

'Gil—'

'No.'

Abby wished very much now that she had stayed in her room, because he turned around and looked at her and it was not the kind of look which you met happily.

'You don't know what I was going to say,' Abby pointed out.

'It doesn't matter. Nothing you can say will make any difference so you might as well go to bed.'

Abby went.

Chapter Twenty-five

Sometimes it's difficult to distinguish between nightmares and life. Sometimes you think you're going to wake up and then you realise that you aren't asleep, that you won't have the relief of waking up and knowing that everything is all right, that your mother is downstairs cooking eggs and your father is walking the dogs in the field and that there will be butter and honey and sunlight and it will be morning. So when Gil found himself on a boat for France, no, let's be clear, he told himself, it's a ship, it's too bloody big to be a boat and the grandson of a boat builder, and the son of a shipbuilder, ought to know the difference in these things; he was on a ship without reason that he could think of, that was when he concluded comfortably that he was asleep and it was just a dream and whatever happened it didn't matter because he would awaken, he just had to get through it.

It wasn't a big ship; it wasn't the kind of ship he built. He saw all the design faults, he saw all the repairs that needed doing. He thought that if he had had any choice, with his knowledge, he wouldn't have got on the damned thing. Worst of all, it didn't balance. Now that was all right as long as the weather was fair, but so often between England and France the weather was bad, but he was reasonably happy about the trip because his brother was there. Edward was actually smiling at him as he hadn't smiled for a long time. Gil couldn't think how long it was. He was happy then. If Edward was smiling, there couldn't be much wrong. Toby was there, too, and they were talking together and laughing and it was like it had been in Toby's garden, at least he thought it was, when the flowers were out and the sun was hot and the wine was cool. They were all going to France, he had known that they were. They were going to build a new life there. The sea was calm like the pond in the park at home, the sunlight turned the water to silk, they sat on deck and drank wine. Toby described the house on the river with its orchard and its garden and its fields, where the hens scratched in the yard and the kittens played in the hay and the unfortunate rabbits sat in their hutch prior to being banged on the back of the neck, cooked and eaten. The dogs slept in the shade during the hot afternoons and friends came to call to take them off to five-course, three-hour lunches in tiny village restaurants. In the evenings the river played its own music and sometimes it rained hard and briefly and refreshed the trees so that the leaves looked polished.

Gil was looking forward to all this, but in a way he didn't want the journey to end. He was tired; he wanted to stay for a little while until he became impatient of the calm sea and the warm air and the way that the ship moved slowly away from England toward the shores of France.

Then it was night-time. They were still at sea and, as they sat outside, it seemed impossible, suddenly mist began to steal from the horizon towards them. It wasn't a slow thing. One minute it was clear and the next the mist was coming towards them, silently moving over the surface of the sea until there was nothing in his vision beyond the ship itself. Soon the calm night was gone. The wind got up and, although the mist cleared slightly so that he could see the size of the waves that were beginning to chafe at the bows, it was as though the ship were held and constricted by that fog. It began to rain, which should have cleared the fog away, but it didn't, and the rain and the waves got all mixed up so that there was water everywhere and the ship began to lurch.

At first he was down below deck. Each time the ship rolled he and everything else in the cabin slid all the way along to the opposite side and he would wait, suspended there on the floor with everything against him, pinned.

There would be a few moments when the ship's side was high out of the water and then the ship would roll the other way and he would slide all the way back across the floor to the other side and everything in the cabin would slide with him. Then he was on deck. He could see the water coming over the bows and he could see the size of the waves. They were so big and so wide that he couldn't see anything above them or anything around them and the water swilled across the decks. Toby was there, smiling, so it couldn't be that bad, and he went below and there was Edward.

'What's it like up there?'

'It's quite a storm, old boy,' he said.

'This isn't fair, you know, Tobe, we are the men who make the ships, we shouldn't have to put up with this.'

'I wish there had been another way. I wish that I had been a bird and could have flown. I didn't ever trust these blessed things.'

'I wish we were in France.'

'We will be soon. The storm can't last much longer.'

He went back up on deck again and the ship rolled and rolled and rolled and rolled and the whole world turned into sea. There was nothing but water. There was no ship to be seen. Then it was cold and he was falling and there was a great wall of salt water.

It was just a dream. He was down below. Toby was up on deck and then he wasn't and Gil knew that the house in France was just as much of a dream as this, that it had never existed and never would exist except in their imagination. It was the nightmare that was real, the storm and the fog and the ship rolling over. He was down below and he realised now that they would not get to France. Funny, but because it was a dream he didn't really care. He could indulge himself. He could think to himself that the world was well lost. He could think that their sons meant nothing to them now, that nothing mattered beyond the love between them. It had been everything. It had been the most important thing in both their lives, so if it should end here, it was right. They had given up everything for one another so it was fitting, comfortable. The October night was not cold and he remembered what he had heard about October storms. They should have thought of that before they set out, he acknowledged. Suddenly it was cold, it was frightening, it was that horrible helpless falling beyond the side of the cabin and he was shouting Toby's name and somebody was screaming.

Gil woke up. He was in his bedroom at Bamburgh House, not the bedroom he had had as a child but the best room in the house. The October sunlight was pouring through the big wide windows where his father used to sleep, the bedroom he had claimed as his right. He turned over.

The bed was soft and reassuring and the sheets were cool on his hot skin. He had thrown the bedcovers off at some time and only the sheet covered him. The curtains had been drawn back by the maid some time since and the windows were open as he preferred them. When he opened his eyes he saw the tray with the tea which she had left and had grown cold. It was late. It was, in fact, Sunday. Abby would have taken Georgina to church by now, so at least he did not have to meet her steady gaze over breakfast. He dismissed the dream. His brother had gone to France with Toby a year ago and, although he had heard nothing, had expected to hear nothing, he had no doubt that they were happy together, having cast off all their responsibilities. He got up, shaved, bathed, dressed and did all the other tedious morning things, then he went downstairs to meet the day.

Abby came back. Georgina reproached him because he had not got up early to go riding, but the day had clouded into rain so Gil could not even promise her that he would go later. He and Abby sat by the fire having a drink before the big Sunday meal. Then a carriage pulled up outside and a man got out. They didn't recognise him, but Gil did when he was announced, it was Mr Emory, Toby's father. Gil hadn't seen him since Toby and Henrietta's wedding and he had aged. Gil wasn't surprised.

He hadn't been able to put the dream from his mind

and now that he was confronted with somebody who would have mattered to it, Gil was most unhappy. He offered Mr Emory a drink and to sit down close by the fire. The man accepted whisky and a seat, but he didn't look straight at Gil and after a minute or two, clutching his whisky tightly in his hand he said, 'I have some grave news, Mr Collingwood. I have had a letter from France. There has been an accident.'

'A shipping accident?' Gil said, unable to stop himself.

Mr Emory looked keenly at him.

'Only in a manner of speaking. It was a boat.'

A boat. It was just a boat. He had been wrong; it was just a dream. Only a boat.

'My son and your brother . . . the boat capsized on the river near – near to their home. They are both dead.'

Mr Emory looked out of the window as though he could see something, whereas in fact the short autumn day was not offering much light anymore even though it was not yet two o'clock. The weather was bad and the days were short.

'All I wanted was a son. Every time we had a child . . . I was so proud of him.'

'You have three grandsons,' Abby said helpfully.

'My son was disgraced before he died. We tried to tell people differently, that he was suffering from some disorder . . . He's better dead.'

Gil was half out of his seat, words were on his lips, but Abby's fingers closed hard around his arm as she said, looking straight at Mr Emory, 'We were both very fond of him and we don't judge.'

'Your generation is extremely lax.'

'I understand that every older generation thinks the same of every younger.'

'In my day a man was a man and a woman was a woman and women did not argue.'

'Insufferable prig!' Abby shouted when he had gone.

She told the cook to give Georgina some dinner and explained to the little girl what had happened. Abby had discovered that if you told children the truth, it was surprising how well they reacted. Georgina remembered Edward only vaguely so she didn't care about that, but she cared that Gil would be upset.

'I thought he might like to go for a walk,' Abby said.

'He won't want his dinner now,' Georgina said, 'and it's a shame when it's Sunday.'

Abby kissed her daughter and went back to the drawing room. He was sitting as she had left him, staring into the fire. 'Do you want to go out for some air?'

Gil glanced at the window. The day was dark and the mist had come down, rolling off the moors just as it had in his dream across the water. It was starting to rain, lightly against the windowpane. He shook his head.

'No.'

'Another drink?'

'That would be good.'

She poured him a large scotch. They sat there and drank too much. It didn't take long; neither of them had had anything to eat since breakfast. The servants had enough sense not to come in and build up the fire. The level on the bottles went down steadily as Abby kept the glasses supplied and by the end of the afternoon he had fallen asleep in her arms. She kept him close and stroked his hair and thanked God for alcohol.

Mr Emory tried to insist that Toby's body was brought home for burial in the family plot just as though nothing had happened. Gil managed to frustrate this aim. It wasn't difficult; the authorities didn't want anything to do with it, so he went to France and made sure that the two young men were buried together as they would have wanted to be. He was glad that he had gone and done what he thought was right, if only because it made him feel better. The worst thing was that when he went to see the French lawyer about what was to be done with the house, he found that they had left the house to him.

'No, no,' Gil said, in the lawyer's office, 'Mr Emory has dependants.'

The lawyer frowned and he looked so much like Mr

Brampton that Gil wondered if it were the same man in different guise.

'Needy people?'

'No, they're very well off, rich—'

'This has been left, as I understand it, to one or to the other if anything happened and then to you. It was their wish. We ought to respect the wishes of the dead. We are a long way from England, Mr Collingwood, in legal terms. Would Mr Emory's family want the house?'

'I shouldn't think so.'

'It is a very nice house.'

It was a very nice house beside a singing river. The smell of lemons and oranges came from the glass house attached and the curtains in all the bedrooms were white. Down the street in the square during the night there was the smell of baking. Gil knew because he stayed in the house where his brother and his brother's lover had been happy. From the hills came the breeze, from the church the sound of a bell, in the square children played and sometimes just before he fell asleep he thought that he could hear the piano at Bamburgh House and see Helen's slender fingers playing Mozart. He caught the colours of her dresses in the corners of the bedroom against the white walls, those dresses she had bought in Newcastle with him when Edward had gone duck-shooting on the Solway and left her there. Sometimes she had just left the room and there was the sound of her laughter down the garden paths and across the river. And in the distance two young men were rowing upstream and singing silly English songs and laughing and all the while the river flowed beyond the windows.

Chapter Twenty-six

Matthew came home for Christmas, full of energy and stories about his new school and with the kind of glowing report that Abby felt sure Gil had never had. He had been top of the class in almost everything and regaled Georgina's reluctant ears with boastful tales of his exploits and doings. Georgina complained to Abby that she wished Matthew would go back to school. Matthew went to Gil in the study one evening and asked if he could go to work with him. Gil was astonished and rather pleased.

'You haven't offered to take me,' Matthew said. 'Other boys' fathers do.'

'I didn't realise you wanted to. I thought you might want to do something else when you get older.'

'What?'

'A doctor or a lawyer or . . . you aren't very old yet.'

'But that's what we do, we're shipbuilders. We're the best shipbuilders on the Tyne.'

So he went to work with Gil, questioning everything, talking to the men, going around the various departments. Only when it was the end of the day and they were back in Gil's office did Matthew say, 'The shipyard gates don't have our name on them like other people's. Why don't they?'

'Because originally two of them belonged to Abby's father, Henderson and he was called Reed, as you know.'

'But the third yard was ours.'

'I didn't want to upset Abby by renaming them.'

'You could call it Reed and Collingwood – or Collingwood and Reed. I don't think she'd mind.'

'I would rather leave it. I don't think it matters what we're called as long as we do the best work and people know it.'

Back at dinner that evening, Matthew said to Abby, 'Don't you think the number three yard should have the Collingwood name on it?'

'Matthew—' Gil said.

'It was my grandfather's, after all. Nothing has our name on it.'

'I don't think people are likely to forget him because of that,' Gil said dryly.

'I agree with Matthew,' Charlotte said.

'You can agree all you like,' Gil said, 'it won't make any difference.'

*

Edward's death had affected Charlotte greatly, Abby thought, and she blamed Gil, though not in front of him. Abby had expected that. Helen and Gil were to blame for every wrong that hit the family, according to Charlotte, though she had to admit that there could be some truth in it. What man would not have looked for some other kind of solace when his younger brother had stolen and seduced his wife? Abby tried to talk to Gil on several occasions, but not surprisingly she thought, he had nothing to say. His mother confined her remarks to her friends and to Abby, but he knew what she was saying behind his back, Abby felt certain.

It snowed heavily the first week that Matthew was at home. Abby watched it from the little room she had adopted as hers for writing letters and seeing the cook and making up menus and sorting out the day-to-day matters of the house. She stopped writing her letter on the Saturday afternoon and watched Georgina outside. She was making snow angels for Gil. Abby thought that her child was the one person he ever really relaxed in front of and only then when he was alone with her. Unobserved now, so he thought, he was making snow angels too and they were laughing. They went on to build a snowman. Abby felt left out. She went and put on her outdoor things and followed them outside. Georgina showed her the snowman and then declared that she was cold and was going inside, her gloves were soggy and her fingers were numb. Gil and Abby walked across the lawns and into the quarry garden. In there it was like a fairytale, the trees laden with snow, the stones brushed with it, the paths white and untrodden until they got there.

He wandered away in front. Abby picked up a handful of snow, squashed it into a snowball and threw it at him. It hit him square in the middle of his back. He turned around and threw one at her just as accurately and then another and then another.

'All right, all right!' Abby said, squealing, and he came to her and brushed the snow from her coat. 'Why do men always do that?'

'What?'

'Compete, mow you down, whatever. You try to get the better of me.'

He moved away again. Abby tried to think what to say. It was the closest they had been since the afternoon when they had received the news of Edward's death and he had fallen asleep with his head in her lap. She threw another snowball at him and he laughed as it missed and went past. Then he came back to her. He looked at her for a moment and then he put one hand firmly into the middle of her back and pulled her to him and kissed her.

Abby had been hoping for conversation, had been trying for weeks to talk to him. She knew that Edward's death had upset him badly and she had wanted to help.

His grieving for his brother was something totally private; he couldn't or wouldn't share it and had told her nothing of what had happened in France. That afternoon when they had drunk too much and he had fallen asleep with his head in her lap had been as close as they had got and he had not even acknowledged it, just woken up, got up and left the room. Until now, that had been all. Now he had hold of her in a very definite way and it was not, Abby knew, a precursor to a meaningful conversation. Within seconds she would have had to struggle to get away and he was pressing on her mouth the kind of kisses which she had forgotten and well remembered, sweet and deep and rather less decent than anything that should have taken place outside. She made a tentative attempt to stop him. This was not a good idea. Somebody might see. It was daylight. It was freezing. There were several inches of snow and even Robert had not been this unsubtle. Gil had been around whores too long, Abby thought.

Being in a bedroom with the windows open to crisp frost was the nearest Abby had come to this. He was not content with kisses and got his hands inside her clothes with the kind of swift expertise which Abby had long ceased to admire in men. Women's clothing was about as intricate as it could be, but it didn't seem to make any difference. You could tell how old or experienced a man was in ways like that and Gil's experience betrayed him.

Abby would have talked to him if she had imagined he was going to listen, but he was past that. He had been beyond conversation since Matthew had gone to school, so there was no chance of that here. She could not help remembering also the lover that he had been, gentle, kind and warm. That was not the man who drew her down into several inches of snow. The ground was icy, wet and unyielding and it had begun to sleet, not big white flakes of snow, but hard like bullets and the sky was a peculiar dark grey, like steel. She said his name a couple of times in protest, but he didn't hear her. The trees where the snow had not covered them were bare and wet and black and the stones in the quarry garden threw huge, jagged shadows across the twisting paths.

Most unhappy now, Abby had to make a decision. Was she going to stop him? Was she going to tell him that she wanted to talk to him, when this was the first time he had come near her in so very long? It was not even that she trusted him to be kind to her any longer. He was too hurt for that. When your worst fears have all come true, what is there left? She knew that Gil had loved his brother with the kind of desperation that would not be dispelled. He had loved Edward without any love in return and that was the hardest thing in the world. She had not forgotten his face or his silence on the day that Edward had left. Gil didn't know how to shed tears, so there had been no release, not even a

word. He had not seen his brother again and now he
never would, neither had he gone to anyone for any kind
of comfort.

Abby was beginning to get extremely angry with herself. Somehow she should have read this situation and
stopped it before it started. He would have understood,
listened. He was not Robert, not insensitive and uncaring so that it would have cost her nothing to deny him.
He had always tasted and felt wonderful to her. Now he
was blind and deaf, only his instincts were working. He
had done this dozens of times to women he paid. Abby
called herself names. She felt stupid. And her body
perversely wanted him, even here. She wished she could
kill him.

Soaked, frozen, furious, Abby knew with a sinking
heart that he was going to do what they called locally
'giving her a bloody good seeing to'; she could tell from
the concentrated way he went about it. Gil was meticu-
lous about everything he did. It wouldn't change
anything, things like this didn't. She felt stupid.

His deft hands had discarded her underwear and
reached her body. It shouldn't have mattered. Robert
had taken her dozens of times when he was drunk,
when she didn't want him to. Gil was not drunk and she
did want him to, only not like this, not from bitterness
and whatever place he had come to in his mind with his
father's death on his conscience and his brother's

hatred. She let him have her and was immediately sorry. He couldn't even be like Robert, careless and clumsy; he had to be himself, accurate and sure. Was this what William had been like? Had he resented and hated his background and his parents and himself so much in the end that he would use Charlotte this hard? Would Gil have noticed if she had made further feeble attempts to stop him? Perhaps he wouldn't have, she thought. Even now, she wanted him. She wouldn't have wanted Robert like this, would have denied him her consent and he had been a gentler man than Gil in lots of ways. Gil was young, not thirty yet, but all the beds he had been in showed on him here. This was not force; it was experience and he made her want him. There was nothing selfish about it in the end. He brought Abby's body to a sweet height and in her mind she cursed him for that final betrayal. It was unfair.

There was nowhere to go when it was over, no blankets to curl into, no pillows to hide against and even then he didn't talk to her. She imagined that even the girls at Mrs Fitzpatrick's got some form of conversation, but he put his clothes back to rights as though nothing had happened and left her there. Abby sat in the snow and cried and called him every name she could think of. Eventually she was so cold that there was nothing to do except fasten her clothes and go indoors and order a hot bath.

*

John Marlowe called in at the office that week and they sat by the fire and drank whisky.

'Allsop's been seen around Newcastle these last few days so just be a mite careful. We don't want your pretty little Missus Surtees back on the streets again, do we?'

'I'm not even certain it was him, John.'

'Who else?'

'It could have been anybody. I just had this idea that it was. I didn't see him clearly.'

'And he likes you so much?' John said.

'I assumed he was dead.'

'Why?'

'I don't know. I hadn't heard anything, nobody had.'

Later, when the whisky had been drunk, Gil made his way back to the country. He thought about Jos Allsop and when he got home he called the appropriate male servants and told them that they were to admit no one without evidence of identity and to stop anybody who came into the grounds, no matter how far from the house. He had already arranged security in his shipyards, with men on the gates and night watchmen on the premises. You lost too much if you didn't look after things.

He called Abby into the study after dinner and told her.

'All I'm saying is be careful and for the next few days keep the children close until I can find out what's happening.'

Matthew burst in at that moment.

'Jonathan sent me a letter today and he wants me to go and stay with him!'

'Matthew, have you ever heard of knocking?' Gil said.

Letter in his hand, Matthew was silenced.

'Go and wait outside.'

Matthew went.

'Try to be kind to him,' Abby said.

'What?'

'He's a small boy. You treat him like an adult.'

'He's very precocious.'

'I wonder where he got that from,' Abby said as she walked out.

When she had gone, Gil cursed himself. He didn't know what to say to her, hadn't known since that day in the garden in the snow. He just wished he hadn't done it. It had made things worse, if they could get any worse. He called Matthew inside and read the short letter inviting Matthew to stay.

'You can't go to Jonathan's, not for a few days.'

'Why not?'

'Because I say so.'

'I'm bored here, there's nothing to do. I hate living in the country with nobody but stupid Georgina. I hate this place and I hate you!' Matthew said and banged the door after him. Gil went after him, got hold of him by the back of his collar and marched him back into the room.

'You're going to hate me a lot more if you aren't careful,' he said. 'You'd better brighten your ideas up, because if you bang the door again like that or say rude things to me I'm going to put you over that desk and beat you. Do you understand me?'

Matthew nodded and then ran. He left the door open that time. Gil didn't think any more about it. He had discovered that work meant you could ease things out of your mind and he had a lot to do before he went to bed, so he worked until it was almost midnight. He heard the gentle click of the door and looked up. White-faced, Abby hovered in the doorway.

'Matthew's missing,' she said.

'He's what?'

'He isn't in his room and he isn't in the house—'

Gil was on his feet, the familiar sick feeling gathering momentum all the time inside him. Within seconds he was dizzy.

'He can't be far,' Abby said reassuringly, 'it's a horrible night.'

'He could have been gone hours, ever since . . . No. Oh God.'

Gil sent the men searching and he rode over to the Charlton household, which was the nearest neighbour. Jonathan was the son of Ralph, whom Edward had been friendly with. All the way there he told himself that this was his fault, but he was sure that Matthew would be there. He was not. The house was in darkness, in silence and though he banged on the doors and got them out of bed, he was without hope by then.

Ralph and all the men he could find offered to help and Gil was grateful. They went to all the houses nearby. He could hear voices calling Matthew's name over the hills, the fellside and the banksides and all the time his mind gave him Jos Allsop and Rhoda. Reason deserted him. It was a cold, wet night. Gil could not believe he had to go through this again and he thought somehow that Allsop would appear and hurt Matthew, that he would have been stalking the house, that he could have persuaded Matthew away, that he might have lured him into Newcastle and kidnapped and killed him. All night he searched and the other men of the district did the same. They found nothing and, just as daylight began, it snowed huge flakes which turned into a storm. He remembered finding Rhoda dead in the snow like some neglected animal and how he had carried her back to the house and how Allsop had reacted. It was all happening again. He didn't want to go back to the house in case someone else had found Matthew dead, or that he had not been found at all and would be discovered cold and still or in some back alley in the city, Allsop having taken out his feelings on Gil's son.

When full day arrived he made his way back to the house, Abby heard him and came into the hall. Her colour was normal and behind her hovered a small figure.

'We found him,' she said, 'just a little while since. I've called off the search. He had hidden to frighten us and fallen asleep.'

It was not relief that Gil felt, it was an overwhelming desire to thrash his child. As he took a step towards her Abby backed with the boy behind her. Gil got her by the arm.

'Come out of the way,' he said.

'I will not!'

Matthew started to cry.

'He's just a little boy. You leave him alone!' She started to fight with him as Gil reached for his son. She was crying, too, but her hands were clenched into fists. Even though she was small and slight, she got in the way quite effectively, but not sufficiently to make the difference in the end. He could have stopped her altogether by knocking her out of the way. It wouldn't even have taken a great effort and Gil could feel the tremendous well of temper surging its way through him. He remembered it. He remembered how he had put the boy out of the second-storey window at school. He remembered throwing men down the stairs at the house in Hope Street. He remembered being in the study with his father and being called stupid and worthless and beaten until he couldn't move. He remembered being thrown into cold rooms and left there for days. And he remembered Helen smiling at him and lying to him and pretending that she cared about him when in fact she had only really cared about his brother. He wanted to break something, to see something bloody and down and destroyed.

Abby had backed as far as the stairs. There was nowhere for her to go now, with the child still behind her. She was fighting with him, but Gil had hold of Matthew and was pulling him out from behind her.

'You won't do it, you won't!' she declared, hanging on. 'I won't let you be William! You're not, you're not.'

He didn't hit her. He released her while she was pushing from him and she fell, the stairs got in the way and he had Matthew to himself, not fighting or crying or protesting in any way. He remembered that too, that horrible resignation, the knowledge that if you cried you would be beaten until you stopped, the awful sick anticipation. The little boy's face was grey-white, the tears had dried and his eyes were all one colour, black with fear, and huge. He was so small, so unable to do anything to stop an adult from punishing him. He was like a terrified rabbit that couldn't move.

The hope for the future if he could learn enough and please sufficiently and contain all the evil feelings. He could be taught that approval and success were all that mattered, that if he was clever enough he could have a house like this and expensive carriages, all the stables full of horses and all the rooms filled with furniture. He could have servants and tables laden with food and a cellar full of wine and his pick of women. He could have the whole world admiring him, he could have everything.

Gil picked the child up and said, 'I think you ought to go to bed, Matthew. You must be worn out,' and he carried him up the stairs.

Abby fussed gently, put the child into bed and talked to him in a soft voice. Gil went back downstairs and into the study. As he opened the door the snow had stopped, the sky had cleared and the sun appeared over the horizon and spilled all over the floor in a mighty surge of dazzling brilliance. There was nothing left to do but go to work, so he went. He wasn't even tired. He spent the day going around the various shops and departments as he sometimes did just to keep everybody lively, and all day the sun streamed in at the windows. The snow had gone from the streets and there was a special buzz about everything because it was Christmas Eve and the men would not be at work for the following two days. In the time before Henderson's influence they had only Christmas Day, but Gil was a believer in holidays and gave them time off at Easter and in the summer and he paid them. He was well hated in the shipbuilding federation for his high wages and lenient ideas and good ships, he thought, smiling. They would have New Year's Day, too, because a great many of these people were Scottish and a great many more felt more Scottish than English and would rather have gone to work on Christmas Day than New Year's, so he accommodated everybody and gave them both. There would be a servants' dance that evening at Bamburgh House and many of the servants would go home for a day or two. He and Abby, instead of having big parties as many people did, would have a quiet time, fetching and carrying for themselves. He pictured them eating in the kitchen and making free of the house as they couldn't when other people were there. They could sit in their nightclothes by the fire if they wanted, he thought. He had planned all this. The plans were ruined. He thought of her falling awkwardly on the stairs, her defence of the child and of the fear in Matthew's face.

He didn't go home. He didn't ever want to go home again. Staying at work was so easy by comparison. The problems could be solved, they were not people, unpredictable and complicated. When it was quiet in the evening he helped himself to whisky and grew used to the idea that Jos Allsop had not abducted or murdered his child. He heard John's heavy footsteps outside his office, so by the time the big man had reached him Gil had a glass ready half filled with golden liquid.

'Get wrapped around that,' he said.

'Cheers,' John said. 'Got some good news.'

'I could take some.'

'Allsop. Found dead in the river this afternoon, belly up like a fish.'

'I couldn't be better pleased. Somebody did him in?'

'Don't know,' John said, frowning and taking his favourite seat across the fire. 'Rumour has it he fell in, drunk. Everything all right with you?'

'Aye, everything's fine.'

'Want to go out?'

'Why not?'

They went to the pub and then they went to Mrs Fitzpatrick's. Gil was rather drunk when he got there and decided that all he wanted to do was go home. John laughed.

'It's all right for some people, they've got it on tap,' he said.

By the time he reached home the drunkenness had worn off with the cold night air. He had expected the house to be in darkness, but it was lit like a Christmas tree. Then he remembered the servants' dance. The hall was deserted. It was evidently over and quiet. People had gone to bed, but Abby was there, wearing a very pretty, low-cut blue dress. She had a mark on her face. People would think he had hit her, Gil thought.

'Just as well I didn't save you the last waltz,' she said.

'I forgot.'

'Of course. What could compete with the delights of the pub and the whorehouse?' She turned away and would have walked up the stairs, but he stopped her. He led her into the nearest room, which was the library. There had obviously been no fire in there for several hours, or possibly at all that day. Nobody went in there except him and on the day of a party people would be unlikely to need books. Abby stood against the door and didn't look at him. Gil had been going to apologise, but that was before he realised about the dance. He wanted to say to her that he hadn't meant to hurt her, that he hadn't intended to, that he hoped the mark on her face hadn't caused her embarrassment, that he hoped the servants had not heard them fighting. It was a vain hope; they had made a lot of noise. Two people fighting like that would not have been ignored by even the least curious servants. Probably all that day there had been talk. Probably they thought he had knocked her over. Her face, to his mind, didn't give enough evidence, it would have been a much bigger mark, but people didn't care about that, they would believe what they chose to believe. He had fought with her and attempted to beat his child. For these things men were not forgiven. The servants' dance, the way she thought he had deliberately stayed away, the drinking was true, the whore . . . he was starting to wish that he was safe in the arms of Chloe or Desirée or somebody who didn't matter, whose name didn't matter . . . these things had not been important on their own, but they were the cap to it, rather like the top of a boiled egg was to some people the dearest part. He wanted to apologise to her, but he couldn't remember how.

She stood there and regarded the side of the bookshelf with rapt concentration.

'It's Christmas,' he said.

Abby stared at the wood. Gil looked at her throat. The way that her dress scooped down like that, you couldn't help noticing at close quarters what a pretty neck she had and the way that her shoulders were so soft and white and her breasts just hidden by the top of the dress would be . . . He wished again that he was back in Newcastle where it was simple, where nobody fought and argued and used the kind of language Abby did, where he could do what he wanted to do to her. All those girls had beautiful bodies because they were expensive. They were all, in fact, more beautiful and much younger than Abby was. He thought of the way she had protected his son against him. She would have fought until she couldn't fight anymore, not just because of Matthew but because she well knew that he did not forgive himself his iniquities.

He put his hands on her waist and slid them around to the back of her dress. There he found the fastenings quite intricate and hidden so that they would not spoil the line of the expensive dress, but he knew these things, had been around women long enough to know how to undress them. That was one problem you didn't have at Mrs Fitzpatrick's: they were half undressed to begin with and because you paid, you didn't have to undress them at all if you didn't want to. They would slowly remove the clothing that they wore if you liked, but he liked to take their clothes off for them. He began to undo the fastenings now.

She tasted and smelled so wonderful to Gil that he wanted her like he had wanted nobody else. Her neck was long and slender and invited kisses all the way down the column of her throat and in the hollows of her shoulders. He could feel the dress loosening from her body, obligingly slipping so that the palms of his hands found the exquisite warmth of her breasts.

'Will you stop it!'

It was only then that Gil realised she was trying to get away. He was not used to that. Nobody did that. He looked vaguely at her.

'What?'

They were on the sofa. He hadn't realised that either, hadn't known that he had put her there, hadn't felt or heard her protesting.

'I'm not a whore!'

'I know that.' But she felt just as good as the girls at the whorehouse, better in fact, much better and, sitting up with her hair tumbled and the dress down to her waist and the angry fired look in her eyes, he was loathe to release her.

'It didn't stop you though, did it? It didn't stop you before, outside?'

Abby was not crying, but her voice was catching as though there was some constriction in her throat. He thought about before, the snow falling and the soft ground and her body so warm against the cold air. He remembered his hands, wet from the snow, finding the heat of her body as it emerged from her clothes and the ecstasy of having her in the stillness. There was no other stillness in the world like that of falling snow. The whole world was stopped and silent and she was his, completely his as if they would not be parted for all eternity.

'You treated me like this then!'

'No. No.' Kissing her now, her body brushing against his shirt, his hands unable to prise themselves away from her. 'Don't leave me. Don't. Please.'

She was off the sofa, pulling her dress up to where it was supposed to be. He couldn't move, tried to be seconds back to where they had been when she was letting him kiss her, touch her. He would not acknowledge that there was a space between them and now the cold night was making its way between them. He knew what that was like, the icy, godforsaken hours of nobody and nothing. He had tried to steal beyond them with women, but he could not forget all those nights and weeks and months and years without Helen, all those days without her, knowing that he had not come from her and would not go back to her, all the time, all the people who meant nothing with their kind and unkind faces, all the ships going down the slipway had not eased the emptiness. Nothing eased it except this.

Abby was angry. Her mind was full of what had happened the previous night. She had never before had to fight with anyone and it had appalled her. When had Gil turned into his father and why had she not noticed it until then? William had been bad-tempered, autocratic, impossible and unforgiving, but she was not Charlotte. She would not stand by and let him beat his son. It was true that Gil didn't hit her, but he caused the circumstances which made her fall and hurt herself and she still had to go on trying to stop him from taking Matthew from her. When the fight was over she relived it, shaking, again and again. Even when Matthew was in bed, where Gil had safely put him, when there was no question of brutality, there had been the possibility and that was enough for her. They had put the child to bed in daylight and then he had actually gone to work. She couldn't believe it. No apologies, no concern. He had left the house, left her to manage as best she could without sleep, his upset child, the staff dance, the Christmas arrangements. Then he had quite obviously stayed out, got drunk, had a woman and finally had nothing better to do than come home. And now . . . maybe there had been no woman. Even somebody young like Gil couldn't have gone without sleep, working all day, got drunk, had a whore, come home and . . . put his mouth and hands on her like this. Abby felt nothing, just cold as though she had been left outside for too long. He was insensitive, like all men were. Robert had done this many times, it didn't mean anything to him; but Gil was not like that, she knew he wasn't, she couldn't have cared so much about him if he had been.

She had begun to resist but he didn't take any notice, pulling the dress down to her waist. He picked her up and carried her over to the sofa and there in the softness of the cushions he put her down. The bloody room was anything but warm and the books smelled like damp books did, sort of mouldy and as though they had never been outside in the fresh air. The whole room had an atmosphere that Abby hadn't noticed before and didn't like now. It was neglected, unwanted, turned aside, cold words on cold pages. The winter wind screamed around the house, making its way down the chimney and into the empty grate and the room was filled with bitter air.

She went. She left him. She didn't say anything. She didn't even say goodnight, as though he had done something unforgivable. The room was so cold, the shadows were so thick, the night was God and nobody could alter it. He made himself go upstairs. He could go back to Chloe tomorrow or the next day and he was safe there. She was young and beautiful and obliging. She tasted good and smelled good and had breasts like apples, round and firm, and a bottom that was neat and high and a waist so slender that he could meet his fingertips around it. She had long blonde hair and bright blue eyes.

He walked out of the library and went upstairs. The night was unforgiving and all the ghosts came at you from the corners when the lights were out. It was easier when Chloe was there. Maybe she would marry him and he wouldn't have to go to bed by himself any more. There was brandy in a glass by the bed and he knew that when he had drunk half a bottle, Helen would not be dead any more. She would just be in another room and Edward would be playing billiards and his mother and father would be having a party. He could soon hear the music and the laughter down below and he could have the ship launch and see the *Northumbria* slide down into the Tyne. It had been the best moment of his life and he could have it back any time. He could have it back any time at all. There it went again, hundreds of Newcastle people cheering and the men throwing their caps into the air and his father standing beside him smiling and the proud look in his mother's eyes and Rhoda . . . He wished Chloe was here. He wished that she was here.

Abby worried. She told herself over and over that he was uncaring and not worth her losing sleep. The night was bitterly cold with a heavy frost and a lot of stars so that both ground and sky twinkled. She stood with the heavy curtains pulled back, but it was cold even though she had kept the fire going in her bedroom. Tomorrow it would be Christmas Day. She didn't decide to leave the room or to go into Gil's room, she just went. She opened the heavy oak door of his room and a blast of freezing air hit her. It was in dark shadows because the curtains were pulled well back and the window was wide open. Abby fumbled about in the dark and finally found the lamp, but it wouldn't light. Eventually she found a candle. That didn't help much, but it gave enough light for her to see Gil.

She had seen Robert in that state too many times not to know how drunk he was. He was unconscious, face down on the bed with one arm under his eyes, fully dressed in neat, expensive clothes. He had blotted everything out with brandy, taken himself into oblivion. She went over, closed the window, pulled the curtains and then she went back to bed.

*

Christmas Day was difficult. She went to church with Charlotte and the children. Gil was downstairs when she got back. He didn't look like somebody who had been drunk the night before, he was just the same and laughed at Georgina's kisses and cuddles. He was too indulgent with her and had bought her far too many Christmas presents, which she unwrapped gleefully. For Matthew a beautiful cricket bat, which he insisted on using, so he and Gil went outside in spite of the weather. One of Abby's presents from Gil was a silver locket containing photographs of her parents. He was good with presents.

They had a big meal and went out for a walk, watching the sun set over the horizon. As the evening drew in she put the children to bed and when she went back downstairs, heard him ordering the carriage.

'Gil!' She went after him into the drawing room. 'Where are you going?'

He looked at her in slight amusement.

'What?' he said.

'If you go . . . if you go to that place . . .'

'What will you do about it? Beat me when I come home, withdraw your favours, leave me? Well?'

'Stay here.'

'What for?'

'Those girls only do it because you pay them!'

'Nice and simple,' Gil said.

'You were drunk last night.'

'That wasn't entirely because you wouldn't let me have you on the sofa.'

Abby hoped diligently that nobody was listening.

'You sleep with the windows open.'

'For the stars,' Gil said and left.

Gil had great hopes of Chloe. He hadn't been there in a long time. She greeted him with enthusiasm and she was so pretty, seventeen or eighteen at the most. She didn't mind the windows open or the whisky or anything at all. From her bed you could hear the sounds of the streets outside and when it was late you could throw back the curtains and see those same stars. They hadn't altered, they were Helen's stars, they went on and on.

He knew the girls. At least, he could distinguish some of them though he tried not to because after a couple of drinks, by candlelight, naked in his arms, each of them became Helen. But tonight it didn't work. Chloe wouldn't turn into Helen. She remained a pretty young girl with a Byker accent, dyed blonde hair and an innocent willingness, in spite of her trade, which Helen had never had. Helen had not looked at him like that, desperate to please. Chloe undressed for him and then she seemed almost like a child. Gil turned away, then he turned back and put her into bed and covered her in bedclothes. The room was freezing. Gil stood by the window and watched the stars and drank brandy and the room grew colder and colder. He went on drinking to try to make the magic happen, but it didn't. All he could see was Abby standing in front of Matthew, protecting him from somebody twice as big as she was who could kill her. He spent most of the night watching the stars from the window while Chloe finally went to sleep and the brandy took its hold on him.

In the morning when he left to go to the office, he caught an anxious look on Chloe's face. He sat down on the bed.

'What's the matter?'

'Nothing.'

'You're supposed to say "I don't want you to go." '

Chloe's face slipped.

'You weren't happy.'

'I was very happy.'

'No, you weren't. I didn't make you happy.'

'And I'm going to complain to Mrs Fitzpatrick, is that it?'

'Maybe.'

'It had nothing to do with you.' He lifted her chin and looked into her clear blue eyes. Then he kissed her on the cheek and gave her a handful of money. 'Go and buy yourself a new dress,' he said.

*

Gil went to the office. Only the watchmen were there and the maintenance people, but the fire burned in his office as it did every day. He had given the men an extra day's holiday. The talk in the clubs, John told him, was that they said he would bankrupt himself. It made him laugh. He liked being here when few other people were. He worked in the silence and drank coffee all day and enjoyed the light-headed feeling that came from eating nothing for too long.

Towards evening he sat by the window and watched the river and debated whether to go home. Mid-evening he heard a noise, assumed that it was John, poured whisky and then realised that the steps were much too light. Abby appeared in the doorway. Gil didn't even get up. He looked into the golden liquid so that he wouldn't have to look at her. She was so beautiful, not as angry as she had been, but there was fire in her eyes. He got up and went to the window. All the shapes outside were defined against the clear sky, all strong and tall and looking as though they would last for ever, when none of them would. They were buildings and ships, and one day none of it would be left.

She seemed to think she could get his attention when in fact the whisky and the night held him inside its magic circle and nothing could get past. The smell of the whisky was sweet and sharp and the night was doing its special floor show with its stars and all its terrors. He thought that, later, when the golden liquid had completely gone, he would be part of it somehow. The view of his shipyard was beautiful; it was possibly the best view in the world. Gil took another swig of whisky and regarded the night. He was prejudiced about the Tyne. He couldn't look at another river and love it like this. He wished he could hold it in his arms. Whenever he launched a ship, he imagined the Tyne taking the ship into its arms like a lover.

'Aren't you going to speak to me?' she said from the other end of the room over by the desk.

'What is there to say?'

'You haven't talked to me at all since you came back from France. You've screwed the arse off me of course, but that's not quite the same thing.'

Gil turned and looked mildly at her.

'One of these days somebody will leather you for your language,' he said.

Abby came to the window.

'You haven't said a single word about Edward.'

'He's dead,' Gil said flatly. That was the first time that he had acknowledged to himself that Edward had died. He had known it in his head, but he had not believed it in his heart. There was a bit of him that still thought he could go any night of the week to the billiard hall they had frequented in the town and there, among the quiet talk and the slow movements of the players, his brother would be across the room, not speaking to him or looking at him, glancing up at Toby from time to time and smiling his slow smile, his fair hair haloed under the low lights above the tables. Toby would be leaning on his cue and suggesting where the next shot should go.

In Gil's mind it was always a night when Edward would suggest after dinner that they should go out. Then they would be in the fuggy warmth of the room and Edward was smiling and there would be another day and another time and another chance. But there was not anymore and never would be.

'Did you go to Mrs Fitzpatrick's?'

'Yes.'

'Why?'

'Because you wouldn't let me "screw the arse off you",' he said.

Abby stood for a few moments as though in admiration of the view and then she said softly, 'That's not true, is it?'

Gil leaned against the wall so that he didn't have to say anything, so that he couldn't even see her except from the corner of his eyes.

'You were never really like that, not like Robert and his friends who would bed anything that looked vaguely female. Why do you go?'

Gil took a sip of whisky and stared out at the darkness of his shipyard.

'When I've had a few drinks, every woman is Helen.'

Abby considered her hands carefully.

'Is that why you put me down into the snow?'

'I wanted you near.'

'That was fairly near,' Abby said.

'It was you I wanted.'

'Sure?'

'Yes.'

'So I'm not Helen. She is dead, you know.'

'Yes, I know.'

'Then why does everybody have to be her?'

He didn't answer.

'You've had a drink or two now. Am I Helen?'

'No, of course not.'

'Then what? What?' She thumped him. 'Goddamn you, talk to me!'

The whisky flew everywhere. Gil put down the empty glass.

'Don't do that!' he said.

'What, this?' she said, thumping him again and he got hold of her. 'Come on then. You've had enough whisky to float a ship. Put me down and make me Helen. She didn't even love you!'

'Yes, she did!'

'When? When she waltzed off to Venice with your brother? When she came back pregnant? When she accused you of fathering Matthew? When she killed herself to spite you?'

'She didn't!' He shook her.

'If she loved you, why didn't she give up Edward and marry you? She never loved you and you know it! And no matter how hard you try, it won't make any difference and no matter how many women you put down in the starlight, it won't alter anything.'

Gil released her when she twisted away from him. She didn't go far, just nearer the window, leaned against it, looking out.

'You can't make people love you, not Helen and not your father, not even Edward.'

Gil couldn't answer that and she turned to him again and said, 'That's the worst of all, isn't it: Edward?'

'I betrayed him.'

'He didn't care about you.'

'There were days . . . when he did. There were times when I thought he did, but I wanted him to so very much. He loved Toby.'

'Isn't that slightly different?'

'I don't know. I don't know where love and touch differs, where it begins and ends, but I know what it feels like when you don't have any, when people don't want you near them or even in their company. People who grow up together have special things between them or they should have, don't you think?'

'I loved my parents, I miss them. Why don't you come home?'

'You don't want me.'

Abby sighed.

'That was just because . . . of what happened. I was afraid. I thought you were going to knock me out of the way and beat Matthew.'

'I was.'

'But you didn't.'

'That was because some termagant got in the way.'

'I'm not that bad. You could have done it.'

'I turned into my father.'

'Almost. Gil—' Abby moved nearer. 'If I hadn't loved you very much I wouldn't have let you put me down into the snow like that. I wouldn't have let anyone else in the world do it – I thought you knew that at least.'

'It wasn't like that,' he said. 'I love you.'

Abby took a deep breath and let go of it.

'So, you weren't just screwing the arse off me.'

He looked disapprovingly at her.

'If you say that once more, I will wallop you.'

Abby grinned.

'That would be a big novelty,' she said. 'I doubt you're capable of it.'

'Just don't.'

'Will you do me a favour then?'

'What?'

'Don't go to Mrs Fitzpatrick's.'

'I didn't do anything when I got there. I haven't been

there since before we left Newcastle. The only woman I've been anywhere near is you.'

She went closer and reached up both hands to his shoulders and kissed him very gently on the mouth.

'Come home,' she said. 'I love you and you have the children and even your wretched mother tolerates you.'

He smiled a little.

'She's got better,' he said.

'She's almost bearable,' Abby said, 'please come home.'

It only occurred to Gil when they got there that since he had come back from France, the piano playing had stopped. Was that why he could no longer conjure Helen's image? Or did it have more to do with the fact that the children, who were supposed to be in bed, heard the carriage and ran down the stairs in greeting? He picked them up and they squealed and giggled and Georgina put her arms around his neck. He took them into the small sitting room, which was the cosiest room in the house. Abby had placed big squashy sofas at either side of the fire. It was high and bright with logs. Gil sat down with Georgina on his knee and Matthew cuddled up to Abby. Gil's mother came in.

'My children went to bed at seven,' she said. 'I don't approve of all these new-fangled ideas.'

'It's the holidays, Grandma,' Matthew said.

'I love Christmas,' Georgina said from the depths of Gil's shoulder, where she was almost asleep.

'Far too many presents,' Charlotte said. 'Your uncle has died. A little respect would be nice.'

'We could go to France in the summer,' Gil said.

His mother looked sharply at him.

'Whatever for?' she said.

'They left us the house. We could go and stay there.'

'You didn't say.'

'The legalities aren't finalised yet.'

'Is it a nice house?' Matthew said, sitting up.

'It's a lovely house,' Gil said, 'by a river.'

'We could go fishing.'

'I could go as well,' Georgina said.

'I don't know that I want to go to a house where—' Charlotte seemed to remember the children and stopped herself.

'He was happy there,' Gil said.

'You don't know that,' his mother said roughly.

'Charlotte—' Abby said.

Gil's mother looked hard at her.

'You spring very quickly to my son's defence, Abigail. When people do that it's high time they were married,' she said and stamped out of the room.

Gil watched Abby press her lips together so that she

wouldn't laugh. They put the children to bed and sat together on the sofa.

'I think she will come to France,' Abby said.

'Only if we get married.'

'I would do anything to please your mother.'

'And me?'

Abby moved closer.

'I could do things for you that Mrs Fitzpatrick has never heard of.'

He laughed. She pushed him over and leaned on him.

'You doubt me?'

'Not for a second.'

'In bed I think. I don't want to be interrupted.'

Abby couldn't help but pause when they passed the doors of the drawing room, but the piano was silent and still. She would not have admitted to him that she sometimes heard Mozart when there was nobody in the room. When they reached her room the fire was burning brightly, but the thick curtains were open. Abby went across and closed out the night, the cold sky, the stars and the bright icy moon. It was what was going to happen inside the room that mattered, she thought, and nobody and nothing could stop her from making him hers. He would belong to her now and nobody else would ever have him again, she swore. She knew a lot about swearing; her mother had taught her. Her father had always proudly said of her mother that she swore better than any docker. Abby went over to Gil and started to undo the buttons on his shirt.

'Did I ever tell you that you have the world's most exquisite shoulders?' she said, and she put her mouth to his warm skin and began to kiss him.

Also by Elizabeth Gill . . .

Nobody's Child

'A wonderful book, full of passion, pain, sweetness, twists and turns. I couldn't put it down. It has a feisty young heroine, two contrasting leading men and a great supporting cast of characters'
Sheila Newberry, author of *The Gingerbread Girl*

When their mother dies and their father, in his grief, burns down their wagon and runs away, Kath and Ella – gypsy sisters – suddenly become orphans. With no one to turn to for help, they face hardship and hunger at every turn. Will their special sisterly bond be strong enough to see them to safety?

Also by Elizabeth Gill...

The Guardian Angel

Alice Lee, middle-aged and unmarried, is the only volunteer when the minister asks his congregation to help young Zebediah Bailey. Zeb is in prison for a ghastly crime, and the townspeople would rather forget than forgive this local lad who lost his way. But Alice dutifully writes to him every week, sending him sweets from the little shop that is her livelihood: Alice Lee's Confectionary. She won't admit she's lonely, but since her parents' deaths making and selling sweets has become her whole world.

Then Zeb comes out of gaol and Alice agrees to take him in, much to the horror of her neighbours. What develops between them is unexpected – intense and bittersweet. It could be a new beginning, or else the undoing of them both . . .